*Welcome
New York...
for luxu
s...*

# PARK AVENUE
# *Secrets*

Three fabulous fairytale-in-Manhattan
stories from Barbara Dunlop, Emilie Rose
and Anna DePalo!

# Park Avenue Collection

March 2012

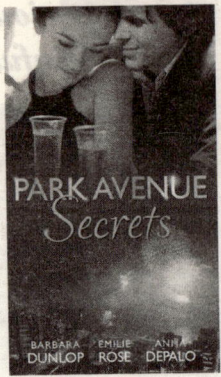

April 2012

# PARK AVENUE
# *Secrets*

BARBARA **DUNLOP**  EMILIE **ROSE**  ANNA **DePALO**

All the characters in this book have no existence outside the imagination of the author, and have no relation whatsoever to anyone bearing the same name or names. They are not even distantly inspired by any individual known or unknown to the author, and all the incidents are pure invention.

All Rights Reserved including the right of reproduction in whole or in part in any form. This edition is published by arrangement with Harlequin Enterprises II B.V./S.à.r.l. The text of this publication or any part thereof may not be reproduced or transmitted in any form or by any means, electronic or mechanical, including photocopying, recording, storage in an information retrieval system, or otherwise, without the written permission of the publisher.

This book is sold subject to the condition that it shall not, by way of trade or otherwise, be lent, resold, hired out or otherwise circulated without the prior consent of the publisher in any form of binding or cover other than that in which it is published and without a similar condition including this condition being imposed on the subsequent purchaser.

® and ™ are trademarks owned and used by the trademark owner and/or its licensee. Trademarks marked with ® are registered with the United Kingdom Patent Office and/or the Office for Harmonisation in the Internal Market and in other countries.

Mills & Boon, an imprint of Harlequin (UK) Limited, Eton House, 18-24 Paradise Road, Richmond, Surrey TW9 1SR

PARK AVENUE SECRETS
© Harlequin Enterprises II B.V./S.à.r.l. 2012

*Marriage, Manhattan Style* © Harlequin Books S.A. 2008
*Pregnant on the Upper East Side?* © Harlequin Books S.A. 2008
*The Billionaire in Penthouse B* © Harlequin Books S.A. 2008

Special thanks and acknowledgement to Barbara Dunlop, Emilie Rose and Anna DePalo for their contribution to the PARK AVENUE SCANDALS series.

ISBN: 978 0 263 89755 5

010-0412

Harlequin (UK) policy is to use papers that are natural, renewable and recyclable products and made from wood grown in sustainable forests. The logging and manufacturing processes conform to the legal environmental regulations of the country of origin.

Printed and bound in Spain
by Blackprint CPI, Barcelona

# MARRIAGE, MANHATTAN STYLE

BARBARA DUNLOP

**Barbara Dunlop** writes romantic stories while curled up in a log cabin in Canada's far north, where bears outnumber people and it snows six months of the year. Fortunately, she has a brawny husband and two teenage children to haul firewood and clear the driveway while she sips cocoa and muses about her upcoming chapters. Barbara loves to hear from readers. You can contact her through her website at www.barbaradunlop.com.

Dear Reader,

In 2006, I took my first trip to New York City. I'd expected the crowds, the skyscrapers, the traffic and the noise. What I hadn't expected was the sheer beauty and magnificence of Manhattan. We toured the Met, climbed to the top of the Empire State Building and strolled through Central Park. The restaurants and clubs were amazing, and everywhere we went, we found the best of the best. By the end of the trip, I realised if a person was going to be rich, they ought to be so in New York.

Enter Reed Wellington, my über-wealthy hero of *Marriage, Manhattan Style*. What better place for his penthouse than 721 Park Avenue, amidst the finest the city has to offer? He should be leading an exceedingly enjoyable life. And he is—until he receives a blackmail letter, is named in a Securities Exchange Commission investigation and is threatened with a divorce. He quickly realises it'll take more than wealth and power to fight his way out of the legal mess and win back his wife, Elizabeth.

I hope you enjoy the story!

*Barbara*

# For the Berry Street and Schoolhouse Girls.
## Sorry I missed the reunion!

# One

Elizabeth Wellington flicked the liberty head, ten-dollar gold coin high into the air above her king-size bed.

"Heads," she whispered to herself in the empty bedroom, her gaze following the coin's twirling trajectory toward the pale, bamboo ceiling mural, "I do it."

If it was tails, she'd wait until next week. At the proper time. When she was ovulating, and her chances of conceiving were at their best.

"Come on, heads," she muttered, picturing her husband, Reed, next door in his home office, studying e-mails or reading a financial report, looking fit and sexy and aloof, his mind firmly locked on the business of the day.

The coin nicked the far edge of the down comforter before bouncing onto the tightly woven carpet.

"Damn." She rounded the four-poster, blinking in vain at the dark burgundy pattern, trying to make out the shiny disk.

After a minute, she kicked off her shoes, dropped to her knees and hiked up her straight, charcoal skirt. Leaning on the heels of her hands, she peered under the bed. Was it heads or tails? And where the heck was the twenty-five thousand dollar collector coin?

"Elizabeth?" came Reed's voice from the hallway.

Guiltily, she jumped up, dusting off and straightening her hair.

"Yes?" she called back, catching a glimpse of the open, satin-lined, rosewood coin collection box. She scooted to the chest of drawers and shut the lid.

The bedroom door opened, and she struck what she hoped was a casual pose.

"Have you seen my PDA?" he asked.

"Uh, no." She moved away from the dresser and spotted the coin. It was tipped up against the nightstand, winking under the glow from the Tiffany lamp.

Reed glanced around the room. "I could have sworn I put it in my pocket before I left the office."

"Did you call it?" she asked, easing toward the coin, planning to camouflage it with her bare foot before his roving gaze landed on it.

She sure didn't want to have to explain this one.

"Can you dial it for me?" he asked.

"Sure." She lifted the bedside phone and punched in his cell number, putting herself between Reed and the coin, careful not to disturb its resting place and ruin the toss.

A tone trilled from somewhere in the penthouse.

"Thanks," he told her, turning for the door.

A few seconds later, he called "Got it" from the living room.

Elizabeth breathed a sigh of relief.

She eased her foot away and checked out the coin's position. It was supported by the wood molding, just a hair off vertical. She upped the light on the three-way bulb and leaned her head down. If the nightstand hadn't got in the way, and the momentum had kept it going, it would have been... Yes! Heads.

She snatched up the coin. The decision was made. She was taking her best friend's advice over that of a trained medical professional.

On the surface, her decision flew in the face of common sense. But her friend Hanna knew more about her life than Dr. Wendell.

Oh, the good doctor knew all about Elizabeth's physical health. He knew her hormone levels and her menstrual cycle. He'd even seen an ultrasound of her ovaries. But he didn't know about her marriage. He didn't know that she'd been fighting since her first anniversary to get back to the honesty and intimacy she and Reed had shared in the beginning.

In the five years since she'd married Reed Wellington III, Elizabeth had learned that the corporation came first, the New York business community second, the extended Wellington family third, with their own marriage somewhere further down the list.

She knew a baby would smooth things out. They'd both wanted one for years. A baby would give them a focal point, something to share, a way for her to fit more neatly into his world, and a reason for him to spend more time in hers. She'd been counting on a baby for a long time. But it was getting harder to convince herself that a baby alone was the answer.

A baby needed a warm and loving home. Children needed to experience intimacy, emotion and authenticity. The further she and Reed drifted apart, the closer Elizabeth came to admitting that even their dream of starting a family wouldn't set things right.

She carefully placed the coin back in the rosewood box, closing the lid and smoothing her fingertips over the whorls and scrolls that decorated the top. Reed had given her the liberty head coin and the rosewood box their first Christmas together. Then he'd added new coins every year. But, as the value of the collection grew, the strength of their marriage declined.

Ironic, really. Back when she had only one coin, they'd joked together, shared secrets, made mistakes and laughed together. More often than not ending up on the bed or the couch or the carpet if no soft furniture was immediately handy.

The first time they'd made love, it was on the padded bench of a gazebo in the massive backyard of his family's Connecticut estate. The dark, clear sky was dotted with stars. They were alone together, and Reed's kisses had turned passionate, his hands roaming the edges of the deep back of her cocktail dress. She'd felt her skin tingle, her nipples tighten and throbbing desire pool in the pit of her stomach.

The time for waiting had passed. They both knew it, and he'd pulled her down on the bench. After long minutes, maybe hours of kisses and caresses, he'd dispatched her panties. Then he buried himself deep inside her. Two weeks later, he'd proposed, and she had enthusiastically talked herself into happily ever after.

Her friends and family in New Hampshire had warned her against marrying a billionaire. His old family money put him in a completely different social class. And they'd told her that her and Reed's expectations of marriage might be completely different. But Elizabeth had been certain their deep love would conquer all obstacles.

Now, five years later, and a whole lot less certain, she moved to the glass balcony doors of her opulent bedroom. Below her penthouse on the twelfth floor of 721 Park Avenue, traffic hummed, and the lights of the cityscape rolled off toward the horizon on this mild, October night. She tugged the heavy curtains closed.

Although she'd recognized the wisdom in Hanna's advice, Elizabeth had felt better putting the decision in the hands of fate. The toss was heads, so the choice was made. She was fighting for her marriage in a different way, starting this minute.

She marched back to the cherrywood chest. The pewter handle was cool under her fingertips as she slid the top drawer open. She thumbed her way through dainty nightgowns and peignoirs, making her way to the bottom of the stack.

And there it was.

Her stomach fluttered as she slid out the red silk negligee she'd worn on her wedding night.

She unzipped the back of her skirt, shimmying out,

tossing her jacket, blouse and underwear on a chair, suddenly anxious to get to Reed. She slipped into the negligee, feeling decadently beautiful for the first time in months. Then she crossed to the en suite, fluffing her auburn hair.

Her eyelashes were dark and thick against her green eyes, her pupils slightly dilated. She freshened her lipstick, stroked some blush over her cheeks, then stepped back to check out the effect in the full-length mirror. Her feet were bare, toenails polished a gleaming copper, and the red silk fell mere inches down her thighs, ending in a band of sheer lace. The neckline dipped low, with more lace that barely camouflaged her breasts.

As a final touch, she dabbed some perfume on her neck and dropped one of the spaghetti straps off her shoulder. Then she stretched to her full five foot five and placed a hand over her fluttering abdomen. Her three-carat diamond winked back at her in the mirror.

Reed was her husband, she reminded herself. She had every right to seduce him. Besides, Hanna would be proud.

She headed across the bedroom, switching off the lamp and padding down the hallway.

"Reed?" she cooed softly, emerging into the doorway of his office, snaking her arm up the cool doorjamb and striking a pose.

Two men looked up from where they were reading a letter.

At the sight of his wife's sexy outfit, Reed's jaw fell open, the words *insider trading* vanishing from his mind. The Securities and Exchange Commission's letter slipped from his fingers to the desktop while, beside him, his vice president, Collin Killian, sucked in a shocked breath.

It took Collin a full three seconds to think to turn away. Reed supposed he couldn't blame the man. It took Elizabeth five seconds to squeak out a gasp and flee down the hall.

"Uh…" Collin began, peering cautiously over his shoulder at the now empty doorway.

Reed swore as he rose to his feet and heard the bedroom door slam shut.

Collin reached for his briefcase. "Catch you later."

"You stay put," Reed commanded, striding across the room.

"But—"

"I just found out I'm being investigated by the SEC. You and I need to talk."

"But your wife—"

"I'll talk to her first." What was Elizabeth thinking? He rounded the corner into the hall.

Collin called behind him, "I don't think talking is what she has in mind."

Reed didn't bother answering.

Elizabeth had no business doing anything *but* talking. He wasn't the one monitoring her basal body temperature, but he was pretty sure they were days ahead of schedule. He missed spontaneous lovemaking as much as she must, but he also wanted to be a father. And he knew damn well she wanted to be a mother. Programmed lovemaking was frustrating. But it was a sacrifice worth making.

He put his hand on the doorknob, forcing himself to pause, steeling his hormones for the sight he knew waited inside. His wife was a knockout, a sexy, sensual, stunning knockout, but he had to be strong for both of them.

He turned the knob and carefully opened the door. "Elizabeth?"

"Go away." Her voice was muffled as she wrapped a terry robe protectively around herself. A stream of light from the en suite backlit her as he shut the door and moved into the room.

"What's going on?" he asked softly.

She shook her head. "Nothing."

He longed to draw her into his arms, maybe slip his hands into the soft terry cloth and pull her tight against his body. It would take so little to nudge the robe open, reveal the negligee beneath, and to gaze on her luscious body. Collin would figure out that he should leave.

"Is it the right time?" Reed asked instead, knowing it wasn't possible that she was ovulating, but still hoping against hope.

She slowly shook her head.

He allowed himself to move a step closer. "Then what are you doing?"

"I thought…" She paused. "I wanted…" Her green eyes blinked up at him. "I didn't know Collin was here."

Reed almost twitched a smile. "No kidding."

Her hand went to her forehead. "He must think—"

"At the moment, he thinks I'm the luckiest man in the world."

She fixed him with a probing gaze. "But you're not."

"Not tonight."

Her gaze slid away.

"Elizabeth?"

She looked back. "I thought… We aren't…"

He was pretty sure he knew where she was going. It was tempting, damn tempting. At this moment, he wanted nothing more than to make passionate love on their big, four-poster bed and pretend none of their problems existed.

He was willing to put off talking about the SEC investigation. But he wasn't willing to compromise on their family. If they made love now, Elizabeth wouldn't get pregnant again this month, and her tears would break Reed's heart.

"Can you hold that thought until next week?" he asked.

Hurt and disappointment clouded her eyes. She opened her mouth to speak, but then she clenched her teeth, compressing her lips and squeezing her eyes shut for a couple of seconds.

When she opened them, her expression had smoothed out, and she seemed under control again. "Is there something going on? Why is Collin—"

"Nothing's going on," Reed quickly assured her.

Nothing but what had to be a completely bogus investigation, which Collin would quash as soon as humanly possible.

Reed hadn't engaged in insider trading, or any other illegal or unethical business practice for that matter. Still, he couldn't help speculating on the maximum sentence. In the current climate for white-collar crime, he imagined they'd try to throw the book at him.

That's why they had to make this go away, and fast.

It had to go away before the press or anybody else got wind of it. Including Elizabeth. Especially Elizabeth.

Their specialist said infertility was often related to stress, and she was stressed enough about trying to get pregnant, not to mention planning their fifth anniversary party. The last thing she needed was to worry about a potential court case.

"I have to head down to Collin's apartment for a little while," he told her.

Her voice went flat, the disbelief evident. "A little while?"

"It's a routine matter," said Reed, vowing to wrap the discussion up quickly.

She nodded. "Of course."

"Why don't you work on the catering menu while I'm gone?" Three hundred guests were invited to the upcoming party; there had to be a million details that required her attention.

"Sure," she said, without enthusiasm. "I'll study the dessert menu for a while."

The sarcastic remark was unlike Elizabeth, and Reed knew he should ask her what was wrong. But he was afraid to get into it, afraid it might lead him to embrace her, to kiss her, to throw all of his good intentions out the window. There was only so much temptation a man could take.

"I'll see you in an hour," he said huskily instead, allowing himself one quick, chaste kiss on her forehead.

His hand brushed her hair, sending tingles of desire all the way up to his shoulder. Her fingers closed over his wrist for the briefest of moments. It was enough to make him question his decision to leave.

But he had to walk out. He'd promised himself he'd do everything in his power to give her a baby. And he would.

Without meeting her eyes, he turned for the door, marched down the hall to where Collin hovered beside the desk, a decidedly uncertain expression on his face.

"Let's go," said Reed, slipping into his suit jacket and leading the way to the penthouse door.

Collin didn't ask any questions. Discretion was one of the things Reed liked best about the man.

"I've got the SEC letter," Collin confirmed as the door closed behind them, and they headed for Gage Lattimer's penthouse. Collin's friend, Gage, had also been named in the SEC's letter as being part of the investigation.

"Envelope, too?" asked Reed. He didn't want a shred of evidence lying around for Elizabeth to stumble across.

"Everything," said Collin, stopping in front of the wide oak door. "And I closed your Web browser."

"Thanks." Reed nodded, giving a sharp knock.

They waited in silence, listening to a clang and clash from inside. The door was finally opened. But it wasn't Gage standing in front of them. It was a tall, attractive brunette with a guarded, almost guilty look in her green eyes.

"Is Gage available?" asked Reed, hoping he wasn't disturbing something. Although the woman *was* fully dressed.

"I'm terribly sorry—" The woman cleared her throat. "Mr. Lattimer isn't in at the moment."

Was that a British accent?

"And you are?" asked Collin.

"Jane Elliott. Mr. Lattimer's new housekeeper."

Reed's gaze caught on the untidy penthouse over her shoulder.

She pulled the door against her back, blocking his view. "May I tell him who called?"

"Reed Wellington."

Collin handed the woman a business card. "Can you ask him to call me as soon as possible?"

"Of course," she replied with a nod, then slipped back into the suite and closed the door.

"I hope he's not paying her much," Reed mused as they turned for the elevator.

"I'd pay her pretty much anything she asked," said Collin.

Reed couldn't help but smile as he punched the call button for the elevator. Then he quickly brought his thoughts back to the problem at hand. "So what in the hell do you think is going on with this?" Reed asked as the doors slid open to an empty car.

"I think maybe you should have paid the blackmail."

Reed drew back. As a wealthy man, he was often the target of both financial appeals and threats. But a particularly bizarre blackmail demand had arrived two weeks ago.

"Ten million dollars?" he asked Collin. "Are you out of your mind?"

"The two could be related."

"The blackmail letter said, 'the world will learn the dirty secret of how the Wellingtons make their money.' It didn't say anything about an SEC investigation." Not that Reed would have paid up in any event. But he might have taken the letter a little more seriously if the threat had been that specific.

"Insider trading is a dirty little secret."

"It's also a ridiculous fabrication."

When Reed first read the blackmail letter, he'd dismissed it as a hoax. There were plenty of lunatics out there. Then he'd wondered if some of their overseas suppliers might be engaged in unethical labor practices. But he'd checked them all out. He could find absolutely nothing to substantiate any "dirty little secret" of the Wellingtons' wealth.

He had no dirty little secret. It was beyond preposterous to suggest he'd engaged in insider trading. And impossible to prove, since he hadn't done it. It wasn't even logical. The vast majority of his and his father's and, for that matter, their ancestors' wealth was derived from the performance of their companies. Reed did very little trading on the stock market.

And what little he did do was recreational, just to see if he could beat the odds. Where was the challenge in cheating? He didn't need the money. And cheating wouldn't be any fun. So why the hell would he engage in insider trading?

"They've got something," said Collin as the elevator came to a rest on the second floor. "The SEC doesn't start investigations on spec."

"So, who do we call?" asked Reed.

As well as being a vice president, Collin was a damn fine lawyer. He inserted his key and opened the apartment door. "The SEC for starters."

Reed glanced at his watch. Nine-fifteen. "You know anybody we can disturb?"

"Yeah." Collin tossed his briefcase on the table of the more compact, one-bedroom apartment that was owned by Wellington International. "I know a guy." He picked up a cordless phone. "You feel like pouring the scotch?"

"On it."

Collin's call was brief.

When he finished, he accepted a crystal tumbler of single malt and sat back in an armchair. "They'll send us a full dossier in the morning, but it's something to do with Ellias Technologies."

Reed recognized the company name. "That was Gage's deal. He thought they were going to go big, so we both bought in." But he couldn't believe Gage Lattimer, his friend and neighbor, would have recommended a stock based on insider information. But he went over the scenario, thinking out loud as he stepped through the deal.

"It did shoot up fast. Particularly when that navigations system—"

A lightbulb went on inside Reed's head.

"What?" Collin prompted.

"Kendrick."

"The senator?"

Reed nodded. "Damn it. How much you want to bet he was on the approval committee?"

The trepidation in Collin's voice was obvious. "Not the one that awarded the navigations contract."

"Yeah." Reed took a swallow of his scotch. "That one."

Collin cursed under his breath.

Reed echoed the sentiment. He hadn't done anything wrong, but if Kendrick was on the approval committee, it would sure look like he had.

"I buy shares in Ellias," Reed speculated out loud. "Kendrick—who the whole world *knows* is an avid supporter of my Envirocore.com—approves a lucrative contract for Ellias. Ellias stock soars. I make a few hundred thousand. And suddenly the SEC is involved."

"You missed a step," said Collin.

"The blackmailer," Reed agreed. If the blackmailer was the one who alerted the SEC, then Reed hadn't taken him nearly seriously enough.

The blackmailer obviously had information on Reed's stock portfolio. He also knew Reed was the owner of Envirocore. And he knew that Kendrick was on the Senate navigation system contract approval committee. What's more, he knew how to put it all together to hurt Reed.

This was no lightweight.

Collin gazed at the storm-tossed seascape on his far wall. "Nobody in his right mind is going to think you broke the law for a few hundred thousand."

"Are you kidding? Everybody's ready to knock old money off their pedestal."

"Can you prove you're innocent?"

Reed scoffed. "Prove that a phone call, a meeting or an e-mail *didn't* take place? I don't see how I can do that."

"Did you call the police on the blackmail letter?"

"I filed it with the rest of the crank stuff." Mistake. Obviously.

"You want to call them tonight?"

Reed nodded. "We might as well get this party started."

# Two

The black-tie hospital fund-raiser at the Bergere Grande Hotel was in full swing on Saturday night. Guests had been served a gourmet dinner in the Crystal Room, and now they were moving through the marble-pillared foyer to the East Ballroom for cocktails and dancing.

Elizabeth had spotted Collin approaching, so she'd quickly set a course for the ladies' room. She knew she'd have to look the man in the eye at some point, but she was putting off the moment as long as possible. She didn't want to think about how much the red negligee had revealed.

She emerged from checking her hair and freshening her lipstick and accepted a flute of champagne from a smartly dressed waiter. Then she concentrated on a series of silent auction items on her way to the main ballroom. She wanted to give Collin and Reed plenty of time to finish their conversation.

Hanna sidled up to her. "So, how'd it go last night?"

Elizabeth bought a little time by putting her head down over an auction item. It was a ruby and diamond choker, and the top bid was ten thousand dollars. She added a thousand and signed her name.

"Nice," said Hanna, nodding to the jewels that were secured in a glass case. "If you win, can I borrow it sometime?"

"Sure."

Hanna latched on to Elizabeth's arm and drew her away from the crowd. "So, did you do it?"

Elizabeth admitted as much with a nod.

"What happened?"

"I crashed and burned."

Hanna's sculpted brows knit together. "I don't understand. Was he asleep or something?"

"I got dressed up in a red, slinky negligee." Elizabeth omitted the part about the coin toss, not wanting Hanna to know she'd had second thoughts. "Then I surprised him in his office."

"And?" Hanna prompted, cocking her expertly coiffed blond hair to one side.

"And Collin was there, too."

Hanna's fingertips went to her mouth to cover her grin.

"Don't you dare laugh," Elizabeth warned in a dire undertone. "I was mortified."

"Were you…exposed?"

Elizabeth sniffed, attempting to regain her dignity. "There was no frontal nudity."

"He saw your butt?" Hanna looked somewhat thrilled at the prospect.

"He did not see my butt. It was a negligee. It was sexy, but it covered everything that counts."

"So, what's the problem?"

"I tried to vamp up my husband, and he left for a meeting with Collin." Elizabeth's gaze slid across the room to where the two men were talking. There were things more embarrassing than having Collin see her in her red negligee.

"Oh," said Hanna, obviously understanding the broader point.

"Yes. *Oh.* Apparently I'm not nearly as irresistible as I'd hoped."

Hanna's red mouth pursed in puzzlement. "What exactly did he say?"

Elizabeth's tone turned sharp, even though she knew none of this was Hanna's fault. "Do we have to dissect it?"

"Of course we have to dissect it. How else are we going to learn from it?"

"Fine." Elizabeth took a breath. Hanna wanted the gory details? "He said 'I have to go meet with Collin. I'll be back in an hour. You should work on the anniversary party catering menu.'" She was beginning to hate that catering menu. "He also said 'Hold that thought.'"

"Ouch," Hanna whispered in sympathy.

Elizabeth peered into the main ballroom. "Let's go find the bar."

"Yeah," Hanna agreed with a rush of breath.

"There are times in a woman's life when she absolutely needs a drink."

They started toward the main ballroom. Elizabeth wanted to hurry and disappear, but she was forced to move carefully in her sleek, silver evening gown.

"Vannick-Smythe at three o'clock," Hanna warned in an undertone.

Elizabeth's gaze flicked to her gossipy neighbor Vivian and made eye contact. "Uh-oh. She spotted us."

Hanna bent her head. "Pretend we're deep in conversation."

"Right."

"I'm surprised she didn't bring her dogs," said Hanna, referring to Vivian Vannick-Smythe's yappy white Shih Tzus. Constantly by her side, the two dogs went uncannily well with the woman's overdyed hair.

"I guess she couldn't get them on the guest list," Elizabeth speculated.

Hanna sputtered out a laugh. "Oops. Here she comes." Then she raised her voice to conversation level. "And what did you think of yesterday's political coup in Barasmundi?"

Elizabeth quickly jumped into the game. "I don't think a woman can hold on to power in West Africa." She resisted the urge to glance at Vivian, as the woman came to a halt beside them. "But if Maracitu can pull off the elections, it'll help stabilize the north, maybe inspire the tribal leaders to participate in democratic rule."

Hanna was a network news anchor, and an all-around political junkie. Elizabeth assumed her ploy was to make the conversation as inaccessible as possible for Vivian.

Luckily, Elizabeth was interested in world politics herself. It was one of the reasons she and Hanna had become such good friends.

Hanna put in, "I don't see how the government can move ahead on the constitutional vote if—"

"Well, I certainly didn't expect to see *you* here." Vivian Vannick-Smythe's drawl overrode Hanna's words.

Elizabeth glanced up to see Vivian's penetrating gaze fixed on her. The hostile tone took her by surprise. "Hello, Vivian."

Vivian sniffed. "At minimum, one would think you'd let the speculation die down."

"What speculation?" Had somebody heard she was trying to get pregnant? Or had Collin gossiped about her failed seduction attempt?

"Why, the SEC investigation, my dear," said Vivian, a flash of triumph in her eyes and a cruel smile fighting its way to life on her face. "I don't know what that husband of yours got up to. And, of course, it's none of *my* business, but when the SEC starts investigating—"

"Vivian Vandoosen, isn't it?" Hanna elbowed her way between the two women and stuck out her hand, giving Elizabeth's mind time to scramble for a foothold on logic.

Vivian's glare all but scalded Hanna. "Vannick-Smythe," she corrected in an imperious voice.

"Of course," said Hanna. "It must have slipped my mind. You understand how it is. I meet so many *important* people in my job, others sometimes get lost in the shuffle."

Any other time, Elizabeth would have laughed at the insulted expression on Vivian's face.

"I'm afraid you'll have to excuse us," said Hanna, linking her elbow through Elizabeth's, all but dragging her away from the stunned Vivian.

"What's she talking about?" Elizabeth hissed under her breath as they passed the fountain, heading toward the patio doors.

"I assumed you knew," said Hanna, making a beeline for the ballroom. "The story won't break until tomorrow."

Elizabeth stopped abruptly. "There's a story?"

Hanna looked uncomfortable. "Bert Ralston is working on it right now."

Elizabeth felt her eyes go wide at the mention of the network's top investigative reporter. "It's that big?"

Hanna nodded apologetically. "Your husband and Gage Lattimer are under investigation for insider trading in Ellias Technologies stock."

Elizabeth was speechless.

"Let's find a drink," said Hanna.

"How... I don't..." Insider trading? Reed would never do something dishonest.

"How do you not know?" asked Hanna, stopping in front of a bar and the uniformed bartender who stood behind a row of sparkling glasses and a garnish tray. "Two vodka martinis."

"He didn't tell me."

Hanna nodded while the man mixed the drinks. "Really."

"Why didn't he tell me?"

Hanna scooped up the drinks and held one out to Elizabeth as they walked away. "Can't help you there."

Elizabeth closed her fingers over the fine stem of the

glass. Her husband was a subject of a criminal investigation, and he hadn't bothered to mention it?

Last night he'd told her nothing was going on. That it was a routine matter. Though clearly Collin knew what was up.

Reed's employees knew more than his wife did. The network news knew more than she did. Even Vivian Vannick-Smythe knew more than she did.

How could Reed have put her in this position?

"Is my marriage already over?" asked Elizabeth, dread welling up inside her.

"I think," said Hanna, obviously choosing her words with care, "you're going to have to ask Reed that question."

Elizabeth took a gulp of the strong drink, determination replacing distress. "That's not the only question I'm going to ask him."

Elizabeth's green eyes glittered like emeralds as she turned on Reed in their penthouse foyer. "How do you not tell me you're under investigation by the SEC?"

Ah, there it was. She'd been uncharacteristically silent in the limo, so he'd known something was up. At least now he could mount a defense.

He flipped on an overhead light, latching the dead bolt behind them. "It's not a serious problem."

Her voice went up an octave. "Not a serious problem? They're handing out twenty-year jail sentences for white-collar crimes these days."

"I didn't do it," he pointed out.

She just smiled mulishly up at him.

"You've got me tried, convicted and jailed." Now, wasn't that a vote of confidence?

"I haven't convicted you. I'm frightened for you."

"You sound angry."

"I'm both."

"You don't need to be."

"Oh, well. Thanks. That makes it all better."

"You think sarcasm's the answer?" He was perfectly willing to talk about this. But he wanted to have a reasonable, rational discussion. Mostly, he wanted to dispel her fears that he might be sentenced to jail.

"I think communication is the answer," she responded tartly. "You know, the part where you talk to me about what's going on in your life. Your hopes, your fears, your aspirations, your *pending criminal charges*."

"How would telling you have helped?" Reed truly wanted to know.

"We could have shared the load."

"You have your own load."

"We're husband and wife, Reed."

"And husbands don't unburden themselves by worrying their wives."

"Sure they do. All the time."

"Well, this husband doesn't. You have enough to think about right now—"

"You mean like the catering menu?"

"Among other things. There was no point in both of us worrying, and I didn't want to upset you."

"Well, I'm plenty upset now."

"You should stop." He was going to take care of it.

It was only a matter of time before this was wrapped up and life got back on track.

"You're joking, right?"

"It's nothing." He stepped toward her. "It'll blow over in no time."

She tipped up her chin to look at him. "What did you do?"

"Nothing."

"I meant to make them suspicious."

"Nothing," he repeated with conviction.

"So, the SEC is conducting random investigations on innocent and unsuspecting citizens?"

Reed drew a heavy sigh. He really didn't have the energy to go into it tonight. It was late and, even though tomorrow was Sunday, he had a conference call first thing in the morning. He wanted to sleep. He wanted her to sleep, too.

She cocked her head to one side. "Ellias Technologies?"

"I bought some shares," he reluctantly allowed. "So did Gage. Their value rose dramatically, and it tripped an alarm bell somewhere. Collin will take care of it. Now, let's go to bed."

"That's all the information I get?"

"That's all the information you need."

"I want more."

"Why does this have to be a thing?" Why couldn't she trust him to take care of it? It was his problem, not hers. Her fretting wouldn't help the situation one bit.

"Reed," she warned, all but tapping her foot.

"Fine." He stripped off his suit jacket and loosened

his tie. "It turns out that Senator Kendrick was on a committee that awarded Ellias Technologies a lucrative government contract."

Her green eyes narrowed. "And they think the senator gave you a heads up."

"Exactly," said Reed. "Are you happy now?"

"No. I am *not* happy now."

He raised his palms in a gesture of defeat. "And *that's* why I didn't tell you. I want you to be happy. I don't want you to worry." Was that so hard for her to understand?

Her lips pursed in that mulish expression that he recognized so well. "I don't need you protecting me."

He moved closer, moderating his voice. "The doctor said you should stay calm."

"How can I stay calm when my husband is lying to me?"

He hadn't lied to her. He'd omitted a small amount of unnecessary information so that she wouldn't get stressed out for no reason. "You're being ridiculous," he pointed out.

She pulled back. "Is that what you think?"

He could see her warming up for a whole new argument. Well, he wasn't buying into that at one in the morning.

"What I think is that Collin is on the case," he stated with conviction. "By next week, it'll be a footnote in my life. And you have much more important things to think about right now."

"Like the catering menu?" she repeated.

"Exactly. And your basal body temperature." He attempted to lighten the mood. "And that little red negligee."

"I do have a brain, you know, Reed."

It was his turn to draw back. Where the hell had that come from? "Have I ever suggested you don't?"

"I can help you solve problems."

"I pay professionals to help me solve problems." That way, he and Elizabeth could lead a calm, uncluttered life.

"That's your answer?"

"That's my answer."

Elizabeth waited for him to say more, but he was happy to end on that note.

Reed was the last to arrive at the lunch meeting in the Wellington International boardroom. Gage, Collin, media mogul Trent Tanford and private investigator Selina Marin were already sitting around the polished table when he walked in.

"Did you get hold of Kendrick?" Gage asked without preamble.

Reed shook his head, shutting the door behind him before taking his place at the head of the oblong table. Fresh-brewed coffee had been placed on the sideboard, and a bank of windows overlooked the fall colors of the park many stories below. "His secretary says he's in meetings in Washington all week."

"He doesn't have a cell phone?" asked Collin.

"He can't be disturbed," Reed quoted, letting his expression tell the room the excuse rang hollow to him. He'd never had a problem getting hold of Kendrick before. In fact, it was usually Kendrick who called him.

"We need his denial," said Trent. "At least, we need

him to publicly deny having given you insider information. And I'd prefer to have it on videotape."

"You'll have it," said Reed, hoping it would be soon. It was in everyone's best interest—including the senator's—to have him on the record in this. In the absence of identifying the blackmailer, Kendrick's backing was their best chance of stopping the investigation in its tracks.

"Did you get anywhere with the police?" Reed asked Selina.

"I had a chat with Detective Arnold McGray." She slid a thick sheaf of paper across the table to Reed. "They've been surprisingly cooperative. Here's the list of blackmail victims in the building."

"The cops are at a dead end," Collin put in. "They're hoping the extra manpower will help."

"Person power," Selina put in.

"Sorry," said Collin with an edge of sarcasm. "I keep forgetting you're a girl."

"Shall I start wearing pink ruffles?"

Reed contemplated Selina's no-nonsense black blazer, white turtleneck, short cropped hair and minimal makeup. With those dark brows and that straight slant to her mouth, she'd look ridiculous in pink.

Reed sighed and picked up the letter, reading the names of Julia Prentice, who before her marriage to Max Rolland was blackmailed regarding her out-of-wedlock pregnancy, Trent Tanford for his relationship with murder victim Marie Endicott, and Prince Sebastian who'd also received a threatening letter.

In the prince's case, the letter writer didn't ask for

any money, and it was eventually proven to be his exgirlfriend. So, the Prince Sebastian incident didn't seem to be related.

"Any connection between mine and the other two?" Reed asked Selina.

"Three different threats," she answered. "Three unrelated incidents. Three untraceable Grand Cayman bank accounts." Then she paused. "Same bank."

Reed allowed himself a small smile. So, the three *were* likely related. That gave them a whole lot more information to go on.

"I'll start looking for connections between the cases," said Selina.

"Any guess as to why mine was ten million and the others were only one?" asked Reed.

Selina gave a wry twist of her lips. "Neither of the others paid up. Maybe expenses were mounting."

"You bet your ass we didn't pay up," muttered Trent.

"You should be flattered," Gage directed his comment to Reed. "The guy obviously thinks you're solvent."

"Flattered isn't exactly how I'm feeling." He didn't need this crap in his life. His life was plenty complicated enough.

"What about Marie Endicott's murder?" Collin brought up the topic they'd avoided so far.

"I don't like speculating about that," said Trent.

Neither did Reed. But ignoring the possibility that the murder was tied up in the blackmail scheme wouldn't change the facts, and it wouldn't reduce the danger.

"The police aren't ready to call it a murder," said Selina. "But that missing security tape makes my hair stand on end. And I think we have to operate on the assumption that they're connected."

"That's a pretty big assumption," said Collin.

"Yeah? Well, I'm preparing for the worst-case scenario." Then she turned to Trent. "I wonder. Did the blackmailer commit murder to set you up? Or did he target you after learning of the murder?"

"My guess would be that he's opportunistic," said Trent. "After the murder, he set me up."

"Generally," said Selina, "there are two reasons for a murder. Passion or greed."

"The blackmailer is definitely greedy," said Reed. "And if he operated on passion, we'd probably have another dead body, not more blackmail letters. He's got to be ticked off at us."

"Fair point," Collin put in.

"But we don't know anything for sure," said Trent.

Trent was right. And Reed wasn't in a position to take any chances. Three people in his building had been blackmailed and one was dead.

He slid the list back to Selina. "Hire as many people as you need. And put somebody on Elizabeth." Then he paused and drew a breath. "But tell him to keep his distance. Nobody talks to my wife about the blackmail." He glanced around the room to drive home his point.

Everybody nodded, and he rose to his feet.

He was keeping Elizabeth safe, but it was also his job to keep her calm. When this was over, they had a family to start. And, God help him, it was going to be over soon.

# Three

"Your marriage is far from over," said Hanna as she and Elizabeth made their way past groups of diners to a corner table in their favorite deli off Times Square.

Out of habit, Elizabeth had ordered a thick corned beef on rye, but she was pretty sure her clenched stomach wouldn't allow her to eat.

"He won't talk to me about anything important," she told Hanna. "He won't make love with me. And when I ask for more information, he gets angry. How can I stay married to a man who won't let me into his life?"

Hanna took a sip of her diet cola. "Stop trying."

The answer set Elizabeth back in her chair. "Stop trying to be married?" That wasn't the answer she'd expected.

"Stop trying to muscle your way into his life." Hanna took a bite of her sandwich.

"That doesn't make any sense." They were married. Elizabeth was supposed to be in Reed's life.

Hanna peeled a paper napkin from the metal dispenser and dabbed the corners of her mouth. "I say this as your best friend, and as someone who loves you dearly—"

"This can't be good," Elizabeth mumbled.

"You've grown a little, well, dull lately."

*Dull?* What the heck kind of a thing was that for a good friend to say?

"You are *way* too invested in Reed and Reed's life."

"He's my husband."

Hanna shook her head. "Doesn't matter. I know you want a baby. And that's admirable. And I know you love Reed. And that's admirable, too. But, Elizabeth, Lizzy, you have got to get a life."

"I have a life."

Hanna gave her a dubious look.

Okay, so maybe working out at the spa, buying designer clothes and planning parties wasn't the most productive life. But Reed did a lot of corporate entertaining. It was important for her to look the part.

"If you had your own life," Hanna continued, "you wouldn't obsess so much about Reed's."

"I don't care what kind of a full, exciting and enriching life I'm leading, I'm still going to care that my husband is under criminal investigation."

"He told you he'd take care of it."

"Of course he told me that. He doesn't want me to worry. He's psychotic that way."

"I think it's sweet."

"*Sweet?* Whose side are you on?"

"Lizzy, you've lost all perspective. It's not about sides. It's about your happiness. Thing is, Reed's life centers around his job, his business associates, his family and friends, and his marriage."

"Not so much his marriage," Elizabeth muttered.

"Maybe. But that's not my point. My point is that your life also centers around *his* job, *his* business associates, *his* family and friends, and your marriage. See the problem?"

"That's not true." It couldn't be true. Elizabeth wasn't some 1950s throwback without a thought of her own.

"Who are your friends? Your old friends? The ones that have nothing to do with Reed?"

Elizabeth searched her brain, conjuring then discounting those people she'd grown up with or met at college.

"My old friends don't live in Manhattan," she finally answered.

After her marriage, it had quickly become difficult to spend time with her old friends. They seemed to think Elizabeth's life was one long party, that money solved everything, that rich people should never have a single problem. And, if they did, they should shut up about it and go shopping.

"And all of his do," said Hanna with an expression of triumph.

Elizabeth eyed her corned beef and decided she could use some comfort food after all. "Your point?"

"All of your current friends are really Reed's friends."

"Except for you."

"You met me through Trent. You remember Trent? Reed's friend."

"This is starting to feel like an intervention."

"That's because it is an intervention," said Hanna.

"Well, I don't need one."

Hanna let out a breath. "Oh, my darling..."

Elizabeth lifted the succulent sandwich. "I don't know why I should take your advice anyway. You were the one who insisted I seduce him last week. And that sure went to hell in a handbasket."

"That's because you did it wrong."

"I did it perfectly. I rocked in that red negligee. Reed was the problem. He was about to be arrested. How can a man concentrate on passion when he's about to be arrested?" Point well made, Elizabeth took a bite of her sandwich.

"You need a job," said Hanna.

Elizabeth swallowed. "Trust me on this. The one thing I don't need is more money."

Hanna waved her pickle. "It's not the paycheck. It's the getting out of the penthouse, exchanging opinions and ideas with other adults, hanging out with people who have absolutely nothing to do with your husband or with getting pregnant."

"And you don't think that will drag us further apart?"

"It'll give you something interesting to talk about when you get home."

Elizabeth was about to protest that they already talked about interesting things, but she stopped herself when she realized how hollow that would ring.

Reed was pretty much a workaholic, and he refused to discuss Wellington International with her. He seemed to think business problems would stress her out as much as SEC investigations. But if she introduced her own business issues, especially if there were problems, she was willing to bet he'd engage in the conversation.

Hmm. Getting a job. Developing an identity. The idea kind of appealed to her. In fact, she wondered why she hadn't thought of it before.

But there was a glitch. A big glitch.

"Who's going to hire me? I haven't worked since I graduated from college." She paused. "With a degree in musical theater."

"We're less than five blocks from the theater district," Hanna offered.

Elizabeth couldn't picture herself as a script girl or a gofer. It would be silly for the wife of a billionaire to take an entry-level position. Not to mention embarrassing for Reed.

"He doesn't have to like it," said Hanna, guessing the direction of Elizabeth's thoughts.

"Wouldn't that pretty much defeat the purpose?" She was trying to save her marriage not alienate her husband.

"What do *you* want?"

Elizabeth suddenly felt tired. "Raspberry cheesecake."

"And after that?"

"A baby. My marriage. To be happy. I don't know."

"Bingo," said Hanna.

"Bingo what?"

"Get happy. Get *yourself* happy. Independent of Reed or a baby or anything else. Make your own life work. The rest will have to sort itself out around that." Hanna paused, her blue eyes going soft along with her voice. "What have you got to lose?"

It was an excellent question. There was little left to lose. If something didn't change drastically and soon, she wouldn't have a marriage. She certainly wouldn't have a baby. She wouldn't have a life of any kind.

Hanna was right. She had to get out there and get a job.

A *job?*

Through the open door of the en suite, Reed watched Elizabeth rub scented lotion onto the smooth skin of one of her calves as she got ready for bed.

"You mean you want to sit on a charity board?" he asked. There were any number of worthy organizations that would be happy to have her support.

"Not a seat on a board," she answered. "I mean a real job."

Reed was stymied. "Why?"

She shrugged, putting the cap back on the bottle. "It'll get me out of the house, into the community, help me meet new people."

"You can get out of the house anytime you want."

This was New York, and she had an unlimited budget. There was no end to the things she could get out of the house and do, and no end to the people she could meet while doing them.

"Shopping doesn't give me the same sense of satisfaction."

He searched her expression, trying to figure out what was really going on. "There's more to life than shopping."

"Exactly." She stood up, replaced the bottle and selected a small jar of cream.

"The Hospital Foundation would be thrilled to have you on board."

"My degree is in theater."

"Then the Arts Board. I can make a call to Ralph Sitman. I'm sure one of the committees—"

"Reed, I don't want you to make a call. I want to type up my résumé and get out there and apply for a job."

"Your résumé?" he asked with disbelief. She was a Wellington. She didn't need a résumé.

"Yes." She turned to the mirror and rubbed the cream onto her forehead.

"You're planning to schlep around the theater district with a copy of the classifieds under your arm?"

"That's how it's generally done."

His voice went dark. "Not in this family, it isn't." If he was lucky, people would think she was eccentric. But some might actually think she needed the money. Like he was some miser who wouldn't see to her needs.

Elizabeth stepped back into the room, her diaphanous gown backlit until she shut off the en suite light. "Excuse me?"

"It's undignified," he told her.

"Earning a living is undignified?"

He tried to stay calm, but he could feel the tension mounting behind his eyes. "You already earn a living."

"No, you earn a living."

"And it's a damn good one."

She stepped forward and flipped back the comforter on her side of the bed. "Congratulations. Bully for you."

"Elizabeth," he pleaded. "What is going on?"

She folded her arms across her chest, unconsciously

thrusting her breasts out against the thin fabric. "I need a life, Reed."

What the hell kind of a statement was that? "You have a life."

"*You* have a life."

"It's *our* life."

"And you're never in it."

"I haven't left New York in months." And don't think that wasn't tough to orchestrate. But he wanted to be on deck for making babies, and he wanted to be around Elizabeth in case she needed anything. It was a tough time for both of them. He recognized that, and he was doing his best to keep things calm and smooth.

"You think this is about your physical presence in the city?"

"What is it about?" He paused. "Please, Elizabeth, for God's sake, tell me what this is all about."

She hesitated, her hands dropping back to her sides. "This is about me wanting a job."

"Doing what?"

"I don't know. Whatever I can get. Script girl, production assistant, gofer." She drew a breath and squared her shoulders. "This isn't negotiable, Reed."

He flipped back his side of the comforter, losing his grip on his temper, feeling the argument slip out of control.

"Great," he intoned. "Our friends and associates will show up to an opening at the Met. They'll all have dates. I'll be stag, because my wife will be the gofer."

"No. Elizabeth Wellington will be the gopher."

"And you don't think that'll be just a little humiliating for me?"

Her jaw clenched. "Then I'll use my maiden name."

"You'll use your real name," he growled.

"Fine." She flounced into bed, tugging the covers up to her chest.

Reed dropped in next to her, more frustrated with his wife than he was with the SEC. She couldn't go slumming backstage at the Met. They'd both be the laughingstock of Manhattan.

He knew he was too angry to argue further tonight, but this conversation was far from over.

He switched off the lamp next to his bed and heard the beep of her digital thermometer. His head hit the pillow, and he closed his eyes.

Her light stayed on. She didn't move. He couldn't even hear her breathing.

He turned and opened his eyes, blinking at her profile in the lamplight, trying to figure out if she was too upset to sleep.

She twisted her neck to look at him, distress clouding her expression. "I'm ovulating."

Reed's stomach clenched. He only just stopped himself from cursing out loud.

Of all the asinine timing.

How could people be expected to live like this?

"Right," he said with a nod, keeping his voice as controlled as possible.

He slid closer to her, reached over her and turned off her lamp, slipping the thermometer out of her hand to place it on the nightstand.

They'd made love hundreds, maybe thousands of times. They could do it now. Piece of cake.

He left his arm draped around her and burrowed his face into the crook of her neck, inhaling deeply. Once, twice, three times, giving them both a chance to get used to the idea of making love.

Her hair was soft against his cheek, and he ran his hand through it, letting his subconscious kick in and memories wash over him. Her scent was one of the first things he'd loved about her. He remembered dancing under the stars, on the cruise in the harbor, the warm June winds flowing over them as she swayed in his arms in that red dress.

Two minutes into the dance, he knew. He knew he was going to love her, knew he was going to marry her, knew he was going to spend the rest of his life taking care of this funny, gorgeous, intoxicating woman.

Now, he kissed the tender skin of her neck. He trailed his fingertips down the satin of her gown, pressing his warm palm against her abdomen. He kissed her shoulder, her collarbone, then moved to her earlobe, drawing the soft flesh between his lips.

He wanted to tell her he loved her, but things were too tenuous between them. He was building a fragile peace, a respite in the midst of the tough conversation that would have to take place in the next few days. He couldn't hope for more than that.

He fluttered his fingertips along the curve of her waist, up her ribcage, skimming the side of her breast. Desire was slowly but surely thickening his blood. He could feel his breathing deepen and the stirrings of need work their way though his body.

He stroked her shoulder, slipping off the strap of her

gown. Then he made his way down her arm, over her wrist, intending to twine their fingers together as one.

But he found a fist.

A tense, tightly clasped fist.

He jerked back to look at her face.

Her eyes were scrunched tight, her forehead creased and her jaw clenched shut.

"Son of a bitch!" He vaulted off the bed.

Her eyes few open, and he was horrified at the grit, determination and aversion in their depths.

He was *not* forcing himself on a martyr. No matter what the cause, no matter what the rationale.

"This is a marriage," he choked out, "not some stud farm."

He grabbed his bathrobe, striding for the guest bedroom.

Alone in the bed, Elizabeth had cried herself to sleep. She'd wanted to make love, wanted desperately to make a baby. But their argument had replayed over and over in her mind while Reed caressed her, until it had shrouded her love for him, and his touch had felt empty.

She knew it would go away. Intellectually, she knew that only minutes or hours would have to pass before she felt secure in his arms once again. But she'd needed some time before lovemaking.

She'd finally fallen asleep in the early morning hours. Then she woke to the sound of the vacuum, and she knew their housekeeper had arrived, and Reed had gone to work.

Part of her couldn't believe he'd left without waking her to make love. But then she remembered his expression as he'd stormed out of the bedroom. She'd angered him. And maybe she'd hurt him. He had, after all, tried valiantly to put the fight behind them and make love.

She was the one who had failed.

She flipped off the covers, showered, dressed and took her car to the Wellington International office tower on Fifth Avenue.

She rode the elevator to the executive floor and paced through the marble foyer without giving herself a chance to hesitate. She'd apologize to Reed. Not for the fight, but for staying so emotional afterward. She was past it now, and she'd tell him so.

If worst came to worst, she'd flash the lacy black camisole she was wearing under her coat dress. She had thigh-high stockings to match, and she'd put on the skimpiest, sexiest pair of panties she could find in her drawer. She wasn't above a little seduction. And there was a fine hotel right across the street.

"Elizabeth." Reed's secretary, Devon, rose from her chair. She shot a quick, uncertain glance at the window through to Reed's corner office. "Is Reed expecting you?"

"It's a surprise," Elizabeth admitted. She hoped a good surprise.

Devon shot another glance at his office, and there was something strange in her expression. "Let me give him a call."

Elizabeth glanced through the window and saw a woman's profile. She had spiky black hair and wore a dark blazer.

"You wife is here," Devon said into the phone.

There was a split second's delay, and then the woman

shot a guilty glance through the window at Elizabeth. She immediately came to her feet.

"Who's that?" Elizabeth asked Devon.

"She's a job applicant," Devon replied, busying herself with some papers on top of her desk.

Something in the atmosphere made Elizabeth feel awkward. "I hope I'm not disturbing something."

"I'm sure it's fine," said Devon.

The door to Reed's office opened, and the woman came out first. She was a strong, no-nonsense type, about five foot seven, with short cropped hair, classic clothes and a self-confident stride.

She nodded to Elizabeth as she passed, leaving a clean hint of a coconut shampoo in her wake.

"I wasn't expecting you," said Reed, and Elizabeth turned back to face her husband.

"Surprise," said Elizabeth, with a smile for Devon's benefit.

He gestured to the open office door, and she preceded him inside.

"Sorry to disturb you," she offered as he latched the door.

"Not a problem." He indicated a pair of leather chairs in one corner of the room, bracketing a low table.

"Who was she?" Elizabeth asked.

Reed waited for her to sit down. "Who?"

"The woman who just left. Devon said—"

"She's a client," Reed said hurriedly.

Elizabeth froze, a terrible feeling creeping into her empty stomach. He was lying. Why was he lying?

"What kind of a client?"

Reed waved a dismissive hand. "She owns a chain of furniture stores on the West Coast."

Elizabeth nodded, depression settling on her shoulders.

"Did you need something?" Reed asked, tone formal and polite.

*I need my husband back.*

She was suddenly at a loss. Did she make the proposition? Did she carry on with the seduction plan? Could she bring herself to make love with him knowing he was lying?

"Sweetheart?" he prompted, his tone more intimate.

"I felt bad about last night." She made her decision in a rush.

"The job?"

She shook her head. "The...other."

"Oh."

She grasped her purse with both hands. "I was thinking, maybe we could..." She glanced around, moistening her dry lips. "Make up for lost time."

He blinked at her.

She forced herself to boldly keep his gaze.

"You're not seriously suggesting we make love *here?*"

"The Oak Castle." She named the hotel across the street.

He glanced at his watch.

"Should I have made an appointment?" she asked tightly.

"Gage and Trent are due in ten minutes."

"Cancel."

"Elizabeth." He held up his palms.

"It's time, Reed."

"It'll wait until tonight."

"But we should have done it *last night*." The words were out before she could think about how they sounded.

"Yeah," he agreed, his gaze going hard. "We should have."

She stood then, feeling supremely stupid for having dug out her black lingerie for a workaholic husband. She didn't know why she had expected today to be any different from other days. Reed was a busy man. He fit her in when he could fit her in, and she'd best not ask for more than that.

He immediately stood with her.

"Goodbye then," she offered, turning for the door, struggling to cope with the hurt of his rejection.

But before she could take a step, an unruly little voice urged her to show him what he'd missed. She fought it for a moment, but then decided to get the last word.

Popping the four buttons on her dress, she turned back and jerked it open.

Reed's eyes went wide and he sucked in an involuntary breath.

"Enjoy your meeting," she told him, redoing the buttons, flouncing out of the office and closing the door before he found his voice.

On impulse, she stopped at Devon's desk. "What was the job?" she asked.

Devon looked confused.

"The woman Reed was interviewing. What was the job?"

"Oh." Devon paused. "Accounting."

"Thanks."

"No problem."

Elizabeth marched to the elevator, meeting Gage and Trent coming the other way. At least the part about the meeting with them was true. Elizabeth didn't know what she would have done if he'd lied about everything.

The elevator doors closed, and the express car whooshed smoothly downward. Truth was, she didn't know what she was going to do about any of it at all. Reed was lying to her. He was lying to her about a woman. She seemed like a woman of substance rather than style, and Elizabeth couldn't help but note the contrast between them.

# Four

Frustration was evident on the face of Reed Anton Wellington II, "Anton" to his close friends, "Mr. Wellington" or "Sir" to most, and "Father" to Reed.

"And you're saying Kendrick never called, never suggested, never even hinted—"

"Never," Reed confirmed, closing the library door in his parents' Long Island mansion. "Not once, not ever."

"It's things like this that can impact the firm."

"I know that, Father."

"It's things like this that can lose millions of dollars."

"I know that, too." Did Reed's father honestly think the broader impact of the SEC investigation were lost on Reed?

Anton moved behind his desk. "You have a good lawyer? You'll cooperate fully?"

"Of course I'll cooperate fully. I have nothing to hide."

Anton stared silently from beneath bushy eyebrows, and a frightening thought percolated in Reed's mind.

"You know I have nothing to hide, right?"

"You wouldn't be the first to succumb to temptation."

Reed was stunned to hear the words from his own father's mouth. "You think I would cheat?"

"I think you have a lot of pride. I think you're very driven to succeed."

"Wonder where I got that from," Reed muttered.

"I need to know what we're dealing with," said Anton.

Reed took a step toward the wide desk. "We're dealing with an innocent man accused of insider trading, and a ten million dollar blackmail attempt."

"Can you prove the blackmail?"

"I'm the third person in my building to be a victim."

"That's not proof."

"No, but the police are working on it. If they find the blackmailer, the SEC will most certainly drop the charges."

"Do they need more manpower?"

Reed shook his head. "I have my own investigation underway, and Collin's put together a legal team."

"Never was too fond of Collin."

"He graduated top of his class in Harvard Law."

"On a scholarship."

"Father, people who receive scholarships are every bit as capable as those who donate them."

Anton harrumphed. "Genetics isn't nothing."

"Don't go there," Reed warned.

"How is Elizabeth?"

Reed threw up his hands. "I swear to you, I am walking out that door."

"I just asked a question."

"You just linked Elizabeth with the middle class. Therefore, in your opinion poor genetics. Don't try to deny it."

"All right. I won't deny it. How is she?"

*Sexy as hell, frustrated as hell, probably mad as hell since it was nearly eight-thirty and Reed wasn't home yet.* "She's fine."

Anton moved to the wide, oak bar and uncorked a decanter of scotch. "You mother and I keep waiting for you to announce that you're expecting."

"I know you do."

When he had two fingers of scotch in each crystal glass, Anton turned back. "Any particular reason why you're not?"

"We'll have children when we're ready."

"Your mother's anxious."

"Mother's been anxious since I was eighteen."

"And now you're thirty-four." He handed Reed a glass of scotch. "You can see why the situation is getting worse."

Reed tried to imagine himself explaining the fertility issues to either of his parents. But he couldn't make the picture form in his brain. Not that he would compromise Elizabeth's privacy in any case, especially not to his parents. She was already intimidated by their opinion of anyone outside their tax bracket.

He downed the single malt. "I have to get home."

"I can have somebody from Preston Gautier sit down with Collin."

"Collin's fine," said Reed. "It's all under control."

At least the SEC investigation was under control. The same couldn't be said of the blackmail. And the same certainly couldn't be said of his current situation with Elizabeth.

Reed could still picture the sexy underwear she'd flashed him in his office. If his meeting had been about anything other than her security and the blackmail case, he'd have chased after her like an eager pup. He'd considered doing it anyway. But then Gage and Trevor arrived, and the real world had closed in.

Elizabeth was on her third margarita in Hanna's downtown loft, blocking out the real world and taking the edge off her humiliation.

"You actually flashed him?" Hanna's laugh was rife with disbelief. "Right there in the Wellington International office?"

"I was wearing underwear," Elizabeth pointed out, stretching out on her stomach on Hanna's leather couch. Hanna was already lounging sideways in an armchair, her shoes kicked off, feet swaying, the slushy drink dangling from her fingers.

"Ever done anything like that before?"

Elizabeth shook her head.

"Bet he was surprised."

Elizabeth nearly giggled at the memory. "I'm pretty sure he was speechless."

"I bet."

Elizabeth's smile faded. She realized the margaritas must be strong or she wouldn't be finding any of this even remotely funny. "I think I was jealous."

"Of what?"

Elizabeth took another sip of the drink. "Okay, this is going to sound crazy. But there was an attractive woman in his office when I got there. He lied about her." She sat up, swinging her feet around to the floor. "He told me she was a client. Devon told me she was a job applicant."

"Uh-oh." Hanna's swinging feet came to a halt.

A few beats went by in silence.

"You think he's having an affair?" asked Elizabeth.

"I absolutely do not," Hanna said with conviction.

"Why would he lie?"

"This is Reed we're talking about. He is not screwing around on his wife."

"Reed's human."

"You have one lie. One little lie, that might not even be a lie. What if Devon made a mistake? What if she thought the mystery woman was a job applicant, and she really was a client?"

"Devon is a crackerjack assistant. She doesn't make mistakes like that."

"Still," said Hanna. "The evidence is way too flimsy to start thinking infidelity."

"What about this?" Elizabeth stood, struggling with her balance for a split second. "Pretend you're a man." She flicked open one of the buttons on her dress. "You're a man, and you haven't had sex in three weeks." She flicked another. "Your wife—your ovulating wife—walks into your office." She flicked the last two. "And flashes this."

Elizabeth opened the coat dress to reveal her sexy lingerie ensemble.

"Wow," said Hanna in obvious awe.

Elizabeth closed the dress. "Does it take a team of wild oxen to keep you away from me? Or is a routine meeting enough to do it?"

"Wild oxen," said Hanna. "Damn, you're in good shape."

"It's the spa membership, my personal trainer."

"I want to join that spa."

Both women went silent as Elizabeth buttoned up and sat back down.

"I still think you're wrong," said Hanna.

Elizabeth desperately wanted to believe Hanna. But there was a sick feeling deep down in her soul that warned her something was going on.

Just then, her cell phone chimed on the table, and she saw it was Reed. She made no move to answer.

"He must be wondering where you are," said Hanna.

"Let him wonder." It chimed again.

"He'll be worried."

"Serves him right."

Hanna moved from the chair and sat down next to her. "Promise me something?"

It chimed a third time.

"What?" asked Elizabeth, clasping her hands together, fighting the urge to answer Reed's call.

"Promise me you'll believe it's nothing until it's not." Hanna reached out to squeeze her hands. "He's a good man, Elizabeth. And he loves you."

Elizabeth took a deep breath, nodded, and reached for the phone, pressing the pickup button.

"Hello?"

"Where *are* you?" Reed demanded, his tone catching Elizabeth off guard.

Her softer feelings for him evaporated. "I'm flashing my underwear for somebody who appreciates it."

There was absolute silence on Reed's end.

Hanna snatched the phone from Elizabeth's hand and raised it to her ear. "Reed, it's Hanna. I'm really sorry. I think I gave Elizabeth one too many margaritas." After a pause, she said, "No. I won't let her drive." She handed the phone back to Elizabeth.

"Hello, darling," said Elizabeth, then she hiccupped.

"You're drunk?"

"A little," she admitted. Not that it changed the facts. Reed was in all likelihood cheating on a drunken spouse, that was all.

"I'm sending a car," he told her.

"Are you drunk, too?"

"No, I'm not drunk."

"But you're not coming yourself?"

"I'm in Long Island. I just left my parents'."

"And if I called them?" Elizabeth couldn't help but challenge. Maybe he was in Long Island, or maybe he was holed up in a hotel room somewhere.

"Why would you call them?"

"I don't know. To say hi. Whatever."

"Elizabeth, it's time for you to stop drinking."

"Sure." She was feeling a little dizzy anyway. And a hangover wouldn't help the job search. And, sex or no sex tonight, she was finding herself a job in the morning and getting started on her very own life.

\* \* \*

Reed waited in the lobby for Elizabeth's car to arrive. Henry was behind his desk, looking nervous about something. The man's gaze twitched from Reed, to the back of the lobby, then out to the sidewalk. Strange.

But then the dark sedan pulled up, and Reed hustled through the double doors to meet Elizabeth.

He helped her upstairs and into the penthouse, tossed her coat on the sofa and took her straight through to the bedroom. There he gently laid her back on their bed and slipped off her shoes.

"You know," she sighed, her eyes closed, hair disheveled, one of her sexy stockings drooping down. "It shouldn't be this hard for two married people to have sex."

"No," he agreed. "It shouldn't be this hard." While she lay with her eyes closed, breathing deeply, he gently removed her jewelry and unbuttoned her dress, his breath catching at the sight of her camisole and skimpy panties.

"Reed?"

"Yes?"

"Promise me something?"

He raised his gaze to her sweet, relaxed expression. "Of course."

"If I fall asleep—" She stopped.

"Yes?" he prompted.

"Let's make love anyway."

He shook his head, allowing himself a tired smile. "Like that's going to happen."

"Good," she said with a smile of her own.

He leaned down. "Elizabeth, I'm telling you no."

The smile turned to a frown. "You're always telling me no."

"I never tell you no."

She had him well and truly wrapped around her little finger. There was almost nothing he could deny her.

"I got all dressed up," she complained.

His gaze dipped down to the black lace highlighting her cleavage. "That, you did."

"Hanna said I looked sexy."

He grinned. "Just how drunk are you?"

She giggled. Then she tilted her chin in determination. "I am getting a job."

"We'll talk about that in the morning."

Her expression changed, and she reached out to him. "Please, make me pregnant tonight." And then her arms went limp, slinking down to the bed, and her body relaxed into sleep.

"Not like this," he whispered, smoothing back her hair and kissing her on the forehead. "Never like this."

He gently removed the rest of her clothes, and tucked her under the covers, stepping back to gaze at her beauty and vulnerability. His cell phone rang, and he quickly opened it, afraid of disturbing her. But she didn't even stir.

Still, he kept his voice low and moved out of the room. "Hello?"

"It's Collin. Selina's at my place."

Reed glanced at his watch. Nine-thirty. "Is anything wrong?"

"Can you come down?"

"Why don't you come up here. Elizabeth's asleep." For some reason, Reed didn't want to leave her alone right now.

"Good enough. Be right up," said Collin, signing off.

Reed pocketed his cell phone then pulled the bedroom door closed. Odds were, they'd completely missed their window of opportunity for this month. Because, he expected it to be twenty-four hours before Elizabeth was feeling remotely romantic again.

And she'd be upset about that.

Well, he was upset, too.

In fact, he was beginning to feel bone weary. The blackmail, the murder, the SEC, all the usual problems at Wellington International. Added to that, his father's values and the persistent infertility trouble were wearing him down. He needed to fix something, anything. But he was operating on every front and, so far, it was to no avail.

For the first time in Reed's life, he wondered if hard work and ingenuity would be enough.

There was a light knock on the front door, and he crossed the foyer to answer it, escorting Collin and Selina to his home office where they took seats around a polished black table.

Reed directed the conversation. "I thought you had somebody on Elizabeth," he told Selina.

She looked startled. "I do."

"She went downtown today. I need a report on things like that."

She jotted down a note in her book. "Sure."

Collin looked at him strangely. "Did something happen while Elizabeth was downtown?" he asked.

"She visited a friend. But I didn't know where she was."

"Just to be clear," Selina added. "Do you want a report on Mrs. Wellington's daily activities or on potential threats?"

Reed took in the expressions on their faces. "I'm not spying on my wife," he protested. But neither did he want her wandering around drunk downtown when there might be a murderer on the loose.

"Perhaps if we changed the nature of the operation," suggested Selina. "Put Joe a little closer to Mrs. Wellington. Say, as her driver? That way, he doesn't have to stay concealed, and he can report to you at intervals."

"I like it," said Reed. "What else do you have?"

"Kendrick," said Collin.

"You found him?"

Collin shook his head. "He's still in Washington, elusive as ever. But some more information has come to light."

"Does it help us?"

Collin and Selina glanced at each other.

"Unfortunately," said Collin, "Hammond and Pysanski also invested in Ellias and made a bundle."

"But, they're—"

"Kendrick's former business partners."

Reed rocked back in his chair.

"It does look pretty bad," said Selina.

Reed couldn't help but defend himself. "Do you

honestly think that if I were going to put together a conspiracy to insider trade, that *this* would be my master plan? A senator giving a heads up on a contract award to four of his closest associates, hoping nobody would notice? It's lame-ass. It's beyond stupid."

Collin leaned forward, eyes hard as he mimicked Reed. "'I'm a smarter criminal than that, Your Honor.' Is that really going to be the cornerstone of your defense?"

"You got a better one?"

"Not at the moment. But if I don't come up with something better than that, Harvard Law School wasted a lot of time and money on me."

"I want this behind me," Reed growled. "There are problems cropping up in the Irish merger, and Germany is talking about changing their safety standards. I don't have time for distractions."

"I'm meeting with the SEC tomorrow," said Selina.

"Take Collin with you."

Something twitched in her expression.

"What?" asked Reed.

She hesitated. "Sometimes Collin cramps my style."

Reed felt his hands curl involuntarily into fists. "There are problems between you two?"

"Stylistic differences," said Collin.

"I take a tough stance. He undermines it."

Reed glanced from one to the other. "You're kidding me?" With all they were facing, these two couldn't get together on their interview techniques?

"Work it out. I want you both in that meeting."

Selina's gaze slid to Collin. He nodded, then so did she.

"Have Joe stop at the office in the morning," said Reed, wrapping things up. "I'll bring him by and introduce him to Elizabeth."

Morning was not kind to Elizabeth.

Rain spattered on the penthouse roof, tapping against her bedroom balcony doors, pounding its way into her fragile skull. She pulled the comforter over her head, praying her housekeeper, Rena, wasn't planning to vacuum today.

Slamming back margaritas on an empty stomach had obviously been a bad idea. It had been a few years since Elizabeth had gotten drunk. And, right now, she was sure it would be many more years before she indulged in more than two drinks in an evening. She blinked open one bleary eye, squinting at the alarm clock. Nine-fifty-two.

She spotted a large glass of water on the nightstand. Sitting next to it were two aspirin tablets. Bless Reed.

She wiggled herself into a sitting position and took the pills. If she could sleep until they kicked in, she'd have a fighting chance of surviving this hangover.

Bless Reed, she thought again. She could forgive him anything at the moment. Well, almost anything.

Though, in the cold light of day, she realized it was unlikely he was having an affair. It wasn't so much her confidence in the strength of their relationship. It was more her knowledge of his core values and principles.

Reed wouldn't cheat.

Even if he wanted to cheat, his honor and principles wouldn't let him.

The rain pulsed harder on the window. She pressed her fingers into her ears and buried her face in the feather pillow, conjuring images of the night before.

Hanna had blended up some fine margaritas, and she'd handed out some sage and practical advice. Plus, it had felt just plain good for Elizabeth to get her anxiety off her chest.

But then Reed had called and annoyed her. Still, when he'd helped her to bed, she'd remembered all the reasons she'd fallen in love with him in the first place. So she'd propositioned him, because time was running out.

Now, she groaned. Time really was running out, and she had no memory past asking to make love last night. She was pretty sure she'd remember it if it had happened.

So, she wasn't pregnant. And it was day three of ovulation. But she didn't think she could even drag herself out of bed at the moment, never mind seduce her husband.

Thunder rumbled in the distance, and the downpour turned torrential. But slowly, ever so slowly, the sound of the raindrops stopped hurting her brain. They became soothing, and the pain went from sharp to dull.

She drifted in and out for an hour, then forced herself to throw off the covers, pulling gingerly into a sitting position. She was tired, but at least she was mobile.

She showered and dressed, and applied a little concealer to disguise the dark circles under her eyes.

She wasn't quite ready for a workout at the gym, but she needed to get the blood flowing somehow. The rain was steady, so a walk was out of the question. She needed to find something to do inside.

The penthouse was empty. Rena was likely out running errands and would be home soon. She didn't like it when Elizabeth cleaned. Baking was acceptable, but baking would fill the suite with aromas.

Not good.

Elizabeth glanced around for inspiration. She caught sight of the living room bookshelf. There was an idea. She could sort through her books, maybe donate some of the older ones to the library. And Reed had hundreds shelved in his office. She'd call Rena on her cell and get her to pick up some cardboard boxes on her way home.

Perfect.

After gathering a sizable pile in the living room, she moved to the office.

Reed liked the occasional mystery or thriller, the kind of book that you didn't reread once you knew the ending. She tugged a couple of his volumes from the eye level shelves and carried them to the black meeting table.

There she paused, wrinkling her nose, trying to identify an unusual smell. It wasn't dust, not leather, not furniture polish. Where had she...

Coconut.

She staggered back in shock.

That woman in Reed's office had smelled of coconut.

"Elizabeth?" Reed called from the entry hall.

The coconut woman had been in the penthouse? Her penthouse? Her home?

"What's with the books?"

She could hear his footsteps starting down the hall.

What did she do? Ignore it? Confront him? Look for more evidence?

Was this why he hadn't made love with her last night? Or yesterday? Or last week?

"There you are." He came around the corner and smiled. "Feeling okay?"

She stared at him in silence, trying to reconcile the man she knew with such reprehensible behavior. While she was desperately trying to save their marriage, had he already ended it?

"There's somebody I want you to meet," said Reed, coming fully into the room.

Not her. Good grief, not her.

"This is Joe Germain."

A man came into view in the doorway, and Reed motioned him into the office.

"Joe, this is my wife, Elizabeth Wellington."

The man stepped forward. He was at least six foot three, with broad shoulders, a burly chest, and very little in the way of a neck. His hair was cropped close, and he wore a dark, neat suit with a dress shirt and tie.

"A pleasure to meet you, Mrs. Wellington." The man held out a strong, callused hand.

"Hello," Elizabeth managed, giving a brief shake, catching a glimpse of a leather holster beneath his suit jacket. Then she met gray eyes, intelligent eyes, some might even say cunning.

"I've hired Joe as your driver," Reed continued.

A driver?

Elizabeth might have been duped, but she wasn't stupid. The man looked like he was half linebacker, half mercenary. He definitely wasn't somebody she'd want to be alone with in a dark alley.

A visceral chill worked its way up her spine.

"Elizabeth?" Reed's confused voice seemed to come from a long way off. "Are you okay?"

She looked back to her husband, her lying, cheating, untrustworthy husband. "I don't need a driver."

# Five

"Elizabeth," said Hanna, her voice chastising as she dunked a tea bag into the teapot at her counter. "You have seriously gone round the bend."

"He insisted, absolutely *insisted* I keep the guy as my driver." Elizabeth had tried every argument in the book to change Reed's mind, but his stubbornness had been off the charts, even for him.

"Maybe he simply wants you to have a driver. You did get pretty drunk last night."

"That guy is *not* a driver."

"He drove you here, didn't he?"

Only because Elizabeth had been too frightened to try to escape. "I think he's a criminal."

"Now, why on earth would Reed hire a criminal?"

Elizabeth hesitated, reluctant to give voice to the fear that had followed her over. But she had to share it with someone. "What if they're right?"

"Who?" Hanna returned to the living area of her loft, where rain pattered on the skylights, and dull daylight gave the airy room a gray atmosphere.

"The SEC. What if Reed has a secret life? What if his wealth really *is* from shady deals with the underworld?" Her mouth went dry and her voice shook ever so slightly. "You know, he's got an awful lot of money."

Hanna enunciated slowly and carefully. "Round the bend, Elizabeth. Reed is a husband and a businessman."

But there were too many inconsistencies lately. He was being far too secretive for this to all be nothing. "Not that much of a husband," Elizabeth pointed out. "He's fooling around with the coconut woman."

"You don't know that he's fooling around with the coconut woman."

"He lied about her. And I know she was in our suite." Elizabeth warmed to the theory. "You know, my parents warned me about rich people. They said they were sly and untrustworthy. They were rich for a reason, and it wasn't hard work and fair trade practices."

"Elizabeth."

"What?"

"You disagree with your parents on that, remember?"

"I was wrong. And look where it got me."

Hanna fought a grin. "You mean with the imagination of a conspiracy theorist? Forget being a script girl. You might want to consider script*writing* as your future career."

"What future career? I'll probably be killed in gangland crossfire before I can ever get a career off the ground. I might know too much already."

"This is insane," said Hanna, picking up her phone. "What's his name?"

"Reed Anton Wellington III."

Hanna shot her a look of dark disbelief. "I mean your driver."

"Oh. Joe Germain. What are you doing?"

"I'm calling Bert Ralston. You give an investigative reporter an hour, and you'll be amazed what he can find out."

Elizabeth plunked back on the couch. That wasn't a half bad idea. At least then Hanna would believe her. At least then Elizabeth would know if she was in any danger from Joe.

How could Reed do this to her? She'd been an innocent young college graduate from New Hampshire when he met her, wooed her, enticed her away from the safe bosom of her family. She never should have borrowed that red dress, or gone on the harbor cruise. Then she never would have met Reed.

Hanna hung up the phone. "You know, you were a lot more fun last night when you were drunk."

"You're not taking this seriously enough," Elizabeth accused.

Hanna rose to pour the tea. "I'm taking this exactly seriously enough. You want vanilla cookies?"

Elizabeth's stomach gave a little lurch of protest. "How come you're not hung over?" she asked Hanna, rising to follow her into the kitchen area.

"Because you outdrank me. How are you feeling by the way?"

"You mean other than facing imminent death by either criminal gang wars or by annoying my driver?"

Hanna carefully poured two cups of steaming tea. "Yeah."

"Bit of a headache. Reed left me some aspirins on the nightstand."

"Yet more evidence of his evil cold-bloodedness."

"He didn't want me to suspect anything."

"Well, that's not working out so well for him so far, is it?"

"That's because of my brilliant, deductive mind."

"It's because of your pickle-brained paranoia."

"I heard the lies. I smelled the coconut."

Hanna's telephone rang and Elizabeth cringed.

Hanna picked it up. "Hello?" She looked at Elizabeth and mouthed *Bert Ralston*. She listened for a moment. Then her brows shot up. "Really?"

"What?" Elizabeth demanded in a stage whisper. Her heart rate deepened in her chest.

"Okay," said Hanna. "Thanks. I owe you one." And she hung up the phone.

"Well?" asked Elizabeth, easing into a chair, because the feeling had suddenly left her legs.

"Joe Germain isn't a driver."

A loud clanging grew inside Elizabeth's head.

"He's a bodyguard."

"What?"

"He's a bodyguard, Lizzy. He works for a national

agency called Resolute Charter. Reed's not trying to hurt you, he's trying to protect you."

An instant rush of relief shot through Elizabeth's body. For a split second, it masked all the other questions. But then they percolated back. "Protect me from *what?*"

"I'm guessing reporters. With Hammond and Pysanski's involvement, this SEC thing is heating up."

Elizabeth had no idea who Hammond and Pysanski were. But Reed wasn't a member of a criminal gang. And her life as she knew it hadn't just ended.

"It doesn't explain the coconut woman," she pointed out.

Hanna slid down into a chair beside her. "If you give it a little time, I'll bet the coconut woman explains herself."

"Dad called here looking for an explanation."

Elizabeth was delighted to hear her brother Brandon's deep voice on the other end of the phone.

"Why didn't he call *me?*" She crossed the living room to curl up in her favorite wingback chair next to the bay window. The clouds were still gray, but the rain had turned to drizzle.

"He thinks the FBI has your phone bugged."

"It's the SEC, and they don't bug phones."

Did they?

If they did, maybe she could get her hands on the tapes and get some information on coconut woman.

"You holding up okay?" asked Brandon.

Elizabeth traced a zigzag pattern on the smooth leather arm. "I'm fine."

Truth was, the SEC was far from her biggest problem at the moment.

"So, you're not worried?" asked Brandon.

"He's got a good lawyer, and they say it's going well." As she finished the sentence, she realized that Reed hadn't in fact said a single thing to her about the case since their initial discussion. In truth, she had no idea how it was going.

"How are things in California?" she asked brightly.

"I hired another vet last week," said Brandon. "And we're advertising for two technicians."

"Business is booming?"

"The practice is definitely growing. We're not in your tax bracket yet, but Heather has her eye on a little house up the coast."

"You're selling the condo?"

"With a growing family—"

"Heather's pregnant again?" Elizabeth hated the pain that filled her chest at the thought of Heather having another baby. She would be thrilled to be an auntie a second time. Babies were nothing but good news. Even if they weren't hers.

"No, Heather's not pregnant. Lucas isn't even a year old."

"Right." Elizabeth was ashamed of her reaction.

"Lizzy?"

"Uh-huh?" She promised herself she'd do better when her sister-in-law really was pregnant.

"I'm sorry you're not conceiving."

Everything inside Elizabeth went still, and a lump instantly formed in her throat. "How did you…?"

Brandon's voice went low and protective, and suddenly they were teenagers again, sharing secrets, laughing and conspiring. "I saw it in your eyes when Heather was pregnant. Then again when you held Lucas. And I hear it in your voice every time we talk about children."

"We're trying," she managed.

"I know. And I assume you have the best medical care money can buy?"

She nodded, then uttered a weak, "Yes."

"It'll happen, Lizzy."

"How long—" Elizabeth stopped herself. It was none of her business.

"Did Heather take to conceive?"

"Yes."

"A couple of months."

Elizabeth reflexively wrapped an arm across her stomach, leaning slightly forward in the chair. She and Reed had been trying for three years.

"I predict," Brandon said into the silence, "that not too long from now, you'll be sitting in my house with a plump, smiling baby wrapped in your arms, and you'll be saying to me 'Thank goodness it took so long. Otherwise we wouldn't have Johnny or Sally or Mary or Tim—the most perfect baby in the world.'"

Elizabeth's throat was so tight, she couldn't speak.

"Lizzy?"

"Three *years*," she moaned, saying it out loud for the first time, feeling the weight of all those failed cycles pressing down on her shoulders.

"It'll happen."

"And what if it doesn't?"

"It's way too early for contingency plans. Trust me. I'm a doctor."

"You're a veterinarian."

"And I spend an enormous amount of my time consulting on breeding issues—dogs, cats, horses, goats."

"I'm not a goat."

"Principle's the same."

There was a muffled rustle on the other end of the phone.

"Elizabeth?" came Heather's breathless voice.

Mortification flushed Elizabeth's body. "You heard?"

"Yes. And I'm about to kill your brother."

Brandon's protest was faint in the background. "I wasn't saying she was a goat."

"Shut up," Heather instructed Brandon. To Elizabeth, she said, "There are plenty of choices."

"I really didn't want this to become—"

"Since you're still trying, I assume Reed's not sterile?"

Elizabeth worked her jaw, but no sound came out.

Heather's voice went muffled. "Of course we can talk about it. We're family. You go check on Lucas."

Her voice came back on the receiver. "Have you tried in vitro fertilization?"

"Uh...no," Elizabeth admitted.

"Artificial insemination? With Reed's sperm, of course."

Once she got past the shock, Elizabeth realized there was something strangely comforting about Heather's matter-of-fact approach. "I've been taking my temperature."

"That's good. Elevate your hips, and don't move for half an hour afterward."

"Right," said Elizabeth, wondering just how far this conversation would go.

Heather's voice went low. "Brandon doesn't know it, but I took my temperature for six months before we tried for Lucas. I knew exactly when I was ovulating. I mean, why take chances?"

"Did you hold off on sex?" Elizabeth could hardly believe she'd asked the question.

"We did. For a little over a week. Of course, Brandon didn't know what I was up to, so he got a little frustrated and confused." Heather laughed. "Never had so many headaches in my life."

Elizabeth smiled, finding the knot in her stomach easing off. "And it worked."

"Like a charm."

"It hasn't for me."

"Nature is fickle," said Heather. "It might take time. And, as for contingency plans, if nothing else works, we'll take your eggs and Reed's sperm, and I'll grow a baby for you."

"What?" Elizabeth coughed out, certain she couldn't have heard properly.

"I'll be your surrogate mother," said Heather with conviction. "We already know I grow the best babies in the world."

Elizabeth's chest filled with emotion, and her eyes welled up with tears. "I don't... You couldn't..."

"Oh yes, I could. And I will."

Elizabeth's sob was audible. She was completely

beyond words. Heather had just made the most generous, kind-spirited offer a human being could make.

"Lizzy, you're my sister, and I love you. And I want you to know that you're a million miles away from exhausting your options." She paused. "Okay?"

Elizabeth nodded, still unable to speak.

"I'm going to take that as a yes."

"I love you, too," Elizabeth whispered.

"Can you come to visit? Is Reed allowed to leave the state?"

The question surprised a laugh out of Elizabeth. "Yes, he's allowed to leave the state.

"Good. Let's make some plans."

"Sure. Yeah. Okay."

"Oops. Lucas is crying. Looks like Daddy's blowing it in there. Bye for now. We'll see you soon!"

Then Heather was gone. And Elizabeth sat staring numbly at the telephone. Her sister-in-law was an angel. She was a saint. And somehow her strength and kindness made Elizabeth feel pathetic.

Elizabeth had once been strong. She'd once had the world at her feet. She was fit and attractive. She had a college degree and a husband to die for. She'd had confidence and energy, and a sense of optimism that told her everything was going to turn out well.

But it hadn't.

And now she had no children, no career, and potentially no husband.

She pictured Reed, wondering what, or who, he was doing right now. Then she banished the vision, remembering Hanna's advice instead. It wasn't reasonable to assume he was having an affair.

It was reasonable, however, to wonder if he was coming home for dinner. She pressed the on button on the phone and dialed his office number.

It rang four times before Devon picked up. "Reed Wellington's office."

"Hi, Devon. It's just me."

"Oh. Hi, Elizabeth." Was there something in her voice? "He just left for a dinner meeting."

A dinner meeting? Was that suspicious? Was he with *her?* "Do you know which restaurant?"

Devon hesitated. "I…"

Damn. It *was* suspicious. "Never mind. I know I wrote it down this morning," Elizabeth lied. "I think it was Reno's…maybe The Bridge…"

"Alexander's," Devon put in.

"Oh, yes. Alexander's. Thanks," Elizabeth said as cheerfully as she could manage, then she hung up and pulled a business card out of her blazer pocket.

Reasonable or not, she dialed Joe Germain's cell phone.

"Might as well make yourself useful," she mumbled while it rang through. It was impossible to get a parking spot near Alexander's at this time of day.

Joe was at her door in less than a minute.

"How'd you do that?" she asked, letting him into the foyer while she slipped on a coat.

"Do what, ma'am?"

"Get here so fast."

"I was in the lobby."

"Lurking?"

One corner of his mouth flexed. "Pretty much."

She hooked her purse over her shoulder. "Is that what you do?"

"Excuse me, ma'am?"

The door closed behind them, and she pulled out her key to lock the dead bolt. "When you're not driving. Do you simply lurk in the lobby?"

"Sometimes I wash the car." He followed her toward the elevator.

"And shoot the bad guys?"

He reached out and pressed the elevator button but didn't answer.

"I know you have a gun," she told him.

"I do have a gun, ma'am."

"Call me Elizabeth. Why do you have a gun?"

"Because this is New York City."

The elevator car arrived, and he gestured for her to go first.

"I know you're not a driver."

"I am a driver, ma'am."

"Elizabeth."

He gave her a look that said her first name wouldn't be passing over his lips anytime soon. "Mrs. Wellington."

"I know you're my bodyguard."

Again, he didn't answer.

"I take it you can neither confirm nor deny you were hired as my bodyguard?"

They started across the lobby.

"Where would you like to go?" he asked in a cool, professional voice.

"I'll pretend I don't know," she offered. "But I think you and I should be straight with one another."

"Am I taking you to dinner? To run errands?"

"Isn't there some kind of special bond? Bodyguard and protectee? One that calls for complete honesty? Considering you may be throwing yourself in front of a bullet for me?"

Joe gave a small sigh. "Visiting a friend?"

"Spying on my husband."

Joe stopped dead.

She took two more steps and then turned and fluttered her lashes. "Is that a conflict of interest for you?"

"No." He started walking again.

"Good. Alexander's Restaurant, please."

Reed paused in the foyer of Alexander's, grateful that Selina's informant had been right.

Third booth past the wine cellar, partially screened by a white, marble pillar, there was Senator Kendrick. He was flanked by two gorgeous young women, and there was an open bottle of Romanée-Conti on the table. No surprise there. The senator was a fairly infamous womanizer. Not that Reed cared one way or the other. The senator's personal life was his own business.

Reed strode confidently past the maître d', rounded the end of the polished bar and came upon Kendrick before the man had a chance to spot him.

"Good evening, Senator." Without waiting for an invitation, Reed slipped into the burgundy velvet booth, sliding up next to the blond woman, helping himself to a breadstick.

The senator's expression faltered, but the woman immediately curved her red lips into a welcoming smile, and she draped a long-fingered hand on Reed's shoulder.

A waiter appeared at the table. "Would you care for a drink, sir? Some wine?"

"Macallan eighteen-year-old," said Reed. "One ice cube."

The waiter nodded and withdrew.

"Reed," Kendrick finally acknowledged with a nod.

"Back from Washington?" Reed asked.

"This afternoon."

"I've been trying to get hold of you."

"I got your messages."

"And?"

"And my lawyers have advised me not to speak publicly on the matter."

Reed cracked the breadstick in half. "Where my lawyers have advised me to *convince* you to speak publicly on the matter."

Kendrick's bushy-browed eyes narrowed.

"I was surprised to read about Hammond and Pysanski." Reed let his gaze bore into the man he'd known and trusted for a dozen years. Not that Kendrick would be the first politician to go bad.

"As was I."

"Something I should know?" asked Reed.

"Should we powder our noses, Michael?" asked the brunette woman.

"No," said Kendrick. "Mr. Wellington won't be staying long."

The waiter set Reed's drink down on the white tablecloth. Then he topped up the others' wineglasses and removed the bottle.

"Reed *Wellington?*" asked the blond woman.

"In the flesh," Reed responded, giving her a brief, polite smile.

"I saw you in the paper just this morning." She sidled a little closer, her arm stretching out along the back of the bench seat. "You're much better looking in color and three dimensions."

Reed took a sip of the scotch, putting his focus on Kendrick. "Do you have something to hide?"

"What do you think?"

"I think Hammond and Pysanski were a very unexpected turn of events."

"That makes me guilty?"

"That makes *me look guilty.*" Reed enunciated each word.

"You go down, I go down," said Kendrick.

"Trent says we get out front of it."

Kendrick shook his head. "I don't want to close any doors."

"What about the other?" Reed didn't have to mention the murder and blackmail for Kendrick to get the point. "I want my family safe, and the more information you can provide—"

"Can't help you there." But there was something in Kendrick's eyes. Something Reed couldn't quite put his finger on. Would Kendrick have to take the Fifth? Was the SEC actually on to something?

Reed downed the drink. "This isn't going to sit well with my board of directors."

"Yeah," Kendrick snorted. "Because losing the Wellington International campaign contribution is my biggest worry right now."

"*Do* you have a biggest worry right now?"

"You mean other than the SEC charges?"

"Of which we're innocent." Reed watched closely for a reaction.

"Like that matters." Kendrick pasted him with a forbidding stare. "You read the papers. You follow the news. Who doesn't want to see a corrupt senator and billionaire go to jail?"

Reed spun his crystal tumbler. "Yeah? Well, I hear you can greatly reduce your chances of being incarcerated simply by not committing a crime."

"That's always been my first line of defense," said Kendrick.

"Then let Trent videotape your statement."

Kendrick shook his head. "No can do."

"I'm going to find out why," Reed warned. He waited a beat, but Kendrick didn't respond.

Then he shoved his glass to the middle of the table and rose to his feet.

# Six

Home from the enlightening stop at Alexander's, Elizabeth stood in her kitchen and struggled to remember the last time she and Reed had eaten in their dining room. Rena was also a cook, and when they were first married, she would make sumptuous four- or five-course dinners. Elizabeth and Reed would indulge in a long, candlelit meal, gazing over the park, talking about the events of the day, their hopes and dreams.

But it had been months since Reed had been home before Rena left for the day. Eventually, the housekeeper had started leaving dinner in the refrigerator for later, tourtière or manicotti—things that were easy to reheat.

Not that Reed would be hungry tonight. Elizabeth was sure he and his little party of four had had a wonderful dinner at Alexander's. While Elizabeth had settled for a banana and a glass of juice.

A key turned in the lock on the penthouse door, and her stomach lurched. She'd been tempted to pack her bags and leave before he arrived. But she kept hearing Hanna's voice asking her to assume it was nothing until proven otherwise. Well, Reed was about to prove it one way or the other.

"Elizabeth?" he called, latching the door shut behind him.

She heard him toss his keys on the entry table, then his footfalls moved toward the living room. She walked out of the kitchen to meet him halfway, glancing at the grandfather clock that showed it was ten-fifteen.

"Tough day?" she asked as he loosened his tie.

"I got stuck in meetings."

"Ahh." She nodded, moving behind the sofa and putting it between them. "With anyone in particular?"

"The last one was with Collin."

"Just Collin?"

Reed peered at her strangely. "Yeah."

"Hmm."

"Have you eaten?"

"Were you at the office?"

He didn't even miss a beat. "Downstairs. Collin's apartment."

She didn't respond.

"We could order something from Cabo Luca." He picked up the phone.

"You didn't eat earlier?"

"Not a thing. I'm starved."

Wow. She'd had no idea her husband was such an accomplished liar.

"Any other *meetings* tonight?"

He paused and cocked his head sideways. "What's this curiosity all about?"

"Just making conversation." She ran her fingertips along the back of the sofa. "Wanting to know about my darling husband's day."

"Tell me about your day. Anything new on the anniversary party?"

"We've chosen the napkins." After only three weeks of deliberation between the party planner, the caterer and the florist. Elizabeth couldn't imagine why her life didn't feel completely fulfilling.

"That's good," said Reed.

"Nothing with Senator Kendrick?"

Reed's eyes narrowed. "Why would you ask that?"

She shrugged. "The SEC investigation."

"I told you not to worry about that."

"Well, I am worried about that. I read the papers. Which, by the way, is my only source of information on this subject."

Reed moved toward her, but she backed off a few steps.

"I saw him briefly, earlier today."

"Just Kendrick?"

"Yes. Trent thought it would be good for me to talk to him alone. If you must know, we want him to make a public statement that we're innocent."

A completely inappropriate chuckle burst from Elizabeth. "Innocent?"

"Of course."

Her throat closed in, and her voice rose an octave. "I don't know what the hell you and Kendrick were doing for four hours with those supermodels, but it sure as hell didn't look *innocent* to me."

Reed drew back, his eyes going wide. "Whoa."

"Who were they, Reed? Or do you even remember their names? A month ago, I would have sworn on a stack of Bibles that you were a faithful husband. And then I thought it was one woman. And now I don't know how the hell many. How long? How long have you been living a lie?"

"Elizabeth!" Arms outstretched, he took two steps forward.

She looped around the end of the sofa. "You stay away from me."

"I swear, I have no idea what you're talking about."

"Swear all you want, Reed. Because I know how well you lie."

"I've been completely faithful." His expression was earnest. If she didn't know better, she'd believe him without question.

"Is that why you wouldn't make love with me? Was it because of her?"

"There is no her. I didn't make love with you because you cringed at my touch. Then I was working, and then you were passed out drunk. I want a baby as much as you do, but I'm not making love to an unconscious wife."

"Then maybe you should have one with someone else." She finished the statement on a sob, realizing how very much the thought of Reed having a baby with someone else hurt her. She loved him. Even through all of this, she still loved him.

It was pathetic.

"Who else?" he demanded, and she could see he was growing angry.

Well, so was she. "I don't know. Take your pick. Maybe that blonde who was hanging all over you in the restaurant, or maybe the—"

"I don't know what people told you. But my meeting with the senator was—"

"*Told* me?" She laughed again, slightly shrill, slightly hysterical. "Nobody had to tell me anything. I was there, Reed. I saw you. I saw her."

"How—"

"My driver. Or should I say my bodyguard. Joe from Resolute Charter. The finest protection money can buy. Did you know he had a gun? Wait. How silly of me. Of course he had a gun. Is he protecting me from irate girlfriends?"

"The blond woman was nobody. I didn't even know her name. She was with the senator—"

"Quit lying to me!"

Reed took a giant step forward, wrapping his big hands around her upper arms. He didn't squeeze. He wasn't hurting her, but she also knew he wasn't about to let go.

"I am not lying about the blonde. I saw her for twenty minutes tops. Call and check with Collin if you want.

"Yes, I hired a bodyguard. But he's also a driver. You want to go out in the city? You want to drink with Hanna? You want to hunt for jobs? Fine. But you're going to be safe while you do it.

"I'm under investigation, Elizabeth. I swear to God I'm innocent, and nobody's going to prove otherwise. But the court of public opinion is an entirely different matter. You could be accosted by reporters or self-righteous citizens, or by anybody else on the street. Joe will keep you safe."

A little of the fight went out of Elizabeth. Was there some logic to that rant? He seemed sincere, offended that his morals had been called into question. And he had conceded on the job front.

"You're okay with me finding a job?"

"Not in the least. But if you're going to do it, you're going to do it. You're not my prisoner, Elizabeth. Although some days I wish you were."

Elizabeth suddenly felt exhausted. Sad and exhausted. What was the truth? What were lies? How was she ever going to recognize the difference?

"How can I believe you?" she asked.

"Can I prove I've never slept with another woman?"

She found herself praying he could. She loved him. She loved him so much.

"No man can prove that," said Reed with a sad shake of his head. "But there's nobody on the planet who can prove I have. I swear to God I've been faithful to you. I love you, Elizabeth." His hands loosened on her arms, and he pulled her into a hug.

Tears dampened her cheeks. "I'm so afraid."

He stroked his palm over her hair. "I'll keep you safe."

"I'm afraid of you, afraid of us, afraid that we're just not going to make it. I *want* to believe you, Reed. I *so* want to believe you."

He pulled back and cupped her face. "What's wrong, sweetheart? What's really going on?"

"I feel like I don't even know you anymore."

He looked puzzled. "You know me better than anyone."

"And you don't know me." She gave a strangled laugh. "Not that there's much to know. I'm nothing. I'm fading."

His tone was heartfelt as he searched her eyes. "You're everything to me."

"But I need to be everything to me. I need to have my own life, my own identity."

His voice went flat then. "So it'll be easier to leave me?"

"Do *you* want to leave *me?*" she asked.

"Never."

But there was still the gorgeous blonde, and there was still the scent of coconut embedded in her brain. "Now would be the time to tell me," she continued. "I won't hold it against—"

*"Never,"* he repeated.

She tried to trust him, tried with all her heart and soul to trust him, but it wouldn't quite come.

"Let's go away," he suggested. "Just you and me. We'll take a trip. We'll reconnect. We'll make love anytime, anywhere, as often as we want. Forget the stupid thermometer."

It was a tempting offer.

Away from New York, she'd have him all to herself.

And if he was having an affair, would he be so willing to leave? Maybe, just maybe, there was hope after all.

"We've already blown this month anyway," she ventured, half to herself.

He smiled. His expression relaxed, and when she looked deep enough into his eyes, she caught a glimpse of the man she'd first fallen in love with.

"Paris," he said, dipping forward. "Or Marseille. We'll rent a chateau and lock out the world."

His lips met hers in a familiar kiss. Her body quickened, and she longed to wrap her arms around him and bury her fears in his strength.

But she couldn't let herself do that. Not this soon. And not this time. They had things to work through besides lovemaking.

She drew back. "Are you serious?"

"Absolutely. I'll book the jet."

Reed had found a chateau for rent in the little town of Biarritz in southern France. It overlooked the craggy beaches, bleached castles and stone walkways of the Atlantic coast. They had their choice of ten bedrooms, the chef came highly recommended and, best of all, there wasn't a blackmailer or SEC investigator within four thousand miles.

He watched while Elizabeth gazed around the arched great room, taking in the bank of French doors and paned windows that revealed a stone veranda. The veranda overlooked the harbor, where waves crashed against the rocks and seagulls called on the afternoon breeze.

It was a cool day, but tourists and residents still dotted

the beach walk. And a few intrepid souls reclined on colorful towels on the sun-warmed sand.

"It's stunning," she said, turning in a circle to view carved wall panels, antique furnishings, rich draperies and crystal chandeliers hanging from twenty-foot ceilings.

After a minute, she grew still, facing him. A wariness shadowed the joy in her eyes.

There was definitely some work to do on their relationship. He wasn't exactly sure where to begin. Elizabeth had misunderstood the blonde hanging all over him at Alexander's. And, he admitted, he could see how that could have happened.

But it was obviously a misunderstanding, easily explained away. And he wasn't sure what he'd done to warrant her suspicion in the first place. Every step he took in life was designed to protect her, to make her life easier and happier. But, for some reason, that wasn't enough.

From what he could tell, this had all started with her crazy idea to get a job. Although why a woman with an unlimited bank account would need a job, he couldn't figure out. Was she bored? Lonely?

He would love to spend more time with her. He'd also love to give her a baby. And he was doing the very best he could on both of those fronts. But he couldn't force a pregnancy, and that unlimited bank account didn't magically regenerate itself. And, lately, the world seemed to throw down challenges as fast as he could rise to meet them.

He felt frustration building within him, but he couldn't give in to the luxury of that emotion. For some reason,

Elizabeth was unhappy. And, as her husband, it was up to him to fix the problem—whether it made any sense or not.

"Are you tired?" he asked gently. "Would you like to take a nap?"

"Could we walk instead?" she asked, turning her attention back to the windows. "Along the shore?"

"Of course," he agreed easily.

She smiled at that, and the frustration eased inside him.

While Elizabeth went upstairs to change into comfortable shoes and a sweater, Reed consulted with the chef on the menu. Jean-Louis also showed Reed a romantic, little dining alcove on the second floor. With a view of the lighthouse and the yachts in the harbor, it would be a perfect location for dinner.

When Elizabeth returned, Reed took her hand, leading her through the wide turret that was the foyer and out to the porch, down a cobblestone path and a short staircase to the beach walkway.

She turned in circles, gazing at the rolling waves and the rock promontories. "This is absolutely gorgeous."

"I think the town center is that way." Reed pointed south to the vintage, stone buildings and the international hotels.

"Let's check it out." Her hand tightened on his as they started to walk.

As they passed other tourists, she asked, "Did you know we have ten bedrooms in the chateau?"

"You counted?"

"I counted."

"It was hard to find a place on short notice." His travel agent had given them a choice of very high end or very low end. High end easily won.

"It seems like we should invite some friends to join us."

"Not a chance." This was their getaway. Theirs and theirs alone.

They came upon a shop with merchandise displayed on the stone sidewalk. Elizabeth ran her hand through a row of colorful silk scarves.

"Would you like one?" he asked, eyeing a bright purple and blue design.

She chose a lemon yellow, so he bought them both.

The next shop sold beachwear.

Elizabeth sorted through a rack of sundresses. "I had the strangest conversation with Heather the other day."

"Uh-huh." Reed checked out a white bikini and matching wrap, wondering if he'd convince her to wear it.

"They know we're trying to get pregnant."

Reed switched his attention from the bikini to Elizabeth, surprised by the revelation. "Did you tell them?"

She shook her head. "Brandon said it was in my eyes when I looked at Lucas and in my voice when I talked about him."

Reed nodded, his happiness dimming a notch. Suddenly, the scarves in the little bag seemed frivolous and inconsequential.

He took her hand and they moved on together in silence.

"Heather..." said Elizabeth, shifting tight against him as they maneuvered around a family of four. Then she took a deep breath and eased away. "Heather offered to be a surrogate mother."

Reed stopped in the middle of the walkway, and his chest contracted painfully. Did Elizabeth know something he didn't? Had there been bad news from Dr. Wendell? Was that what all this job and infidelity nonsense stemmed from?

"Why?" he demanded in a hoarse voice.

Elizabeth urged him to the edge of the path, out of the crowds, where a cliff dropped down to the crashing waves below.

"Were there more tests?" he probed. "Did you find out—" He couldn't voice the question.

"No more tests," she said quietly. "But it's been three years."

Reed braced his hands against the waist-high rock wall, clenching his fists and pressing his knuckles against the rough stone. Sure, it had been three years. But the first eighteen months or so, they weren't really trying for a baby, they simply weren't trying not to have a baby.

He'd assumed it would happen naturally. Thousands of women got pregnant every day of the year. Many of them weren't even trying; some were actively trying to prevent it.

And then there was him and Elizabeth, both with above-average intelligence, both healthy, both hardworking. Both of whom would be stellar parents. Yet they had to contend with charts and graphs and invasive tests, and still nothing happened. And now their family members were beginning to speculate.

"I *hate* this." He fixed his stare on the endless ocean. "It's none of Brandon's business. It's none of Heather's business. There are *way* too many people in our bed."

Elizabeth placed a hand on his tense forearm. "She was only trying to—"

"I don't care," Reed ground out. "I want it to stop. I want you and only *you*. I want it the way it used to be, with you purring and perspiring—"

"Reed."

"—arching and moaning—"

*"Reed!"* She pasted him with a censorious look, glancing meaningfully around at the families out shopping.

He swallowed. "I miss you."

"I miss you, too," she whispered, leaning against his arm, a sheen coming over her eyes.

"I don't want us to be self-conscious about making love."

"I know."

"My parents—" He stopped himself. Elizabeth didn't need to know his parents were also waiting with baited breath for any sign of pregnancy.

"They may not be crazy about my pedigree," she continued his train of thought. "But they definitely want you to procreate."

"My parents are snobs."

"You *think?*"

He chuckled at the tone of her voice, turning to brush a few stray hairs from her soft cheek.

Her skin was flushed, her smile wide, and the sunshine off the Atlantic highlighted her green eyes. "Can we talk some more about sweating and moaning?"

Arousal instantly hit him in the solar plexus. "Not here we can't."

"Back at the chateau? In one of our ten bedrooms?"

"I noticed the master bed was a four-poster," he pointed out, suddenly anxious to get her back there.

Her smile widened even further.

"And we have these new silk scarves." He waggled his eyebrows suggestively.

"I hope you're hinting that I should wear them."

He moved closer to rasp in her ear. "Among other, more interesting things."

"You've got to be joking."

"Why?" Lovemaking should be playful and fun.

With the heel of her hand, she playfully hit him in the shoulder. "You seriously want to tie me to the bed and have your way with me?"

"Absolutely." A sensual, compelling picture rose in his mind.

She coughed out an unintelligible protest.

"Trust me," he told her.

"Reed."

"Trust me." He pulled away and grasped her hand, urging her back along the walkway toward the chateau.

# Seven

At the chateau, Jean-Louis was clearly delighted to see them. And when Elizabeth saw the beautiful table he'd prepared, and inhaled the luscious scents wafting from the kitchen, she knew making love would have to be postponed. She excused herself to change, finding her clothes freshened and hanging in the closet of the master bedroom.

She changed into a black cocktail dress then met Reed at the bottom of the formal staircase.

He gallantly held out an arm. "Would you care to accompany me to the wine cellar?"

She grinned to herself, feeling sexy and playful for the first time in months. "Can I trust you in the wine cellar?"

He grin broadened. "Come on down and find out."

She pretended to hesitate, but he turned them both into a short hallway that ended with a wood-plank door.

The stone staircase beyond it was narrow, and the light was dim. Reed kept a firm hold on her waist as they made their way to the bottom. There, he switched on an overhead light, and she drew in a surprised breath at the rows and rows of dusty wine bottles.

"We're looking for row eight." Reed led her down to the third rack.

"What are we looking for?" she asked.

"This," he announced, and his hands closed over her hips, lifting her to sit on a ancient, hewn-beam table in the middle of the aisle.

"What—"

He silenced her with a kiss, moving between her knees and wrapping his arms tightly around her.

His lips were cool and soft, moist and parted. His tongue gently explored the recesses of her mouth, and she felt shards of arousal work their way out from the pit of her stomach to the tips of her fingers and toes.

His hands moved to her bare knees. His kisses explored her neck, her ears, her shoulders, while she gripped his upper arms for support.

His fingertips circled higher on her thighs, leaving a burning trail of want behind them.

"I had a feeling I couldn't trust you down here," she breathed.

"You can trust me completely." But his fingers hooked around her panties, tugging them down.

She gasped and grasped his forearms. "Not here." She glanced around at the cold, dusty room.

He chuckled. "No. Not here." But he pulled her panties to her ankles, peeling them off over her heels. Then he tucked them firmly into his inside pocket.

He gazed hotly into her eyes. "Later."

"But—"

He silenced her with a finger across her lips. "We're on vacation, Elizabeth. We can play."

He lifted her down from the table, smoothing her skirt back into place. Arm still around her, he guided her toward the narrow staircase.

"Reed?"

"Yes?"

She tipped her head to look back at him. "The wine?"

"Right."

Elizabeth leaned back against the solid table, content to let Reed choose the year and the winery. If there was anything her well-bred husband knew, it was good wine.

She watched the play of his muscles as he reached into the bins, considering and returning bottles. She shifted down the table to bring his profile into view. There was no doubt he was a gorgeous man, and a slow pulse of sexual arousal remained steady in her bloodstream while the cool air circulated around her bare legs.

She couldn't help but picture the big, four-poster bed. The silk scarves also tickled their way into her imagination, making her shiver. She and Reed had more complex problems than a long night of pleasure could solve, but reconnecting sexually wouldn't hurt. It might even help. And it could definitely be satisfying.

"After you," he said, gesturing to the staircase with one of the bottles he'd chosen.

They made their way back to the second floor, where a young French woman assisted Jean-Louis in serving them an artichoke and baby greens salad. It was followed by pumpkin soup, bay shrimps, salmon, a cheese tray, and finally the most heavenly torte she'd ever tasted.

By the time the final dishes were cleared away, Elizabeth had kicked off her shoes and curled up in the rich, velvet upholstery of the big, Louis XV chair.

"Come here," Reed rumbled, a half smile on his face and heat smoldering deep in his midnight-blue eyes.

Elizabeth's sexual arousal returned in a rush. She set down her coffee cup, uncurled her legs and padded the length of the table to Reed's chair.

He took her hand, drawing her down into his lap. Pulling back her loose hair, he feathered soft kisses into the crook of her neck.

Footsteps sounded in the doorway, and she stiffened at the sight of Jean-Louis.

Reed's hand closed around Elizabeth's wrist, keeping her from jumping off his lap.

"We won't require anything further tonight," he told the chef.

*"Bonne nuit, monsieur,"* intoned Jean-Louis with a respectful nod.

"Oh, it will be," Reed whispered to Elizabeth as the door closed behind the chef.

"That was embarrassing," said Elizabeth.

"Exhibitionism not one of your fantasies?"

She drew back in astonishment. Sexual fantasies were definitely not a subject of discussion in their marriage. "No."

He chuckled and resumed kissing, his spread fingers delving into her hair. "Noted."

"Seriously, Reed. I'm not—"

"Noted," he repeated. "I'm not going to forget."

"But—"

He anchored her head and kissed her deeply on the mouth. His other hand stroked behind her knee, teasing its way up her thigh, reminding her she was naked under the little black dress.

Her arms snaked around his neck, and she breathed his name, leaning into another deep kiss, reveling in the play of his lips and tongue on her swollen mouth.

Her breasts rubbed against his broad chest, nipples coming erect, growing sensitized against the fabric of her clothes. Her skin began to tingle, itching, aching to be touched.

His hand cupped her bare bottom, sliding toward the small of her back, bringing the hem of her dress up to her hips. He began an intimate exploration, and perspiration soon slicked her skin.

She went for the buttons of his dress shirt, popping them from their holes, splaying her hands over his chest, starting an exploration of her own.

"I've missed you," he groaned.

She nodded, but words were beyond her capability right now. His skin was taut, his muscles firm, the fire in his veins transmitting itself to her very core.

His palm slipped back down her leg, covering her thigh, caressing her knee, exploring the curve of her calf, then teasing the arch of her foot. Her head dropped back, and his kisses found her neck. He made his way down her chest, while her hands moved to grip his shoulders, stabilizing her position.

He nudged her neckline, moving the fabric out of the way, kissing her nipples through the thin silk of her bra, leaving wet circles that cooled and puckered her skin unbearably.

A groan made its way up from her core, and his hand convulsed against her waistline.

"I love you," he whispered against her breast. "I am madly and passionately and completely in love with you."

"Oh, Reed."

"No matter what happens—" He pulled back, straightening, scooping her into his arms while her body throbbed with need. He carried her the length of the hallway, pushed open the master bedroom door, then closed it firmly behind them.

The lights were out, but the shine from the town and the glimmer of the lighthouse gave the room a luminous glow. Reed sat her on the edge of the bed. Then he stripped off his jacket and tie, his shirt still hanging open. He came down on one knee in front of her, parting her legs and easing between.

He hooked his fingertips into the top of her bra and tugged her forward. She came easily, kissing his mouth, running her fingers through his neat hair, shifting forward so that her dress bunched up and she came in contact with the bare skin of his abdomen.

He rolled her dress up over her head, unclipped her bra so that it fell between them. Then, his eyes boring into her body, he laid her back on the bed. He stroked his hand up the center of her belly, over her navel, between her breasts and across her shoulder.

His mouth followed the trail, leaving hot, moist spots along the way. Finally, he slid up beside her, lips coming down on hers, arms wrapping around her, pulling her solidly against the strength of his body.

His cotton shirt trailed over her skin, further sensitizing her belly, her breasts, her nipples. His hand circled down, touching her downy curls, lower still, until she gasped and arched off the bed.

His kiss deepened, and she convulsively dug her fingernails into his back. Her eyes closed. Her toes curled. Her thighs began to quiver, and her lungs struggled to keep up with her need for oxygen.

Then something brushed softly over her face.

She opened her eyes to see a yellow haze.

Reed stretched out her right arm, then trailed the scarf along it, wrapping the soft fabric loosely around her wrist.

He was joking.

He had to be joking.

But what an odd time to decide to be funny.

He moved her other arm, and she felt the same sensation along it. Something shivered deep down in her core.

"Reed?"

"Trust me," he whispered.

Then he rose, stripping off his shirt, his slacks and everything else.

She lay still, not moving her arms, not moving a thing, taking in every inch of his magnificent body as diffuse light played off the planes and angles of his muscles. His chest was broad, shoulders strong, arms toned, hands capable.

He leaned over her, and she swallowed.

Gripping her upper arms, he shifted her to the center of the bed, her head cocooning in the deep pillows. He placed one knee on either side of her stomach, without putting any weight on her.

He stretched her right arm out again.

He was not serious. He was *not*.

He wrapped the other end of the scarf around the bedpost.

She tried to talk, but her throat had gone dry, and the words turned into a rasp. She wasn't scared. She wasn't angry. In fact, she was sort of…

He stretched out the other arm.

"Reed," she tried, wiggling her hips.

He centered himself over her, capturing her gaze, looking directly into her eyes. "Do you think I'll hurt you?"

She shook her head.

"Do you think I'll do one single thing you won't like?"

She shook again. She wasn't scared. In fact, she was turned on. She was well and truly turned on at the thought of giving him free rein over her body.

"Do you trust me?"

She nodded.

He smiled. "Good."

Then he kissed her mouth. She opened wide, welcoming his tongue. Instinct told her to hug him, but she kept herself still instead.

He kissed her jawline, her neck and shoulders. He made his way to the tip of one breast, then drew the nipple into his hot mouth. She groaned, and arched, and he moved to the other. Sparks of hot sensation traveled the length of her body, flushing her skin, making her blood burn with need.

She hissed his name. But he took his time, indulging in her belly, her thighs, her knees, all the way to her ankles. On the way back up, he moved to the inside, closer, slower, until he hit the center, and she nearly arched off the bed.

Her breaths became pants, and her head thrashed from side to side. Her thighs moved apart, knees bending.

"Now, Reed," she finally cried.

He levered up on his arms, settling over her, pushing inside in one smooth stroke. And she gave a guttural groan. Her arms automatically went around him. The scarves fell away, and she realized he'd never tied a single knot.

She wrapped her ankles across the small of his back, trapping him to her, rising to meet him, reveling in the barrage of sensations she'd nearly forgotten could exist. Her need drove higher, her body grew hotter, as their slick bodies came together over and over again.

A roar grew in the depths of her brain, and a pulse at the base of her spine became insistent. It throbbed harder and faster, radiating out to engulf her limbs.

She moaned his name and tightened her body around him as his rhythm came harder and faster, until rockets exploded behind her eyes and warm honey seemed to fill every crevice of her body.

Then the pulse slowly subsided, and her limbs grew limp. Her legs fell down to the bed, and her lungs worked double-time to recover.

Reed smoothed her hair from her face.

"You're gorgeous," he said.

"I love you," she affirmed.

He pulled her tight, rolling them both, so she was cushioned by his body. Then he flipped a comforter over her back and tucked her head against his shoulder, stroking her hair, his chest rising and falling with his own deep breathing.

Their time in Biarritz was like a second honeymoon. As the days drifted by, Reed watched the tension ease from Elizabeth's expression. They walked the beaches, rented a yacht, tried windsurfing, and visited the funky little shops that dotted the town. They even bought and shipped home an oil painting of the local lighthouse.

They made love every night, most mornings, too. He felt like they were finally reacquainting themselves with each other's bodies. He dreaded going back to the fertility charts and programmed sex.

He was surreptitiously checking with Selina, Collin and Devon several times a day. He'd kept the communications quiet, not wanting to break the spell for Elizabeth. But he knew that issues were beginning to pile up on his desk, and their vacation had to come to an end.

Elizabeth resettled against him on a sofa in a little nook they'd found in the turret on the third floor of the chateau. The sofa faced a curved bank of windows that showed off the brilliant orange sunset over the ocean. A storm was forecast overnight, and Jean-Louis was reluctantly whipping up a gourmet pizza so they could dine casually.

Let it rain, and let the waves blow in. Reed was looking forward to a cozy evening with his fabulous wife. It was their last evening in France. Elizabeth didn't know it yet, but the jet was already on its way to the Biarritz airport.

"Why can't it always be like this?" she asked.

"Sunset?"

"I mean, us. Together. No worries, no problems."

Reed couldn't help but smile at her wistful voice. "Well, for one thing, we'd run out of money."

She straightened to look at him, curling her legs beneath her in slim jeans and a loose, sea-green sweater. "Would we?"

"Of course."

"Maybe we could sell off a few companies. Or maybe you could hire a manager to run them?"

"It doesn't work that way." Everything in his conglomerate was interconnected. It was also interconnected with his father's companies. Wellington International as a whole was worth a lot more than the sum of its parts.

"Then, how does it work?" she asked.

Reed wasn't sure how to explain the complexities of his job.

"The companies depend on each other," he told her. "And someone needs to watch out for the big picture."

"What about Collin?"

"Collin has his own job. He can't do mine, too."

She harrumphed out a sigh. "I think you're getting too puffed up with your own importance. They didn't miss you this week."

"A week's not very long." And he'd been monitoring quite a number of things via his laptop and cell phone.

"I like spending time together," she said.

"I like spending time together, too."

There was a light rap on the door. "Mr. Wellington?"

"Yes?"

The solid door creaked open, revealing one of the housemen. "A phone call for you, sir."

"Obviously something important," Elizabeth sassed.

"Obviously," he agreed, giving her shoulder a quick rub before getting up from the sofa. He was keeping his cell phone turned off most of the time, and he'd asked the office not to contact him through the chateau unless there was an emergency.

This better be good.

The uniformed man pointed to a telephone in the corner of the room, and Reed perched himself on a tiny, French provincial chair.

"Hello?"

"Reed, it's Mervin Alrick calling."

Reed was shocked to hear Elizabeth's father's voice. "Mr. Alrick?"

Elizabeth swiveled her head to look at Reed, brows knitting together in a question.

Reed shrugged in answer.

"I'm afraid—" Mervin cleared his throat. "I'm afraid I'm calling to give you some terrible news."

Reed's chest tightened in dread, his thoughts going to Elizabeth's mother. "Yes?" he asked slowly.

Elizabeth leaned forward, cocking her head, a look of concern growing on her face.

"It's Brandon."

"Brandon?"

Elizabeth came to her feet.

"Brandon and Heather were in a car accident on the coast."

"Are they okay?" Reed reached for Elizabeth, and she moved forward to take his hand.

"What?" she whispered.

Reed gave his head a little shake, concentrating on the call.

"I'm afraid—" Mervin cleared his throat again.

"Mr. Alrick?"

"They've died."

Reed felt like he'd been sucker punched. *"They?"*

"Both of them." Mervin's voice broke, while Reed pulled Elizabeth against him.

Watching his expression, her eyes had gone wide with fear.

"You'll tell Elizabeth," Mervin rasped.

"Yes. Of course. We'll be there as soon as possible. And Lucas?"

"Is fine. He was with his babysitter."

"My jet's in France. We'll go straight to San Diego."

"Yes…well…" Mervin was clearly struggling for control.

"We'll call you soon." Reed disconnected.

"Reed?" Elizabeth's voice was paper dry.

He turned to face her, bracing one hand on each of her shoulders.

"Why do we have to go to—"

"It's Brandon," said Reed, hating what he was about to do to her. "He was killed in a car accident today."

Elizabeth shook her head in denial. "No. No. That doesn't make sense."

"Heather was killed, too."

Elizabeth took a step back, still shaking her head.

"I'm so sorry, sweetheart."

Brandon was her only sibling, and she'd adored him.

"It can't be," she whispered, even as her eyes welled up with tears.

Reed stepped forward and pulled her back into his arms. She struggled against both his touch and the cruel reality of the situation. "No. No. I can't believe it. I won't believe it."

"I need to get hold of Collin." Even as he rocked her, Reed reached for the phone. "He'll contact the jet and make arrangements."

Elizabeth let out a low, keening moan that nearly broke Reed's heart.

"We have to get to California," he told her firmly. "Lucas needs us."

She stilled, looking up. "Lucas?"

"Lucas is fine. He's with a babysitter. But we need to get to him."

She gave a jerky nod, tears flowing freely down her cheeks. Reed wrapped one arm firmly around her shoulders, and used the other hand to dial Collin.

# Eight

Elizabeth moved through the next week in a state of shock, picking up Lucas, consoling her parents, attending the funeral in California.

Thankfully, Reed handled the legalities of the will. While her brother had named her as Lucas's guardian, he had named Reed executor of the estate. Between Reed and Collin, she needed only to sign papers and direct the packing up of Lucas's things.

She briefly met with Heather's parents after the funeral. They were nearly paralyzed with grief. They barely spoke, but held Lucas as long as possible, clearly struggling with the fact he was moving to New York.

Finally, she was back in the penthouse. Lucas's nursery was set up and decorated, and he was settling into a routine with Elizabeth. He still seemed sad and confused at times, but started crawling around the apartment, pulling up on furniture and showing Elizabeth how many changes she'd have to make to protect both Lucas and their antiques.

After a while, when he curled up in her lap for his bottle or drifted off to sleep in her arms, she actually caught herself smiling. There was a permanent hole in her heart for her brother and sister-in-law, but Lucas needed her, and she'd do everything in her power to make sure he grew up loved and protected.

She kissed his silky hair, carefully shifting him to her shoulder to carry him to his crib. His nap was late today. He'd been restless and fussy, chewing on everything he could find. His cheeks were pinker than usual, and his bottom gum was swollen red.

The poor little thing was getting a tooth.

Elizabeth came carefully to her feet.

There was a knock at the door, and he had startled in her arms. She quickly cooed, praying he'd stay asleep.

Rena appeared from the kitchen, drying her hands on a towel.

Elizabeth signaled with a finger across her lips, and the housekeeper glided silently toward the front door, while Elizabeth trundled Lucas down the hall. She laid him carefully into the crib.

She left the bedroom door ajar and padded back down the living room. There, she found Rena with a courier envelope in her hands.

"It's for you." She handed it over.

The return address was for a California law firm. Elizabeth sighed. Some new will detail no doubt. The tears that were never far from the surface burned the backs of her eyes.

"I'll be in Reed's office." The envelope felt heavy in her hands. But it was better to get it over with.

She pulled the tab on the courier envelope as she walked into the office, releasing a thick sheaf of official-looking documents. There was a seal on the top sheet, and it was addressed to her.

She scanned the opening paragraph, frowned, went back and read it slowly.

As she read on, her heart all but stopped in her chest, and emotion squeezed her in a painful vise.

Heather's parents wanted Lucas. This was a legal notification that the Vances were contesting the will. They wanted Lucas back in California, wanted to raise him themselves, wanted to defy Brandon and Heather's wishes and rip Elizabeth's nephew from her home.

She galloped through the package, then reached for the telephone, her hand shaking as she dialed Reed's number. Unanswered, the call bounced to Devon's desk and Elizabeth asked for her husband.

"I, uh…" Devon hesitated. "He's out of the office."

"I'll try his cell."

But all she got was his voice mail. She left a message, as another knock sounded on the door.

"Mrs. Wellington?" Rena appeared in the office doorway. "Hanna Briggs to see you."

Elizabeth nodded. "Send her in."

Hanna was breezing into the office in seconds. "Baby asleep?" she asked. Her smile faded when she took in Elizabeth's expression.

"Take a look at this." Elizabeth shoved the papers across the desk.

With a puzzled frown, Hanna scanned the papers. Then she looked up. "They can't do that."

"They're doing it. They think they'll be better parents than me."

"That's ridiculous."

"They claim they've seen Lucas every day of his life, that San Diego is a better place to raise a child, that Lucas knows them better. Add to that, they're experienced parents, where I—" Elizabeth's voice broke. "I'm only experienced in buying designer clothes and planning parties."

Hanna reached across for Elizabeth's hand. "That's crazy."

"They're not wrong. I do buy designer clothes and plan parties. And until last week, I hadn't changed a diaper in my life."

"Well, that's it then. Because, I'm sure a diaper changing contest will be the first thing the judge thinks of when determining custody."

"You know what I mean."

"I do. But you're getting ahead of yourself again."

Elizabeth understood Hanna's point. She'd gotten ahead of herself when she thought Reed was cheating, and when she thought Joe might be a criminal.

"I can't get hold of Reed," she said.

"He's probably in a meeting."

"He's always in a meeting."

Things had definitely been better between them physically since they returned from France. But she could feel them slowly slipping back into their old routine. Although nine-month-old Lucas kept her busy, she couldn't help but notice that Reed's evenings were filling up with business obligations.

"You should call Collin," Hanna suggested.

"You hate Collin."

"Only because he's a lawyer. But they do have their uses."

Elizabeth thought about that. Should she wait for Reed? Or should she get things rolling on her own? She did want to develop some independence.

Getting a job was out of the question for her now that Lucas had arrived. But that didn't mean she couldn't start standing on her own two feet.

The strength and self-assurance of the coconut woman had wedged itself firmly into Elizabeth's mind. For some reason, she knew deep down in her soul that Reed respected that kind of a woman.

"Collin it is."

When the line connected, she heard female laughter, then a voice that sounded vaguely like Reed's. Elizabeth's spirits lifted.

"This is Collin."

"It's Elizabeth calling."

"Oh. Hello, Elizabeth." The background sounds suddenly stopped. "How can I help you?"

"Are you by any chance with Reed?"

"Not at the moment. Do you need to get him a message?"

Too bad. "Actually, I need some legal advice."

There was a pause. "Sure."

"I received a notice today that my sister-in-law's

parents are contesting my brother's will." She gave him the details.

"Does Reed know about this?"

"I haven't been able to get hold of him."

"I'll have him call you." And the line went dead.

Elizabeth replaced the receiver and frowned at Hanna. "Not a lot of help." Then, remembering the opening to the conversation, she said, "It's funny. It almost sounded like—"

The phone rang on the desk. She grabbed it quickly. It was Reed.

She felt a rush of relief. "Did you get my message?"

"From Collin?"

"I thought you weren't with Collin."

"I'm not. He called me."

So Reed picked up the calls from Collin, but not the ones from her? "Where are you?" she asked.

"What's going on? Collin said the Vances contacted you."

Elizabeth explained the contents of the letter.

"Collin's going to come by and pick up the package," said Reed. "I don't want you to worry about it."

"How can I not worry about it?" She glanced at her watch, noting that it was nearly five. "Aren't you coming home now?"

"Not for a while. I've, uh, got a conference call with the West Coast."

"I see." Elizabeth didn't disbelieve Reed. Problem was, she didn't completely believe him, either. There was something in his tone that didn't quite ring true, something that made her feel he was searching for excuses.

She didn't like feeling this way. But the further they got from Biarritz, the more her confidence faded. If he loved her the way he said he did, shouldn't he be rushing home? Shouldn't Lucas and she be the most important things on his mind?

Reed hung up the phone and looked across the table at Collin. "Can you head for the penthouse and pick up those documents?"

Collin immediately rose. "You bet."

Reed cursed the fact that he couldn't leave right now. Elizabeth had too much on her plate. She was working round the clock to care for Lucas, while struggling to get over her brother's death.

Collin left the boardroom as Gage Lattimer walked in.

"What's up?" Gage took the chair across from Reed.

"This," said Reed, sliding his latest problem across the table. It was another letter from the blackmailer.

"Don't touch it," he warned Gage. If he hadn't obliterated them by opening it, the police might be able to raise fingerprints.

Gage read the short letter.

*Hammond and Pysanski are the beginning. I'm the only one who can stop this now. Pay up!*

When Gage looked up, his eyes were thunderous. "Who is this guy?"

Reed shook his head. "Trent stopped the Hammond and Pysanski connection from being reported in the media."

"Is it somebody close to you? Or somebody connected with the police?"

Reed had no idea. But this was a very disturbing turn of events. "If he's either of those things, you have to wonder how deep the frame-up goes."

"You think he could actually nail you?" Gage paused. "Or me? Why isn't he shaking me down?"

"Whoever did this has been thinking about it for a long time. Maybe he's planted evidence against me but not against you."

"I'm merely collateral damage?"

Reed coughed out a laugh. "Maybe. Or maybe he thinks I'm worth more money."

"You are."

"There you go."

"Ten million," mused Gage. "How long would it take you to raise that kind of cash?"

"Five minutes," said Reed honestly.

Gage nodded as Selina breezed into the room.

She reached into her briefcase, pulled out a plastic bag, and tweezered the letter safely inside. Then she sealed it, sat down and turned it so that she could read.

"I'll take this to a private lab. I doubt we'll get fingerprints. The operation has been too sophisticated so far to make a mistake like that."

"What about the police?" Reed asked her.

"I'm not putting this into the bowels of their backed-up crime lab. I'll get to them later."

"Any more clues? Anything else at all to go on?"

"I'm still following up on Hammond and Pysanski. In my opinion, we have a better chance of clearing up the SEC thing than finding the blackmailer. It we cut the SEC investigation off at the knees..." She snapped her fingers in the air. "Poof, the blackmail problem is gone."

"For me, anyway," said Reed. The blackmailer undoubtedly had other victims in mind.

"And, since you're the one paying my salary, you're the one I care most about."

"And me?" Gage put in, in a voice tinged with mock offense.

"You'll be a collateral victory," said Selina.

"You heard me say that?" asked Gage.

"I hear everything." She gave her attention back to Reed. "Something triggered this second letter. We're going to have to go over the details of your past few days."

Reed nodded in resignation, desperately worried about Elizabeth, and hoping Collin was taking good care of the will issue. Lately, it seemed as if Reed were being dragged simultaneously in a dozen different, yet crucial directions.

Elizabeth sat in the wingback chair opposite Collin.

"On my preliminary read," he was saying, the legal documents in his hands, "I'm feeling very optimistic. But I have a friend who's a member of the bar in California. I can get him to fly out tomorrow so that we can start on a proper plan of defense."

Elizabeth nodded, grateful to Collin. He was cool and controlled, and his expertise shone through at every turn in the conversation. But she couldn't help thinking that Reed should be here instead. It should be her husband who was offering comfort and advice, not his lawyer.

Then she berated herself for that train of thought. Hanna was right. Elizabeth needed to stand on her own two feet.

"I'd like to meet with your friend," she told Collin, squaring her shoulders. "I'm available anytime."

"I'll set it up."

The penthouse door opened, and they both turned to see Reed stride in. "What did I miss?" he asked.

Elizabeth glanced at her watch. It was nearly nine.

"I read the package," said Collin, coming to his feet. "I'm going to ask Ned Landers to fly in tomorrow."

Elizabeth stood to face Reed. "It's all under control. You don't need to worry."

Reed drew back sharply. "That's—"

"I know you're busy," she put in. Then she turned and reached out to shake Collin's hand. "Thank you very much for your advice, Collin. I appreciate your taking the time."

"Not a problem," he answered. "I'm always available for you, Elizabeth."

At the other side of the room, Reed stayed silent.

"Good night," Collin said to them both.

As soon as the door shut behind Collin, Reed turned on Elizabeth. "What the hell was that all about?"

She blinked at him in surprise. "What?"

"'I don't need your help, Reed,'" he simpered. "'It's all under control.'"

"It *is* all under control. Collin says we're in a very strong position. He says the Vances would essentially have to prove we're unfit parents to win in court."

"It's nice to know what Collin had to say, but what about what *I* have to say?"

"You weren't here."

"I had a meeting."

"You *always* have a meeting." She cringed at the sarcasm in her voice.

Reed's tone grew stronger. "I would have been here if I could."

"Keep your voice down."

He drew an exasperated breath. "I want the details."

She pointed to the papers on the round table. "Help yourself."

"I also want to know exactly what Collin said," he warned, scooping up the paperwork.

"I'll tell you everything I remember."

His eyes narrowed, and he peered at her.

"What on earth is the matter?" she demanded.

He was acting as though he were jealous of Collin.

Reed was stonily silent for a long beat. "I don't like being replaced by my lawyer. This is *our* problem, not your problem alone."

"I can take care of it, Reed. I'll have professional help."

His complexion turned ruddy. "So, you don't need me? Is that what you're saying?"

"Isn't that exactly what you said to me?" Even as she lobbed the volley, Elizabeth silently acknowledged that she didn't want to have this fight. Lucas was what mattered. All of her energy and emotional resources needed to be directed at him for the time being.

Reed turned sharply, and marched down the hall into his office.

Now she'd done it. The closeness they'd shared in France was officially a distant memory, and the cool formality from before their trip had turned to hurt and anger. And it was her fault. Fawning over Collin's presence had been a passive-aggressive slam at Reed's absence.

She screwed up her courage and followed him down the hall, carefully sliding open the door.

"Reed?" she ventured.

Without looking up, he grunted an acknowledgment.

"I'm sorry."

That got his attention.

"We should work on this together," she said calmly. "And I do appreciate your perspective."

"He's my son, too, you know."

Her eyes clouded, and she blinked rapidly. "Of course. I thought you were too busy. I was trying…"

Reed let the sheaf of papers flatten on the desk. "I'm sorry I was late." His jaw tightened. "Things are complicated…at the office right now."

She nodded, even though she didn't understand what he meant. But then she never had been privy to the intricacies and machinations of Wellington International. "Lucas is what matters."

"Yes, he is. We're his parents now, Elizabeth, and we need to ensure his well-being. On all fronts."

A tear slipped down her cheek. "Why are they doing this?"

Reed shook his head. "Grief over Heather? Maybe a desire to cling to a little piece of her?"

"But Brandon and Heather chose *us*." Elizabeth didn't know the Vances. They could be selfish or mean-spirited, they might even be fanatical about something. There was a reason her brother and sister-in-law had entrusted Lucas to her care, and she wasn't going to let them down.

"And the court will see it that way," said Reed. "We'll talk to Ned Landers together."

"Together," Elizabeth agreed. But a little part of her couldn't help wondering if Reed would make the meeting.

# Nine

Ned Landers advised Reed and Elizabeth to carry on with their ordinary lives. The only leg the Vances might have to stand on is if they could paint Reed and Elizabeth as unsuitable parents. That task would be all but impossible.

Although Elizabeth had been focused on Lucas, her party planner and neighbor, Amanda Crawford, had carried on with the anniversary party plans. Ned recommended that they go ahead with the party. It sent a signal that their marriage was strong, and that they had a good support network of friends and extended family, helping to paint them as a stable family unit.

Hanna had volunteered to babysit Lucas for the

evening, insisting that she was the only one he trusted and that she hated big parties anyway. Elizabeth knew that was true, so she went along with the plan. For some reason, Reed had also insisted Joe Germain spend the evening in the penthouse.

Hanna had protested the arrangement. That is, until Joe showed up at the door and she got a good look at the tall, übermasculine man.

Elizabeth supposed Joe was a handsome man, in a caveman kind of way. Although, if a woman were turned on by physical power, Joe was about as good a fantasy as a girl could get.

Judging by Hanna's speechless, wide-eyed stare, she had a thing for physical power.

"Thanks for coming, Joe," said Reed, appearing from the kitchen.

Joe headed for Reed, giving Hanna a curious nod of greeting as he passed.

Hanna's gaze locked on the rear view of Joe.

Elizabeth elbowed her friend. "Down, girl. I don't think he's allowed to make out on duty."

"How would you know?"

"It must be in the handbook or something."

Hanna grinned. Then her gaze drifted up and down Elizabeth's red satin evening gown.

"You're going to knock 'em dead," said Hanna. "I wish I had your clothing budget."

"I feel pretty spoiled tonight," Elizabeth admitted. Reed had insisted that her gown be custom-made and dramatic.

Hanna gathered Lucas from Elizabeth's arms.

"There are a couple of bottles for him in the refrigerator," said Elizabeth, smoothing his hair and kissing his chubby baby cheek as she ran down the instructions.

"Yes, Mommy," Hanna sing-songed, and Elizabeth's thoughts went immediately to Heather.

"Sorry," Hanna whispered.

"It's all right. We have to move forward. And I guess I'm the one to do it."

"You're doing beautifully," said Hanna.

Elizabeth took a breath, and Reed appeared at her side.

"Ready?" he asked.

"I don't know how regular parents do this," said Elizabeth, reluctant to leave little Lucas.

Joe stepped up. "I'm trained in fire safety, first aid, defensive driving and, well, hand-to-hand combat."

Reed grinned. "See that? We have absolutely nothing to worry about."

"Do you change diapers?" asked Hanna, obviously trying for a joke, but her voice came out breathy.

"Whatever's necessary," Joe said easily, lifting Lucas with a deft gentleness out of Hanna's arms and tucking him against his shoulder like he'd been doing it all his life.

Elizabeth wasn't sure, but she thought Hanna might have fallen instantly for Joe.

Reed held out an arm to Elizabeth. "Shall we?"

She smiled up at him, determined to enjoy her evening. She linked her arm into his as they turned for the door.

"Is Joe single?" she whispered under her breath.

"I think so. Why?"

Elizabeth glanced back at Hanna's expression. Her friend looked liked she'd been dropped straight into her deepest fantasy.

\* \* \*

It wasn't often that Reed imagined himself in a science fiction story. But, at the moment, he would take it very kindly if somebody would please *beam him up.*

"I understand that these things can happen," continued Vivian Vannick-Smythe, a halo of feathers that served as a hat quivering around her lined face while she gesticulated her story. "And I'm certainly not one to stand in judgment."

Reed choked back a laugh at that statement.

While Vivian carried on about the SEC investigation and how it was all about her, he scanned the crowd for Elizabeth, wondering why, since this was their anniversary party, he'd spent so little time with her. Then he saw her dancing with Prince Sebastian. The man was holding her too close for Reed's taste. If not for the Prince's European sensibilities and the fact that he was getting married in Caspia on New Year's Day to his American assistant, Tessa Banks, Reed would have had words with the man.

"I think the reputation of the entire building is at stake," Vivian prattled on. "And if I were you—"

"You're not me," Reed pointed out.

Vivian took an imperious breath, the feathers jiggling again. "If I were you, I would do everything in my power to bring a speedy end to this embarrassing episode."

"You don't think I'm already doing that?" he asked.

Her eyes narrowed. "You should think long and hard about how you go about protecting your family, your friends and your neighbors...."

Reed drew back from her shrewd expression and the odd turn of phrase.

"From the crushing embarrassment of being associated with an accused criminal," she finished.

"Right," said Reed. "The crushing embarrassment of my neighbors is my primary concern at the moment."

"Good evening, Reed," came a familiar male voice.

Vivian's head came up, her self-confidence instantly evaporating.

"Good evening, Father," said Reed.

Anton stared Vivian down until she mumbled something unintelligible and scooted away.

Reed resisted the urge to thank his father.

"Elizabeth is looking well."

Reed turned his attention to the dance floor, agreeing that his wife looked incredibly beautiful, particularly considering everything she'd been through. "She's coping the best she can."

"I understand she's taking care of her nephew now?"

"Our nephew," Reed corrected.

"Yes, of course. And there are some grandparents in the picture?"

Reed gazed at his father's inscrutable expression. "You mean the Vances?"

"I understand they'd like to raise the boy."

"Lucas. His name is Lucas. And we're his legal guardians."

"Do you think that's wise?"

An uncomfortable feeling wedged its way into Reed's stomach. "It's not a matter of wise or unwise, Lucas *is* our responsibility now."

"Unless the grandparents win the court case."

"They won't."

His father squared his shoulders and set his jaw. "I wonder if you've thought this through."

Reed waited to see where Anton was going.

"Have you considered the impact this…nephew—"

"Lucas."

"—will have on your future children?"

And then Reed got it. And it was horrible. "Please tell me you're not suggesting—"

"He's not your natural-born son."

Reed coughed out a hollow, disgusted laugh. "You're worried about his pedigree? You're worried that he will somehow detract from…what? Their inheritance? Will his bad breeding somehow rub off on them?"

Anton's eyes turned to flints and he put his infamous intimidation mask in place. But it wasn't about to work on Reed.

"I'm adopting Lucas," Reed said firmly. "He'll have every legal right of any other child I may or may not have in the future."

The mask slipped. "He'd be your eldest son. The Wellington heir."

"Yeah," said Reed. "How about that."

"I can't let you—"

"There is nothing, *nothing* you can do to stop me." He leaned in, making his point loud and clear. "And, believe me when I tell you, it is not in your best interest to try."

Then he turned and walked away.

"Reed?" Collin appeared by his side, falling into step.

"Where's the nearest bar?"

Collin pointed to one corner of the ballroom, and Reed started in that direction.

"You okay?"

"Fine," said Reed, forcing himself to switch gears. His father was his father, and there was nothing he could do to change that. He could only protect his family as best he could from the man's interference.

"What's up?" he asked Collin.

"They've set a court date in California," Collin told him. "In three weeks."

Reed digested the new information as he ordered their drinks. "What are Ned Landers's thoughts?"

"He's somewhat worried about the Vances' existing relationship with Lucas. They have documentary and pictorial evidence of having seen him nearly every day. They set up a scholarship trust fund for him mere days after his birth—"

"I could set up a scholarship trust fund," said Reed. Trust fund, hell. He was about to make Lucas a boy-king.

"Too little, too late," said Collin as they moved to a quieter spot with their drinks. "Besides, our argument isn't that you've been close to Lucas since his birth, it's that you and Elizabeth were Brandon and Heather's choice as guardians. Economic wherewithal is self-evident. You just need to keep your head down and your nose clean."

Reed knew what he meant. The SEC investigation.

"Innocent until proven guilty," Reed pointed out. "Surely a judge understands that."

"They'll try to use it."

"Let 'em."

"Don't get hostile," Collin warned.

"I don't need to get hostile. I'm in the right."

"And don't get cocky. Some judges see wealth as a handicap, not an advantage."

"Because I'm rich, I'm de facto strange?"

"Something like that."

"That's bullshit."

"Hostile again," Collin warned.

"Maybe you should go to the hearing instead of me."

"You mean with you?"

"I mean instead of me." The night the legal papers had arrived bloomed in Reed's mind, surprising him with the rush of anger it provoked. "You did a good job taking my place with my wife on Wednesday."

Collin stood stock-still, his martini halfway to his lips. "Don't be an ass."

"Elizabeth seemed pretty grateful."

"You sent me," Collin pointed out.

"We both know why I wasn't there."

"You accusing me of something?"

Reed squared his shoulders. "Is there something to accuse?"

Collin nodded to Reed's drink. "How many of those have you had?"

"Not nearly enough."

"You actually think I'm putting the moves on your wife?"

The blunt question stopped Reed in his tracks. "No." Of course not. The very idea was ridiculous.

"Good. Because if I want your wife I'll tell you straight up. Then we'll duke it out."

"Seems fair," said Reed with a shrug, acknowledging that his anger with Collin was completely misdirected. "But I think I could probably have Joe kill you."

"True enough," Collin agreed easily. "But first, we have to deal with this court date."

"Yeah." Reed swirled the ice cube in his glass. "I don't know what the hell happens if that doesn't go our way."

"Odds are with us on that one." Then Collin nodded to the foyer. "Wish I could say the same thing about the SEC investigation."

Reed followed Collin's line of sight, catching Selina hovering in the archway. Her jaw was compressed, and her eyes were hard.

"Damn," Reed muttered. He glanced to the dance floor where Elizabeth was in the arms of another lucky partner who wasn't Reed. "Tell me, when does this party get fun?"

"Want me to come with you?"

Reed shook his head, placing his empty glass on a nearby tray. "I want you to keep an eye on Elizabeth. Run interference if you need to."

"You got it," said Collin, moving off as Reed headed for Selina.

"What's going on?" he asked her, putting a hand on the small of her back and moving her to one side.

"It's Hammond and Pysanski." She sounded almost breathless.

"What about them?"

"There's evidence—dates, purchases and profits—that this isn't the first time one of Kendrick's committee decisions has netted them a windfall."

Reed glanced back into the ballroom, realizing for the first time that Kendrick and his wife hadn't shown up for the party. Had Reed underestimated the significance of this problem to Kendrick? Was it possible the senator was actually guilty?

Reed moved closer to Selina, lowering his voice. "Go on."

"Hammond put fifty thousand dollars into a company called End Tech in 2004. Two months later, the company won a federal contract for wireless R&D. Both Hammond and Pysanski bought into Norman Aviation right before a big helicopter award in '06. And, last year, Hammond went big on Saville Oil Sands just in time for the stock split."

Reed swore.

"Yeah," Selina agreed. "Add that to Ellias, and you've got yourself one hell of a pattern to put in front of the jury."

"And Kendrick can be connected in each case?"

"His committee made the pivotal decision every time."

"I'm screwed," said Reed, gripping the back of his neck.

"You're innocent," Selina pointed out.

"Tell that to a jury of my peers, after the prosecution shows them pictures of my real estate holdings and my airplanes."

She glanced away. "Okay. It's a challenge all right."

It was the first time Reed had seen even a hint of anxiety in the woman's eyes.

He leaned in, wondering just how much of a problem this new evidence would be. "Selina?"

Her teeth came down on her lower lip, and she gazed at him with a frankness that said more clearly than words they were in big trouble.

Whirling in the arms of her neighbor, Trent Tanford, Elizabeth caught yet another glimpse of Reed in the foyer. He was in deep conversation with a woman she couldn't place. The woman wasn't dressed for the party, but wore a pair of jeans and a blazer. Elizabeth could only see the woman's back, but Reed's expression was intense.

He touched the small of the woman's back and moved her off to one side, out of Elizabeth's sight. The song ended, and Elizabeth quickly thanked Trent, crossing behind a marble pillar for a better look.

Several friends stopped her to chat, and she was briefly distracted by a glimpse of Amanda Crawford. The normally vivacious and bubbly woman looked upset. She was cloistered in a corner with a very pregnant Julia Rolland, and the two looked to be having an intense discussion.

But then Reed came back into view. He was still talking with the mystery woman. Elizabeth took a few more steps. Then, suddenly, the woman turned.

Elizabeth's stomach plummeted to the floor. For a second, her limbs were paralyzed and a roaring in her ears nearly drowned out the music.

It was the coconut woman.

Reed had stepped out of his own anniversary party to have an intimate conversation with the woman he'd lied about at work and brought into their home. What was going on?

What had he done?

"Elizabeth?"

She blinked a man into focus in front of her. Gage.

"Care to dance?" he asked, holding out a hand.

No. Elizabeth did not want to dance. She wanted to rant and rail, and scream at fate, scream at Reed, demand an explanation for what looked absolutely damning.

"Sure," she said instead, and let Gage's strong arms pull her into the rhythm of the music.

She tried to ignore Reed, but that was impossible. The conversation was still going on. Reed looked angry. Coconut woman looked upset. Then Collin joined the two of them. Collin, the traitor. Had he been routinely covering for Reed's trysts?

How long had this been going on? Had Biarritz been some kind of a trick?

"Uh, Gage, that woman in the foyer with Reed. Do you know her name?" Elizabeth was proud of how even she managed to keep her voice. "We met at Reed's office a few weeks back, but I'm embarrassed that her name's slipped my mind."

Gage hesitated long enough to make Elizabeth want to sock him. Was he in on it, too? Was there a conspiracy of silence among rich, powerful men? Did they all keep a mistress? Had she been hopelessly naive all these years?

"I think it's Selina."

Elizabeth waited, taking in the discomfort on Gage's face.

"She's connected to law enforcement somehow," he said.

Right. First Selina was a job applicant, then a client, now in law enforcement? Elizabeth wasn't stupid. This was a conspiracy, and she couldn't trust anyone.

"That sounds right," she said with a bright smile. She blinked, searching the room for something else to concentrate on while the song finished.

She spotted Amanda again. The woman still looked upset, but this time she was talking to Alex Harper. While Elizabeth watched, Alex touched Amanda on the shoulder. The woman's lips compressed. She turned away, and Alex's smile turned to a frown. It looked like he called her name, but she kept walking.

Then finally the dance ended. Elizabeth gave her husband one last fleeting glance then slipped out a side door.

"I didn't expect you this early." Hanna hopped up from the sofa as Elizabeth entered the penthouse.

"I missed Lucas," Elizabeth lied, hoping she'd successfully hid evidence of her crying jag while she was in the back of the limo. In case her eyes were still red, she busied herself hanging up her coat and putting her purse away.

"He was a doll," said Hanna. "And Joe really does change diapers."

"Pediatric protection detail," Joe put in, levering up out of his chair.

"But you were right," said Hanna in a breezy voice. "He's not allowed to make out while he's on duty."

Elizabeth sputtered out a laugh. "You propositioned my bodyguard?"

"I'm your driver," Joe corrected.

"He's a stickler for the rules," said Hanna with a saucy shimmy.

"Would you mind driving Hanna home?" Elizabeth asked Joe. The faster they left her alone, the faster she could fall apart.

"Not at all," he drawled. "There's a…little matter we need to finish."

"I…"

Elizabeth smiled, amazed that she could be happy for her friend when her own life was crashing down around her.

"Good night, Elizabeth," Joe offered as he propelled Hanna toward the door.

"I'll call you." Hanna waved.

"Lock up," he advised as he let the door swing shut.

Elizabeth turned the dead bolt and took two steps back. Then, she stopped, bracing a hand on the entry table and closing her eyes as the world spun around her. She felt genuinely dizzy.

What on earth did she do now?

The spinning stopped, and she walked into her home. She took in the furniture they'd had custom-made, the paintings she'd so lovingly chosen, the wrapped package leaning against the wall. It was the painting they'd purchased in France, when everything seemed like it would work out.

What was Reed thinking? How could he make such tender, passionate love to Elizabeth while coconut... Selina was waiting in New York?

She made her way down the hall, listened by Lucas's door, then turned into the office. There, she did something she'd never done before. She opened Reed's laptop and booted it up.

It took only three tries to guess his password and get into his e-mail. She scrolled through hundred of entries, until she came to the dates they'd been in France. Selina Marin, Selina Marin, Selina Marin. There were dozens of e-mails from her, and dozens of answers from Reed.

Elizabeth didn't have the heart to read any of the messages. The last faint hope that she'd somehow been mistaken was gone. Reed had a mistress, and Elizabeth's life was a lie.

# Ten

Reed couldn't understand why Elizabeth had left the party. If she was worried about Lucas, she should have said something. As it was, he'd been left in the embarrassing predicament of having to make her excuses.

Unlocking the penthouse door, he found himself struggling for patience. "Elizabeth?" He kept his voice low, not wanting to disturb Lucas if he was asleep.

"Elizabeth?" he tried again, dropping his keys on the table. Her purse and coat were here, and Hanna and Joe had obviously left.

He started down the hall, glancing into the office, Lucas's room, then, finally, the master bedroom.

"There you are." He stopped short, seeing an open suitcase on the bed. "What's wrong?" Had there been some news? Was she going to California?

She didn't answer, didn't look at him. Her cheeks were streaked with tears, and there was a stiffness to her walk.

"Elizabeth?" He moved toward her, arms out, fear rising in his throat.

"Don't touch me!" she snapped, jerking back.

"What? What's wrong?"

"You know perfectly well what's wrong." She met his eyes for the first time, and he was floored by the anger he saw reflected in her depths.

"What?"

She yanked open a drawer. "Don't play dumb with me."

"I'm not *playing* anything. Why are you packing? Where are you going?" His heartbeat thickened in his chest. Something was terribly wrong.

"Selina Marin. Name mean anything to you?"

Uh-oh. Had she heard about the blackmail? Was she afraid for Lucas? "I didn't want to tell you," he began, "because—"

"You don't think I can guess why you kept it a secret?"

Well, yes, of course she could guess. "There were so many things going on. You had so much on your mind."

Elizabeth gave a hysterical little laugh, then pressed a shaking hand against her mouth. "You think I was too *busy* to hear about your mistress?"

For a split second Reed was too stunned to react. "My *what?*" His harsh shout woke Lucas, and the baby cried out.

Elizabeth immediately moved for the door.

Reed grabbed her by the arm. "What the hell are you talking about?" he thundered.

"Let me go."

He released her, and she darted to the nursery.

Reed followed. "I have no mistress," he hissed from behind.

Elizabeth picked up the crying baby, rocking him against her shoulder.

"Did you hear me?" Reed demanded.

Elizabeth turned as Lucas's sobs subsided. "You're caught, Reed."

"Caught doing what?"

"I know she's not a client. I know she's not a job applicant. I know your friends and your staff have been covering for you. You lie when you say you're in meetings—"

"I do *not* lie."

"Keep your voice down."

"I do not lie, Elizabeth. When I say I'm in meetings, I'm in meetings. I can't always share the subjects with you, but that's for your own good."

She harrumphed a sound of disbelief. "How long, Reed? How long have you been sleeping with Selina Marin?"

"Selina Marin is a private investigator."

"There we have it," said Elizabeth. "Career number four for the intrepid Ms. Marin."

"She is a private investigator. And I'm not sleeping with her."

"Prove it."

Reed almost laughed. Elizabeth was as bad as the SEC, asking him to prove something didn't happen?

"I saw the e-mails," said Elizabeth.

"What e-mails?"

"The e-mails from France. You wrote to the woman every damn day. How could..." Tears welled up in Elizabeth's eyes, and she turned away.

Reed dragged a hand through his hair, wondering how everything in his life could get so far off-track. He could see that Lucas's eyes were fluttering closed, so he backed out of the nursery, giving Elizabeth a chance to settle him again.

He waited in the hall, his mind ticking through possible scenarios that had led her down this path. He had to come clean about the blackmail. He realized that. But how on earth had she interpreted Selina's PI activities as an affair? Surely it took more than business e-mails to the woman for Reed to be tried and convicted.

Elizabeth exited the nursery, pulling the door partway closed.

Reed reached out to her. "Come and sit down."

She shook her head.

"Please? Something's gone so far wrong, and we're not going to work it out unless we talk."

"I don't want to be lied to."

"I'm not going to lie."

She gave a little laugh. "A liar telling me he's not going to lie. How could I possibly doubt the sincerity of that?"

"Elizabeth." Now she was frustrating him.

"I'm done, Reed. It's over."

"How did you see the e-mails?"

She looked momentarily stricken. "I hacked into your computer."

"The password wasn't there to keep you out."

"You e-mailed her from Biarritz every single day. While you... While we..."

Reed remembered full well what they'd done in Biarritz. "Did you read them?"

Elizabeth shook her head.

He reached for her hand, but she jerked away.

"I'm being blackmailed, Elizabeth."

"Because you're having an affair?"

Reed clamped his jaw and counted to ten. "Let's sit down."

She set her lips in a mulish line.

"Do you want to know the truth?"

She blinked rapidly. "I want to know the truth. I need to know the truth. Don't lie to me anymore. Please, Reed. I couldn't stand it."

His heart contracted, but this time when he reached for her hand, she let him take it. He led her to the living room, to the wingback chairs in the bay window where they'd be facing each other.

"I'm being blackmailed," he began. "Last month, I got a letter demanding ten million dollars or 'the world will learn the dirty secret of how the Wellingtons make their money.' I ignored it. Then the SEC investigation started, and we realized it was connected to the blackmail. We also realized that my blackmail could be connected with Trent and with Julia and—here's the biggest problem— the police can't rule out that Marie Endicott's death wasn't a murder and wasn't connected to the blackmails."

"And you didn't tell me?" Elizabeth's voice was small.

"I didn't want to worry you. You were trying to conceive."

"How could you not tell me?"

"There was nothing you could do."

"I could have given you moral support."

"Yeah. Right."

Her expression turned thunderous, and she started to stand.

"I meant, I'm man enough not to burden my wife with my problems."

"So you burdened Selina instead."

"Yes. And Collin and Trent and the New York State Police Department."

"But not me."

"Elizabeth."

"I'm not made of spun glass, Reed."

"We were trying to get pregnant. The party was taking a lot of your time. Then the SEC thing hit, and there was Lucas. And I didn't think you needed to know there could also be a murderer on the loose. Dr. Wendell specifically said no stress. A murderer is stress, no matter how you slice it."

"So you hired Joe."

"Selina hired Joe."

Elizabeth shook her head sadly. "Let me make sure I've got the picture. You're not sleeping with Selina."

Thank goodness she finally got that part right. "I'm *not* sleeping with Selina."

"You're sleeping with me."

"As often as humanly possible."

She didn't smile, and he regretted making the weak joke.

"With Selina, you're sharing your troubles, your fears, your aspirations and your secrets."

Reed wasn't sure how to respond to that.

"And while we were in France, you were tying me to the bedposts—"

"—I never really—"

"—while discussing the weighty matters of our personal lives, our marriage and our future with *her*." Elizabeth's voice rose to a fever pitch. "You know what I think, Reed?"

He was afraid to ask.

"I think you're married to Selina and having a fling with me." She rocketed out of her chair.

He jumped up. "That is completely unfair. *Completely.*"

Elizabeth turned on him. "I bet you spend more hours in a day with her than with me. And is there anything about you she doesn't know? She's chasing down a murderer, so I bet you have to give her all the details."

"You're bastardizing—"

"Do you lie to her about where you are? Who you're with?"

"Will you please settle—"

"I don't just want to share your bed, Reed. I need more than the few minutes you can spare around your other obligations. I need more than the scraps of information you deem safe to share with me. I need *you*, Reed. I need to share your life.

"You are sharing my—"

"This *isn't* a marriage. You and I have none of the fundamental pieces that couples need to build a life together. Yeah, we're good in bed. You can completely push my buttons. I even liked the silk scarf thing. But I need more. I need all of you. I cannot, I *will* not play second fiddle to your 'professionals.'

"I'm going to finish packing, Reed. Then Lucas and I are leaving."

"No, you're not."

"Yes, we are. And you can't stop us."

"*I'm* leaving," Reed said in a low, firm growl. "It's nearly midnight. You are *not* going to drag a baby out of bed and cart him off to a hotel in the middle of the night. I'll leave. You two stay here."

He didn't wait for her answer, simply headed for the door and left the penthouse. He had no other option. If she'd made up her mind, she'd made up her mind. He'd been the best husband he knew how, and if that wasn't good enough, the only thing left to do was step aside.

Elizabeth had just settled Lucas in his baby swing when Hanna arrived at noon the next day. "All I can say," she purred as the door clicked shut behind her, "is that Joe Germain sure knows how to take care of a girl's body."

"Good night?" Elizabeth asked, feeling exhausted from her own sleepless hours of tossing and turning. She knew in her soul that things couldn't continue with Reed, but she missed him desperately, especially in their big bed.

When she thought about the fact that he'd never be there again, that his strong arms would never wrap around her, that she'd never feel the satisfying, naked weight of him on top of her ever again, she wanted to collapse in a heap and cry her eyes out.

Hanna, however, was smiling. "Joe is the sexiest, toughest, most inventive man on the planet."

Elizabeth tried for a smile. "I never would have put you two—" She swallowed. "I never would have—"

"Lizzy?" Hanna peered into her eyes, concern growing on her face. "What the hell?"

As Elizabeth felt a fresh rush of tears, Hanna helped her to the couch, sitting down next to her and curling up her jean-clad legs. "What happened? The Vances? Lucas?"

Elizabeth shook her head. Her throat was raw and her chest felt like it was being squeezed by a giant rubber band. "Reed," she managed.

"The SEC thing?"

"I don't understand."

Elizabeth forced her emotions under control. She had to stop this. It was what it was, and no amount of crying would change that. "Reed and I split up last night."

"He was *not* having an affair. I know this."

"He might as well have been. He won't share his life with me, Hanna. The man was being blackmailed for ten million dollars, and he never even mentioned it. But to her—" Elizabeth's voice shook. "With her, it's a dozen e-mails a day."

"Like online sex?"

"Like online life. To me, he lies, he evades, he protects. She gets his hopes, his fears, his dreams. I want that," she said, stabbing her thumb against her chest.

Hanna cocked her head. "But he's not sleeping with her."

"No."

"And he is sleeping with you?"

"Was."

"And there's no way to fix the other? I mean, now that you know about the blackmail…"

"There'll be something else. Something else he worries will upset me, things he needs to keep secret for my own good. He's got this unbelievable protective streak, and he absolutely refuses to treat me like an adult. I could help. I could have helped."

"With the blackmail threat?"

"Yes."

"Yes. Well, of course. Because with your extensive experience with criminal investigative techniques, and your training in hand-to-hand combat…"

"You sound like Joe."

"Have you tried to talk to Reed?"

"Until I'm blue in the face." But nothing convinced Reed to let her in. If she couldn't get in, she couldn't be his wife.

"Do you still love him?" Hanna asked softly.

The tears that had dried up threatened again. "It's not like an on/off switch."

"I'm telling you," Reed said, rising to his feet and raising his voice so that Collin would get the point. "It's over. I left her at her request."

"And I'm telling you," Collin replied, "it *can't* be over for three more weeks."

"It's not like I won't support her. She can have anything she wants."

"That's not the point, and you know it."

Reed did know it. He simply didn't want to accept it. "To make her happy, I have to stay away."

"To protect her, you have to go back." Collin dropped back down in the guest chair. "The judge will want to see an intact family. You want Elizabeth to keep Lucas? You put your ass back in that penthouse and keep it there until the court case is over."

"It doesn't work that way," said Reed, trying to imagine Elizabeth's reaction if he showed up at the front door. "You don't understand. You've never been married."

"I'm not giving you marital advice," said Collin. "I'm giving you legal advice. Sleep on the couch. Eat at restaurants. You work eighteen hours a day anyway. It's not like you'll have to see each other."

Collin's accusation came too close to one of Elizabeth's complaints for Reed's taste.

"I don't work eighteen hours a day."

Collin snorted. "How many times last month did you have business dinners?"

Reed scanned back in his mind. "A few."

"Seventeen, to be exact. Devon showed me your schedule."

"Seventeen?" Reed turned the number over in his brain. Add to that his Chamber of Commerce functions, the two nights he gave speeches, and a couple of business trips to Chicago, and it started to add up.

He tried to picture his last dinner with Elizabeth. They'd eaten together at the anniversary party, of course. But he'd dealt with a flurry of problems while she danced with other men.

"Let me make one thing perfectly clear," said Collin.

"I have absolutely no designs on your wife." He paused while Reed's eyes narrowed. "But I'm glad she did it. If I was her, I'd have left you a long time ago."

"Wellington International doesn't run itself," Reed pointed out. He didn't attend business dinners because he'd rather be there than at home. They were important. They were necessary. Particularly when you were dealing with out-of-town guests or other cultures, the social aspect could make or break a deal.

"Don't you think I know that?"

"So, what's your solution?"

"My solution is to stay single."

Reed dropped back into his chair. "Looks like I'm about to do the same thing."

"But not for three weeks."

"Right," Reed reluctantly agreed. For Elizabeth, for Lucas, he'd be a man about it. She was going to resist. But he'd make her understand it was for her own good.

The last person Elizabeth expected to knock on her front door was Reed. It was surreal for him not to use his key. Plus, she'd been picturing him in her mind for so many hours, it was almost a shock to see him in person. Frustratingly, her heart gave a little lift. She squelched it.

He made no move to come in.

"Sorry to disturb you," he said instead, sounding formal even for Reed.

"No problem," she managed. "Lucas just went down for a nap."

Reed nodded. "I…uh…"

Did he need something? His clothes? Elizabeth struggled for the right way to behave.

"Can we talk?" he asked, looking very serious.

Her heart did the little lift thing again. "Sure."

She stood to one side and motioned him in, telling herself that nothing had changed. She could not, would not let him sweet-talk her into trying again.

He walked through the doorway and dropped his keys in their usual spot on the table. There was something about the unconscious act that tightened her chest and clogged her throat.

"What did you want to talk about?" She knew her only hope was to get this visit over with quickly. The pain of having him here was too intense, and she knew she was in for a fresh crying jag after he left.

As long as she could make it that far…

She sat down at one end of the sofa.

"I've been talking to Collin," Reed began. "He thinks…well, for Lucas…" He paced to the bay window.

Her stomach hollowed out. Reed wasn't going to fight her for Lucas. Please God, not that.

He didn't meet her eyes. "For the sake of Lucas, and the court case, and to maximize our changes of defending ourselves against the Vances, we should stay together until custody is settled. Three weeks."

Elizabeth was speechless.

Reed, here? Them, together, but not?

Reed slowly turned to look at her. "Elizabeth?"

"I…" she tried. How could she do it? How could she possibly see him every day while she was trying to get over him? It would be horrible, painful, impossible.

"I can't," she managed, her voice cracking.

His jaw clenched. "I know. That's what I said to Collin."

So, Reed had already refused. That was good. They'd find another way. A way that didn't require her heart to be shredded for twenty-one long days.

His blue eyes turned flat with determination. "But we have to."

A small whimper escaped from her, and she shook her head.

He crossed back to her, coming down on one knee. "If we separate, it gives the Vances exactly what they need. Their lawyer will use it to destroy our case. It puts Lucas at risk, Elizabeth."

She closed her eyes, fear and despair roiling within her. She wanted to throw herself into Reed's arms. She wanted his soothing voice to assure her that everything would be okay.

But he couldn't. And he never would again. She was on her own this time, and she had to be strong for Lucas. Her nephew, and her brother's last wishes were all that mattered now.

"I'll sleep on the couch," Reed offered. Since they'd set up the nursery, there was no spare bedroom.

"I can sleep on the couch," she croaked out, realizing the words told him she'd given in. Not that there was a choice. Logic told her that Collin was right. How could they present the better environment for Lucas if they were in the middle of a divorce?

Reed was shaking his head. "You need your sleep. You have a baby to take care of."

"And you don't?" She found an ounce of strength

somewhere to argue with him. "You have a corporation to run, criminal charges to defend against, and a blackmailer on your trail."

Reed unexpectedly gave a dark chuckle. "We're fairly pathetic, aren't we?"

She frowned. It was way too soon for humor.

"Sorry." His hand moved toward her face. He was going to brush her hair from her cheek, like he'd done a thousand, maybe a million times before. But he checked himself just in time. "I'm going back to the office. I'll probably be late."

Elizabeth watched him leave. The door swung shut behind him. The silence closed in around her. And the horrible feeling that she had made a terrible mistake by leaving him pounded relentlessly through her brain.

She didn't move until Lucas cried from the nursery.

Then she dug deep and found a smile for the baby, changed him, gave him his bottle and a handful of dry cereal. Together they built a block tower on the living room floor and watched a cartoon movie.

Rena took weekends off, so Elizabeth cleaned up after Lucas. By the time she gave him a bath, tucked him in, did his small load of laundry, and made up his bottles for the morning, she was dead on her feet.

After changing into a nightgown she settled down with a comforter on the sofa. Despite Reed's protests, she would sleep out here. It was less lonely than the bed.

She stared at the city light pattern on the high ceiling, telling herself she'd had no choice but to separate from Reed. Sharing such a minuscule portion of his life was worse than sharing none of it at all.

When his key turned in the lock, she closed her eyes, pretending to sleep.

She knew the exact second he spotted her. His footsteps froze, and he took a sharp breath. Then he moved to the side of the sofa.

"Elizabeth?"

She didn't answer.

"I know you're awake."

How could he possibly know that?

She heard him crouch down beside her.

Astonishingly, there was a trace of humor in his voice. "When you're asleep, you snore."

Her eyes opened. "I do not."

"It's very quiet, and very ladylike, but you definitely snore."

"You are lying."

He gazed the length of her body under the comforter. "What are you doing, Elizabeth?"

"Sleeping."

"My wife's not sleeping on the couch."

She struggled up onto her elbows. "Well, you're way too tall. I barely fit."

They both stared at each other in defiance.

"We have to share the bed," he finally stated.

"We can't share the bed."

"It's a big bed. I'll stay on my side, you stay on yours."

She gave her head an adamant shake. "That's crazy."

"Is there anything about this situation that's *not* crazy?"

She couldn't come up with an immediate answer.

His arms swept under her shoulders and knees.

"Reed!"

He lifted her. "You need your sleep. I need mine. And there's only one way to get it." He started for the bedroom.

His arms felt too good around her. His body felt too good against her. She had to fight to keep from melting into his strength. Twenty feet, ten, five, finally.

He stopped at the edge of the bed. He didn't immediately put her down, but stared into her eyes for a long moment, making her want all the things she couldn't have.

"Sleep well," he finally murmured then laid her gently down on the comforter.

Within seconds, he'd disappeared into the en suite. The fan began to whirr, and the water drummed against the floor of the shower.

Elizabeth buried her head firmly in her pillow and sobbed in utter frustration.

# Eleven

Elizabeth awoke to silence. She'd slept deeply, and it took her a second to figure out why she had a sick feeling in the pit of her stomach. But then she remembered. Reed was leaving, and the pain came flooding back in force.

Morning sunshine fought its way through the bedroom curtains, confusing her. Lucas usually woke her up by seven. *Lucas.* Her gaze flew to the bedside clock, and she discovered it was nearly ten.

What was the matter with Lucas?

She sprang out of bed and jogged down the hall in her wrinkled nightgown.

His crib was empty. Panic clawed at her throat. But then she heard it. The gurgling sound of his voice. And then Reed's voice.

"The trick," Reed intoned, "is to make sure your foundation is solid. That means we use the red blocks first."

Lucas cooed in apparent agreement.

Elizabeth made her way down the hall. She stood in the doorway for a minute, watching the colorful tower go up before Reed spotted her.

"Good morning," he said, no inflection in his voice.

"Why didn't you wake me?"

He usually headed into the office first thing.

"You were tired," he said, keeping his attention focused on Lucas and the blocks.

"I could have—"

"You were tired." There was a snap in his voice this time, and his annoyed gaze met hers.

She cleared her throat. "I can take it from here."

"No problem," he said. "I wasn't planning to go into the office today."

Elizabeth blinked, trying to make the words compute.

"I've invited my parents for dinner."

Raw panic hit her system. "You did what?" Anton and Jacqueline *here?* In the middle of this? Her gaze flew around the slightly messy room.

"I invited my parents for dinner," he repeated.

"Why?" she wailed. "Rena's off. Did you call a caterer?" She rushed toward the kitchen. Was the Alençon tablecloth ironed? Did they have fresh candles? What about a centerpiece?

"I told them we'd send out for pizza."

Elizabeth stopped in her tracks, turning to stare at Reed. "Is that supposed to be a joke?" She really wasn't in the mood.

"No joke. They want to meet Lucas."

"You are planning to serve Anton and Jacqueline Wellington take-out pizza?" They were the reigning king and queen of New York society.

"I did warn them."

"You can't do this. I'll be mortified. They'll think I'm the worst hostess in the world. They already don't like me." Not that it mattered. They weren't going to be her in-laws much longer.

Reed came to his feet. "You worry too much."

"No. I don't worry nearly enough."

"I'll grab a six-pack to go with it."

"You absolutely will not. I'll going down to Pinetta's to pick up some filets. Do we still have that black labeled merlot in the wine rack?" Where was her purse?

Reed grasped her arm to stop her. "You're in your nightgown."

Elizabeth glanced down. She took a breath. "I'll change first...of course."

"You're not changing." He gave his head a shake. "I mean, you're not rushing out for filets. I told them pizza, and we're serving pizza."

"Why are you doing this to me?" Was he punishing her for leaving him? She searched his expression. "Do you hate me that much?"

He instantly let go of her arm, his gaze fixing on the wall behind her. "I don't hate you, Elizabeth." He seemed to gather his thoughts. "You're busy. You're exhausted. And you're upset. I've chosen this moment to take a stand against my father. If he wants to visit Lucas on short notice, he can do so while noshing on take-out pizza and sipping a beer."

The fight went out of Elizabeth. "So this is about you and your father? Not about punishing me?"

Reed's eyes narrowed. "*Punishing* you?"

She swallowed. "For leaving you."

He stared down at her while Lucas clattered blocks in the background, and a muscle ticked to life near his temple. "I would never, *ever* do a single thing to harm you. You are my wife, and I will protect you until you force me to stop. Understand?"

Her chest tightened painfully, and Elizabeth felt teary all over again. "Yes," she whispered. "We can serve pizza."

Reed could tell that Elizabeth was nervous.

He'd relented and allowed Elizabeth to order a centerpiece and use a tablecloth. And he would admit that it was entertaining to watch his mother tackle a slice of pizza on Wedgewood China with sterling silverware. She had pronounced it delicious. Elizabeth obviously hadn't believed her.

She was still jumpy after dinner when his mother climbed onto the floor in her linen pantsuit to play with Lucas. Elizabeth rushed to her side when Lucas grabbed a handful of Jacqueline's silk blouse, aiming it toward his mouth.

Jacqueline calmly untangled Lucas's chubby fingers and gave him a toy, which he immediately stuck in his mouth. Jacqueline laughed, but Elizabeth didn't relax her vigil.

Reed handed his father a second glass of German beer and sat down in the other wingback chair.

"Your mother and I have been talking," Anton began, setting his tall glass down on the round table between them.

Reed braced himself. He let his gaze rest on sweet, adventurous Lucas and elegant, compassionate Elizabeth—both of whom he loved to distraction. Somehow, some way, he was going to protect them from his father's narrow-mindedness. Even if he had to send them to live in France.

Anton's voice went gruff. "I was out of line the other day."

Reed turned to stare at his father's stern profile. Anton was also fixating on the cluster of people on the carpet.

"Excuse me?"

"About Lucas," said Anton. Then he cleared his throat. "I was out of line to suggest that you shouldn't adopt him."

Reed couldn't believe his ears. "You've changed your mind?"

"As I said. Your mother and I were talking."

Reed's mother? His mother had actually changed his father's mind about something as significant as the heir to the Wellington dynasty? Reed looked at Jacqueline with new respect.

Anton lifted his glass from the table and took a sip. "The baby makes your mother happy."

"Lucas," Reed prompted.

"Lucas," Anton acknowledged.

"He makes Elizabeth happy, too," said Reed, wondering if he should take a page from Lucas. A sappy smile. A big hug. A clap of his hands. Maybe Reed had been trying too hard as a husband.

"You should go to California," said Anton.

Reed turned his attention back to his father. "To do what?"

"Talk to the Vances. They want something. Find out what it is."

"They want Lucas," said Reed.

Anton shook his head. "They say they want Lucas. You find out what they really want."

"You're not suggesting this is a shakedown." It was preposterous to suggest that the Vances would use Lucas to get money. They obviously loved him.

"Your mother tells me babies are wonderful. But she also tells me that once you've raised your own, you want grandchildren. You don't want to start over.

"The Vances want something." Anton nodded to Elizabeth and Lucas. "This is your family. You go find out what it's going to take to fix the problem."

Reed considered his father for a moment. "You get a lot of advice from Mother."

Anton shot him a censorious look, and Reed braced himself for the fallout. But then his father's expression unexpectedly softened. "Yes. Well. That's just the way it is. The jet's at JFK. I took the liberty of clearing the schedule for tomorrow."

It took Reed all of thirty seconds to realize that the Vances weren't looking for a bribe. They loved Lucas, and they only wanted what was best for their grandson. After finessing his way around the issue for a good thirty minutes, in desperation, Reed had decided to put all his cards on the table.

He told the Vances about his and Elizabeth's infertility, of the strain it had put on their marriage, of her deep love for her brother, and her passionate desire to adhere to Brandon and Heather's final wishes.

He didn't brag about his wealth, but he didn't downplay it, either. Lucas would live in the finest areas of New York. As he grew, he would have access to private schools, culture, travel, a thousand experiences that would enrich his life.

Then, lastly, he admitted the problems he and Elizabeth were facing in their marriage. But he pledged to the Vances that he was going to do everything in his power to keep his family intact. As the words poured out of him, he knew they were absolutely true. He was going to fight tooth and nail for Elizabeth. He loved her, and he would find a way to win her back.

Margarite Vance cracked first. She admitted her deep fear that Reed would take Lucas away from them. Unlike Reed, they weren't wealthy, and California was a long way from New York. They didn't want to be parents, but they desperately wanted to be grandparents. They wanted to be a part of Lucas's life, to watch him grow.

Reed had immediately pledged his jet, his corporate account at a dozen Manhattan hotels, his parents' guest rooms on Long Island, and he offered to send Elizabeth and Lucas to California as often as possible. He explained that he would like nothing better than for the Vances' house to be Lucas's second home when he and Elizabeth needed to be away.

In the end, the Vances had enthusiastically agreed not to contest the will. Reed had wanted to promise a visit for the weekend, but he knew he needed to talk to Elizabeth first.

On the flight home, he grew more and more eager to talk to Elizabeth, and he thought of more and more things he wanted to say.

But, at the airport in New York, he was met by Collin and Selina. They both fell into step with him as he marched toward his limo at the passenger pickup.

"Go away," he told them, determined that for *once* Elizabeth would come first.

"We need to talk to you," said Collin.

"I don't care," said Reed. He was going home, and nothing was going to stop him. He'd pay the damn ten million dollars if that's what it took.

"It's important," said Selina.

"So is my life." Reed pushed open the airport door, coming out onto a floodlit, rain-soaked sidewalk.

"This is about your life," said Collin.

"We have information," said Selina.

"I have a marriage to save," Reed countered, spotting his driver. He marched out from under the awning. The driver rushed forward with an umbrella, relieving Reed of his briefcase.

"We can tell you in the car," Collin offered.

Reed heaved a sigh. "We're going straight to the penthouse. I'm not going to the office, or the police station, and we're not stopping for anything but traffic lights." He looked pointedly at the driver. "And even those are optional."

The man grinned. "Yes, sir."

He glanced back at Selina and Collin who were rapidly developing a drowned rat look.

"Get in," he grumbled.

"It's important," Selina repeated, as they settled into their seats, an apology in her tone.

"It's always important," said Reed. "That's the problem with my life. If I was deciding between Elizabeth and the things that weren't important, I wouldn't have a problem, would I?" He didn't wait for an answer. "But every day, nearly every hour, something that is vitally important grabs my time and attention. I spend my evenings with you two and with Gage and Trent, because if we don't work this out, I might be going to jail. A blackmailer might extort money. Somebody might even die.

"And so I do my part," Reed continued. "But you know what? It stops here. I'm going home to Elizabeth. You two tell me what I need to do to make that happen."

Selina glanced at Collin. "Do you want to tell him or shall I?"

Collin gestured that Selina should go ahead.

"It's the Hammond and Pysanski connection."

"Don't tell me. It's getting worse?" Reed absolutely could not get a break.

"I spent the last two days in Washington," said Selina. "I found out that each of Hammond and Pysanski's purchases were made in the forty-eight hours following the committee's shortlisting of the project in question."

"How many companies on the shortlist?" Reed couldn't help asking. Had Hammond and Pysanski bought into the shortlisted companies on spec?

"Usually three to five," said Selina. "But it looks like the unofficial decision coincided with the shortlist. Because they bought into the right company each and every time."

Reed was dumbfounded. "So, Kendrick is guilty."

"At first I thought it was Kendrick, too. But then I found this." Selina pulled a sheet of paper out of her briefcase. "One of the senator's aides, Clive Neville. With each transaction, the day after the Hammond and Pysanski stock purchase, ten thousand dollars was deposited to Clive Neville's account."

"A payoff?" asked Reed.

Selina nodded. "But you and Gage bought your shares a week before Hammond and Pysanski," she said. "*Before* the shortlist." She smiled at him.

"So it's over?" Reed asked.

Collin slapped him on the shoulder. "It's over."

The limo came to a halt in front of 721 Park Avenue.

Reed handed the bank printout back to Selina. "Well done, team. I hope you don't take this the wrong way. But, goodbye." Reed beat the driver to the door handle and stepped out into the rain.

"You know," said Hanna, topping up their wineglasses with a merlot, "there *is* another option."

"No, there's not." Elizabeth was out of options to save her marriage. All that was left was to save herself. Reed was never going to change. That's why she was taking such drastic action.

Hanna set the empty bottle on the coffee table and leaned back at the opposite end of the sofa. "You could tell him you were wrong, that you love him, and that you want your marriage to work out."

"Yeah," came a deep, male voice, and Elizabeth nearly dropped her wine into her lap. Hanna's eyes went wide, and she twisted toward the penthouse foyer.

"You could do that," said Reed, dropping his keys and sauntering into the room.

"Reed." Hanna swallowed around a dry rasp.

"Hello, Hanna."

"I am *so* sorry," she offered in obvious embarrassment. "I was... We were..."

Reed shook his head. "Don't be sorry. If I thought you'd convince her, I'd leave and let you go at it."

"She won't convince me," said Elizabeth with conviction. It was nearly ten o'clock, and today was just another example of Reed's hectic schedule. He'd flown to Chicago for a meeting. Clearly, he'd spent the entire day there. Just as clearly, he'd had more important things to do than tuck Lucas into bed.

Maybe it was her own fault. Maybe she simply wasn't interesting enough to come home to. Maybe she should have gotten a job years ago and become a more interesting wife for him.

Then again, how would he know whether she was interesting or not? The man wouldn't even show up for a conversation.

Reed picked up the wine bottle, raising his eyebrows when he saw it was empty. "Shall I open another?"

Hanna struggled to get to her feet. "I should really go, and let you two—"

He forestalled her with his palm. "Stay put. You're

obviously on my side. It looks like you two have a head start, but I'd love to joint the party."

Hanna gave Elizabeth a questioning look, which Elizabeth answered with a shrug. It wasn't like she and Reed had any big plans for being alone. In fact, it was probably better to have Hanna here as a foil until bedtime, or at least until Elizabeth got slightly intoxicated.

"Bring on another bottle," she told him.

Reed gave her a genuine smile, and the force of it shot all the way to her toes. She immediately rethought her strategy on getting intoxicated. It could be dangerous to be around him without all her faculties intact. She set her wineglass down on the table.

Reed headed for the wine rack in the dining room.

With him out of the room, Hanna hit Elizabeth with an expression of stark curiosity.

Elizabeth held her palms up in a gesture of confusion. She'd never seen Reed in a mood like this.

He strode back into the living room with an open bottle of wine and three fresh glasses. "The eighty-two Chateau Saint Gaston," he announced with satisfaction.

Elizabeth blinked.

Hanna choked. "Did you just open a ten thousand dollar bottle of wine?"

Reed pretended to study the label. "I do believe I did." He poured them each a glass of the Saint Gaston.

Still standing, he held his glass aloft. "A toast," he said.

"Please don't," begged Elizabeth. She didn't know what he had in mind, but she didn't like the reckless look in his eyes nor the cocky set to his mouth.

"A toast," he said in a softer voice, looking straight into her eyes. "To my gorgeous, gracious, intelligent wife."

"Reed," she pleaded.

"I lied to you today."

So what else was new?

"I wasn't in Chicago."

Something shriveled up inside Elizabeth. The man lied recreationally. She couldn't have cared less whether he was in Chicago.

She waved a dismissive hand. "Whatever. Salute." She lifted her glass to take a drink.

"Uh, uh, uh," he tisked. "This is a ten thousand dollar bottle of wine. Let's have a little respect."

She heaved a frustrated sigh. Maybe she should just go to bed, get to sleep before he decided to join her there. Maybe, just maybe, she'd feel stronger in the morning.

"I was in California," he continued.

Elizabeth waited for the point.

"Ironically, on the advice of my dear father, I went to see the Vances."

She froze. "No." He hadn't compromised their case. He wouldn't.

"And while I was there," he said, "I realized that you, dear Elizabeth, are absolutely right, and I am completely wrong."

He perched himself on the armchair cornerwise to her. "I promise I will never lie to you again."

Elizabeth searched his eyes. They were warm and soft and loving, but she didn't know what to say. "Thank you," she tried.

His lips stretched into a smile before he tipped his glass and took a sip.

Elizabeth followed suit, but she couldn't taste a thing.

"I love you," Reed said to her.

"Hey," Hanna put in, coming to her feet. "I really think I'd better—"

"Drink your wine," Reed ordered. "I might need you later."

She sat back down.

"Where was I?" he asked.

"Are you drunk?" asked Elizabeth, trying desperately to make sense of his behavior. This wasn't the Reed she knew.

"Oh, yes. Now I remember. The Vances are not going to contest the will."

Elizabeth was afraid she hadn't heard that right. "What?"

He nodded his confirmation, slowing down his words. "The Vances are not going after custody of Lucas. And, no, I'm not drunk."

A pulse of optimism hit Elizabeth for the first time in weeks. "How did you…?"

"Skill, intelligence and guile. Plus a really fast private jet."

"Quit messing around," Elizabeth ordered. This was a serious conversation, not a joke.

"Oh, I think I'll mess around a little longer." He took another sip of the wine, holding his glass back to study the legs. "Worth every penny."

"Go, Reed." Hanna applauded in a reverent tone.

"Thank you," said Reed. "Now, will you help me convince her I'm worth sticking with?"

"He's worth sticking with," Hanna said to Elizabeth.

"Traitor," Elizabeth muttered, but even she was running out of excuses to leave him. He might have lied about Chicago, and he might have been gone all day long, but he'd done it for Lucas, and he'd done it for her.

"She told me you were great in bed," Hanna offered.

"Hanna!" Elizabeth was horrified.

"Well, that's one in my column," said Reed.

"Damn straight," said Hanna.

"There's one more thing." He sobered, all traces of joking gone, his attention fixed completely on Elizabeth. "I'll be home evenings from here on in. Or I'll work part-time. Or I'll sell my companies. Or we can move to freakin' Biarritz if that will make a difference."

Elizabeth's throat thickened up. "What are you saying?"

"I'm saying that I'm prepared to put as much effort into my marriage as I put into my business."

Elizabeth was speechless. Her heartbeat sped up and her chest went tight. She stared at Reed in utter astonishment. "Seriously?"

Hanna stuck out her foot and nudged Elizabeth in the knee. "I think the word you're looking for is *yes!*"

# Twelve

Elizabeth and Reed were on their way to the bedroom when Lucas stirred. Reed went into the nursery to rock him back to sleep, while Elizabeth all but floated into their bedroom.

Reed was staying. They were going to work things out. He'd decided their love was worth fighting for, and if there was anything her husband could do, it was to achieve whatever goal he set for himself.

Though they'd slept in their bed together hundreds of times, she knew tonight was special. It was the beginning of a whole new marriage, a whole new family.

She pulled open the top drawer of the bureau, and her gaze caught on the rosewood coin box. She slowly lifted the lid, pulling out the liberty head, ten-dollar gold coin, and hefting its weight in her palm.

"Heads," she whispered to herself, "I do it."

Tails, she'd do it anyway. This time, she didn't need to flip the coin.

She slipped it back into its holder and pulled out the red silk negligee she'd worn on her wedding night. Appropriate, since this was another new beginning.

She removed her clothes, but as she was about to slip the soft silk over her head, her gaze caught another flash of fabric in the drawer. Lemon yellow and bright blue and purple. The silk scarves they'd bought in France.

Elizabeth paused. She set the negligee aside, fingering the texture of the scarves. And then she smiled. This wasn't her honeymoon. It was a different beginning, a different relationship, a relationship based on authenticity instead of fantasy.

She wrapped the lemon yellow scarf over her breasts, tying it at the back like a bikini top. Then she fastened the blue and purple one low on her hips, sarong-style, leaving most of one thigh and hip bare. She combed her hair, dabbed some perfume, then waited, standing in the middle of the room.

Reed walked in and stopped, his gaze trailing up and down her body. "We going to Tahiti?" he asked.

She sauntered toward him, walking her fingertips up his chest, snaking her arms around his neck. "I think we're going to nirvana."

A gorgeous smile spread across his face. One arm snaked around to the small of her back, tugging her tight. His other hand cupped her bottom through the soft silk.

"I do love you," he whispered as he bent to kiss her lips.

She tipped her head back, opening her mouth, meeting his hot tongue in a tangle of passion and desire that she couldn't hope to contain. And she wouldn't. It was all honesty all the time from here on in.

She pushed his suit jacket off his shoulders, letting it fall to a heap on the floor. Then she attacked his shirt buttons while he nipped and nibbled his way along her shoulder. His hand slipped under the sarong, toying with her heating skin.

He cupped her breast, strumming his thumb over her hard nipple. "I so love these scarves," he breathed.

"Versatile," she agreed.

He chuckled low, then his tone turned to a growl. "Nobody, nowhere, no how is ever going to stop us from making love. I don't care what the science says, *this* is right."

She nodded her agreement, gasping as his finger slipped inside.

"Too fast?" he asked.

"No. Just right." She grappled with his belt buckle, and he shucked his clothes, pulling her onto the bed in a flurry of caresses, kisses and silk.

When she was naked, he stretched her arms over her head, stroking his fingertips from the wrists all the way to her toes and then back again.

She shuddered at the sensations, freed her hands and caressed the play of his muscles, from his shoulders to his abs and beyond.

He rolled on top of her, settling between her legs, his body teasing her sensitized flesh. He took one nipple into his mouth, drawing out the caress as she squirmed beneath him. Then he laved the other, then moved to her mouth, kissing her long and deeply.

He drew back, gazing down into her eyes as he slowly pushed into her. She felt the pressure, then the heat, then the fullness, and then he stopped. They stared at each other for a frozen moment of perfect communication.

Reed flexed his hips, and sparks shot off in her brain. She tipped her head back, exposing her throat to his kisses. Her hands tangled in his hair, and he murmured her name over and over while time stopped and he drove them higher into the atmosphere, past the moon and the stars, to the outer stratosphere until the entire universe exploded around them.

Elizabeth woke to the sound of Lucas's gurgles and coos in the nursery. Reed's arm was across her stomach, holding her firmly back against his body.

"Good morning, gorgeous," he whispered against her hair.

"Good morning, handsome," she responded.

He planted a series of tender kisses on the back of her neck.

"There's a baby waking up," she warned him, the buzz of desire forming instantly in her belly.

"Can't resist me?" he teased.

"I don't want to resist you," she corrected.

He moaned. "Oh, *that's* what I like to hear."

"But I have to get Lucas."

"I'll get Lucas. You go lounge in the bath for a while."

Elizabeth glanced at the clock. "You'll be late for work."

She felt him shrug. "So, I'll be late for work. Who cares?"

She turned onto her back to stare up at him. "Reed, you don't have to prove—"

"What are they going to do? Fire me?"

"I'm just saying—"

"Bath," he repeated. "What does Lucas eat for breakfast?"

"Oatmeal." She searched his expression. "Are you really…"

"What did you think I meant last night?"

"That you'd get home earlier in the evenings."

"And the rest?"

The part about working part-time or selling his companies or moving to France? "I thought it was a terrific speech."

Some of the light went out of his eyes. "I was serious, Elizabeth."

"Okay." She nodded, realizing he was completely serious. "Okay, husband of mine. Our baby eats oatmeal for breakfast. Sometimes he gets it in his hair. Sometimes he gets it in my hair." She jammed her thumb in the direction of the en suite. "And I'm going to take a very long bubble bath."

"Good for you."

She wrapped her arms around him and held him close, drawing the hug out until Lucas's little voice turned demanding. Then Reed pulled back the covers, and Elizabeth headed for the bathtub.

While the water splashed and foamed its way to the top of the oversize bath, she brushed her teeth, combed her hair, and twisted it into a messy knot on top of her head. She retrieved a soft terry robe from the closet and hung it on the hook on the back of the door.

Rain spattered on the bathroom window, while the small room filled with the scent of roses. Elizabeth took a deep, cleansing breath, glad that the month of October was coming to a close. November was going to be so much better. Maybe they would go to Tahiti.

She slipped a toe into the hot water, then her ankle and calf. The steam caused a sudden wave of vertigo, and she steadied herself on the towel rack. But it passed, and she lowered herself into the luxuriant water.

They'd only had Lucas for three weeks, but already she appreciated the simple pleasure of time for self-indulgence. She pictured Lucas in the high chair, and Reed heating up the oatmeal. She smiled. There would be happy months and years ahead of them.

Months.

Elizabeth blinked.

She sat up, sending a wave of water over the edge of the tub, splashing onto the tile floor.

October was almost over.

Her cycle was off.

Her cycle was way off, and she'd been dizzy getting into the tub, dizzy three days ago in the penthouse foyer. She counted on her fingers.

No way. *No way.* They'd missed her prime ovulating days. They'd gone against all the advice of their doctor.

Yet, still…

Her hands started to shake as she made her way out of the tub. She pulled open the lower cabinet, digging through the bath crystals and shampoo, finally finding an open box containing the second of two pregnancy tests.

She frantically checked the expiration date. She was in under the wire. Then she scanned the instructions, followed them and set the little wand down on the counter, backing away.

From across the room she stared at the little window for three minutes, dripping wet, while the color arranged itself against a white background.

When the time elapsed, she moved forward.

Two lines.

She blinked.

There were *two lines*. She was pregnant. Lucas was going to have a brother or a sister. She and Reed were going to have a baby.

She sat down on the edge of the tub. Her legs were shaking, and a chill came over her body. When the weakness subsided, she wrapped her arms around her abdomen. There was a baby in there. A tiny little baby was growing inside her.

A warm glow enveloped her body.

She stood and wrapped the terry robe around her. Then she tightened the belt and all but floated down the hall to give Reed the good news.

"Iron, calcium, vitamin A, and a good source of fiber," he was reading out loud.

She rounded the corner.

"I kind of like it myself," said Hanna.

Elizabeth stopped short at the sight of Reed, Joe and Hanna surrounding Lucas's high chair.

They all turned to stare at her bulky robe and messy hair.

"Why does this keep happening to me?" she asked.

"Gotta say, babe," Reed said as he gave Elizabeth a kiss on the cheek, "you looked a lot better last time."

Hanna laughed. Even Joe gave a smile.

"Are you on duty?" Elizabeth asked him. If he was going to be hanging around their house, she supposed he'd better get used to her in a bathrobe.

"Just visiting." His hand brushed Hanna's, and Hanna held his fingers for a brief instant.

"Ahh," said Elizabeth.

"I forgot to mention that Selina and Collin solved the SEC problem," said Reed.

Elizabeth spun around to look at him. "It's solved?"

"Yes."

"You're off the hook?"

"It was one of Kendrick's aides. I can give you all the details."

"You're not going to jail?" she confirmed.

Reed nodded.

"And I don't need a bodyguard anymore?"

"Not anymore."

"Those are all the details I need."

Lucas banged his hands on the high-chair tray and chanted a single note.

"So…" She glanced around at the little group. "There's something I need to mention."

They all waited.

"I'm pregnant."

It took a second for her words to sink in.

Hanna squealed and Joe offered congratulations.

Reed simply looked flabbergasted. Then, finally, "How on earth…"

"In Biarritz, I guess," said Elizabeth. It had been scientifically possible, but given her and Reed's history, getting pregnant had seemed highly unlikely.

"Did you do something different?" asked Hanna.

Joe quickly elbowed her.

"That's not what I meant," Hanna protested.

"He tied me to the bedposts," said Elizabeth.

Hanna hooted out a laugh. Joe guffawed.

"I can't believe you said that," Reed told his wife, laughing deep in his throat.

Elizabeth shrugged. "I'm just trying to be honest. And, hey, it worked."

His arms went around her, and he drew her close. "From here on in?" he murmured against her ear. "This honesty thing is just between you and me."

Elizabeth grinned at his words, squeezing him tight as her world settled into a permanent glow of happiness.

\* \* \* \* \*

# PREGNANT ON THE UPPER EAST SIDE?

EMILIE ROSE

Bestselling Desire™ author and RITA® Award finalist **Emilie Rose** lives in her native North Carolina with her four sons and two adopted mutts. Writing is her third (and hopefully her last) career. She's managed a medical office and run a home day-care, neither of which offers half as much satisfaction as plotting happy endings. Her hobbies include gardening and cooking (especially cheesecake). She is currently working her way through her own "Bucket List" which includes learning to ride a Harley. She's a rabid country music fan because she can find an entire book in almost any song. Letters can be mailed to: Emilie Rose, PO Box 20145, Raleigh, NC 27619, USA, or e-mail: EmilieRoseC@aol.com.

Dear Reader,

I adore Manhattan. But then who doesn't? When I was offered the opportunity to work with some of my favourite Desire™ authors on a series set on Park Avenue, refusing never crossed my mind. The only thing more fun would be taking another trip to New York City—and that is definitely on my agenda.

For a laid-back southern girl there is nothing like the energy of the city that never sleeps. I love visiting places I've seen on TV or in the movies like Times Square, Central Park and Ground Zero to name but a few. I'm sure my practice of smiling at everyone I pass marks me as a tourist, but so what? When I go to Manhattan I'm there to have fun, see the sights and yes, the people, and that brings a smile to my face that I can't smother.

My only regrets: I haven't managed to catch a Broadway play or get to a baseball game on my trips north. So look out New Yorkers. I'll be back and I intend to hit both a Yankees and a Mets game—both just short train rides away—and catch a show or two. Keep your fingers crossed that I don't sing a show tune on the way out of the theatre. Trust me, that would be bad.

*Emilie*

Starting over is never easy, but I've been fortunate to have friends to help me through the transition. You know who you are, and you have my infinite gratitude for making the process as painless as possible.

# One

"Are you stalking me, Alex Harper? You're an attorney. You should know better." Amanda Crawford frowned at the too-handsome-for-his-own-good man standing beside the rows of mailboxes in her apartment building.

Alex feigned innocence. Badly. His coffee-brown eyes glinted with mischief, shooting off tiny gold flares in his irises, which in turn set off corresponding sparks below her navel. She clamped down on the unwelcome response.

He withdrew his hand from his black overcoat pocket and dangled a brass mailbox key in front of her. "I'm here to pick up Julia's mail. It's not all being forwarded to Max's place, and since I was going to be in the neighborhood I offered to stop by."

As excuses went, Amanda could almost accept that one. Julia, her former roommate, had married Alex's best friend just over three months ago. But Amanda had been seeing far too much of Alex to believe mail call was his only motive for turning up at 721 Park Avenue on a Saturday night at the exact moment she returned to her apartment building. No matter where she went lately he managed to make an appearance.

"The post office makes change-of-address kits for exactly that purpose. I'll send a few to Julia. Better yet, I'll fill them out myself."

Melting snowflakes glistened in Alex's dark hair, and he stood close enough that she caught a whiff of his cologne. She'd always been a sucker for Calvin Klein MAN, especially when applied to a tall, well-built body.

*Stop it. You're all business all the time now, remember? No men to divert your focus. Especially not* this *man.*

At five foot ten in her bare feet plus her three-inch-heeled Stuart Weitzman ankle boots, she shouldn't have had to look up at anyone not affiliated with professional basketball. But with Alex she did.

"I'll take care of Julia's mail since I still live here," she insisted. "Besides, I have more upstairs."

"I'll come up and get it and deliver it when I meet them for dinner later."

*Walked right into that one, didn't you, Amanda?*

Disgusted by her slip, she turned and stalked across the marble-floored lobby toward the elevator. Henry the doorman sat in the center of the lobby behind his big mahogany desk, with the phone receiver pressed to his ear. She waved as she passed and his beady eyes followed her.

Alex kept pace beside her. "Why don't you join us tonight?"

"No thanks. I'm busy." Not exactly true. All she had

planned was an evening of combing her accounts and trying to find the money to cover her most pressing bills, but she didn't want to encourage Alex by accepting. Not that a womanizer like him apparently needed encouragement. She'd given him none and yet here he was. Again.

"When are you going to stop playing hard to get and go out with me, Amanda?"

"Never. And I'm not playing. I *am* hard to get. Impossible, in fact. So have a little pride and stop asking." She stabbed the call button and caught Alex's inspection in the ornate gold-rimmed mirror hanging on the Tiffany-box blue wall.

"I never give up when I truly want something. Or someone."

She attributed the shiver working its way up her spine to the record-breaking cold November weather outside the glass lobby doors. Alex's deep voice and the interest in his eyes had nothing to do with it.

"Especially when she's equally as interested."

She caught her breath at his audacity. And his insight. "For someone who is supposedly brilliant, you missed the mark on that one."

Amusement mingled with disbelief in his eyes. "Did I?"

Why bother to lie? He wouldn't believe her anyway. She ducked her chin into the fox collar of her cashmere coat and repositioned herself so she couldn't see him or his reflection.

She had to admit she found Alex's pursuit incredibly flattering, but she was smart enough to recognize a relationship train wreck when she saw one. In the dictionary of dating, Alex's name defined the words *temporary* and *heartbreaker.* Getting involved with him would be a disaster on a major scale. Not something she needed to add to her already infamous and blotchy relationship résumé.

"Why is it the party girl—"

"Party *planner*," she corrected instantly. Oops, that had sounded a little snippy and defensive. But he'd hit a hot button. Her disapproving parents had railed long and hard about her unacceptable career. If she heard *Get a real job or marry money* one more time she wouldn't be responsible for her actions.

"—parties with everyone but me?" he continued as if she hadn't interrupted.

She squeezed into the elevator even before the doors finished opening. He followed her into the car, crowding her toward the back wall. She put as much room between them as possible, which meant he literally had her backed into a corner. Not her idea of fun.

"Other people pay me for my services."

"That's what it takes? I have to hire you?"

"Yes."

"Good to know."

Trying to ignore him, she flipped through her mail and grimaced. Bills, bills and more bills. No surprise there. Her business, Affairs by Amanda, continued to grow, but unfortunately not fast enough to cover the balloon payment coming due on her bank loan.

If she didn't land a lucrative and highly visible event contract soon she'd have to consider closing her doors or—a fate worse than death—beg her parents for a loan to tide her over. Either way, her father would need a larynx transplant because he'd wear out his voice box lecturing her about disgracing the venerable Crawford name. Not that she hadn't heard that speech a thousand times already.

The elevator opened. She exited with Alex's shoulder bumping hers. The contact acted like a blaring alarm clock on every cell of her being. She absolutely detested his ability to affect her this way.

Honestly, the man had nothing going for him...aside from being rich, smart and gorgeous. It had even been rumored he had a sense of humor. But she could and would continue to resist his advances.

She dug her keys out of her Carlos Falchi python tote bag and shoved them into 9B's lock. It turned smoothly. The building might be prewar, but the security was modern era. If not for her friend Julia's connections, Amanda could never have found herself at such a prestigious uptown address. The real question was how long could she afford to stay without a significant boost in income.

"Wait h—"

"I'd love to come in. Thanks." Alex's chest bumped her shoulder when he reached past her to push open the door. The usual unwanted frisson of awareness hit her.

Why him? Why did Alex Harper have to be the one to ring her chimes?

She stared at him for five seconds, debated the wisdom of letting him in and then decided it wasn't worth arguing. He'd be gone in minutes. She left him behind and crossed the living room to the brushed stainless basket where she'd piled Julia's magazines and mail. When she turned with the bundle in hand, Alex was right on her heels. Her breath caught at his nearness. She shoved the mail forward, jabbing him in his flat belly, in an attempt to make him back off.

"Here you go. Thanks for picking it up. I'll show you out."

He stayed planted, his big body blocking her path to the door. His gaze held hers as he accepted the stack of letters and magazines. His fingers grazed hers. That fleeting contact hit her like a speeding subway train, quickening her pulse, shortening her breath and knocking her silly with lust.

And then he blinked his ridiculously thick lashes, releasing her from his spell. He scanned the pale pink and white high-tech decor of her living room. She could swear he zeroed in on each new addition. The votives, the trio of bubble-glass vases she'd picked up at an estate sale for next to nothing, the lime-green-beaded sari she'd draped over the back of the white sofa and the new raspberry tasseled lampshade.

"You've made some changes since Julia moved out."

"A few." He'd been in the apartment dozens of times, but not recently and never without Max or Julia as a buffer. Funny how he seemed to take up more space and air when it was just the two of them. "You don't want to be late for dinner."

"I have time."

She gritted her teeth in frustration.

"I want more than Julia's mail from you, Amanda."

As if she didn't know that already. Nevertheless the words sent a quick thrill through her. She'd considered *more* with Alex a time or two during her weaker moments. *More* would probably be pretty darn good with him considering all the practice he'd allegedly had. But the man and the timing were all wrong. She had to work on organizing her life before she could allow someone else into it.

She folded her arms and rocked back on her heels. "Really? Now there's a surprise. But there's this little word. *No.* N. O. I'm sure you're familiar with it since I've shared it with you so often."

The corners of his mouth twitched as if he fought a smile. She would bet a month's rent—which she didn't have to spare—he enjoyed their little verbal duels. Why else would he provoke her every time they met?

"You'll change your mind when you hear my proposition."

A proposition. Again, no surprise. Nonetheless, her mouth dried because she really was going to have to say no. Again. And each time it was a little harder to squeeze out that single syllable. "I doubt it."

He took off his coat and draped it over his forearm, revealing a charcoal Brooks Brothers suit, blinding white silk shirt and ruby power tie. "I need Affairs by Amanda."

He'd employed the one line that guaranteed she'd hear him out rather than kick him out. "For what?"

"Harper & Associates just landed a substantial public settlement. I'd like to reward the staff for their hard work."

He definitely knew how to tickle a girl's interest. A party for his firm could be good for business. His and hers. "What kind of event?"

"A couple hundred guests including friends, clients and a few celebrities to make it interesting. Choice of venue is yours, but I'd prefer something upscale like the Metropolitan Club."

Size and visibility. Class and clout. A-list guests who might be persuaded to use her services for their future affairs. Not exactly money in the bank, which she desperately needed, but the exposure could be just the boost her business required.

As a millionaire finance attorney, Alex had the kind of

connections she could use. Not that she didn't have her own connections. But his were better.

She knew there would be strings. A wheeler-dealer like Alex would always have strings. She curved her fingers in a "give me more" gesture. "Details."

He named a budget that made her salivate. "The catch is I'd like to do this within the month. The sooner, the better."

"That could be problematic." But a boon for her finances.

"If you're not up to it I can go elsewhere."

A power play. And he knew exactly what he was doing. She didn't miss the challenge in his eyes or in the angle of his chin. "What makes you think I'm available on such short notice?"

"Julia mentioned you'd had an unexpected cancellation."

A huge engagement party had gone kaput. The bride-to-be had run off with the groom's youngest brother. Not pretty. And while Amanda would get to keep the deposit to cover most of her losses, there would be little left after she paid the vendors and her employees.

She ought to turn Alex down. He was demanding and impatient and a workaholic like her father. He'd be hell to work with unless he stayed out of her way. And she doubted he would.

But she couldn't afford to say no.

"If I do this, your party is all I'm doing. Is that clear?"

One dark eyebrow hiked and his delectable mouth tilted mischievously. "Amanda—"

"Don't 'Amanda' me. I have no intention of being your latest accessory."

His slow, confident smile hit her below the three-inch-wide patent leather belt she'd cinched over her lavender cashmere tunic sweater. "But we'd be so good together."

That's what she was afraid of. He'd be amazing. Right up until the moment he dumped her. And she'd be left with yet another failed relationship. Wouldn't her parents love to rub that in her face?

"But as you pointed out, I'm an attorney. I know better than to force my attentions when they're not welcome. Meet me tomorrow to discuss the party details. Park Café. Four o'clock."

She sputtered at his pushiness. "That's less than twenty-four hours."

"Long enough for you to know if you can pull this off." He turned on his heel. His long strides carried him out of the apartment. The door shut quietly behind him.

She had her work cut out for her, but she'd be darned if she'd back down from the challenge he'd issued.

She couldn't afford to.

Amanda shifted her laptop case to her left hand, braced herself for another onslaught of Alex's charisma and pushed open the door of Park Café.

The upscale coffee shop was her favorite, and not just because of its close proximity to the building where she lived. If she ever had to have a last supper, she wanted it to be one of the café's double chocolate chip walnut muffins—preferably fresh from the oven while the chocolate chips were still gooey.

She waved to Trish, the barista. The warmth enfolding Amanda had everything to do with leaving the blustery outside behind and nothing—*absolutely nothing*—to do with spotting Alex unfolding his tall frame from a chair at a corner table.

He'd dressed casually for a Sunday afternoon in

charcoal wool trousers and a dove-gray cable V-neck sweater that made his shoulders look a mile wide. She caught a glimpse of the black T-shirt he wore between the cashmere and his skin.

*Don't think about what's next to his skin.*
*Keep the meeting on a business footing.*
*And if he flirts, ignore him.*

Easier said than done when even his smile invited her to break rules and promised she'd love doing it. Why did the man tempt her to throw caution and common sense out the window?

He pulled out a chair for her and nodded toward her briefcase. "You came prepared."

"I'm good at what I do. That's why you're hiring me. I brought a list of venues and dates that we can get within the next four weeks. Needless to say, it's a short list since the most desirable locations book up months or years in advance. I can pull up pictures of the spaces online since the café has wireless Internet access."

Trying to make connections with vendors on a Sunday had been absolute hell. But she'd done it by calling in every favor she was owed. This job was that important.

"I've ordered your usual. Trish said to tell you she'd start your latte when you walked in the door and a fresh batch of muffins would be out of the oven in five minutes."

Her usual? She'd met Alex here with Julia and Max a few times, but she hadn't realized he'd noticed she always ordered the same thing. Most likely Trish had told him. "Thank you."

She set her case on the table and extracted her computer. While the laptop booted up, Alex stepped behind her to help her remove her coat. Each touch, no matter how fleeting, hit her with a charge of electricity. Static electricity, no doubt.

*Who do you think you're fooling?*

He draped her coat over his on the spare chair. She sat quickly to get away from his heat and shoved a sheet of paper across the table the moment his behind hit the chair.

"Here are the sites, dates available, room capacities and prices. We'll have to act fast to snap up whichever one you choose because we're capitalizing on cancellations. Once we select the location we'll start on the menus.

"The Metropolitan Club is available for one day only, but I think the Trianon Suite at the Carlyle Hotel would be a better option. That time and date don't conflict with any of the other high-profile events going on in Manhattan."

"The Trianon it is."

That had been too easy. "Do you have your guest list?"

He extracted it from his coat pocket. Amanda took it and scanned the names. Adrenaline rushed through her. If she could convince just two or three of these people to hire her, Affairs by Amanda would be in the black for a long time to come. Alex definitely moved with the in crowd.

A shadow fell across the page. She glanced up and stifled a groan. Curtis, her lying, thieving ex, stood by the table. It took every ounce of civility she had to hide her less-than-happy-to-see-him reaction.

"Hi, 'Manda."

"Hello, Curtis. I can't talk right now. Could you please excuse us?"

The jerk didn't move. "I stopped by your apartment."

"Curtis, I'm working."

"Your balloon payment is coming due this week. Do you have enough money to cover it?"

Her cheeks burned. She did not need Alex to know she had financial issues. He might change his mind about hiring her.

"I don't have time for this discussion now. Later, okay?"

Curtis shoved his hands in his pockets and rocked back on his heels as if he had no intention of going anywhere anytime soon. "I could loan you some cash if you're strapped."

The money Curtis wanted to loan was probably her own. She had to get rid of him. "Why don't I let you talk to my attorney about that cash?"

She knew she was bluffing, but she saw her threat register in his eyes. And then she saw him dismiss it. His lips curled in a smirk. "Now, 'Manda, there's no need to get nasty. We both know you're not interested in making a fuss that would draw your parents' attention to your…difficulties."

Damn. Double damn. She glanced at Alex, and his dark, speculative gaze held hers for perhaps ten seconds. Then he shoved back his chair and rose.

She'd lost him, his business and her much-needed fee. Her stomach sank. Amanda racked her brain for a way to salvage the situation and came up empty. She grimaced an apology.

But instead of storming out of the coffee shop, Alex offered Curtis his hand in a friendly gesture. Surprised, Amanda searched his face. The hard glint in his eyes and his looming posture were far from amicable. In fact, she'd never seen Alex look so ferocious.

"I don't believe we've met. I'm Alexander Harper, Amanda's finance attorney."

Curtis's eyes widened. His mouth opened. The color

leached from his face and he winced. Amanda realized Alex must have crushed his hand. As soon as Alex released him Curtis shuffled back a step. He glanced warily from Alex to Amanda and back, then squared his shoulders.

"Curtis Wilks, Amanda's boyfriend."

"Ex-boyfriend," she corrected. "When you cancelled the lease on our apartment without telling me and then moved out while I was out of town, you ceased to be my anything."

He'd left her high and dry, and with a stack of bills. Since they had been splitting expenses equally, her name had been on all the utilities though not the lease. She'd been doubly screwed. She'd had to move and cover their debts. If Julia hadn't needed a roommate, Amanda wasn't sure where she would have ended up.

Curtis seemed to gather himself. "Yes, well, about that loan—"

"If Amanda needs anything she'll get it through me. Understand?" Alex's cold tone gave new meaning to the word *frostbite*.

Amanda blinked up at him. She wasn't used to anyone coming to her defense, and she kind of liked it. Even if he had lied about being her attorney.

Curtis took another step back. "Uh yeah, sure. See y'round, 'Manda."

Not if she saw him first, to quote the cliché. She watched him leave the shop.

"Pack up. I'll change our order to go," Alex said.

"Why?"

"You're going to tell me what's going on. And I don't think you want to discuss your financial status in a crowded coffee shop. We'll go to your place."

Having him back in her apartment wasn't a good idea. "I'd really rather not discuss my private affairs at all."

"If you don't level with me, Amanda, then our business is finished."

She sighed. What choice did she have? "My place it is."

# Two

"Let's have it," Alex said the moment Amanda finished hanging up their coats. She hadn't looked him in the eye once since leaving the coffee shop.

She carried the bag of muffins to the kitchenette and fished around the cabinets for plates. After placing a muffin on each dish, she retrieved utensils and carried the lot to the small glass-and-steel high-top bar table. Her movements were deliberate and graceful, but he didn't need his body-language-reading skills to recognize she was stalling.

"Amanda?"

Her wary grey eyes finally met his. "How much has Julia already told you?"

Not nearly enough. No matter how hard he'd tried to pry information out of his friend's new bride, Julia had stayed closemouthed about anything that mattered about her former Vassar roommate. The only details she'd shared had been useless stuff he'd already figured out.

"Only that your split with Wilks has left you disinterested in a new relationship."

And Julia had only volunteered that because Amanda continued to shoot Alex down at every turn despite the obvious chemistry between them. He knew women too well to misread the awareness he saw in Amanda's eyes.

She ruffled her short blond hair with her fingers. The strands fell more or less back into place, but she didn't run to a mirror to check it. Amanda's lack of primping was just one of the things he liked about her. Her long, lean body didn't hurt, and the fact that she was confident enough to wear sexy-as-hell heels despite her height was a total turn-on.

"You heard Curtis. I have a banknote coming due and I'm running a little short. But that won't affect my ability to plan this event for you."

A wise man would back away from a company in financial trouble. But he wasn't feeling wise at the moment.

He shoved his hands in his pockets. "Do you need a loan?"

Her eyes widened and then her long lashes fluttered down. She focused on peeling the paper off the muffin. "I'll talk to the bank about an extension. Now, about your party—"

He wasn't going to let her change the subject that easily. "Spill it, Amanda. All of it. And then I'll decide whether or not we'll do business."

Her chin tilted in a defensive angle. "I am very careful about budgeting and planning ahead. We'll have a contract. You don't have to worry that I'll take your deposit and pay my creditors and stiff the people we engage for your event."

"I wasn't. But if you're so good with budgets how did the shortfall happen? Is business slow? I've heard nothing but accolades about your work."

She shoved her dish aside with a wistful glance at the muffin she'd crumbled into a messy pile. Instead of looking at him, she concentrated on wiping her chocolate-dotted fingers on a paper napkin. Stalling again.

"It's my fault, really. I made the mistake of allowing Curtis to help me set up the books and accounts for Affairs by Amanda.

"It worked well for a while. But then my operating capital started disappearing. At first I didn't notice because the amounts were small and I was too busy building my client list to pay attention, but then bigger chunks went missing. I questioned Curtis and he claimed I'd underestimated the costs of several major items. But I *never* underestimate. I always *over*estimate by five percent, just in case. When I asked for the receipts in question he told me he'd have to find them. Then he moved out while I was away for the weekend and left me holding all the bills."

Her case sounded typical of many others he'd handled. The embezzler started with small amounts to test the waters and then grew bolder and took more. "There are legal avenues for handling this situation."

"I know. But there are three reasons I've chosen not to go that route. Curtis knows them. One, I don't have the money to pay lawyer fees right now, and two, as Curtis said, I'd rather my parents not hear about this. Three, I may be convinced Curtis is responsible for the missing money, but proving it is another story. The questionable invoices mysteriously vanished when he did. And I had given him access to my accounts, so that makes me at least partially responsible."

His first instinct was to take her case pro bono. But he also intended to sleep with Amanda, and that was a conflict of interest he'd learned the hard way not to repeat. So as much as he'd personally love to nail the Wilks weasel, he had to hand this off.

He extracted his checkbook, a business card and a pen from his inside coat pocket. "I'm writing the name of one of the associates from my firm on the back of my card. Call him."

"Alex, I can't afford—"

"He'll defer payment until settlement." Alex would make sure of it—even if he had to guarantee the fees himself. "And I'll loan you the money to make your payment."

"I don't think—"

"You don't want to damage your credit by asking for an extension."

"Well…no."

"Do you want to let Wilks get away with this?"

"Of course not. But, Alex, you don't have to do this."

"What are your other options?"

She grimaced. "I could ask my father for a loan."

"You said you didn't want your parents to find out. Will your father hand over a chunk of cash without asking why you need it?" He barely waited for her to shake her head before going for the closer. "I want you handling my party, Amanda. If you're worrying about your finances, you'll be distracted and you'll give me less than one hundred percent."

And she'd be less likely to fall in with his plans.

He wanted Amanda Crawford for more than just sex, although that played a large part. Her networking expertise was unparalleled. The woman knew how to work a room better than anyone he'd ever met. She was exactly who he needed by his side to build the powerful connections that brought in clients and put money in the bank. She'd be an asset to his career for as long as their affair lasted, and it wasn't an ego trip to know he would be equally beneficial to hers. The fact that she wasn't interested in a permanent relationship only enhanced the attraction.

He opened his checkbook. "How much do you need?"

She hesitated. "Are there strings attached to the loan? I mean, do you expect me to sleep with you?"

Full disclosure wouldn't be in his best interest at this point. "When we share a bed it will be because you're tired of fighting the chemistry between us, not because of misplaced gratitude."

Her pupils expanded and her lips parted. "You sound convinced that will happen."

"It will."

"But you want something from me."

Smart lady. "I could use your connections. You introduce me to potential clients and I'll do the same for you."

She inhaled deeply as if preparing to argue, but then shook her head and blew out a long, slow breath. "I can do that. But, Alex, I never took you for the knight-in-shining-armor type."

Taken aback, he straightened. "I'm not."

Her lips twitched into a small smile and her eyes sparkled as if she had a secret. "I don't believe you."

A corner of his brain urged him to accept her change in attitude and use it to get ahead in the game. "Believe whatever you want. Give me an amount."

After a moment she did. He wrote the check and tore it out of the book. It was his job to get everything in writing, but discussing a repayment schedule would kill the deal faster than bleach killed germs. From everything he'd learned about her she would reimburse him. But if she didn't, he wouldn't miss a few thousand. And it wouldn't be the first time a woman cost him.

"Pay me back when you can."

Looking a little suspicious and a lot stunned, she took the check and business card. "That's it? You're just handing me money?"

"That's it."

"Thank you."

And then she surprised him by throwing her arms around his neck. Her body bumped his. He hugged her back, learning the feel of her lean length pressed against him, her breasts on his chest, her warm, smooth cheek against his and her soft hair tickling his ear. His libido howled like a wolf, but there would be time for that later. He released her the moment she eased back on her heels.

"Thank you again, Alex. I don't know what to say."

Her scent lingered in his nostrils. "Say yes to dinner."

She gasped, and her cheeks pinked.

"We never did get around to discussing the party," he reminded her.

She nibbled her bottom lip and then nodded. "Yes. To dinner."

Her measured tone said, "And only dinner." He fully intended to change her mind. But not tonight.

Success would take patience. And strategy. Luckily, he excelled at both.

Amanda couldn't believe she was nervous. But her damp palms were a dead giveaway. She pressed them to her flannel trousers.

Did Alex consider this a date? He'd certainly steered the dinner conversation away from planning his event, and he'd done so with such skill she hadn't even realized it until the taxi ride back. Each time she'd tried to stay on task he'd eased the conversation from the topic to people or places they both knew—people who would be at his party. Tricky.

Would he try to kiss her good-night?

Would she stop him this time?

He'd shown her a side of himself today that was different from what she'd seen before. She'd always considered him more ruthless shark than noble rescuer. Now she wasn't so sure she'd read him correctly.

*Oh, please. Are you twenty-eight or eighteen?*

As usual, Alex invaded her personal space the moment he entered her apartment. He stood with his hands in his coat pockets but close enough that she could see each blade of dark beard stubble and the fine lines in his lips. She yanked her gaze away from his mouth and tamped down the anticipation vibrating along her nerve endings. Her hands trembled as she unwound her scarf and hung it up along with her coat.

"Dinner was nice. Thank you."

The hole-in-the-wall Italian restaurant was new to her

but apparently not to Alex, who had been welcomed by name and immediately shown to a table despite the line of customers waiting to be seated. He couldn't have made a reservation because he couldn't have known she'd accept his invitation. She hadn't even known until the words had tumbled from her lips. And he couldn't have called ahead because he hadn't been out of her sight between her acceptance and their arrival at the family-run place.

"You're welcome. It's nice to share a meal with a woman who eats."

She flushed. She'd definitely done an embarrassing amount of that by packing away a salad, veal parmesan, crusty bread, her chocolate gelato and then some of Alex's pistachio.

"May I take your coat?"

"I'm not staying. Make the calls tomorrow morning and meet me for lunch to tell me what you've set up."

She scrambled to claw through her surprise or dismay or whatever it was and recall her calendar. Her Monday was lamentably open. She had a couple of small events in the works, but nothing more urgent than Alex's. "I could confirm by phone."

"No." Flat. Nonnegotiable. Bossy.

Her hackles rose, but she ignored them. "Where, then? My office?"

"Mine." He pulled out his BlackBerry and punched a few buttons, then slid it back into his pocket. "I should be finished by twelve-thirty."

His hand curved over her shoulder, strong and sure. The heat from his palm permeated her sweater. A shower of tingles rained down from the point of contact. He leaned closer. She caught her breath and swallowed the sudden rush of moisture to her mouth.

"You did a good job, Amanda. Your ideas thus far are top-notch. I'll see you tomorrow." His fingers tightened briefly and then he released her. She stood as still as a statue as he let himself out of the apartment.

No kiss? She stared at the closed door. She wasn't disappointed he hadn't attempted to kiss her good-night.

She wasn't.

This was business. Only business. And that was a good thing. Exactly what she wanted. She didn't have room for complicated relationships in her life at the moment, especially not with a finance attorney who probably thought she was a complete idiot for getting herself into her current predicament. She'd bet the trust fund she wouldn't come into until she turned thirty that Alexander Harper never made stupid mistakes with *his* money.

Tension poured from her muscles like sand through a broken hourglass. She headed for her bedroom, shed her clothes and took a long, hot shower. She conditioned her hair and shaved everything that needed shaving. She'd had to give up waxing to save the salon costs and because she was too much of a wimp to wax herself at home. She had a half-used waxing kit in the vanity cabinet as proof of her cowardice.

But the antsy feeling wouldn't leave her alone. Wrapped in a lavender towel, she padded into the bedroom, snatched up the phone and dialed Julia's new number. Her friend answered before the second ring.

"Moving pretty fast for a pregnant lady, aren't you?" Julia laughed. "You're just lucky I had the receiver parked on my mountainous belly. You sound out of sorts. What's the matter?"

She and Julia had known each other too long to miss the nuances in each other's voices. Julia heard Amanda's distress as clearly as Amanda heard her friend's happiness. "Go ahead and have me committed."

"Why? Are you dating Curtis again?"

"If I were that stupid I'd commit myself." She took a deep breath and confessed in a rush, "I agreed to plan an event for Alex Harper."

"And that's bad because…?"

"You know why."

"He's in hot pursuit. Yes, it's so tragic when a handsome, intelligent, wealthy guy wants you."

"Hey!"

"Amanda, you two can't keep your eyes off each other when you're in the same room. Max thinks Alex is a great guy. And I know you need someone to boost your confidence after that jerk Curtis. I say go for it—the party and anything else Alex is offering."

So much for her friend talking her off the celibacy-sucks ledge. "You know my goal. Get my life back on track and make a success of my business before I hit thirty."

"And come into all that money."

"I have to prove I can make a success of my business before then. Otherwise, my parents will just think Granddad's money bailed me out."

"Amanda, that's two years away. One brief affair is not going to set back your schedule."

"Says the woman who ended up pregnant after a *very* brief one-night stand."

"Ooh. You only fight dirty when you're running scared. Just remember Alex isn't the forever type."

"No kidding." She couldn't keep the sarcasm from her voice.

"In fact, he's quite a hound dog. Take precautions. You can't be celibate forever."

With her track record it would probably be her best option. "Why not?"

"Besides the obvious—that sex is fantastic with the right partner?"

Well, yes, there was that. "He's not the right person."

"You don't know that. Give the man points for persistence and reward his efforts already. Watching you dance around each other is exhausting me, and my poor, pregnant body is already on a hormonal roller coaster without watching all that longing in your eyes. Do him already."

She rolled her eyes. "You're not helping."

"Yes, I am. You're just not willing to admit I'm giving sage advice."

Admit to her newlywed and now aggressively matchmaking friend that she was attracted to Alex Harper?

Amanda would rather walk naked through Times Square.

At twelve-twenty-six the next day Amanda pushed open the heavy gold-stenciled glass door of Harper & Associates.

Alex's firm epitomized the affluent type of client Amanda longed for. Perhaps, she thought, she should consider targeting more corporate clients instead of focusing primarily on private affairs.

Her D&G pumps sank into the thick carpeting as she crossed to the cherry reception desk that had been polished to a mirror shine. A twenty-something blonde greeted her with a face and a toothy smile worthy of a beauty queen. "Good afternoon. May I help you?"

Amanda smiled back. "Amanda Crawford for Alex Harper."

"One moment please." She swiveled away and spoke quietly into a headset before turning back. "His assistant will be right with you. Would you care for a beverage?"

A stiff shot of something to calm her nerves would be good. "No, thank you."

"There she is now," the receptionist said, drawing Amanda's attention to a compact, midforties brunette charging down a wide corridor in her direction.

"Ms. Crawford? I'm Moira Newton. I'll take you to Mr. Harper's private waiting area."

Amanda followed her into a room that reeked money, from the wainscoting to the clean-cut lines of the leather and cherry furniture to the original artwork on the walls. If a room could instill a client's confidence in its owner, then this one would.

"Alex will be with you momentarily. May I get you anything while you wait?"

"I'm fine. Thank you."

"I'll take your coat."

Amanda shrugged off the garment, handed it over and sank into a deep wing chair tucked in the corner.

Moira hung her coat in a small closet hidden by the paneling, then sat behind a desk that fronted the remainder of her work space, which was discreetly concealed in a large alcove.

Moments later the muted timbre of Alex's voice scattered the butterflies that had been resting in Amanda's stomach. A door on the far wall opened and a harassed-looking, balding man stepped through, followed by Alex. As yet unnoticed, she drank Alex in as the men said their good-byes.

From the aggressive angle of his jaw to the straight set of his shoulders, Alex radiated self-assurance. His black tailored suit accentuated his height and athletic build, and his white shirt brought out his olive complexion. His dark hair swooped back from the side part, the ends covering his collar at his nape. Traditional, conservative clothing and furnishings, but the deliberately in-need-of-a-trim hairstyle hinted at a rebellious side. And her rebellious side snapped to attention.

*Business only.*

The client left. Alex turned and nailed her to the chair with his direct gaze. "Hello, Amanda."

How did he unsettle her with nothing more than a slow perusal and a *hello?* She had to work on shutting down that reaction.

"Alex." She dipped her head in greeting and rose, lifting her laptop case. "I have confirmations and contracts, and I need signatures."

"Come in." He extended his arm, gesturing for her to precede him.

His spacious office contained the same high-end furniture but had a slightly more relaxed atmosphere. A subtle hint of his cologne hung in the air. In addition to the desk and bookcases, he had a boardroom table set up in front of a bank of windows. He led her to that table. "Have a seat."

His knuckles brushed her shoulder blades as he seated her in the chair closest to the glass. She hid her shiver by reaching into her briefcase, extracting his file, then admiring the view of the Manhattan skyline.

"We have the Carlyle Trianon Suite for Saturday, the

twenty-second. We need to choose a theme and send out invitations immediately. If you have e-mail addresses for the people on your guest list I can also send out a blanket 'save the date' notice tomorrow."

He leaned back against the edge of his desk and crossed his ankles. His unwavering gaze pinned her to her chair. "Moira can give you the addresses. You look beautiful today."

Her brain tripped. She couldn't remember what she was supposed to say next. How did he fluster her so easily? "Thank you."

She dropped her gaze to the papers in her hand and struggled to regain her footing. "I have—" A knock at the door interrupted her.

"That should be our lunch. Eating in will allow us more time. I hope you like Greek food."

Lunch in an office shouldn't seem intimate. But it did. "A working lunch is a good idea. We have a lot to cover. And I love Greek food."

He opened the door to reveal Moira with a brown paper bag in one hand and tableware in the other.

"Need help setting up?" his assistant asked.

"We can handle it." He took everything from her, then placed the bag on the table and opened it. A delicious aroma saturated the room.

Amanda's mouth watered as he removed the lids from containers of feta, tomato and spinach salad, followed by farmer's bread and artichoke moussaka. He crossed to a small wine refrigerator tucked beneath a counter in the corner and returned with a bottle of Dry Creek Valley Zinfandel, which he opened and poured into two glasses.

She'd learned to keep a clear head when around Alex. "I don't usually drink when I'm working."

"The wine goes well with moussaka, but I'll get you a bottle of water if you prefer." He retrieved two bottles from a different refrigerator and set them on the table.

After scooping generous portions onto plates, he surprised her by shoving the containers to the opposite side of the table and sitting beside her instead of across from her. Their shoulders brushed as he adjusted his chair.

Too close. How could she concentrate with him touching her?

He lifted his glass and twisted in his seat. "To an enjoyable and profitable relationship."

"I'll drink to that." She lifted her glass and clinked her rim against his.

She took a sip. The zesty fruit-and-berry flavor of the cool liquid slid smoothly down her throat. She would have to be careful because she liked this wine too much, and that could get her in trouble.

Alex looked at her over the rim of his glass. "I'll need you to act as my hostess."

Her heart skipped a beat. She snapped her gaze from the food in front of her to Alex's. "You can't find someone else at this late date?"

"I want you, Amanda."

# Three

*I want you.*

Alex's firmly stated phrase, delivered in close proximity and with direct eye contact, made Amanda's insides quiver.

*He means for the party.*

*No, he means more than that. But you're ignoring the "more" part. Remember?*

"I—I can hostess." Usually she facilitated events from behind the scenes, but it would be much easier to make those much-needed connections by Alex's side.

"I will, of course, cover the cost of appropriate attire."

God, he smelled good. "Alex, you don't need to do that."

"This evening will be as important for me as it will be for you. Buy yourself something."

Definitely bossy and not what she needed. "If I don't have anything suitable I'll consider it."

The hard look he shot her should have sent her scurrying to comply. Instantly. But she ignored it thanks to practice. She'd learned to deal with a similar look from her father. She reached for her fork. "This looks yummy."

"Aglaia's is one of my favorite places. Eat. Then we'll talk."

The salad was delicious, perfect in flavor and texture, as were the other dishes. They consumed the meal in silence. Unfortunately, the lack of conversation made it far too easy to get hung up on each shift of his body and each bump of his elbow, and it drove her to her wineglass more often than her water bottle.

Had she ever noticed he had great hands? Long fingers, blunt nails, sparse dark hairs on the backs. She couldn't remember experiencing this all-consuming awareness with anyone else.

*Get a grip.*

Finally, Alex forked the last bite of moussaka between his lips, chewed and swallowed. "Last night you said we had to choose a theme for the party. What did you have in mind?"

So he had listened before changing the subject.

He angled in his chair, his right thigh nudging her left. His heat penetrated the thin layers of their clothing and her thoughts snarled. She struggled to untangle them. Under the guise of shifting her empty plate out of the way she put an inch or two between them.

"That depends on whether you want a formal, traditional sit-down meal or something more relaxed and fun."

"Which do you recommend?"

"Your office is formal and conservative. If you want this to be a reward then I'd go for a 'festive drinks and hors d'oeuvres' event. You said your employees worked hard. Let them mingle and loosen up a little."

He reached for his wine, pursed his lips and sipped. She found her gaze locked on his mouth again and pried it away.

*You really must stop doing that.*

She fumbled for her water bottle, hoping the chilled liquid would satisfy her sudden oral fixation. The last thing she needed was more wine. Her head was already spinning, and she wasn't sure alcohol was the cause.

"Would you consider a masked ball? You could still have a formal affair, but donning masks allows everyone to let down their guard a little."

His left eyebrow hiked.

"Not full costume," she rushed on before he could object. "More of a Mardi Gras in November. We could even have New Orleans cuisine and music, if you like."

"Sounds like a good plan. Can you get a jazz band?"

"I've used a couple of good ones before. This afternoon I'll call and see if either is available. Since we've decided on a theme, I have invitation and decoration suggestions."

She reached for her laptop, booted up and then picked up the paper file. Inside she'd tucked samples for several different party themes in different pocketed folders. As soon as he made choices she could enter the info online and e-mail it to her supplier.

Alex rose and carried the plates to the wet bar in the corner. When he returned he sat down closer than before, his long legs bracketing her chair and his arm resting along the back of her seat. His position hemmed her against the table. If she leaned back she'd be in his arms— one of the places she'd been avoiding for the past three-plus months and intended to continue avoiding.

She fought to block out his nearness and focused on pulling up the images on-screen. "Here are sample schemes."

She clicked her mouse, scrolling through each page. He leaned closer. His breath teased her cheek and stirred the hair at her temple. Her mouth moistened and her pulse quickened.

"Stop. Back up." He spoke quietly, directly into her ear.

It took a few seconds for her brain to relay his words to her fingers. She cleared her throat. "This page?"

"Yes."

It was no surprise he'd chosen the most conservative of the bunch. She extracted a sample from the folder. "This?"

"Yes."

She picked up a pen with a hand that wasn't as steady as she would have liked and made a note, then did the same on the computer. "With that I'd recommend these."

She flipped to the next item on her list. Thank goodness the program she'd installed prompted her or else she would be floundering. What was wrong with her? She loved planning events. And yet today she could barely connect the dots.

*Concentrate.* "I'll make sure to order an assortment of spare masks for the guests who don't bring their own. Would you like for me to get one for you?"

"Amanda."

She turned her head at his low-voiced but commanding tone. Their faces and lips were scarce inches apart—the closest they'd been to date. The temptation to close the distance between their mouths streaked across her mind. She forced her gaze to his eyes and dragged a slow breath into her lungs.

Lambent desire flickered in his dark chocolate eyes. "You know what I want."

Did she ever. Her pulse rate rocketed. She swallowed and nodded. "I have a pretty good idea."

"I trust you to make the decisions to make it happen." Firm. Decisive. Not at all seductive.

What? Confused, she blinked and sat back.

"We've covered the basics," he continued. "I'll leave the rest in your capable hands."

Work. He was talking about *work?*

*Of course he is. That's why you're here. Remember? Get your head out of the ozone, Amanda Crawford.*

"I'll get right on it." She hastily closed her laptop, then grabbed the file folder and stacked it on top.

Alex shifted again, leaning forward so that his chest and arm pressed her back and shoulder, enfolding her in his warmth and scent. "Before you go, I have something I know you can't resist."

Her heart thumped like a bass drum, the beat reverberating off her eardrums and her gaze drifted back to his mouth.

He reached across the table and extracted two small boxes from the take-out bag. "Baklava. Two kinds. Walnut and chocolate. I couldn't neglect your sweet tooth."

She wasn't disappointed. *She wasn't.*

Yes, she was.

*What is wrong with you? Do you actually miss him trying to get into your pants? How perverted is that?*

But she was touched he'd noticed she had a weakness for sweets. Had Curtis? Had any of the men who'd blemished her relationship record in the past decade? Regrettably, no.

And what did that say about her taste in men and her

ability to choose them wisely? Nothing good. Which was why her sudden yen for Alex Harper was bad news.

She transferred her attention to the flaky confections cut into bite-size diamonds.

"Go ahead, Amanda. Dive right in. You know you want to."

Exactly. And that was becoming a big problem.

The police again?

Amanda's steps faltered on the marble floor as she entered her lobby early Monday evening. She hoped the police presence was more of the same old unsolved investigation and not some new occurrence in the apartment building.

As she passed under the massive crystal chandelier on the way to the elevators she nodded a silent greeting to Detective McGray, who loomed over the doorman's desk. His green eyes and lean, paunchy body looked tired and harassed.

The detective had been haunting the building since a former resident had been found dead back in late June. At first the police had believed Marie Endicott's death to be a suicide, but now they suspected foul play. The possibility of someone being murdered in the building gave Amanda the creeps. She shivered and shifted her attention to the doorman.

Poor Henry was sweating and mopping his face with a handkerchief despite the frosty air Amanda brought *whoosh*ing in on her heels. She couldn't blame the guy. The hard-eyed detective could make anyone squirm. McGray had certainly rattled her cage when he'd questioned her after the woman's body had been found.

Amanda hadn't even known the deceased. But she'd heard everyone in the building had been questioned. And then there'd been an even more uncomfortable Q&A in July when Julia had received a blackmail letter from someone threatening to spill the news of her pregnancy.

Amanda stepped into the waiting elevator. According to her former roommate, the scandals of 721 Park Avenue's residents could keep the tabloids busy for years. Yet another reason to keep the Curtis situation quiet. She wasn't ready to involve Alex's associate and risk exposing her predicament.

Which brought her thoughts back to Alex. As if they'd strayed far from that taboo subject lately. She sighed and leaned into the corner as the elevator shot upward. His enticement with the baklava had almost led her to create a scandal of a whole different kind. How she'd managed not to lick the man from head to toe right there in his office when he'd fed her a bite of chocolate baklava was still a mystery.

Kudos to her for having the good sense to invent another appointment and rush out of there before she devoured him and his baklava. Her willpower was stronger than she'd suspected. But it was worrisomely shaky.

The doors opened. She straightened and prepared to exit but stopped. Jane Elliott, penthouse B's housekeeper, stood in the opening. Amanda glanced at the floor number. Six. "Hi, Jane. Going up?"

Jane hesitated and then stepped inside and hit the button for the penthouse. "Yes. Good evening, Amanda."

The doors slid shut. Amanda briefly wondered who Jane had been visiting on the sixth floor and then shoved the question into the "none of her business" category.

She looked longingly at the housekeeper's long, curly

hair and wished—not for the first time—that her baby-fine hair would hold a curl. But no. She might have inherited her mother's height and build, but she'd been cursed with her father's flyaway locks and pale coloring instead of the thick auburn hair and sultry looks that had made her mother a top fashion model for two decades before she'd traded in that career to become a successful clothing designer.

Bad hair. Just one more way to disappoint her overachieving parents. As if she needed another way.

She shook off the negative thoughts. "Detective McGray is back in the building. I haven't missed anything new, have I?"

"I'm not aware of any new occurrences," Jane replied. The doors opened again. "Are you visiting Gage—Mr. Lattimer, I mean?"

Amanda's gaze shot to the numbers. "Oops. No. My mind was wandering. I guess I forgot to push the button for my floor."

"Good night, then." Jane left the elevator.

"Good night." Amanda stabbed the 9 button. The doors closed. She smacked a palm against her forehead.

Alex had taken over her brain, and she couldn't afford to mix business with her personal life again. It wasn't as if she didn't have a clear pattern to show her the error of her ways.

During her senior year in high school she'd fallen head over heels for Heath, the star quarterback. She'd almost flunked her last semester and that would have cost her her acceptance to Vassar if her father hadn't bailed her out by having a long talk with the dean. Amanda suspected there had probably been a deep-pocketed donation along with the discussion.

And then while in college she'd met Douglas at an art gallery. Talk about being stupidly distracted. She'd been young, naive and totally trusting. Douglas had been thirty-two, suave and so attentive. He'd swept her off her feet and taken her to Vegas. Instead of marrying her like she'd expected, he'd proceeded to gamble away the majority of the money she'd inherited from her grandmother on her twenty-first birthday. When the money had run out, so had he. She'd had to call home for airfare. Hadn't *that* been embarrassing?

By the time Curtis rolled into her life, her parents considered her truly stupid and irresponsible. And she'd proven them right. She'd been distracted by the whole falling-in-love myth and she'd trusted too much. Apparently her hormonal stupors caused her to miss critical details—details that still could cost her Affairs by Amanda.

But the hormonal stupors induced by Heath, Douglas and Curtis were like mild colds compared to the full-blown flu version Alex brought on.

Maybe a little inoculation would cure her.

*No. Don't go there.*

She couldn't afford to lose her business. That meant she couldn't lose her head. Because if she lost Affairs by Amanda she'd be forced to admit to her parents and herself that she was a failure.

"Alex." The flash of hunger in Amanda's eyes when she opened her door later that Monday was gratifying. The frown that followed was not. "What are you doing here and how did you get upstairs without Henry buzzing me?"

"I'm here because I heard you're a Monday night

football fan. And Gage Lattimer brought me up. He lives in the penthouse."

She gave him a patient look. "I know who Gage is. You took a lot for granted assuming I'd be at home and free tonight."

"I did, but I brought food, beer and fresh Krispy Kremes to make up for it."

Her gaze dropped to the bags in his hands. Indecision filled her face. She shifted on her bare feet, drawing his attention to her fuchsia-painted toenails. "I don't think—"

"And another party proposition."

He had her. Whether it was the donuts or the party that sealed the deal didn't matter. He saw capitulation soften her grey eyes before she opened the door wider, albeit with obvious reluctance. "Come in. But only if you're pulling for the Giants."

He grinned. "I have season tickets. Box seats. Fifty yard line. Be nice and I'll take you to a game."

That earned him a smile. What more could a guy want? Amanda was smart, sexy, a networking genius. And she liked football.

He scanned the place for competition as he followed her in, but he didn't spot any sign of a date. He had taken a risk showing up uninvited tonight, but his previous strategy wasn't working. He'd needed an adjustment. The exercise mat on the floor clued him in to her evening plans and explained her T-shirt, cotton pants and lack of makeup. Not that she needed to paint a face like hers.

He handed over the beer—an imported brew that Julia claimed was the only brand Amanda would drink. "Shove that in the refrigerator while I unpack the rest. The game doesn't start for an hour. That gives us time to eat and talk about my brother's birthday party."

*His brother.* The lie didn't slide as easily off his tongue with Amanda as it would with anyone else. For some reason he wanted to tell her the truth. He wanted to claim Zack as his son. But revealing that secret would cause nothing but trouble and could possibly hurt Zack. Besides, it was nobody's business.

"The party you wanted to discuss is for him?"

"Zack's going to turn eighteen in a few months. I'd like to throw a big bash, one he'll never forget. And I'll need your help for that." He shrugged off his coat and tossed it over the back of a bar stool before extracting the Chinese food containers and lining them up on her kitchen counter, but Amanda's eyes drilled the donut box. He handed it to her.

"Dessert first?" she asked with a wistful look in her eyes.

How could he deny her? If she would look at him like that they'd both be naked and busy. "Go for it."

She wasted no time ripping open the top, pulling out a glazed donut and biting into it. Her eyes closed and her head tilted back. "Mmm. Oh, my God, these are amazing."

Her throaty words hit him below the belt with a kick of arousal that nearly took him to his knees.

*She'll look like that in bed.*

He couldn't tear his eyes away as she greedily consumed the rest of her prize. She didn't lift her lids until she'd finished the last sugary bite. Her tongue swept her lips, but white flakes of glaze clung to the corners. She lifted one finger to her mouth and licked.

He wanted that job.

Screw strategy. He grabbed her hand, carried it to his

mouth and lapped her sticky fingertip with his tongue. Her breath hitched. But she didn't slap him or yank her hand away. Without taking his eyes off hers he moved from the first sweetened digit to the second. His tongue swirled around the tip, and then he pulled her thumb into his mouth and repeated the process. Her pupils dilated and her lips parted.

He had to have her mouth. Now. Releasing her hand, he closed the distance between them.

"You have more sugar here." He dipped his head to lick it away.

She leaned into him, lifting her chin in silent invitation. She didn't have to ask twice. He traced the sugary outline of her lips. It wasn't enough. He covered her mouth with his and delved into her silky warmth. The sweetness of the donut gave way to the unique flavor of the woman in his arms.

He'd been waiting months for this. He caught her waist and pulled her closer, crushing her against his chest and deepening the kiss. Her hands rested briefly on his shoulders, her short nails digging into his muscles and then her arms slid around his neck. She opened her mouth wider for him and her tongue sought his, slick and sweet, warm and wet.

She fit against him even better than he'd expected. Need rumbled up from his gut to his throat. He mapped her spine, her waist, her hips. She was long and lean and hot. His fingers found silky bare skin between the hem of her shirt and the waistband of her pants.

She gasped and lifted her head. But she didn't pull away. Her passion-darkened eyes sought his. "I— We shouldn't do this, Alex."

"It's long overdue."

Her gaze dropped back to his mouth. Regret flickered across her face. "I don't sleep with my clients."

"Should I fire you?" he teased.

She stiffened and panic widened her eyes. "You'd do that?"

He rubbed her back soothingly, enjoying the smooth warmth of her skin. "No. I honor my promises. And I promise you, Amanda, this isn't a mistake. We're going to be magnificent together. In bed *and* out."

Indecision flitted across her features. And then she sighed. Her fingers threaded through his hair. She pulled his face back to hers. Whatever he'd expected, it wasn't the aggressive, carnal, no-holds-barred kiss she planted on him.

She devoured him with the same intensity she'd given to the baklava at lunch and the donut tonight, and he was more than willing to be consumed. He cupped her butt and pressed her hips to his. If she hadn't known where he wanted this to go then his growing erection was a dead giveaway. Damn, she was potent.

By the time she lifted her head and slid her hands to his pectorals, his heart was slamming like a wrecking ball against his chest wall.

She licked her damp lips. "This is crazy. I don't have time for a man in my life right now. For the next few years, my career is my priority. Alex, if you can't handle this being temporary then we need to stop. Now."

Her frankness momentarily took him aback. But her willingness to speak freely was one of the things he liked about Amanda. Was she joking? What man would say no to a brief, passionate affair? Temporary was his specialty.

"I can handle it. Where's your bedroom?"

For a second she hesitated, looking as if she might change her mind, but then she took his hand and led him across the living room. His gaze dropped to her butt in the thin knit pants. Nice. Firm. Rounded.

Her bedroom was as pink and white and feminine as the rest of the apartment. A thick, white faux-fur rug covered the floor. Filmy white drapes, tied back with brightly colored silky-looking scarves, hung behind a platform bed in a makeshift headboard. He'd never been one for bondage, but he couldn't help thinking those scarves could come in handy later. He would like to tie her up and pleasure her until she begged him to stop.

Right now he was too impatient to play sexy games.

He yanked her hand, spinning her back into his arms. Their bodies and mouths slammed together, lips parting, tongues clashing. She met him stroke for stroke. Her fingers dug into his waist. Her pelvis nudged his. She wasn't shy or coy, and her boldness was an incredible turn-on. He whisked her shirt over her head. Before he could savor her pale, smooth skin she attacked his shirt without hesitation.

Dressed, Amanda looked deceptively lean, but she had curves. Not overblown. But subtle, exquisite. Perfect. He wanted to linger, to savor her breasts above her lavender lace bra, but he'd wanted Amanda for months and hunger snuffed out patience. The bra gave way with a flick of his fingers. He tossed it aside and caught one puckered pink nipple in his mouth, the other in his hand. She tasted good. Smelled good. Her pale skin was warm and silky soft against his lips.

Her fingers speared his hair, flexed into his scalp with an energizing tug. Then she lightly scraped her nails across his shoulders and down his sides. His muscles rippled in the wake of her touch. Her nimble fingers encountered his belt. The leather gave way quickly, followed by the button and zipper of his pants. She had him so aroused he could barely concentrate.

Apparently he wasn't the only one in a hurry. Her palms flattened against his hips and shoved the fabric of his pants and boxers over his butt and down his thighs. Her caress sent a shock of need through him, making him grit his teeth and struggle to fill his lungs.

He released her long enough to kick off his shoes and the remainder of his clothing, and then he ripped her pants down her long legs. The tattoo he uncovered when he removed her bikini panties caught him by surprise. "A martini?"

She nibbled her bottom lip as if she expected him to be repulsed by the ink. "An appletini. It's a reminder that life's supposed to be fun."

With one finger he outlined the tilted glass just below her left hipbone and then knelt and sipped from the inked rim. He lifted his gaze to hers and rose. "It's sexy as hell. Tasty, too."

Her slow smile and the desire in her eyes decimated what was left of his control. "So are you."

And that's when he realized he might be in trouble. A little of Amanda Crawford might not be enough.

# Four

Alexander Harper had been hiding a body to die for beneath his custom designer suits.

His wide shoulders, ropey muscles and washboard abs had Amanda salivating for the feel of those brawny arms wrapped around her. She bisected his smooth chest with her fingers, drawing a line between his pectorals to the goody trail below his navel and the dense dark hair surrounding his erection. His stomach quivered beneath her touch and his arousal twitched, begging her to curl her fingers around his thick length. She wasted no time in doing so. His breath whistled.

"Amanda." The man actually growled.

She grinned mischievously up at him and stroked him from base to tip. "Yes?"

His pupils expanded and his skin flushed. "You're playing with fire."

"That's okay. I like it hot." She just hoped her desire for Alex didn't burn her before it burned out.

Experience told her this was a mistake, but she couldn't stop now. He'd monopolized her thoughts for three long months and she ached for him. Her thumb found a slick droplet pearling on his engorged tip and spread it around. She leaned forward to lick his tiny, brown nipple.

One strong arm banded around her, yanking her flush against his hot torso. His other hand stabbed into her hair, fisted and tugged just hard enough to force her head back. The combination of his scorching heat, his strength and his controlled aggression robbed her breath. His kiss was hard, bordering on rough, his passion barely contained. And she loved it. How long had it been since anyone wanted her so intensely? Had anyone, ever? She couldn't remember. But she doubted it.

She released his erection, wound her arms around his neck and relished the heady desire racing through her. She loved that Alex was taller and broader than she. Both Curtis and Douglas had been her height. She'd felt like an Amazon with them. But not with Alex. He was bigger in *every* way, and he loomed over her, making her feel dainty, desirable and feminine and not the least bit delicate.

He skimmed her curves, kneaded her bottom. His tongue and hands worked magic, arousing her beyond anything she'd ever experienced as they flexed into her flesh. She kissed him back, tangling her fingers in his hair and arching as tight against him as she could get. It wasn't close enough. She wanted to wind herself around him but settled for lifting her leg, sliding it up the outside of his hair-roughened, rock-hard, muscled thigh and hooking it around his waist. He grasped her knee and arched his hips, plunging deep inside her. The shock of his sudden penetration filled her, forcing the breath from her lungs on a moan of pure ecstasy.

He withdrew and then rocked upward again and again, nearly lifting her off the ground with each thrust. Her heart raced and every muscle in her body clenched with need as he drove deep, so deep inside her.

Alex swung her around and her world tilted. She felt herself falling. She clung to his shoulders and whimpered into his mouth, but he didn't drop her. He eased her onto the mattress. Cool sheets pressed against her back, but it was the hot body above her and driving into her that held her rapt attention.

She tore her mouth free to gasp for air and buried her face in his neck. She couldn't resist a nibble. He smelled good, tasted good, felt good. Around her. Over her. Inside her. Tension coiled below her navel. She squeezed him tight internally and externally, clasped his tight buttocks and pulled him in deeper still.

His groan reverberated against her chest. With each thrust he teased exactly the right spot, and she was getting close, so close. He captured her shoulders and barrel-rolled them sideways until he was on his back and she straddled him on her knees.

"Finish us," he ordered hoarsely. His hand found her breasts.

She'd never been much for taking orders, but when he tweaked her nipples like that, sending darts of pleasure straight to her core, she would do pretty much anything he asked. She rose above him and then sank down, taking as much of him as she could. Over and over she filled herself with him, rose and dropped, swiveled and rocked. Again and again. His blunt-cut nails raked down her belly to comb through her pale curls. He found her center and buffed her with his thumb.

She wanted to wait, to savor, to explore the tension twisting tighter with each caress, but it had been too long. She couldn't hold off. Ecstasy exploded through her, radiating outward in shock wave after shock wave. Her muscles contracted, whipping her forward until she and Alex were face to face, breast to breast, her palms planted beside his head. She lost herself in the hunger burning in his eyes, hunger for her that beat anything she'd experienced before. He gripped her hips as he thrust upward, harder and faster, and then his eyes squeezed shut and his body bowed off the bed as release jerked through him, setting off a series of tiny aftershocks inside her.

Their rapid breaths mingled as she stared at the handsome face beneath hers and tried to right her world. She'd had sex with demanding, impatient, workaholic Alex Harper. And she was absolutely certain she was going to regret that...in a minute.

But right now she felt too damned good to worry that Alex Harper had just given her the best sex of her life.

Alex Harper was a *god* in bed. Amanda could have lived without that knowledge.

Muscles quivering, she fell back on her pillow and stared at the ceiling, trying to catch her breath and listening to Alex doing the same beside her. Wow.

The road to hell was paved with good intentions. And she had paved miles of it last night. She'd meant to send Alex packing the second he'd arrived. But the fresh, still warm donuts, along with the possibility of another party contract, had defeated her.

And then she'd meant to kick him out when he licked her fingers, igniting a blaze inside her. But she hadn't been able to say the words *no* or *go*.

She'd planned to send him home after they made love the first time. And again after the second. But somehow they'd ended up sharing dinner while watching the second half of the Giants game *naked* before climbing back into bed, where he'd held her until she'd fallen asleep.

Third time the charm? Could she rally her willpower this time? And did she really want to?

Starting a Tuesday morning with multiple orgasms beat an alarm clock any day of the week. She smiled to herself and turned her head to find Alex's dark eyes focused on her.

Her heart skipped a beat. Having him here felt too good. Too right. "You should go."

"In a minute. Right now I don't think I could stand." He delivered the words with a rueful but naughty smile that practically turned her wrong-side-outward.

The scent of their lovemaking permeated her bedroom. The lingering fatigue of a busy night weighted her muscles. Amanda wasn't sure she had the strength to crawl to the shower and prepare for her morning appointment. Alex had even farther to go.

"How will you make it to Connecticut and back in time for work?"

"I keep a spare suit at the office. I'll shower here. With you."

A thrill raced through her, but she choked out a laugh. "I don't have to be psychic to know how that'll end up. With both of us being late for work."

He grinned and rolled onto his side. But then his smile faded. He gently brushed the hair off her cheek and tucked it behind her ear. "Come home with me this weekend."

Her lungs refused to work.

"We never discussed Zack's party. He's a great kid. If you meet him you'll get a feel for what he likes, and we'll have a better chance of surprising him with something that'll blow his mind."

*Work. He's talking about work. Focus.* "You want this to be a surprise party?"

"Yes. Spend the weekend at my place. You can meet Zack and my parents."

She recoiled. The last thing she needed was for her mom and dad to get wind of her dating Alex. He would be the only man she'd ever hooked up with that they would consider suitable. And she was throwing him back just as soon as she came to her senses.

"Alex, we don't have and will never have a meet-the-parents kind of relationship."

He shook his head. "That's not what I'm implying. You need to visit my parents' house. That's probably the best place for the party if we want to keep it under wraps. If after you see the place you don't like that idea, then I'd like to have the party somewhere else in Greenwich so Zack's friends can come. You'll have to help me choose an alternate location."

Why did he keep making offers she couldn't afford to refuse? She sighed. "If I say yes to spending the weekend with you, you're not going to take it the wrong way and think this affair is more than temporary insanity, are you?"

He rolled over her, planting his knees between hers and propping his elbows on either side of her body. His eyes held hers and his breath teased her lips. Desire stirred anew. "This relationship will last only as long as it's beneficial to both of us."

And with his body intimately connected to hers it was hard not to appreciate the benefits of their association. But uncertainty nagged her, tensing muscles that had been completely lax just moments ago.

She forced herself to relax. She needed this job and any other that Alex could throw her way. She could handle whatever else came up. And he was hellaciously good in bed.

"Okay. I'll come to Greenwich with you."

Amanda had known Alex was loaded, but she hadn't expected his home to be a large estate at the end of a winding, white-fenced, paddock-lined road in the Greenwich backcountry.

She followed him into the sprawling stone center hall colonial Friday evening and paused in the two-storied marbled and wainscoted foyer. To her left she could see a living room with a soaring stone fireplace, a wet bar and a suede sectional sofa.

"Alex, this is nice."

"Were you expecting a bachelor pad?"

She wrinkled her nose. "You do have a reputation as a guy with a short attention span."

"Is that why you kept playing hard to get?"

"I told you I wasn't playing. I *am* hard to get. Not that you'd know it by this week's performance."

His lips tilted in that sexy, I'm-going-to-get-you-in-trouble-and-you're-going-to-love-it smile that made her insides hum like a beehive. He set their bags at the foot of the stairs and strolled toward her, lazily, but with a predatory glint in his eyes that quickened her pulse. "I have no complaints with your performance."

Her body flushed from her center to her fingertips, which she pressed to his chest to stop the embrace she saw coming. "Nor I yours, but we'll never get the details of your party finalized if you don't quit distracting me."

Alex had come to her place two of the past three evenings after work under the guise of planning his party. He'd spent the nights, but not working on arrangements. She hadn't started regretting the involvement yet. But she knew she would. Her relationships always came back to bite her.

He captured her hand with his, lacing their fingers. "I'll give you a quick tour."

"Don't we have to be at your parents' for dinner soon?"

Mischief glinted in his eyes. She'd seen that look often enough recently to know it meant he wanted her naked, and if she gave him about three seconds' leeway she'd want it, too. Anticipation made her pulse stutter.

"That's why you're getting the abbreviated tour. Otherwise I'd be showing you my bedroom from beneath the sheets. You wouldn't see much of the house that way." The man oozed sexuality.

Desire pulsed through her. She tamped it down. "Lead on."

Her heels tapped out a beat on the hardwood floors as he whisked her past a cherry-paneled study, formal living and dining rooms and through the gourmet eat-in kitchen with black-granite countertops. The place begged for a family to fill it and for a woman to soften the stark decor with a vase of flowers here and there or a few knickknacks or framed photographs.

Did Alex plan to marry and have children? She'd never heard of him staying with anyone long enough to get close to settling down. But why own a place like this if he didn't plan to start a family?

*And why do you care?*

*You don't.*

She followed him outside onto a limestone-tile patio. Her breath clouded the cold night air. Outdoor lighting illuminated a lap pool that had to be at least fifty feet long. In the shadows beyond the subtle glow she caught hints of lawn and in the distance a low stone wall like the one out front. Evergreen trees mingled with the bare-limbed deciduous variety—one of which had a huge branch perfect for a rope swing. Alex's home would be the perfect place to raise children.

*Children.* She'd never thought about having them. And couldn't now. Her life was a mess. Until she had that straightened out, she couldn't think about adding complications. But she suddenly wondered if she was missing out.

*Of course not. What do you know about good parenting? Nada.*

She hugged her coat tighter around her to ward off the frosty air. "You said bring a swimsuit, but it's too cold to swim."

"I have a hot tub if you want to brave it later." He pointed toward a sheltered corner of the patio. "But my parents have an indoor pool. Tomorrow we can swim with Zack, and you can try to get a feel for what kind of party he'd like."

He led her back inside and up the stairs to a vaulted-ceiling bedroom decorated in black, white and grey. A king-size bed with a raw-silk pewter bedspread and a massive, carved cherry headboard took up only a quarter of the large room. A gas fireplace with a cozy sitting area had been centered on the wall opposite the bed, and French doors led to a Juliet balcony overlooking the pool and large backyard. She suspected the view from the windows would be beautiful and green in summer.

The room reminded her of Alex. Luxurious, but no frills, no clutter.

Her gaze returned to the bed she'd be sharing with him. It didn't bother her that she'd be just one of many to pass through it.

*It didn't.*

Yes, it did. And that made no sense. She had no claim on him. And didn't want one.

"Is this where you entertain your women?" She wanted the catty words back the instant she said them. Why had she said them? She wasn't usually the type to blurt out her thoughts.

"I don't bring women here. I go to their place. You might have noticed the express-train commute and climbing into a cold car at the depot isn't exactly romantic." Alex left his Mercedes at the station every day before heading for Manhattan.

She smiled. "I can see how a forty-minute ride on the express train could kill the mood."

He stroked a fingertip along her jaw, sending ripples of arousal through her. "Has it killed the mood?"

Not even close. She would much rather stay here, strip down and make love with him in front of a roaring fire than eat with his family. Family dinners, in her opinion, were rarely comfortable affairs. But that wouldn't help her get Affairs by Amanda on a firmer financial foundation.

"Ahem. What time are your parents expecting us?"

"Soon. I'll save the tour of the third-floor gym, sauna and steam shower and the basement for later. As much as I'd prefer to keep you here—" he dipped his head to indicate the bed "—we need to go."

She appreciated his restraint because apparently she'd lost hers—and her perspective right along with it. This weekend was all about business. And that meant meeting his well-connected parents was high on her to-do list.

Like it or not.

If Alex's home had been impressive, Amanda found his parents' French Chateau–styled waterfront mansion in Old Greenwich downright intimidating even in the dark. Well-placed landscape uplighting illuminated the sheer scale of the place.

Her stomach felt as if she'd swallowed a witch's bubbling cauldron of some hot brew. Why was she nervous about meeting his parents? They were merely prospective clients, not prospective in-laws, and she'd grown up in affluent circles.

It was because of the job, the connections and the possibility of tapping into Greenwich society's deep pockets for future events. The results of this meeting could make Affairs by Amanda financially secure.

But she'd interviewed for jobs with society's movers and shakers before, and those hadn't made her this nervous. And thanks to her family and her Vassar education, she knew many über-wealthy people. But still, the unexplainable butterflies tormented her.

The front door of the house opened and a tall, lanky, dark-haired teen came out. Despite the frosty temperature he wasn't wearing a coat over his short-sleeved Giants T-shirt. Unsmiling, he strolled toward the car as they climbed out.

"He looks just like you," she told Alex, when he joined her at the end of the long walkway.

Alex's eyes narrowed and his face seemed to tense. Why?

"I take it that's your brother?"

"That's Zack."

She noted and disregarded the odd note in Alex's voice. Bringing a woman home to meet the folks implied things they didn't want implied. Was he as uncomfortable about this as she? "He's cute. As I imagine you were at seventeen. I'm sure you were a lady-killer in training."

He shot her an odd look but said nothing, since Zack had reached them. Alex held out his upraised hand, grasped palms with his brother in a boys-from-the-hood kind of handshake and then the males slapped each other's back in an almost-hug. Zack, obviously playing it cool, didn't crack a smile, but his excitement over seeing Alex sparkled in eyes the same brown shot with gold as Alex's.

"Amanda, this is Zack. Zack, my *friend* Amanda Crawford."

She shot Alex a quick questioning glance. What was that about? The emphasis he'd put on the word *friend* implied they were more than friendly, and she didn't want to give his family the wrong impression. Sure, they were lovers at the moment, but that would soon change. This was merely business with benefits.

Amanda offered her hand. "It's nice to meet you, Zack."

The teen surveyed her from head to toe. Did she detect a tinge of resentment in his eyes? He briefly shook hands. "You, too."

Zack turned his attention back to Alex. "The 'rents are waiting inside."

Alex placed a hand in the small of her back and guided her up the walk and into the house. The foyer was as opulent as the outside of the house had led her to expect. The decor emitted an old-money feel with an intricately patterned hardwood floor, classic antique furniture, luxurious Persian carpets and artwork by Albert Bierstadt and Frederic Church on the soaring wainscoted walls.

Her stomach twisted tighter with each echoing step as she and Alex followed Zack's loping stride into a paneled den. A man and woman rose with welcoming smiles on their faces from the sofas that flanked the brick fireplace. It was easy to see that Alex and Zack had inherited their mother's coloring and patrician bone structure. The blue-eyed blond man was the exact opposite coloring-wise of the woman by his side.

"Mom, Dad, this is Amanda Crawford. Amanda, my parents, Ellen and Harry Harper."

Alex's mother immediately stepped forward and pulled Amanda into an exuberant hug. The warmth of her greeting took Amanda aback. And then Ellen put her at arm's length, clasped both of Amanda's hands and beamed as if she'd just been voted Time's Woman of the Year. "We are so glad Alex has finally brought someone home."

Apprehension tickled Amanda's toes.

"Mother, I told you this wasn't—"

"Oh, hush, Alex. Go pour us drinks, darling. I can't wait to get to know your Amanda better."

Amanda's uneasiness multiplied. She gave Alex a fix-this glare. He shrugged and she wanted to smack him. Instead she forced a smile and turned back to her hostess when Alex surprisingly complied with his mother's command.

"Thank you for inviting me to dinner, Mrs. Harper."

"Ellen. We don't stand on formality here. And we're happy to have you."

As soon as Ellen released her, Alex's father took her place and captured Amanda's hand in both of his. "It's nice to finally meet you, Amanda. Your father and I have known each other for years. He's spoken of you often. When I talked with Theo this afternoon I told him you were coming home with Alex tonight. We couldn't be more pleased."

Amanda barely stifled a groan. The evening couldn't get worse. Alex's parents and hers thought there was more to this relationship than party planning and stellar, though temporary sex. When it was over, she'd have to listen to her parents' lectures about yet another failed relationship.

Oh, joy. She couldn't wait for that.

# Five

Amanda Crawford was a professional charmer. The past two days had only reinforced Alex's opinion that she was the woman for the job of increasing his visibility and connections. No other woman would do.

His family's overexuberant welcome Friday night had thrown her, but after one panicked glance at him, she'd sailed in like a trouper and worked her magic for the remainder of the weekend, putting everyone at ease and keeping the conversation flowing. She'd even teased Zack out of his surly mood—a mood Zack seemed to exhibit more often than not these days.

Amanda was smoother than the Rémy Martin Louis XIII cognac he brought out to celebrate special occasions. It was only because Alex knew her agenda that he'd recognized the subtle, skillful questioning she'd employed to tease Zack's hobbies and interests from him this weekend.

Pulling out his BlackBerry, Alex made a note to schedule some one-on-one time with Zack to get to the bottom of the bad attitude. It frustrated him that he could give only brotherly advice. Eighteen years ago he'd wanted nothing to do with fatherhood and would have readily paid for an abortion. And that would have been a mistake. Now he wanted to claim his son, to tell Zack how proud he was of him. But that could never happen.

Shoving away the nagging thoughts, he put his Black-Berry away and studied Amanda's profile as the taxi neared her apartment building. She had her face turned toward the window, apparently enthralled by the gently falling snow or the bustle of pedestrians. More likely ignoring him.

Except for Amanda Crawford, women didn't ignore him.

He could feel her putting distance between them. In fact, he had felt the chill since they'd boarded the train to Grand Central Terminal. She'd wanted him to stay in Greenwich, let her travel home alone. But he always saw his women to the door.

The only downside to the weekend was when they'd said good-bye three hours ago, after Sunday brunch. His mother had been wearing a smug smile that told him she was already planning a wedding. His and Amanda's.

That wasn't going to happen, but she refused to believe him no matter how many times he'd told her he spent too much time dealing with the financial fallout caused by nasty divorces to be interested in signing up for that headache. It concerned him that his mother had bonded so quickly with Amanda. But that was partially his fault. He'd never taken a woman home before.

The taxi pulled to a stop at 721 Park Avenue. Alex climbed from the car and turned to hand Amanda out of the vehicle. The sight of her long legs beneath a short cashmere dress hit him, along with memories of her kneeling above him in bed, wrapped around him in the shower and stretched out on the rug in front of his fireplace. His heart kicked into overdrive.

He stepped to the back of the car, paid the driver and took Amanda's suitcase from the cabbie before she could reach it.

"Alex, there's no need to walk me up. Take the taxi back to the station."

"We need to discuss Zack's party. I want to know what you and my mother cooked up when she banished the men of the house to play billiards."

Amanda hugged her coat tighter around her middle. Snowflakes settled on her fuzzy pink knit hat. "Nothing earth-shattering, but she and Zack gave me some ideas to work with. We have plenty of time to plan his birthday. Your company party is a different story. You change the subject every time I bring that up."

"Correction—I've put the event in your capable hands and I trust you with the details."

"I know you said you wanted me to handle everything, but I'd really like your input on a few items. Carte blanche sounds like a good idea to an event planner, but I've learned the hard way those kinds of events rarely live up to the expectations of the one who's footing the bill. You have expectations whether you realize it or not."

Since he wasn't ready to say good-night, he'd play along. "We'll grab a couple of coffees and your favorite chocolate muffins, and you can tell me what else you've come up with."

Talking wasn't all he intended to do. The minute she

finished her muffin he'd untie the knot at the waist of her plum colored dress and unwrap her, one pale, delicious inch at a time. If he could wait that long.

His hunger for her these past three months had bordered on an obsession. Why hadn't having her—repeatedly—lessened his need? It was a weakness he wouldn't tolerate, and that meant getting past it.

Amanda's less-than-enthusiastic expression would give a less confident man performance anxiety. But he knew he pleased her in bed. She wasn't shy about expressing her pleasure or asking for what she needed. And that turned him on like nothing else.

"It's been a long weekend, Alex. I need to prepare for the upcoming week and—"

"Invite me up, Amanda."

Her lips parted at his gruff tone. She held his gaze. He could tell she was considering refusing. He stepped closer, invading her space, and nudged his thigh against hers, earning a gratifying hitch of her breath.

"Fine. You can come up for a few minutes."

They made a quick, silent detour to Park Café and then returned to her building. The doorman watched them from the moment they entered, his narrowed gaze falling on Amanda's suitcase in Alex's hand.

"Hello, Henry," Amanda greeted him.

The doorman nodded. "Good afternoon, Ms. Crawford, Mr. Harper."

Alex nodded a greeting and escorted Amanda across the white marble-floored lobby and around the doorman's desk. He had learned to trust his first impressions of people and there was something about the man's eyes and body language that bothered him.

Amanda looked up at Alex as they crossed the lobby. "I cannot get over how much your brother looks like you. It's almost as if he's a carbon copy. He has your coloring, your gestures and even a similar speech pattern."

The back of Alex's neck prickled. She had spent a lot of time with Zack. Had she guessed the truth? "We're brothers. Siblings have similarities."

"Since I don't have any brothers or sisters I wouldn't know. You both look exactly like your mother. I couldn't find any trace of your father in either you or Zack."

He didn't want to pursue this conversation. He hit the elevator call button since her hands were full with the coffee and muffin bag and her oversize tote bag.

"Did I tell you how much I enjoyed having you in my bed all weekend?" He leaned toward her and pitched his voice low so Henry couldn't overhear.

Her breath caught and desire expanded her pupils, igniting a burn in his gut. She darted a quick glance over his shoulder toward the doorman's desk and then hit him with a small naughty smile that knocked the air from his lungs. "You might have mentioned it. Once or twice."

Hunger pulsed through him. "I want to stay tonight, Amanda."

Her cheeks flushed. The elevator doors opened. She hustled into the car, pivoted on her spike-heeled ankle boots and faced him as the doors closed. "You have to stop doing that. We're temporary, remember?"

He stroked her jaw with a fingertip and then bent to sip from her lips once, twice, a third time. It wasn't enough. Not nearly enough. He drew back until only the tips of their noses touched.

"Stop telling you I want you? Or stop spending the

night? I'm not moving in, Amanda. I want to be lost in you again. We're good together."

Her head tipped back to rest against the wall. Staring up at him, she swallowed, licked her lips and inhaled a shuddery breath.

"You can stay tonight. But, Alex, when your party ends, we end. Okay? I'm not looking for forever. And neither are you. Let's not try to make something out of this temporary diversion that it's not. Your parents already think… Well, you're going to have to convince them that it's not going to happen."

Interesting to be on the receiving end of that comment for a change. Interesting. But not enjoyable. "No. It's not. I don't do marriage."

He wanted her for more than a few weeks, but he'd worry about changing her mind later. At the most they'd last a few months. He'd never met a woman he wanted to spend the rest of his life with. Not even Zack's mother. Especially not Zack's mother. Chelsea Brooks was one devious, deceitful, greedy bitch. Too bad he hadn't known that before their affair.

But Amanda wasn't like Chelsea in any way. He leaned as close as the carrier of coffee Amanda held between them would allow and lowered his head. She met him halfway. Her lips parted and her tongue met his. Silky, slick, seductive. Need rose within him. He angled his head to deepen the kiss. Her scent filled his nose. Releasing her suitcase, he burrowed his hands beneath her heavy coat to the warmth of her waist and dug his fingers into the soft cashmere of her dress. His palms wicked up her heat, spreading it up his arms and through his torso.

A few months of this would be enough.

It would have to be. But at the moment his hunger for her seemed insatiable.

A chime announced they'd reached Amanda's floor. He lifted his head and inhaled a sobering breath a second before the doors glided open. The interruption was a good thing, since he wasn't into public displays of affection.

How did she do that to him? Make him forget where he was and that the elevator probably had security cameras? In his business, image was everything. He couldn't afford to be caught with his pants down—literally *or* metaphorically. But then again, no one at 721 Park cared what he did. He wasn't a resident. And in Greenwich he kept a low profile. The press ignored him to focus on the celebrities who made their home within the town's borders.

He released Amanda, grabbed the handle of her suitcase and followed her out. He had to admit he found the slightly dazed look in her grey eyes gratifying. Nice to know he wasn't the only one in a hormonal fog.

But like the weather, this fog would eventually lift.

Why had she let Alex talk her into this? Amanda asked herself as she unlocked her apartment door.

*Because he gave you that look—the one that deep-sixes your ability to think. A look he's probably been perfecting since he was younger than Zack.*

*And he bribed you with a muffin.*

*God, you're easy.*

After sixty almost uninterrupted hours of Alex's company, she needed to get away from the man. Watching him interact with Zack, she'd seen a side of him this weekend that she could have lived without—a caring, gentle, understanding side that had gone a long way toward eroding Alex's player image. And she couldn't afford to see him as anything less than a player. Alex was all about temporary and so was she. She liked it that way.

She shouldered open her door and marched straight into her kitchen, where she deposited her tote, the coffee and the bakery bag on the table. Alex followed.

"Have a seat. I'll get your file. It's in my office."

He caught her elbow as she passed. "Eat first. I know you like your muffins hot and fresh from the oven."

"That's because the chocolate chips will still be gooey and delicious." Thinking about it made her mouth water. She shrugged out of her coat. He took it from her and laid hers and his over the back of the extra chair.

*Get it over with. Feed him. Update him. Get rid of him.*

While she grabbed plates from the cabinet he tore open the bag. The scent of chocolate and roasted walnuts filled the room. Her stomach growled as she climbed onto one of the high stools. Alex did the same beside her. Their knees bumped beneath the table, sending a spray of sparks northward.

Good grief. She'd exhausted a year's quota of orgasms this weekend. How could she still get all shivery and hot from just bumping knees with the man?

Doing her best to ignore him in his charcoal cashmere V-neck sweater and snug black jeans, she peeled away the muffin's paper. Melted chocolate quickly coated her fingers. If she were alone she'd lick her fingers. But with Alex here she had to act like less of a glutton.

She rose to find some napkins, but Alex caught her wrist, pulling her between his splayed knees. His desire-filled gaze locked with hers as he lifted her hand to his mouth and laved her fingertip with a slick swipe. She shivered with want. He moved on to the next messy fingertip and the next.

Her eyelids grew heavy and drifted closed. Not good. Lack of sight only accentuated her other senses. She lost herself in his scent, the brackets of his strong thighs around her hips, the hot caress of his tongue swirling around each fingertip and the feel of his hand on the thin skin of her wrist. He couldn't possibly miss her racing pulse beneath his thumb.

She forced her eyes open. He finished the left hand and moved to her right. Desire flushed his cheekbones with dark color, making her feel hotter and gooier than the muffin's melted chips.

But she didn't protest because she couldn't find her voice. He dipped his finger into a glistening melted chocolate spot in his muffin and then painted her lips with a slow sweep. The intense concentration of his dark eyes on her mouth made breathing nearly impossible. He bent his head and licked and nibbled off the chocolate.

She nearly collapsed into a puddle at his feet.

*Stop him. Stop this. Wanting him this much can't be good.*

The warm, wet, slow pass of his tongue dragged a moan from her. He took advantage of her parted lips to deepen the kiss. She savored the delicious combination of chocolate and Alex. But then he drew back. Relieved to escape the onslaught—and yes, a little disappointed, too—she stared at him.

A slow smile worked its way across his lips. He pinched off a morsel of muffin and brought it to her lips. "Open."

She dumbly complied. The rich, chocolaty taste filled her mouth. Her taste buds did their usual dance. But she would rather be tasting the man tormenting her. She swallowed. As if he'd read her mind, his mouth covered hers again. He devoured her mouth with sips, nips and swirls. Her thoughts whirled like fruit in a blender. He had her off balance mentally and physically.

A tug at her waist sobered her. She jerked back. "What are you doing?"

"Wait and see." He pulled again at the tie of her wrap-around dress. Cool air swept her torso as he brushed the fabric aside.

Her still-sticky fingers kept her from grabbing her dress as it slid off her shoulders and caught at her elbows. She'd never get chocolate stains out. "We're supposed to be going over your part—"

He smeared a streak of chocolate just above the lace of her bra, dipping into her cleavage.

"Hey!" And then he bent to lap it up. Her protest turned into a groan. "Working, Alex. We're supposed to be *working*."

But the heat inside her intensified, liquefying her knees. Her legs weakened. She grasped the table's edge to keep herself upright. He painted another melted chocolate chip stripe on her other breast, then laved her clean. His fingers hooked her bra straps and lowered them to her upper arms, baring her nipples, which he circled with more chocolate paint. The heat of his moist mouth enclosed her, the suction tugging at the desire deep in her belly and pulling forth a response she thought he'd exhausted.

She bit her lip on a whimper of want. She would never be able to eat her favorite food again without remembering this.

"Touch me," he ordered against her breast.

"Hands. Chocolate. Cashmere." She couldn't retrieve more from the mush he'd made of her brain.

Alex stood, ripped his sweater and the T-shirt he'd worn beneath it over his head and tossed them.

Food sex. A new one for her. New and exciting. But then sex with Alex had been an adventure each time. One she'd have to end. Soon.

She crumbled off a corner of the moist cake and swiped her finger through a melted morsel. Debating her options, she decided to plant a fingerprint on each flat nipple. Holding his gaze, she bent to lick him clean.

His pupils expanded and his hands fastened on her waist, tightening and releasing as she worked zealously to cleanse his skin. He groaned. "Watching you eat your muffins has been driving me crazy for months."

Stunned, she straightened. "Watching me eat turns you on?"

"It's the sensual way you savor each bite. I knew you'd wear the same expression when I was inside you."

Heat rushed through her, and her pulse quickened to double time. "I do?"

"Yes. Drop the dress." His low voice rumbled over her skin like the roar of an approaching motorcycle.

She had to be out of her mind to comply. They were here to work. But work would have to wait. She dropped her arms by her side and let the dress go. The soft fabric drifted down, caressing her calves as it passed to puddle around her ankle boots.

Alex unfastened her bra and sent it on the same path, leaving her in nothing but her lavender lace thong and shoes. He devoured her with his gaze, lingering over her breasts, slowly sweeping her belly, her hips and her thighs before taking an equally meandering return trip.

His hands bracketed her waist and stroked a swath of heat, first upward to tease the undersides of her breasts and then downward, dragging the thong to her knees as he passed. He bent to press an openmouthed kiss over the tattoo on her left hip, stealing her breath, and then he lifted her onto the stool she'd abandoned and whisked her lingerie over her ankles. He splayed his hands on her knees, separated them and stepped between her thighs. His arms banded around her, bringing them chest to scorching chest as his mouth branded hers in a hot, wet, carnal kiss. His tongue plunged deep.

His hands swept her back, her waist and finally her breasts. He stroked and tweaked her nipples until hunger consumed her and she squirmed with need. His hands traveled lower, finding her wetness and igniting a fire no amount of moisture could put out. Alex had great hands, she'd grant him that. And a great mouth. And a great—

The nip of his teeth on her neck cut off her thoughts. She arched into his touch, relishing each stroke of his fingers until she teetered on the edge of release and she would need more than just his hand.

He had on too many clothes. The supple skin of his back goose-bumped beneath the light rake of her nails. His buttocks clenched under her caress. She dragged her fingers around the inside of his belt, opened the buckle and lowered his zipper. Impatient to pleasure him as he was her, she shoved his pants and briefs over his hips and curled her fingers around his erection. His hot, silky flesh thickened and pulsed with the stroke of her hand.

Alex broke the kiss on a hissed inhalation and

withdrew a condom from his pocket before letting his pants fall to the floor.

Striving for mental distance, she nodded to the packet in his hand. "You keep those on you at all times, huh?"

"When I'm with you, yes. Otherwise, no. I'm too old to think like a kid who's always prepared on the off chance he might get lucky."

Not what she wanted to hear. That made him sound as if he weren't a player. She reminded herself they had only thirteen days left. Less than two weeks to gorge herself on Alex's talent in bed, the shower, the hot tub, or in the kitchen, as the case may be tonight. And then she would quit him cold turkey. Part of her wanted to store up as much sexual satisfaction as she could until then. Another part warned her to pull back now before she became as addicted to this man as she was to Park Café's chocolate muffins.

Her needy, demanding side won the argument. She curled her fingers around his nape, threaded them through his hair and pulled him forward for another kiss. Alex didn't hesitate to step up to the plate. You had to like a man who was confident enough not to be threatened when a woman turned aggressive.

He let her set the tone for the kiss. Or maybe he was just as desperate and edgy and needy as she was. Their teeth clashed. Their noses bumped. But his soft lips, slick tongue and dexterous hands kept her fire stoked.

One corner of her mind heard the condom wrapper tear. A tiny part realized he was taking care of protection, but her pulse roared when he grasped her hips, dug his fingers into her bottom, and pulled her to the edge of the high stool.

He nudged her entrance, slicking his tip in her moisture, and then he thrust forward. She tore her mouth from his to gasp as he filled her. When he withdrew, she dug her nails into his buttocks and pulled him back. He slid deep again and withdrew over and over. His teeth nipped her neck, making her gasp as a shock of longing bolted through her. She tilted her head to grant him better access.

Her pleasure built, fueled by his thumb circling her center. She wound her legs around his hips, savored the steam of his breath on her neck, her jaw, her cheek. And then orgasm reverberated through her like blasts from a bass speaker, making her body pulse and contract.

Alex's hands tightened on her bottom, his tempo increased and his mouth covered hers in a desperate, edgy kiss. His groan filled her mouth as he stiffened with his own release.

Every cell in her body felt alive and aware of this man and of this moment. Why hadn't any other man ever felt this good or made her feel this good?

It wasn't fair that she'd finally found one who rocked her world. And she couldn't keep him. He was too much a part of that restrictive world she'd grown up in.

The one in which she'd never fit.

# Six

A cell phone jarred Amanda from sleep. She rolled over and blindly, groggily slapped around the nightstand until her fingers closed around the device. She fumbled it open.

"Hello." Cracking an eyelid, she looked at her digital clock. Five-thirty. Who would be calling at this ungodly hour on a Monday morning?

"Amanda, darling." Her mother's voice shattered what was left of her sleepy haze. "I am so proud of you."

Not words she'd heard from a parental unit before. Was she dreaming? A warm glow suffused her…until she started wondering what she'd done to earn that rare proclamation. Nothing came to mind.

A strong arm banded her waist, pulling her back under the covers. Heat blanketed her back. Teeth nipped her shoulder, awakening her in an entirely different way.

Alex. He'd stayed the night. Again. She'd worry about

that later. But now she couldn't stop herself from leaning back into him and savoring his embrace and the morning arousal pressed against her buttocks.

She forced her attention back to her caller. "Good morning, Mother. What are you talking about?"

The hand skating from her waist to her breast distracted her, but felt too good to stop him. Alex knew exactly how and where to touch her to reap the maximum benefit. The kink factor of enjoying having Alex naked against her when her mother was yapping in her ear was off the charts.

"I'm talking about your association with Alexander Harper. I'm so glad to see you finally coming to your senses."

The words snuffed out the kindling glow. Amanda sat up, dislodging Alex's arm and lips. A chill that had nothing to do with the blankets falling away from her bare skin rushed over her.

"My friend at the paper says you spent the weekend with the Harper family."

This was not good. Not good at all. Her parents would expect more than a fling, and she couldn't deliver anything more than another disappointment. She glanced at Alex and found his questioning dark eyes trained on her. "What friend? What paper?"

"She writes for the Greenwich society column. They're running a story on the weekend's happenings, and apparently you and your beau were seen all about town."

*Her beau?* "It's not what you think. Alex and I were looking for a location for his brother's birthday party. And don't tell anybody that because it's supposed to be a surprise party."

"You can concoct whatever tale you wish, dear, but my friend says you and Alexander were quite friendly in the photos they snapped."

Amanda cringed at the emphasis. Yes, she and Alex had held hands and, yes, they'd sneaked in a few heated embraces and kisses during the walk around town. How could she help it? He was too sexy. But she would have kept her hands and lips to herself if she'd known someone was spying and that the news would get back to her parents.

Mental memo: No more PDAs.

"Amanda, your father and I approve wholeheartedly. A man like Alexander would be such an asset. He's exactly what you need, and he makes enough that you'd be able to give up that business of yours."

Amanda gritted her teeth to hold back a groan at the jab at Affairs by Amanda. As often as she heard the barbs, they should bounce right off by now, but they still hurt like someone ripping off a scab. "Mother, you're not willing to give up your business. Why should I be willing to give up mine?"

"Because mine makes scads of money and it's respe—"

"Respectable. Yes. I know." Why did she bother to rehash this argument over and over? She would never win.

But she wanted to. That's why she kept trying.

Alex caught her attention as he rose from her bed, all lean, long, muscular and naked. His golden skin, lightly dusted with dark whorls of hair, mesmerized her. Her gaze fell to his erection. Desire licked her insides, shocking her since she still had her mother yapping in her ear.

How twisted was it to want to reach out and touch someone intimately with your mother on the phone?

"Amanda!"

Oops. What had she missed? "I'm sorry, Mom, what did you say?"

"I said you need to bring him home for dinner."

Amanda's stomach turned. "I don't think that's a good idea."

"He comes from a good family."

"Yes, I know. But—"

"He owns a house and a successful law firm. I don't think your previous disasters owned more than their clothes."

Ouch. But in most cases true.

"You have to grow up sometime and quit this party nonsense. You could do worse than Alexander Harper. In fact, you have. Often."

Another scab ripped off leaving her raw and bleeding. She couldn't handle this kind of abuse without caffeine. "Mom, I have to get ready for work now. I'll call you back when I have time to chat."

No, she wouldn't.

"Get me a list of dates when Alexander can visit, and your father and I will check our calendars." Her mother disconnected, leaving Amanda in a funk she knew would ruin the rest of her day. Talking with her parents always did.

"Problem?" Alex asked, as he returned from the bathroom.

"Nothing I can't handle." She threw off the sheet and rose.

He snagged her around the waist and pulled her close, molding his naked frame to hers. One big palm cupped her bottom and kneaded. "Join me in the shower."

"Alex—" Desire hit her hard and fast, followed by a crazy chaser of an idea.

What if she kept Alex around? Not forever, but for a

while. Just until she got Affairs by Amanda on a firmer footing. Her parents might get off her back.

There would be hell to pay when the relationship ended....

But wouldn't it be worth it to have her parents' approval for as long as it lasted?

She studied his face and weighed the risks. "Apparently news of our relationship is about to hit the Greenwich papers. Perhaps we should consider extending our affair until after Zack's party. It will make the planning easier to keep secret."

His eyes narrowed. She waited for him to voice the questions she could see forming.

"Works for me," he said instead.

She hoped she didn't live to regret extending her temporary affair.

> Deposit one million dollars in the Grand Cayman account listed below or the truth about your "brother's" true parentage will be made public.
>
> Do not go to the police or you will regret it.

Tension invaded Alex's muscles and a chill enveloped him Wednesday afternoon as he read the single sheet of boldfaced type.

Who'd sent this?

He scanned the letter again, but it yielded nothing more than the demand and banking information. His name and office address had been typed. There was no return address on the letter or the envelope and no identifiable handwriting.

The red-stamped *Confidential* inscription on the left

side of the envelope didn't trip any triggers. He received mail marked this way on a daily basis. It was the nature of his business. Usually there was nothing personal in the contents, but Moira had decided long ago to pass those letters on to him unopened. He returned them to her as soon as he discovered they fell under her jurisdiction.

Which led him back to who could have done this. Less than a handful of people knew the truth about Zack's parentage. He and Chelsea. His parents. The attorney who'd handled Zack's adoption. But his parents wouldn't do this, and the attorney was too straitlaced and respectable. That left Chelsea.

Was Zack's birth mother up to her old tricks? She'd sold Zack once already. In the past eighteen years she'd shown no desire whatsoever to get to know their son or even to meet him. And she had spending issues. The woman burned through money like a California wildfire rips through the canyons during a drought.

Chelsea was greedy. She'd come to him for money several times since their split. But he'd never believed her to be stupid. She'd have to know she'd be the first he'd suspect. He dropped the letter on his desk, picked up the phone and punched out her number.

"What the hell are you trying to do?" he asked, as soon as she answered.

"Alex? What are you talking about?"

"The extortion letter."

"What?"

"Did you write a letter threatening to expose Zack's parentage?"

"No! I— No. I wouldn't do that." Her shock sounded genuine.

"It wouldn't be the first time you tried to squeeze money out of my family. Nor the second. Or even the thir—"

"Alex, I didn't. I swear it. The gallery is doing well now. You should stop by and see it. We could do dinner afterward."

The suggestive lilt of her voice did nothing for him. She'd tried to trap him into marriage almost nineteen years ago, and she'd periodically made a play for him every few years when she was between men. But he wasn't interested in opportunistic women who put a price tag on their children.

Usually he ignored her advances because reacting in any way seemed to encourage her. "I'm not interested, Chelsea. In your gallery or anything else you're offering."

"Not even if I offer you an amazing opportunity to invest in a fabulous new artist?"

Was that what she was calling her need for money these days? "No, thanks. Who have you told about Zack?"

"No one. I promise. That's not a part of my life I care to share."

That he believed. He ended the call.

If it wasn't Chelsea or one of her cronies, then who could it be? Alex stood and paced to the windows. Apprehension twanged his nerves like guitar strings. He had to protect Zack. No matter what the cost. Otherwise, this would hurt his "brother" and possibly push Zack from surly to outright rebellious.

What should he do?

Pay the money? No. Crooks always came back for more. Then what? Ignore it? Call the police?

The only permanent solution was to eliminate the threat. That meant going to the police no matter what the note said. But he couldn't trust just anybody with something this volatile.

So who could he trust?

A private investigator might work, but that could take too much time.

The detective who'd interviewed him twice after Marie Endicott's murder at 721 Park seemed like a straight-up guy. Perhaps Arnold McGray could recommend someone within the department who could discreetly handle this case.

Alex dug in his wallet for the detective's card, but before he could reach for the phone his intercom buzzed.

He didn't have time for interruptions now. "Yes?"

"Amanda Crawford is here for your lunch appointment."

Amanda. The current crisis had knocked her pending arrival out of his head—a first since thoughts of her had taken up residence in his brain several months ago. His interest in her should be waning by now, but the leap of his pulse said otherwise.

*Because you've yet to utilize her to further your career.*

Right.

Could Amanda be behind this? Since the weekend in Greenwich she'd remarked more than once on the similarities between him and Zack.

"Alex? Should I send her in?" Moira's voice interrupted his thoughts.

"Yes." Amanda didn't seem the type to stoop to extortion or bribery. But she was short of cash and she'd just spent the weekend with his family. Had she guessed Zack's parentage? He didn't know how that was possible, but that could be why she'd suddenly agreed to extend their affair when she'd been adamant only a few days ago about ending it.

His office door opened. Moira ushered Amanda in. He searched Amanda's face for a sign that she'd sent the extortion note or that she knew who had. But her grey gaze met his directly and her smile looked sincere. A slight flush pinked her cheeks. Nothing about her slender body wrapped in a fuzzy powder-blue sweater and a short suede skirt looked evasive or expectant. She carried her ever-present briefcase and wore the requisite ankle-breaking heels—this time in the same suede as her skirt.

If not her, what about her crooked ex? Had Amanda shared her suspicions with Curtis Wilks?

"I'll bring lunch in when it arrives," Moira said, before backing out and closing the door.

Amanda took two steps into the room and then stopped. Wearing a puzzled expression, she searched his face. "Is something wrong?"

He wasn't about to tell her. "No."

She shrugged, crossed the room and swung her briefcase onto the desktop. The movement sent the extortion note flying. With rapid reflexes, she bent over the desk and slapped a hand over the fluttering page to keep it from falling to the floor. The move made her short skirt rise up and gave him an arousing glance at the back of her lean thighs.

"Caught it." She slowly straightened with the sheet in her hand. Before he could snatch it from her, her gaze fell to the letter. Her eyes widened as she read the large font and then she lifted her gaze to his. Her shock appeared authentic, but there was a trace of something else in her eyes—something missing from her expression—that made his gut clench. Amanda displayed a total lack of surprise.

"Alex, what are you going to do?"

"That's none of your business."

She stiffened. "I'm not trying to pry. But you have to do something. This would hurt Zack if he doesn't already know."

Apprehension chilled him. He struggled to keep his churning emotions from showing. "If he doesn't know what?"

She bit her bottom lip and her expression turned cagey. "That he's not your father's son."

How had she found out? And what would she do with the information? "Why would you think that?"

"Besides the almost-eighteen-year age difference between the two of you?"

"Yes."

"While you men were doing guy things, your mother mentioned something in passing about how much she regretted missing your high school graduation but that she couldn't be there because she'd been living in Paris when Zack was born. She seemed to regret the slip, so I didn't pursue the topic. But after reading this… It seems to confirm what I thought."

"And what did you think?"

"That maybe your parents had separated for a while and that your mother might have had an affair during their time apart. That's nothing to be ashamed of. A lot of couples have trial separations."

His mother had lived in Paris with Chelsea during the pregnancy. Was Amanda telling the truth and merely curious or was she fishing for details? With so much at stake he couldn't afford to take chances.

"You guessed incorrectly."

"Okay." She sounded unconvinced. She nodded to the letter. "Then what does this mean?"

He took the letter from her. "Don't meddle. This doesn't concern you."

"Well, *excuse* me for caring. What will you do? To protect Zack, I mean."

"I'll handle it."

"I like your brother, Alex, and it's obvious your father adores him. Will Harry help you?"

"Help me what?"

"Come up with the money."

The back of his neck prickled. "You expect me to pay this?"

"What choice do you have? It says don't go to the police."

He weighed her words, her expression and her body language. Was she hiding knowledge of the perpetrator? Did she know more than she was letting on? If she was, he couldn't see it.

"Did you send the note?"

She flinched and then paled. Dark red spots filled her cheeks. "You think I would bribe you? Or hurt Zack?"

She held up a hand before he could reply. "Don't answer that. The fact that you even asked the question says it all. You don't know me. All we have is good sex. And we won't have that for long."

The frost in her voice matched the outside temperature. She opened her briefcase with sharp, decisive movements. "Perhaps we should get to the real reason for my visit. Your party is only ten days away."

"By all means." Because until he got to the bottom of this he couldn't trust her or anyone else.

* * *

Amanda's head was reeling and her heart... Her heart was in serious trouble. She was falling for Alex Harper. Why else would his nasty accusation hurt so badly?

How she'd managed to get through the past hour she would never know. Carefully blanking her expression, she kept her eyes on the number panel above the doors as she took the elevator down from Alex's office after the tense lunch meeting. The darn box stopped on almost every floor, increasing the urgency of her need to escape the high-rise. Her blood pulsed in her ears.

She could not, would not fall for Alex Harper.

Too late?

Maybe.

No. Not too late. She wouldn't let it be too late.

But a sense of doom settled over her. Why did she always fall for the wrong guys? Did she have a masochistic streak? Did she like pain and suffering and relationship train wrecks?

Apparently so. She certainly drew disastrous romances like Times Square does New Year's Eve revelers.

How could Alex sleep with her, loan her money, hire her and introduce her to his family if he distrusted her so much? She'd barely hung on to her professional demeanor during the past hour as that question had tumbled around in her brain.

The elevator finally reached the ground floor. Amanda spilled out of the cubicle and into the lobby with the rest of the crowd. She numbly followed them through the revolving glass doors, onto the sidewalk and straight into a cold wind that cut so deeply she tugged her coat tighter.

Undecided which way to turn, she paused on the

concrete. Should she go home to wallow in her discovery alone or somewhere else? She needed a chocolate chocolate chip muffin and a latte. Or a raspberry martini. Definitely a martini. Maybe two.

*Lovely. The man's driving you to drink in the middle of the day.*

Would Julie be up for an afternoon of hooky? Amanda pulled her cell phone from her pocket and headed toward her apartment, but then remembered Julie was pregnant. Her former roomie wouldn't drink alcohol. And drinking alone wasn't a habit Amanda wanted or needed to acquire. She shoved her phone back into her pocket.

"Amanda!" a deep voice called from behind her—a voice she didn't want to hear at the moment. She quickened her stride.

"Amanda, wait."

An uncooperative crosswalk light and a steady stream of taxis trapped her between escape and Alex.

She knew the instant he stopped behind her, even before he gripped her elbow and pulled her out of the flow of pedestrians who surged forward now that the light had changed—five seconds too late.

Alex swung her around to face him. "I'm sorry."

The apology surprised her. She hadn't taken Alex for the apologizing type. And then she noticed he'd come after her without his coat. He had to be freezing. She was cold even with her coat, scarf and hat.

"I'm worried about how Zack will take this and how badly he'll be hurt. I don't know how to protect him. I shouldn't have accused you. But I have no idea where this threat is coming from or how to deal with it."

Hmm. A man who admitted uncertainty. Interesting.

And rare. The men of her past had always bluffed their way through any ignorance—even though it usually came back to bite them.

Alex's obvious love and concern for his brother eased some of her pain. "What 'this' do you mean? That Zack is not his father's natural son? Yes, that will upset him initially, but your father accepted Zack, loves him and raised him as his own. Zack will get over the hurt when he remembers that your father was there for him when it counted."

"I never said Zack wasn't my father's."

"You didn't have to. He's clearly your mother's child."

If anything, Alex's face tensed even more, and the cold wind painted ruddy stripes on his cheekbones and tossed his overlong hair. He looked like he had something to say, but remained silent and shoved his hands into his suit coat pockets. She fisted hers against the urge to smooth his windblown locks, to tangle her fingers in the strands and pull him close for a kiss that would curl her toes and chase away the chill.

That he'd shut her out after sleeping with her for the past nine days stung. She shifted in her boots. "You should go back inside, Alex. It's too cold to be out here without your overcoat."

He looked ready to argue, but nodded instead. "I'll see you tonight."

She had to pull back while she still could. Letting him spend so many nights at her place was guaranteed to only order up a dose of heartbreak.

"No. I think…I want a little space, Alex."

His eyebrows lowered and he searched her face. "What about the cocktail party Friday night?"

She fought a grimace. She'd forgotten about the

charity affair Alex had asked her to attend with him. Accompanying him to a rich-and-famous-filled event would give her another opportunity for exposure and to make connections—one she couldn't afford to refuse. And she'd promised. She always kept her promises.

"I'll be ready at seven."

But by Friday she'd have her game plan established and her walls firmly back in place. Never again would she make the mistake of forgetting Alex Harper was temporary.

Because today he'd given her a taste of what his eventual dismissal was going to feel like. And she didn't like it.

# Seven

"Detective." Alex extended his hand across the paper-stacked desk and shook hands with Arnold McGray.

"Harper." The lean but paunch-bellied, fortysomething detective with salt-and-pepper hair and disillusioned green eyes rose and returned the greeting with a firm grip. "Have a seat and tell me what brings you to my turf."

"I received an extortion note today. I realize extortion is outside of your homicide sphere, but I was hoping you could direct me to someone within the department who could handle this discreetly."

McGray perked up. "Did you bring it with you?"

Alex pulled the clear plastic bag from his coat pocket and passed it across the desk. Before sitting down in a scarred but sturdy wooden chair in front of the desk, he removed his overcoat and draped it over the back of the second chair.

"If your note's related to 721 Park, then it's part of my investigation until I determine otherwise." Without opening the plastic McGray scanned the text, flipped it over and studied the envelope. "What's the secret the perp's threatening to expose?"

Did the detective really need to know?

"Could lead to motive," McGray said, as if reading his doubts.

True. Alex checked over his shoulder to make sure they wouldn't be overheard. "Zack is my son and not my parents'."

"And that's not common knowledge?"

"No."

The detective took a moment to scribble on the pad beside him. "Besides you, who's touched this letter?"

"My assistant, any number of Harper & Associates mailroom employees and Amanda Crawford."

Without moving a hair McGray suddenly seemed more alert. Tension entered his body and his gaze sharpened. If Alex hadn't witnessed the change he would have missed it. "Crawford. Leggy blonde. Lives at 721 Park?"

"Yes."

The detective jotted another line on his pad and then looked up. "And why would she have handled this?"

"She was in my office shortly after I received it."

"Personal relationship or business?"

"Both."

"She have an ax to grind with you?"

"Not that I know of."

"What about with the deceased, Marie Endicott? Anything between the women?"

"I don't believe they knew each other."

"What about Endicott's lover? Crawford know him?"

"Marie had a lover?"

"She was having an affair, and we suspect it was with someone in the building. But Trent Tanford's been ruled out as a suspect, despite the pictures all over the papers preceding Endicott's death of the two of them." He tapped his pen on the desk. "Could Endicott's lover have been someone Crawford was interested in or believed she had prior claim to?"

Alex didn't like the turn of the conversation. The protective surge he felt toward Amanda surprised him. He reined it in. "No. Amanda is relatively new to the building. She was seeing someone else before she moved in. Curtis Wilks."

McGray made a note and then his green eyes narrowed on Alex. "You spend a lot of time at 721. Were you seeing Endicott?"

Alex sat back abruptly, his defenses on full alert. "Are you accusing me of something?"

McGray wiped a hand over his face. "No. And there's no need to start sounding like a lawyer. I'm just asking questions. The damned investigation is going nowhere."

"You've asked me that question before and I told you I have friends at 721. I wasn't involved with Marie Endicott. I've heard she fell or was pushed from the roof. Is that correct?"

"Yes."

"Perhaps you should check the security video."

"The roof video is missing and the visitor log for the night in question is empty. Harper, I don't think your case is related, but it could be. There have been other extortion attempts at 721 recently, so I'm going to hold on to this and let our guys—our *team*—compare the font and paper to the others. Until we've ruled out a connection I'm going to have to assume there is one."

He'd known about Julia being threatened with the exposure of her pregnancy, but he hadn't known about any other incident. Did that put Amanda at risk? He needed to warn her.

"Who else has been threatened?"

McGray rose, clearly ending the interview. "I'm not at liberty to say."

Of course McGray wasn't allowed to discuss an open investigation, but Alex had needed to try. He'd already learned more from the detective today than he'd known previously. Alex stood. "I need a quick response. Can't you check for prints or do a DNA analysis on the saliva on the envelope seal?"

McGray's lips flattened in disgust. "This isn't TV, counselor. You know the real world doesn't solve cases in an hour."

"Right. You're understaffed and overworked, but Zack—"

"You're not dealing with an upstanding citizen here, Harper." He thumped the note with a knuckle. "Don't expect him or her to follow the rules. My advice is to tell your son the truth before someone else does. Kids are resilient. They bounce back. He'll get over it."

"That's not an option." Because unlike what Amanda had said, Zack's birth parents hadn't been there for him. His mother had sold him, and like a damned, dumb kid his real father had taken the easy way out.

And that was a mistake Alex could never forgive himself for making. And after almost eighteen years of deceit Zack would never forgive him. Every bond the two of them had forged would be irreparably shattered.

And Alex refused to go there.

Amanda looked good standing beside Alex at the Metropolitan Club, and she knew it. But knowing they made a striking couple, with him so dark and her so fair and both of them tall, didn't lessen the tension between them—a tension that hadn't been there before he'd received the threatening note two days ago.

Alex's height and the breadth of his custom-tailored tux-clad shoulders made her feel delicate and feminine—something she didn't often experience with her stature and addiction to four-inch heels. But long ago she'd realized all the cute shoes were heels, and she couldn't deny she was tall. So why fight it?

Alex's hand on her waist guaranteed her acceptance into this über-rich fund-raising crowd milling about the grand renaissance revival dining room with its ornate columns and marble-and-gilt-accented decor. Only four hundred of the city's elite had been invited to the ten-thousand-dollars-a-ticket event.

In the past hour Alex had introduced her to several prospective clients and managed to plug Affairs by Amanda numerous times without being too obvious. She gave him points for that. In turn, she'd made a few connections for him that he didn't already have. Her parents were actually good for something—not that they'd ever put in a good word for her business with their friends. If anything, they'd do the contrary. But they had exposed her to a few city bigwigs over the years.

She and Alex made a good team. Not something she

needed to dwell on, though, given the temporary nature of their alliance.

Alex snagged a couple of fresh flutes of champagne from a passing waiter, offered one to her and leaned down. His lips touched her ear and she shivered, almost spilling the golden beverage. The chill between them hadn't nixed his ability to arouse her without effort.

"Have I told you that you look amazing?"

Warmth coursed through her. Warmth she tried to tamp down because come hell or high water she was going to dodge this emotional bullet. And the only way to dodge it was to not get in any deeper with Alex.

"Once or twice. But thank you. It's not something I ever tire of hearing." Nor something she heard very often from her hypercritical parents. She had enough pride to hope the greedy way she sponged up Alex's compliments wasn't pathetically obvious.

Smoothing a hand over her red dress, she scanned the crowd rather than look into Alex's eyes and reveal how much his words had meant to her. She'd bought her designer gown in a secondhand shop. It had still had the tags on it and never been worn. It fit so perfectly it could have been personally designed to drape Amanda's body without alterations. But her mother would be appalled at the idea of Amanda wearing someone else's castoffs.

Dominique Crawford always offered Amanda free clothing—an offer Amanda almost always turned down, because the gesture wasn't made from the goodness of her mother's heart or from any maternal love. No, Dominique wanted to dress her daughter for two reasons. One, for free advertisement of her Dominique Designs, and two, because until she'd heard about Alex she'd thought

Amanda had horrible taste—not just in men—and she wasn't shy about sharing her opinion.

Her mother's frequent phone calls over the past five days attested to her approval of Alex, and Amanda was running out of excuses for not scheduling the requested dinner.

"Showtime," Alex murmured, his breath stirring her hormones along with the hair at her temple. She pasted a smile on her face and turned to see who was approaching. Her parents were cutting a direct line toward them across the marble floor and closing fast. Her good mood evaporated. Her heart thudded with panic. She glanced toward the exit, but her path was packed with well-heeled guests. Too late to make an escape.

Her mother, smiling her best camera-ready smile—faux though it might be—approached with arms extended and issued the requisite air kiss near Amanda's cheeks. "Amanda, darling, you didn't tell me you'd be here tonight."

A deliberate oversight. Otherwise, she'd known her mother would miraculously wrangle a ticket to the sold-out event. But apparently her mother had other sources, because this wasn't one of her usual charities. She had no reason to be here except to snoop on her daughter.

"Hello, Mother. Dad." And because she couldn't avoid introductions, she took a deep breath and prepared to plunge into what promised to be certain disaster.

"May I introduce you to Alex Harper? Alex, my parents, Dominique and Theodore Crawford."

Both were well-known, her mother on an international scale in the fashion industry and her father as a Wall Street CEO.

Alex's grip on her waist tightened. His fingertips slipped beneath the low cut fabric on her back sending awareness skipping up her vertebrae. "It's nice to meet you, Mr. and Mrs. Crawford."

"Dominique, please." She offered a beringed hand which Alex shook once. "Perhaps now we can schedule our dinner. Amanda has been quite difficult about setting a date."

Alex shot Amanda a quick questioning glance. No wonder. She hadn't mentioned her mother's invitation. Another deliberate omission. "Amanda and I have both been busy. Call my office and I'll see what my assistant can do to work you in."

Surprised that he'd backed her, thereby earning even more bonus points, she smiled up at him.

Her mother appeared to handle his evasion well, but when she turned a critical eye on Amanda, Amanda's smile slipped. She braced herself. "Darling, that dress—"

"Doesn't Amanda look amazing?" Alex kissed Amanda's temple and pulled her close to the hard, lean line of his body. His warmth and support seeped into her. "She's easily the most beautiful woman here tonight."

Her mother arched a brow. "I wouldn't say that."

"I would." Firm. Decisive. A don't-argue-with-me tone combined with a drilling stare that probably worked wonders on witnesses in the courtroom. "You have a beautiful, talented and very smart daughter. Congratulations."

Amanda could have kissed him. But that would definitely give her parents the wrong idea.

Surprisingly her mother blinked first. "And what have you two been busy doing besides spending time in Greenwich?"

Not a subtle bone in her mother's body. Dominique always probed, always pried, always pushed.

"Amanda is planning a couple of events for me. She's doing a great job." His knuckle dragged along her spine, making her shiver. Getting turned on in front of her parents was definitely new and uncomfortable territory.

Her mother's eyes narrowed, taking in Alex's protective stance. There would be hell to pay for this little act later. Once Amanda and Alex parted ways her mother would want to know how her daughter had managed to let a good one slip through her fingers.

Dominique turned to her husband. "Did you know the Vandercrofts are here? I must say hello. Nice meeting you, Alex. I look forward to our dinner."

And then she sashayed off with her husband in her wake. Tension drained from Amanda like water being released from a dam.

Alex had gone to bat for her—something none of the guys from her past had ever done. At that moment the ledge slipped out from under her and she fell head over heels for Alexander Harper. Womanizer. Millionaire. Heartbreaker.

He kissed her, briefly but firmly right on the mouth for anyone at the stuffy gathering to see, and for once she didn't care how her parents would interpret the gesture.

"Let's get out of here." His low-pitched voice rumbled over her exposed nerve endings.

"What about working the crowd? I haven't introduced you to the mayor yet."

"Invite him to my party. I'll meet him then."

Her heart took a swan dive and landed right in a hot spring of desire. This crash was going to hurt. But she would survive it, just as she'd survived every other one.

"Lead the way."

\* \* \*

He had to be out of his mind to leave the gala before he'd maximized the connections he'd paid good money to make.

But Alex lost enthusiasm for networking when the excitement in Amanda's eyes turned to anxiety. Sure, she had sucked it up and pasted on a smile, but the overwhelming urge to convert her smile back into a genuine one was as unexpected as it was unwanted.

He didn't need any more drama in his life. He had enough with the threat to expose Zack's paternity. Amanda's mother was a first-class drama queen. A real bitch. He'd recognized her type instantly from his frequent exposure through work. Money battles brought out the worst in most people.

If her parents were that critical it was no wonder Amanda didn't want them to know about her financial problems. Compared to his parents, who'd always put their children first and often at great personal sacrifice, Dominique Crawford's open disrespect and criticism had been hard to swallow. Alex relaxed his tensed muscles. He'd been angry on Amanda's behalf.

"I've missed holding you, Amanda." He dragged a fingernail down the tense line of her spine and relished the hitch of her breath, her shiver and the flush returning to her pale cheeks.

"You're sure you don't mind leaving early?"

The hunger he found in her gaze as she looked up at him made him suck a sharp breath. "I'm sure I'd rather be in your bed tasting you than here drinking inferior champagne."

Her lips parted, and her pink tongue appeared briefly to dampen them. The need to taste her hit him hard. But public displays of affection were not appropriate here and he'd already slipped up once. Amanda had a bad habit of edging past the steel barriers he locked around his emotions. A wise man would cut her loose and move on. But the rewards of having her by his side outweighed the risk of slipping again. She'd made a couple of introductions for him tonight that could prove lucrative if he followed up on them. And of course he would. Business always came first.

Lacing his fingers through hers, he led her toward the entrance. The time it took to retrieve their coats dragged, making him impatient to hold her. He finally got her outside in the blustery cold air, inside the wrought-iron colonnade tucked out of sight of paparazzi and gala guests. He yanked her close and covered her lips, catching her frosty breath in his mouth. Amanda opened to him instantly and kissed him back, not trying to hide her desire or temper her hunger. She tasted of champagne and her own addictive flavor.

Her fingers clutched his coat at his waist, pulling him closer. He liked that Amanda didn't play games. What she wanted, she took without apology but also without the greediness of other women he'd known, because she returned the pleasure she received tenfold. And it made him so hot he needed to shed his overcoat and grind her against the cold wall before he spontaneously incinerated. He considered dragging her the ten blocks to her apartment at a run.

Instead, he eased back and pulled in enough air to clear his head. "Your place. Now."

Her shiver shook him to the core. She spun away from him and stalked through the gates to the street.

What the— Had he offended her?

"Taxi!" she called out and he grinned. Amanda definitely didn't play games. She was bold and blunt, sometimes too blunt, like the times she'd told him to go bother someone else. But her resistance had only increased his determination to have her. She'd been well worth the battle.

A taxi cruised to a stop in front of them. Alex opened the door and followed her in, giving the cabbie her address. And then, because he couldn't resist in the privacy of the car, he pulled her into his lap. The layers of their coats and clothing did nothing to block the arousing pressure of her butt against his growing arousal—especially when she met his gaze and shifted, slowly, deliberately, to settle herself more comfortably in his lap. Desire burned through him.

She unbuttoned her coat in the hot, stuffy cab and the simple seductive releasing of the five buttons from collar to hip seemed as erotic as hell. The fabric parted, revealing the thigh-high slit in her gown and intensifying the heat in his groin.

That slit in her dress had driven him wild all evening. With each step she'd taken she'd flashed him with her mile-long legs and stiletto heels. He'd become distracted more than once with the mental image of her wearing nothing but those shoes.

Keeping his eyes on the rearview mirror to make sure the taxi driver wasn't watching, he spread his palm over her knee. Amanda's breath hitched audibly. He inched his way up her thigh, caressing her smooth, warm skin and he wondered how far he'd go. How far she'd *let* him go.

The fact that they were not alone added to the risk of discovery and heightened his excitement—not something he'd experienced before. He wasn't a PDA kind of guy. But Amanda, the craving for her mouth and the feel of her skin, was corrupting him. Waiting another five minutes to have her seemed impossible.

As his hand inched higher her breaths quickened, as did his, until he was only inches from her panties, from her appletini tattoo. He bent his head, burying his mouth and nose in her neck. He inhaled her fragrance. Not cologne. Pure Amanda. He sipped from her soft skin, swirled his tongue over the pulse pounding beneath her jaw. Her short nails dug into his thigh and her breath hissed.

His thumb eased under her silk dress, reached the crease where the elastic leg of her panties should have been and encountered…only skin and curls. Hunger for her exploded in his gut, in his groin and pulsed heavily through his veins.

Amanda's passion-filled eyes telegraphed her need in the darkened cab. Then the cab swerved, jarring him, forcing his thumb into her damp folds. His control jumped the tracks like a derailed train. He sank deeper into her slickness.

"Ten fifty," the cabbie said from the front, jarring Alex from fantasy to reality.

He reluctantly removed his hand and allowed Amanda to slide from his lap, which she did with excruciating slowness. He dug for his wallet, handed the driver a twenty and followed Amanda from the car without waiting for change. She hugged her coat around her and hustled for the glass-and-mahogany doors of 721. He followed more slowly, trying to recover his control and staggered by how close he'd come to losing it. In a cab.

This affair would have to end before he made a fool of himself. But it wasn't going to end tonight.

The doorman greeted them. But Alex didn't want to waste time in the lobby. He nodded at the man, hooked his arm around Amanda's back and hurried her toward the elevator.

Inside the car he backed her up against the wall, tucked his knee between hers and pinned her with his chest. Conscious of the security cameras and the guy watching downstairs, he reined himself in.

"You're not wearing panties," he whispered.

She smiled. Wickedly. Seductively. "No, I'm not."

He eased his hands inside her coat and around her waist and then down over her bottom, pulling her hips to his to let her feel how she affected him. The fall of her coat would conceal his actions. "If I'd known that at the gala I wouldn't have lasted five minutes."

She rolled her eyes. "Oh, please. You wouldn't have left without meeting the top ten on your list."

The accuracy of her remark surprised him. "Why would you say that?"

"Because I've watched you at every party we've attended since we met. You always have an agenda. I can almost see you ticking off your mental list. And then when you've finished it, you always come after me. The only reason you were willing to leave tonight was because you'd checked off your must-meet people before my parents arrived."

The woman was dead on target. She read him too well. "You've been watching me?"

Her gaze remained locked on his, but her cheeks pinked and her lashes fluttered over her grey eyes. "You know I have. And just so you know, my pantiless state has nothing to do with you and everything to do with the lines of the dress."

"I don't believe you."

The elevator doors opened behind him. He straightened and released her, allowing her to precede him to her door. She glanced at him over her shoulder as she pushed her key into the lock. "Believe what you want. I know the truth."

"The truth is that you want me as much as I want you."

Her sassy smile faded. "Yes, I do."

She turned away to open the door and then stepped inside. When her gaze met his again, the worry had left her eyes and the teasing tilt of her lips had returned. "The question is, what are you going to do about it, Alex?"

"This." He swept her into his arms, kicked her door closed and carried her straight through to her bedroom. Once he reached the side of her bed he shoved off her coat. The garment and her evening purse hit the floor. He wanted her naked. Now. And he wanted inside her. He dropped his own overcoat and tux jacket and reached for his tie. The fabric snagged and refused to loosen.

She batted his hands away, untying the knotted snarl he'd made of the black bow tie. Next she started on his shirt, releasing one button at a time and then yanking it from his pants and shoving it from his shoulders. Her short nails scraped down his chest, dredging up a firestorm of need and making his muscles jump.

When her fingers hooked behind his waistband, he sucked a lungful of air, caught her hands and put them by her side. Too much. Too soon. He studied her dress, found the zipper down the side of the curve-hugging, strapless red gown and eased it south. Her clothing fell to the floor, leaving her bare except for her heels.

He clamped his teeth on a groan. Seeing her naked

never failed to deflate his lungs. He fought for breath, for control, for reason. Amanda made him lose his head.

She smiled, scooped up her garments and strolled across her room to drape coat and dress over a chair. She was teasing, stalling, but he savored every wiggle of her hips, and he'd bet she had added that extra sway to her gait because she knew his gaze was glued to her incredible rear view. Amanda was long and lean, but curved where it counted. The woman had the kind of butt made to wear a thong…or nothing at all.

And then she pivoted, slowly, like a runway model. He drank in her breasts, their nipples tight and waiting for his hands, for his mouth. His gaze rolled over her narrow waist, the tattoo on her hip near the pale blond triangle of curls and down those mind-wrecking legs. His hands fisted against the need to grab her and toss her on the mattress.

Looking at her creamy skin from a distance wasn't enough. He kicked off his shoes and shed his attire with record-breaking haste. When he was bare she strolled back toward him with a hips-rolling, make-his-tongue-hang-out stride. Her eyes telegraphed her desire, exponentially increasing his own.

How did she reduce him to testosterone insanity so easily? But she'd had that effect on him from the first day they'd met. Even after she'd told him to get lost. *Especially* after she'd told him to get lost. Women who knew his income bracket and background didn't push him away. But wanting Amanda was more than just the need to acquire what he'd been denied.

She lifted a hand toward his face. He captured it and carried her wrist to his lips. Stringing a trail of kisses up her pale inner arm, past her elbow, to the tender skin of her bicep, he relished each gasp and each shudder he wrenched from her. He enjoyed the heavy fall of her lashes drifting across her cheeks and the warmth of her skin against his lips. He savored her taste on his tongue.

Amanda draped her arm around his neck and stepped into his embrace, the way she'd done on the dance floor tonight, only now his tux and her dress weren't between them.

Her flesh curved into his, searing him. Her flat belly brushed his erection, sending a megawatt of electricity charging through his system. She swayed against him, as if dancing to a tune playing in her head, and he could barely breathe, barely think, barely stand.

When she lifted her lips, he didn't refuse the invitation. Her mouth was soft, her tongue wild. The ravenous kiss consumed what was left of his control. He swept her into his arms and eased her onto the bed, following her down and blanketing her with his body. The funky, fuzzy fabric of her comforter tickled his knees and shins and forearms. But it was the slick welcome of her body that blew all but one of his fuses.

Damn. Damn. Damn. How did she make him forget the most basic rules? He withdrew. "Condom."

Amanda twisted beneath him, opened the small carved jewelry box on her nightstand and withdrew a condom packet. She'd been keeping them there since he'd started sleeping over.

Palming his chest, she shoved him back until he knelt between her knees and then she planted kisses along his hipbone while applying the protection. Her tongue licked a path of fire along his flesh, making his stomach muscles quiver while her hand stroked latex down his rigid shaft.

He gritted his teeth against the jolt of pleasure but a groan seeped through.

Reclining again, she opened her arms and smiled that smile at him—the one that made steam rise from his pores. He loved that she'd turned a stupid mistake into sexy foreplay. But that was Amanda. She had a way of pulling something unexpected to keep him on his toes. A guy could get used to that. If he'd let himself.

But he wouldn't. He couldn't.

He bent and kissed her hard and fast on the mouth, but then slowed his pace as he strung nips and kisses down her neck, over her collarbone, from one nipple to the other. She writhed beneath him as he made his way down the center of her abdomen, past her navel, to the swollen flesh buried in her curls. He sucked her bud into his mouth and flicked it with his tongue. Her flavor registered simultaneously with her moan.

He alternated laving her, sucking her and gently nibbling until her knees bent and her back bowed—the sign he'd been waiting for that told him she was clinging to the edge. He freed her to rise up so he could sink deep inside her. Slick and hot and wet, she surrounded him. He withdrew, returned, withdrew again and then he reached between them and stroked her.

Release crashed over her, contracting her internal muscles around him and filling his ears with her cries of pleasure. He struggled to make it last. Sweat broke out on his skin as he brought her to orgasm a second and third time. He started to shake with the effort of holding back, and then her lids lifted. Smoky grey eyes caught and held his as she reached out and hooked his nape with her hand. She dragged his mouth to hers and bit his bottom lip then sucked it into her mouth. And blew his restraint straight to hell. He couldn't pull back. Couldn't dam the flood of pleasure.

Orgasm pounded through him, slamming him with wave after blinding wave of sensation. When it finally ended, he collapsed to his elbows over her. Winded. Drained. Sated.

Her lips curved into a satisfied smile and something wrenched in his chest. That's when it hit him.

It was going to be hard to let Amanda Crawford go.

# Eight

Heart pounding, Amanda dropped her PDA back into her briefcase Monday morning, reached for her desk calendar and counted back again. But modern technology hadn't failed. The numbers didn't change on paper.

Her period was late.

Not late enough to panic. Yet. She'd give it another day or two. And then she'd panic. If she had to.

Which she wouldn't.

*But you're never late.*

She took several calming breaths and reminded herself there was a first time for everything. And being late didn't have to mean anything. She'd been under a lot of stress lately. And stress messed up body clocks, didn't it?

But what if it wasn't stress, the nagging voice in her head insisted. How could a slip like this have happened? When had she and Alex ever not used protection? She searched her memories of the hot, steamy, slow and fast encounters and—

The first time. That first time in her bedroom they hadn't used a condom.

Her stomach sank at the memory. She braced herself against the kitchen counter. How could they have been so stupid? And how could she not have thought about it even once since that day two weeks ago? She was never careless about birth control or safe sex. Never.

She pressed her hands to her belly and gulped for air.

She couldn't afford a baby. She could barely support herself, and until she had her financial mess unraveled—

The bathroom door opened, severing her thoughts. She lowered her hands. Steam billowed out, followed by Alex wearing only a lavender towel low around his hips. The feminine color did nothing to lessen the masculine impact of his broad shoulders, ripped abs and long, muscular legs. Her pulse kicked erratically in appreciation.

No matter how strong her reservations, after Friday night at her place they'd spent the entire weekend together in Greenwich. When they'd managed to climb out of bed, he'd taken her to Round Hill, an old Continental Army lookout point with a great view of the Manhattan skyline. They'd strolled hand in hand past the exclusive boutiques and restaurants of Greenwich Avenue, people watching, window-shopping and discussing alternative venues for Zack's party. The Harpers' home was still an option, but Amanda had wanted to come up with something more special for Zack's big day.

Alex hadn't left after returning Amanda to her apartment last night. She hadn't been able to get enough of his company. She might as well admit it. She was putty in his hands. What Alex wanted, Alex got. Eventually. From her, anyway. How she'd held out as long as she had was a miracle.

But this...

She opened her mouth to spill the bad news, and then closed it again. Why ruin his day on a maybe? She'd worry enough for both of them. She'd take a pregnancy test first. And then she'd tell him *if* there was anything to tell.

There wouldn't be.

He walked toward her, stopping a foot away. "I'll be tied up in court all day and I have a client dinner tonight."

"That's okay. I have several appointments today and I'll be very late getting home." Her level tone pleased her. No trace of panic tinged her words. She hoped her expression didn't give away her tormented concerns.

He finger-combed his damp hair. His biceps and pectoral muscles flexed, and his towel slipped down, revealing an inch of the thick dark hair in his groin. He looked so sexy her mouth watered and her internal muscles clenched. She struggled with the urge to stroke her fingertips down his still damp chest.

"Then I'll head for Greenwich tonight." He stroked her jaw line. "Unless you want to give me a key."

Shock knocked her back a step. "No."

That hadn't sounded good. She'd practically shouted at him, and from the tightening of his lips, he wasn't crazy about her reaction. But she couldn't repeat the mistake she'd made with Curtis and Douglas of trusting too much. Both men had cost her self-respect and cash. She didn't think she'd ever trust a man enough to give him access to her home or her heart again.

"I'm sorry, Alex. I don't want to go there. We're temporary. Remember?"

He didn't correct her.

*Did you want him to?*

*No.*

*Maybe.*

After a tense silence he nodded. Even though he hadn't moved, he'd withdrawn so far he might as well be standing on the opposite side of the room. "I'll call you in the morning."

"The masks I ordered are due to arrive tomorrow. I'll stop by to get your approval. I'll check with Moira for a good time first."

"That will work." His dark gaze ran over her lime tunic sweater and black miniskirt, tights and boots. And with just that slow look he quickened her pulse and her respiratory rate and turned her insides into a jumble. "You seem in a hurry to get out the door. I'll lock up if you're gone when I get through dressing."

Avoiding an awkward good-bye appealed on so many levels.

"Thank you." So formal. They spoke like acquaintances rather than a couple who'd been entwined like mating snakes less than an hour ago.

But then Alex had withdrawn immediately after making love to her last night. She'd fully expected him to make an excuse and leave. But he hadn't. And this morning he'd reached for her again, but put that same distance between them after satisfying her so many times could barely walk on her wobbly legs. He hadn't joined her in the shower—a first since he'd started staying over.

What did that mean?

He probably had his mind on work. He'd mentioned a complicated case going to trial this week. Or with his party only five days away, maybe he was prioritizing that who-he-must-connect-with list. Because even though this was a company party, he'd invited quite a few influential outsiders.

Whatever the cause of his tension, she wasn't going to increase it by blurting out her fears. She'd stop by the pharmacy and pick up a pregnancy test on the way back from her morning appointment. She could take the test tonight…or tomorrow…or maybe she'd just wait a few more days to make the purchase. She was probably jumping the gun anyway. Why even waste money on the test?

*Coward.*

He took a step toward her. She planted a palm on his chest and his heat seeped up her arm and into her core. She was too rattled to handle another one of his meltdown kisses at the moment.

"We'd both better get going if we don't want to be late."

She had absolutely no idea how Alex would react to the situation. If there was a situation. Would he want a child? Would he pressure her into having it if she didn't want to? Did she want to have a baby even though it would totally mess up her life at the moment?

*Boy, wouldn't your parents love an illegitimate grandchild?*

*Not.*

So not only did she have to find out if she was pregnant, she had to decide whether or not to share the test results with Alex. Not doing so seemed devious and underhanded. But telling him and knowing his ability to talk her into almost anything…

His hand covered hers, his fingers laced through hers and then he lifted their linked hands to his mouth. He nibbled on the fleshy pad at the base of her thumb and her hormones went haywire. Darn him, he knew that made her knees week.

Her heart raced. She snatched her hand away and cleared her throat. "Well, then, have a great day. I'll see you tomorrow."

She scooped up her coat and briefcase and bolted. There were decisions she just couldn't handle at the moment. Later, when she was dealing with facts instead of just terrifying, life-altering possibilities, she'd be more mature. But at the moment she felt more like a hysterical eighteen-year-old than a mature woman of twenty-eight.

"Moira had to step out for a moment," the Harper & Associates receptionist told Amanda on Tuesday afternoon. "You're welcome to go back to Mr. Harper's private waiting room if you'd like."

Becoming a frequent visitor to Harper & Associates evidently carried some perks. She was now trusted to go places without an escort.

"Thank you. I will." Amanda wheeled the rolling attaché down the hall and into the now-familiar room. She shed her coat, hung it in Moira's closet and crossed to her favorite chair tucked out of the way in the corner. But she was too agitated to sit.

Instead, she walked to the window. Worry churned in her stomach as it had been doing since her discovery yesterday morning. She'd found the courage to buy the pregnancy test kit, but chickened out before using it and hid it beneath her bathroom cabinet where she wouldn't have to look at it until she was ready to take the plunge. She hated her cowardice, but reminded herself a day or two's delay wouldn't change the outcome.

Focusing on a tourist helicopter in the distance, she tried to block out her personal mental clutter and concentrate on business—the one area of her life that was mostly under control thanks to Alex's loan. She'd brought an assortment of the Mardi Gras party favors for Alex's approval. It was merely a formality. She didn't expect him to object to any of the materials. Her favorite supplier had done its usual top-notch job.

Alex's office door opened, and the anticipation of seeing him raced through her like a lit fuse. She really needed to work on putting some emotional distance between them, but her heart wasn't receiving the message.

A svelte, expensively dressed and glammed-up redhead strode into the opening, stopped and turned back to the room she'd vacated. "I'm glad you called, Alex. It's good to see you again. I've missed you."

She had a smoky, sultry voice and her tone was far too intimate for a client/lawyer conversation.

Prickles of unease tickled Amanda's nape like a spiderweb.

"Keep this between us," Alex's deep baritone said, as he stepped into view. He didn't look Amanda's way.

"You know I'll do that. For you, I'd do *any*thing."

Amanda's spine snapped straighter at the emphasis on *any*. The woman's body language said she wasn't talking about bringing him chicken soup when he had a cold. Her pale fingers with red-tipped nails caressed his black lapel and then adjusted his ruby tie. And he let her. This man who didn't like PDAs let the woman mess with him. Never mind it was his private office.

"I don't want this to get out," he added.

"Neither do I."

Alex's visitor rose on tiptoe, cupped his cheek and then kissed the corner of his mouth. She lingered far too long for Amanda's peace of mind, and then Amanda's worry turned into something ugly and uncomfortable and shocking. Something that made her need a stiff drink or three.

Jealousy? Was she *jealous* of Alex and this woman? She couldn't be. That emotion implied deeper feelings—the kind of feelings that led to wanting something…permanent. And painful.

She wasn't ready for that and probably never would be.

She studied Alex and the woman. Their familiarity implied there was definitely something between them. But what? A current relationship? History? Whatever their connection, the woman wanted more of it. She wanted Alex. That desire was evident in every line of her seductively garbed body.

Had Alex decided to move on when Amanda refused to give him a key yesterday? For all she knew he might have an entire ring of women's keys. He'd certainly asked for hers easily enough. And hadn't Julia warned her repeatedly of his reputation as a player? That was one of the main reasons Amanda had avoided him so long.

"So about tonight…" the redhead purred, looking up at him through her lashes.

Pain stabbed Amanda in her chest. She gasped. Alex had claimed he had another business dinner tonight. Had he lied?

He turned and spotted her. A trace of red lipstick lingered on his skin. "Amanda."

She felt used, discarded, hurt. Betrayed. He had a date tonight and he'd lied to her. Struggling for composure and clinging desperately to her pride, she squared her shoulders. "I'm here for our appointment."

"Chelsea, you know the way out." His dark gaze never left Amanda's. Amanda made a painful note of the lack of introduction. Who was this woman Alex didn't want her to meet?

"Of course I do, since I come here so often." The coquettish tone returned.

The witch's barb hit the target again. Amanda fought to conceal the hurt. But she couldn't help wondering if she'd gotten herself possibly pregnant by a two-timing, womanizing jerk. And if she had, then what?

The woman left, but the ache in Amanda's heart didn't lessen and the knot in her stomach intensified with each passing second.

There was only one possible cause for her current misery. She'd fallen for Alex Harper, womanizer extraordinaire. To make matters worse, she might be carrying his baby.

Her parents were going to love this.

"I'm glad you're here, Amanda. Come in."

Alex's words made her jump. How could she tell him about her pregnancy concerns now? She couldn't. Not today. Maybe never. Was there even anything to tell? She prayed there wasn't. Her child—if there was one—deserved better than a guy who juggled women like a day trader does stocks and bonds.

*Concentrate on the job, Amanda.*

She forced her limbs into motion, snatched the handle

of the rolling attaché in a knuckle-numbing grip and dragged the case into his inner sanctum. The room smelled like him and *her*. A trace of the woman's heavy cologne lingered. The corner of his desk where Amanda and Alex had almost made love—*had sex*—pulled her gaze like a magnet. Had Alex and the redhead—

*Never ask a question to which you don't want to know the answer.*

Redirecting her attention to the task at hand, she flipped open the latches of the case and very carefully laid a representative assortment of masks and beads across his desk. She couldn't think of a word to say. She dredged her brain for the reason for her visit and finally pulled a few thoughts together.

"Take a look at these samples. If they're not right I can reorder by five this evening to get replacements in time for Saturday's event."

"Amanda." He cupped her shoulder. She jumped out of reach.

"Don't."

His eyebrows lowered. "What's wrong?"

"When I'm in an intimate relationship I am exclusive. For health reasons I refuse to share."

His eyes narrowed. "What are you implying?"

The red smear drew her gaze like a light does moths. "You're wearing her lipstick."

He removed a handkerchief from his inner pocket, wiped the telltale spot, then looked at the stained cloth. "Chelsea and I are not together."

"I don't believe you."

His shoulders snapped back. "I won't waste my time trying to convince you."

"Who is she?"

He seemed to weigh his response carefully. "Someone I knew years ago. We were involved, but we aren't any longer."

That qualified as an evasive answer. "Not by her choice."

"Chelsea has always wanted what she couldn't have."

And Chelsea wanted Alex. Her make-him-notice clothing and do-me-now heels made her intentions to entice him abundantly clear. Had Alex been tempted? While he hadn't kissed the witch back, he hadn't moved away, either.

Amanda rolled a shoulder, feigning disinterest. "Whatever. But from now on you and I are business only. I won't sleep with you anymore."

Because she couldn't share a man she'd fallen in love with. *Love.* The admission sent another round of aftershocks through her. How had this happened? She didn't want to fall in love. She sucked at it. Her three previous relationships were proof of that.

She turned away quickly and straightened the rows of party junk on his desk. Her hands were far from steady and no matter how hard she tried she couldn't stop the tremor. She hoped Alex didn't notice.

He moved into her peripheral vision. "What about our agreement?"

Dread curdled in her stomach. She stilled her frantic rearranging and risked looking at him. "Which agreement? The loan? You told me there were no strings attached."

"I'm talking about our mutually beneficial introductions and you hosting my parties."

Her heart was ripping in two and all he cared about were his stupid parties? Her throat burned and nausea decided to make an unwelcome cameo appearance. She was so tired of being used by the ill-chosen men in her life. And so sick of choosing unwisely. She had to work on that.

*Forget it. Go back to the no-men rule for a decade or two.*

"I'll do what you paid me to do. But no more."

He lifted a hand and stroked her cheek before she could jerk out of reach. The brief contact hit her like a Taser, locking her muscles and jamming her thoughts so she couldn't escape.

"We're good together, Amanda."

She had to get out of here before she lost it. "And we still will be. On a professional level."

Unwilling to take the time to wait for him to examine the samples or to repack her attaché case, she backed toward the door. She wouldn't need that case again before Saturday anyway. She only used it when she had heavy stuff to lug around.

"Have a look at the masks, beads and other party favors. If you want any changes then have Moira call me by four-thirty this afternoon. I'll fax any other pertinent information to you between now and Saturday. I have another appointment." *Liar.* "I have to go."

The pain on Amanda's face ripped Alex apart. He didn't want her to leave. Not yet. Not like this. He wanted to tell her the truth. All of it. The realization made him uneasy. He'd never wanted to share Zack's parentage with anyone except Zack. The risk for his son to get hurt was too high. But with the threat of blowing the Harper family's privacy to hell hanging over his head, he wanted Amanda to hear it from him first.

The urge to share didn't mean he was falling for her. He only needed Amanda's opinion on how to handle the situation. The police and his parents were giving him no help. And he wanted Amanda to stay and wash away the stench of Chelsea's self-absorbed personality.

Amanda was as open and honest as Chelsea was devious and conniving. Amanda would never lie to him or keep something from him the way Chelsea had eighteen years ago when her actions had robbed him of the power to make a decision that had affected the rest of his life, the rest of Zack's life. He would never ever let a woman do that to him again.

"Stay." Besides the off-the-Richter-Scale sex, he enjoyed Amanda's company. Too much? Probably. But he had to love—*like,* he amended—a woman who not only understood the intricacies of football but could also throw on a designer gown and network like a pro before stripping down to skin and driving him out of his mind.

The novelty of their attraction would eventually burn out, but he'd had three calls already as a result of Amanda's introductions Friday night. He didn't intend to let her go this soon.

Shaking her head, she backed toward the door. "I can't."

"You asked Moira to block off thirty minutes."

"Something came up." There was an unfamiliar quiver in her voice and she wouldn't meet his gaze. A strange idea implanted itself in his head and wouldn't let go.

"Are you jealous of Chelsea?"

She jerked and stared at him as if he'd said something insane. "Jealous? Why would I be jealous? We're temporary, remember? I told you at the beginning that I didn't want anything more from you."

The statement should have filled him with relief. Temporary was his MO. Instead, her words left him feeling...off balance. He searched for a firmer footing, lifted a hand and traced her jawline with his fingertip. The hitch of her breath rewarded his efforts. He loved touching her soft, smooth, satiny skin.

"We are a potent and effective combination."

She stepped out of reach. "You're a client. I should never have let this become personal. From here on out we'll focus on our professional relationship and you can go back to your Chelseas. It was only a matter of time before you did anyway, Alex."

She yanked open his door and stormed out. He wasn't ready to let her go. He strode after her.

"Alex," Moira called out. "Bill Hines is on line one."

Hines would be Harper & Associates' largest corporate account—if Alex could land him. Torn between work and following Amanda, Alex stopped in his waiting area. His gaze followed Amanda down the hall, but duty turned his feet away from the door.

Business always came first. Success meant power. And he could never get enough of that.

But for the first time he wanted to say to hell with the climb to the top.

# Nine

Amanda focused on Julia's rounded belly and sent up a silent prayer that she wouldn't be in the same situation in a few months.

Not that she had anything against children. She'd never really thought much about having them. The idea of getting married and having a family had always been a hazy, distant "someday" possibility. But the present timing couldn't have been worse. She prayed this was a false alarm. But deep in her heart she suspected it wasn't.

She fluffed her hair and shifted her gaze from Julia's stomach to her so-radiant-it-hurt-to-look-at face and then back to her plate. The two of them had elected to sit on the floor and eat at the coffee table, but Amanda's favorite food just wasn't ringing her chimes tonight.

How could two intelligent college graduates both end

up accidentally pregnant? That just didn't happen in the real world.

Okay, it did. But not to her.

*Please don't let it be happening to me.*

She needed someone to talk to. Her whole sordid story hovered on the tip of her tongue, but she just couldn't find the courage to confess her worries to Julia. Not yet.

"Are you okay?" Julia asked.

Amanda blinked—innocently, she hoped—at her friend. "Why wouldn't I be?"

"You're very quiet. That's not like you."

"I'm a little distracted by Alex's party." And the late period. And Alex. And the fact that she really missed having him in her bed…and her body.

She couldn't remember ever having something she couldn't share with her friend, and when she'd come over to Max and Julia's penthouse loft for a girls' night of takeout Chinese, she'd been determined to discuss the situation and her options.

She knew Julia wouldn't judge or condemn her because her former roommate had been caught in exactly the same position. Julia's pregnancy hadn't been planned, either. It had been the result of a passionate one-night stand with Max seven months ago. Julia had already had to swim through those murky "what if/what'll I do" waters. She'd since married the father of her baby and couldn't possibly be happier, if her glowing face was an indicator.

But marrying Alex wasn't an option for Amanda. She sucked at relationships, had lousy judgment in the male selection department and was a rotten example of not-so-happily-ever-after to her parents. Not to mention, Alex wasn't interested in marriage. And then there were her money issues, her determination to avoid workaholics like her father and—

*Don't dwell on shortcomings.*

*Hard not to when the list is so long.*

Even though she knew Julia would offer her unbiased guidance, Amanda wasn't ready to share her secret. For pity's sake, she couldn't even bring herself to use the test kit until she knew where she stood with Alex.

Was she on her own in this decision? Or not?

Was the redhead a factor…or wasn't she?

Julia rubbed her tummy. "Is Alex staying out of your hair and out of your bed?"

Amanda jerked in surprise. Her kung pao chicken fell from her chopsticks and landed with a splat in her lap. Oops. Life had been so hectic she hadn't filled Julia in on the status change over the past two weeks.

"Um. Alex is Alex. He's never going to change," she hedged, and snatched up a paper napkin to blot at the mess clinging to her sweater—more to avoid Julia's perceptive blue eyes than to clean what was probably going to be a permanent stain.

"Well, yes, but his interest in you has outlived any of his other relationships that I've heard about."

"Probably because I didn't fall all over him." In the beginning. She searched for a safer topic. "The RSVPs are rolling in, but I'm surprised some of our neighbors haven't responded. I haven't heard from Carrie and Trent or Sebastian and Tessa."

"That's because they're all out of the country. Carrie and Trent are on a prewedding honeymoon in Caspia. They won't be back in time to attend."

Disappointed, Amanda frowned. How could she

have missed that her second-floor neighbors weren't even in the building? Had the affair with Alex filled her head with smog?

"A *pre*wedding honeymoon? Isn't that a little backward? Honeymoons come *after* the wedding for most people." Although she had no room to object if her neighbors did things a little out of proper order. She could be the poster child for bending rules. Besides, thinking outside the box was a requirement for a good party planner.

"Prince Sebastian and his fiancée Tessa gave Carrie and Trent the trip as a wedding gift, and Sebastian and Tessa are over there with them, showing them around the country. We have very generous neighbors." The wistful tone of the last phrase caught Amanda by surprise.

"Do you miss living at 721?"

"Yes and no. I miss you and our friends, but not the intrigue. And I have Max. His place isn't too shabby," she added, with a twinkle in her eyes.

"No. Not shabby at all." Amanda's gaze swept the large room with its wide-planked oak floors, a fireplace flanked by loaded bookcases and the oversize furniture. Julia's new digs couldn't be more comfy and inviting. "And soon you'll have your baby."

"Not soon enough."

A buzz from the intercom interrupted them. Julia lumbered to her feet, crossed the room and pushed the button. "Yes?"

"Julia, buzz me in." Alex's deep voice filled the room.

Amanda's stomach plunged.

"I need to see Amanda," he continued.

Wide-eyed and near panic, Amanda shook her head vigorously. She wasn't ready to see him today. This afternoon's introduction to jealousy had rattled her cage. She'd never been jealous before. Ever. And she didn't like it. Not at all.

*Why not?* Julia mouthed silently.

Too much to explain. Again, Amanda shook her head and held up her hands in the universal stop sign.

Julia sighed and turned back to the intercom. "What makes you think she's here?"

"Max told me."

Amanda winced. Max had been nice enough to clear out and let them have a girls' night, but this killed any gratitude she might have felt toward him.

"You can come up." Julia pushed the door release button. She turned to Amanda. "I'm not going to lie to him. He's Max's best friend. Do you want to tell me why you're avoiding Alex? Or should I ask him?"

Amanda debated for thirty seconds before admitting defeat. Julia would never let her out of the loft without a total confession. "We were sleeping together. Now we're not. I'm late. And I think he's two-timing me with a gorgeous redhead."

Julia's mouth dropped open at the rushed summation. She sagged against the wall beside the door. "Couldn't you have mentioned this earlier instead of chitchatting about nursery colors?"

Amanda grimaced. "I should have, but I—I didn't know where to start. And now I don't know what to do." A knock halted her words. Alex was here. The urge to run sent a boost of adrenaline through her muscles. But Julia wasn't giving her the option of avoiding him.

Julia reached for the doorknob but paused and pointed an imperious finger. "You're not leaving tonight until I get every detail. And I mean *every* one. You've been holding out on me."

Resignation settled over Amanda. There were some things you just had to endure, like trips to the dentist, visits with the parents and getting grilled by best friends. Thoroughly unpleasant, but survivable.

She rose from her seat on the floor and wiped her hands down her thighs. Inhaling deeply, Amanda braced herself. "Okay."

Julia nodded and opened the door.

There was no way for Amanda to prepare for the impact of Alex's dark gaze slamming into hers. For several hammering heartbeats, he stared and she couldn't breathe or move her locked muscles, and then he glanced away briefly to greet Julia before turning back to Amanda. "We need to talk."

She wet her lips and swallowed in a futile attempt to ease her dry mouth. "I think we've said all there is to say."

"Now, Amanda." His firm, inflexible voice made her wonder if he had a bit of a stubborn streak. But then what male didn't? And he had been as persistent as a pigeon in Central Park in chasing her. So yes, he definitely had a stubborn streak.

But she wasn't going have this conversation in front of Julia. Amanda reluctantly walked toward him. "Not here. Outside."

"Wait," Julia called out. "You are not leaving. I'll give you some privacy."

As much as Amanda appreciated the support, she wanted to handle this situation her way, and that meant not telling Alex about her late period yet. Maybe she'd tell him after his party. If it was still necessary. But Julia had no way of knowing that and she might unintentionally blurt out something.

Amanda shook her head. "We're just going to step out for a moment. I'll be back to finish our dinner. I promise."

Not that she expected to be able to put another bite in her churning stomach. But she'd promised to give Julia details and she would keep her promise.

Alex held the door for her and then followed her out into the hall. For several seconds his dark eyes pinned her in place, probing, seeking, wanting. Oh, yes, the want was there plain to see and it kindled a reciprocal need in Amanda.

Tension stretched between them. Tension and awareness. A trace of his cologne underlain by his own scent teased her senses, and her clothing suddenly weighed heavily on her overly sensitized skin. Every breath dragged the fabric over her like a caress.

How could she still desire him if he'd two-timed her? Had she no brains whatsoever? No self-preservation instinct? No pride? Sure, he'd claimed there was nothing between him and the redhead, but she'd seen the connection.

She refused to squirm or look away from him. Instead, she folded her arms and leaned back against the wall, feigning calm she wasn't even close to experiencing. If she managed to bluff her way through this confrontation she wouldn't have to see him again except at his party and his brother's. The rest of the details could be phoned in.

Her heart would have time to heal. And she'd have time to make decisions.

"Alex, what could possibly be so important that you had to tell me in person rather than call or send me an e-mail?"

Moving as fast as a striking snake, he planted a hand on the wall on either side of her head and then his mouth covered hers. Shock held her immobile for a few heartbeats while his lips plied hers with a skill she'd come to appreciate and crave, and then her brain kicked in.

How dare he! She shoved against his chest, but instead of moving away he slowly bent his elbows, closing the gap between them. The weight and heat of his body ironed her flat against the wall, trapping her hands between them. His heart beat rock-steady, if somewhat rapidly, against her palms. His hips and thighs nudged hers.

Hunger rumbled to life inside her and she couldn't kill it any more than she could slow her quickening pulse or keep her lips sealed when he stroked them apart. His tongue twined with hers, slick and seductive, familiar and arousing. He coaxed a response from her that she was shockingly willing to give. Her heart raced and heat flooded her.

How could she give this up? She'd never been so physically in tune with a man before. Her hands slid to his shoulders and then his nape. Supple skin and soft hair teased her fingertips. She stroked his jaw, savoring his evening beard.

He lifted his head slightly. "You can't e-mail this."

Before she could gather her wits and escape, his lips returned with devastating, protest-robbing results. So much for resisting. He sucked her bottom lip between his teeth, nipping it lightly before easing back until only their foreheads and the tips of their noses touched. "We shouldn't be doing this."

"You can try to deny the chemistry between us, Amanda, but it's not going to work. We are a dynamic team. In bed and out. I'm not letting you go. Not yet."

Reason rallied slowly, kicked into gear by a weak wave of indignation. "You can't make me keep seeing you."

"Is that a challenge?"

The glint in his eyes sent a warning shiver over her. She was already on shaky ground. She didn't need to goad him. "No. It's a statement of fact. One you know as a lawyer not to cross."

He eased back a few more inches, allowing her precious breathing and thinking room. "How many calls have you had as a result of our night at the gala?"

Smart man. He hit her in the weakest spot of her dump-him-and-run argument. But then she'd never doubted Alex's intelligence. They were a good team. And it wasn't his fault her feelings had crossed the lines they'd established.

"Four," she confessed reluctantly.

His dark eyes said I told you so. He caught her chin in his fingers and forced her to meet his gaze. "Chelsea is not an issue."

The need to believe him almost overcame her good sense. "Then tell me who she is. Because it's as clear as Waterford crystal that you've slept with her."

Shadows filled his eyes. "It's not my story to tell. Others could be hurt. But we haven't been intimate in over a decade."

She searched his steady eyes, his face. Was she being stupidly gullible? Probably. Silently calling herself a fool, she conceded defeat. "I believe you."

"Then we're still a team."

A statement. Not a question.

She inhaled slowly, deeply, praying for the strength to refuse him and finding none. "We're still a team. For now."

But would her secret—her possible secret—turn him against her?

\* \* \*

"I'll have a hard time keeping my hands off you tonight." Alex's comment from behind her in the opulent Trianon suite startled Amanda seconds before his warm, firm grip settled on her waist. He pulled her back against his muscled frame.

She tried and failed to suppress her body's spontaneous-combustion reaction to him and neutralized her expression. Using the process of turning to face him to her advantage, she stepped out of his grasp, but it was too late. The heat of his touch had branded her.

With his broad shoulders and lean build Alex looked totally edible in his black custom-tailored tux with a snowy white shirt and black tie.

She'd tried to get him to wear a colored bow tie to go with the festive Mardi Gras mood, but he wasn't the wild-colors type. And honestly, the stark black and white worked extremely well on him. It also reminded her that while she might be something of a free spirit, he was essentially conservative and traditional.

*Except in bed.* She quickly snuffed that thought but not soon enough to prevent a flicker of arousal from igniting at her core.

His conservative tendency was just one more reason they should not have a child together. They'd argue constantly on how to raise it. Like her parents had argued about her. In the end she hadn't fit in with either of their blueprints for her life and she'd disappointed them both. There was nothing like continuous, disappointed scowling to put a damper on life.

"Alex, the dress is beautiful. Thank you." She stroked a hand over the metallic ombré silk of the evening gown.

"You're welcome. It suits you." His appreciative gaze poured over her like heated massage oil, reinforcing his statement.

"I couldn't have chosen a more perfect dress for myself if I'd tried."

When the delivery man had handed her the box yesterday Amanda had thought her mother was up to her old tricks again, and she had come very close to refusing to accept the package. But then she'd caved and opened the lid for a quick peek, fully intending to return the garment. It had been love at first sight—even before she'd found the card from Alex tucked inside.

While her mother always sent dresses intended to showcase the Dominique apparel line's newest designs, Alex had bought a dress that made the most of Amanda's physical assets. The plunging surplice bodice enhanced her smallish bust and the empire waist and hip-molding skirt accentuated her height and slender build. A slit from the hem to her upper thigh opened when she walked and flashed her legs and silver heels.

"I adore the colors." Almost as much as she adored the man who'd chosen the dress. *Don't go there.*

To distract herself from that unwelcome thought, she glanced sideways at her reflection in the tall, arched gold-leaf mirror on the wall behind the reception table. The fabric of the bodice was a pale lavender—the exact shade of the orchid on her bedside table. The color graduated to darker shades as if the hem had wicked up a deep, luscious midnight-sky purple.

"Turn around."

Amanda hesitated at Alex's low-voiced command, but then complied when his hands cupped her shoulders and tried to turn her to face the mirror. She instinctively resisted, but reminded herself she was working for him tonight and that meant doing what he asked—within reason. She pivoted. He removed his hands, reached into his pocket and then lowered a glittering gold chain around her neck. A large briolette-cut amethyst settled between her breasts and the cool metal rested on her skin.

"A perfect match to the dress." His fingers teased her nape as he fastened the clasp sending a shiver of awareness down her spine.

She met his gaze in the mirror. "Alex, you shouldn't have."

His lips touched the side of her neck and her pulse skittered wildly. Her heart hiccuped even faster when his teeth grazed the cord of her neck. "You worked hard. You deserve it."

She'd never be able to resist him if he kept this up. She clutched the stone in her fingers and once more pulled away from the sensory overload Alex induced, and faced him. "It's my job."

Holding her gaze, he stroked her cheek with his fingertips and she all but melted at the approval in his eyes. "It's more than your job. You live for the thrill of pulling all the details together, the same way I do with a complicated court case. And you're very good at what you do, Amanda."

How could he make her stomach flip-flop with nothing more than a few kind words and a hot glance? It was disgusting how easily he aroused her.

"Thank you. For the compliments and the necklace."

Flustered and pleased, she reached across the table for the plain black half mask she'd purchased for him. "Your guests should start arriving any moment. Put this on."

His fingers brushed hers as he accepted the molded fabric and a sliver of need worked its way up her spine.

"Our guests. We're going to wow them tonight." He dragged a knuckle down her bare arm, leaving a crop of goose bumps in his wake.

She dampened her lips and reached for her white, feathered and sequined mask. She'd been hustling around all afternoon trying to put the finishing touches on the gala setup. But the hardest work was done now. Every detail had been checked and double-checked. That left her with nothing to keep her from dwelling on how much she desired the man in front of her and how complicated their lives would get if the pregnancy test delivered the wrong answer.

*Don't think about that tonight.*

*You are the queen of denial.*

She slipped on her mask and studied Alex in his. The masks immediately kicked up the naughty factor. Through the small openings Alex's brown eyes glittered with excitement, anticipation and hunger. The latter sent a ripple of awareness over her and made her wish they had a few minutes to explore whatever it was that mischievous twinkle implied. Her pulse quickened.

Approaching voices provided a grounding distraction. Alex blinked, and instantly what she'd come to recognize as his professional face replaced the passion.

Reed and Elizabeth Wellington, Amanda's neighbors who resided in one of the two penthouses at 721 Park, rounded the corner looking as wrapped up in each other as newlyweds. They didn't appear to notice Amanda or Alex until they were only a few yards away. The couple hadn't looked nearly as happy at the fifth anniversary party Amanda had organized for them last month at Cipriani

42nd Street, but tonight Elizabeth's face glowed with happiness. Being pregnant certainly agreed with Elizabeth.

"Hello, Amanda. Alex." Elizabeth kissed Amanda's cheek and gave her a quick hug, then did the same to Alex. It was almost as if Elizabeth couldn't contain her joy.

Amanda air-kissed Reed's cheek after the men shook hands. "How's Lucas?"

"He's a great kid," Reed replied. "He's ten months old now."

In addition to welcoming their own baby in seven months, the couple was in the process of adopting Elizabeth's nephew after the death of the child's parents. The process hadn't been smooth sailing, but judging by their expressions, whatever headaches they'd been through had been well worth it.

Amanda indicated the table displaying the Mardi Gras masks. "We're glad you could make it tonight. Please choose a mask and go on in. You're the first to arrive, so you'll have the dance floor to yourselves until the others arrive. Be sure to ask the band to play you a slow, jazzy tune."

Elizabeth and Reed chose masks and disappeared into the Trianon Suite, with matching smiles of anticipation on their faces.

Alex dragged a fingertip down Amanda's spine, whipping up waves of want. She loved it when he did that and every single time it made her hot. "We should have had a slow dance before our guests arrived."

Amanda looked into his eyes and the desire she saw made her breath catch. How could he look at her like that if he wanted that Chelsea woman? Maybe he'd told the truth about his relationship with the redhead. She hoped so. "Maybe we can have a dance after everyone leaves."

"I'm not waiting until the end of the night to hold you."

The determination in his low-voiced statement made her stomach flip and her pulse flutter. "I don't want you to."

More fool her. This was going to be a *big* relationship train wreck if she didn't find a way to pull back emotionally. But a tiny part of her wanted to savor every moment just in case. Just in case disaster struck and she found herself pregnant.

Ellen and Harry Harper arrived next. Amanda smiled. She enjoyed Alex's parents' company, and she hoped the night wasn't too hectic for her to find time to talk to them. But she couldn't help but be curious about the mystery surrounding Zack's parenthood. If Ellen hadn't had an affair, then what was the secret worth a million dollars?

Alex's hand settled on Amanda's waist—a circumstance his parents didn't miss. Ellen beamed and Harry nodded. But they'd barely exchanged hellos before another group of guests arrived.

Amanda spent the next two hours in a hypervigilant state as Alex's hostess. Even when he left her side it was as if some internal radar made her aware of his location, and it annoyed her that she couldn't seem to turn the Alex-detection system off. Each time their eyes met across the room her heart hiccuped.

She really had it bad for him and that wasn't good.

"Hey, you. How's it going?" Julia waltzed up beside her, accompanied by Elizabeth Wellington.

"Great. The Mardi Gras theme seems to be a big hit with Alex's employees. The incognito factor relaxes people, and everyone's having a good time if the number of smiles I see beneath the half masks are any indication."

"You always throw a great party, Amanda," Elizabeth said.

"Please feel free to shout that from the rooftop anytime, Elizabeth. Better yet, take out an ad in the *Times*." She winked at the women. "Where are your men?"

Julia dipped her head to indicate an area on the far side of the room. Amanda followed her gaze. Max and Reed had joined Senator Kendrick and the mayor. All the men's expressions were intense, as if they were cooking up a business deal.

"It's always sad when a marriage ends," Elizabeth said. "I read in the gossip section of the paper that the senator and Charmaine, his wife of thirty years, are divorcing." The tinge of pain in Elizabeth's voice hinted at the difficulties she and Reed had been through. "Not too long ago I thought Reed and I were headed down that painful path."

Amanda nodded. She'd noticed the tension while planning the Wellingtons' event. "I'm glad you managed to work out your issues. It's depressing when any relationship ends. They all leave scars—even if ending them is the best option available."

And she had the history to prove it.

Gage Lattimer, Reed Wellington's business partner and the occupant of the other 721 Park penthouse, joined the men. Usually Gage was a loner, but tonight Amanda had seen him working the crowd. He appeared to be having a good time.

"Gage has been a social butterfly tonight. He looks quite cheerful for a change. Do you think something or *someone* has gotten into him? It would be great if he'd settle down."

Julia's expression turned curious. "He had a bitter

divorce years ago. It'll take him awhile to put that behind him. Max claims Gage came away from the bitchy ex with a really hard shell. Good luck to the woman who tries to crack it."

Julia handed her plate to a passing waiter. "I want another dance with my husband before I go home and crash. Pregnancy is exhausting. I've never had so many early nights."

"That sounds like a wonderful idea," Elizabeth seconded. "Again, a lovely party, Amanda."

The women left Amanda alone. Moments later a tap on her elbow caught her attention. Alex's father and mother stood beside her.

"You're good for my son, Amanda," Harry announced. "I've never seen Alex look happier."

Amanda's gaze jerked across the room and slammed into Alex's heated regard. Her breath stalled and her insides warmed at the desire he made no effort to conceal. How unlike Alex to come out of his conservative shell and reveal his hunger in a public forum.

"I hope this means we'll see a lot more of you in the future." Harry's voice pulled her attention back to him.

"You'll definitely see more of me as we plan Zack's birthday party."

And they'd see a lot of her if she was carrying their grandchild.

She still hoped she wasn't.

It would be different if Alex loved her. Then the bad timing and the fear of being as lousy a parent as hers had been wouldn't be as anxiety-inducing. With his assistance she'd be able to hire help so she wouldn't have to neglect Affairs by Amanda, and her bad parenting examples would be counteracted by Alex's great ones. She truly envied him and Zack their parents.

Ellen stiffened and paled. Amanda followed her gaze to the entrance of the ballroom. The redhead from Alex's office stood poised in the doorway in a drop-dead, gorgeous, black form-fitting, cleavage-revealing dress.

Amanda's stomach pitched as if she'd gone over the top of a roller coaster. What was the woman doing here? There hadn't been any Chelseas on the guest list and because of the space limitations this was an invitation-only event.

What could she possibly want? Or maybe the question was *Who?* Amanda couldn't decide whether to ask Alex if he'd privately invited the newcomer or just insist the woman leave.

"Excuse me," Harry said and then stalked toward the interloper. His long, purposeful stride reminded her of Alex's. So maybe the son had inherited a characteristic from his father after all. Ellen stayed beside Amanda, but the smile she'd been wearing seconds ago had turned brittle.

Amanda glanced back at Alex to see if he'd noted Chelsea's arrival, but he was still deeply engrossed in a conversation with the senator.

Mr. Harper hustled Chelsea to an anteroom. Seconds later Amanda heard raised voices. They weren't loud enough to make out the words, but the argument drew the guests' attention—and Alex's. Amanda hurried across the ballroom to ask them to quiet down. Before she arrived the door opened and Mr. Harper escorted the redhead out. Twin dots of angry color marred Chelsea's beautiful face. Amanda felt no sympathy for her.

Harry didn't pause as he passed. "Good night, Amanda."

Alex's mother followed them out of the ballroom.

Amanda stared after them. What had that been about?

She searched for Alex and found him still with the senator, but he was tense, tight-lipped and definitely not looking like the happy host at the moment.

She'd have to intervene if she wanted to save the situation. But one thing was certain. That woman had put a damper on the event and Amanda wasn't going to rest until she found out why and what power Chelsea held over the Harper family, Alex in particular.

# Ten

The new, unsmiling Alex of the past hour had surprised and confused Amanda. The only thing that shocked her more was when he dropped her off at her apartment door and turned away without kissing her good-night or asking to come in.

*Let him go,* she told herself as she studied his stiff back. But she couldn't. He was upset and she needed to know why and to help him with the issue if she could.

"Alex?" He paused in the hall, but didn't face her. "What's going on? Chelsea's appearance at the party cast a pall over the remainder of the evening—and not just because she wasn't on the guest list. She upset your parents and you."

After several seconds he turned to face her, one clearly reluctant but deliberate step at a time. His jaw looked rigid, as if he had his teeth clenched. "Inside."

He followed her into the apartment and closed the door but didn't sit. Instead he walked the strip of hardwood floor between the front door and the bedroom hallway and back again. Amanda waited, her own tension increasing as the seconds ticked past. She'd bet he looked very much like this when he was in court. Cool. Composed. Determined.

He stopped in front of her. "Chelsea reappears in my life every few years, usually when she needs money. This time she's calling her demand an 'investment opportunity' in some artist her gallery represents."

He thought Chelsea only wanted money? He couldn't possibly be so naive, could he? "Did she send the blackmail note?"

His eyes narrowed. "That's an astute question. One I've asked myself. But after talking to her neither the police nor I believe so."

"Then why did her presence tonight upset everyone? And why would she keep coming back for more money and expecting to get it?"

He took a deep breath and loosened his tie. The fabric whistled through his collar as he ripped it free and then stuffed it in his pocket. Next he removed his coat and tossed it over the back of a chair. His usual smooth moves were jerky and abrupt as if tightly leashed anger drove each action.

"Chelsea is Zack's mother."

Amanda gasped in surprise.

"And I'm Zack's father."

Her knees buckled. Head reeling, she sank onto the sofa. She hadn't seen that coming. But it explained so much, like the closeness between the "brothers" and the times she'd caught Alex studying Zack as if he were searching for something or soaking up details. "Oh, Alex."

"Chelsea has never been a part of Zack's life and couldn't care less about him. She's never even met her son and doesn't want to meet him now."

"How could she do that? He's an amazing young man. Smart and funny and sweet."

"I agree."

Amanda did some mental math. The numbers weren't good. "You were very young when she got pregnant."

"Barely seventeen. I wasn't ready to be a father. For a number of reasons I didn't believe the baby was mine, and I offered to pay for an abortion. By then I'd learned enough about Chelsea to know she'd make all of us miserable. I wasn't willing to marry her."

Amanda decided her possible pregnancy was not something she needed to spring on him now. Dread curled in her stomach.

"Chelsea went behind my back to my parents and threatened to not only make a public fuss about her pregnancy but to terminate if they didn't cough up a million dollars. My parents were horrified, both by the possible scandal that could have irrevocably damaged my father's reputation and by the idea of losing their first grandchild.

"Instead of letting Chelsea end the pregnancy they not only paid her the money she demanded, they decided to adopt Zack. My mother had always wanted more children but couldn't have them. She claimed Zack was her second chance."

Typical of a man, Alex had focused on the facts and not the emotions wrapped up in the events. "How did you feel about that?"

"What I wanted didn't matter. I was powerless. Completely and totally powerless." The anger and frustration in his voice said more than his words. It didn't bode well for her situation. If there was a situation.

His frustration also explained why he was such a workaholic now. He wanted the power he'd been denied back then.

"Mom cooked up an elaborate scheme. She and Chelsea moved to Paris until after Zack was born. As soon as a paternity test confirmed Zack was mine, my parents started the adoption procedure. My father visited Paris often enough during the pregnancy so that when my mother returned with a newborn, no one doubted that Zack was my father's child."

"And it helped because he looks just like you."

He inclined his head. "You mentioned that before. That's why I suspected you of the extortion note. You and my mother hit it off so well I was afraid she'd let something slip and you'd decided to capitalize on the information."

"She did let something slip, but I misinterpreted it. You don't think I'm capable of extortion now?"

He shook his head. "I haven't since we first discussed it."

She should take comfort in that, she supposed. "And you've told no one else about Zack's parentage?"

"Never. Not even Max knows."

But Alex had trusted her. The knowledge warmed her. "Then who could be behind the note?"

"I don't know. But I must find out before Zack is hurt."

The shock would be hard on the teen. "You should tell him, Alex."

"You're the second person to suggest that. I don't agree. Right now Zack trusts me. He's going through a rough spell, and he comes to me with problems he won't discuss with anyone else. If I tell him I abandoned him, I'll blow that trust."

"You didn't abandon him."

He fisted his hands by his side. "I didn't live up to my responsibility as his father. I took the easy way out and let my parents pay for my mistake. Hell, I didn't even want him to be born. When I think about not having him in my life and what I would have missed if Chelsea had done as I asked—" His voice cracked.

She fell a little deeper in love with him at that moment. Alex would be a wonderful father. But given his history with Chelsea, Amanda wasn't sure they would have even a slight chance at a healthy relationship if she turned up pregnant.

Chelsea had trapped him and used him and she'd taken his money. Amanda had used Alex for his connections and accepted a loan from him. She hadn't trapped him. Yet. And she didn't want to. But two black marks out of three didn't look good.

"Alex, you were little more than a child yourself."

"It doesn't matter. I wasn't there for Zack."

"I think you're wrong. I think you have been there for him from the moment you made the decision to relinquish him. I've seen the closeness between you. That doesn't develop without a lot of love and trust. But if you don't tell him and he finds out from someone else, his sense of betrayal will only be worse. You and your parents should sit down with him."

"I want him to know. I've wanted to tell him for years. But I don't want to lose him." The agony on his face revealed how much he struggled with the dilemma and responsibility. "Everyone he loves and trusts, me and our parents, have been living a lie."

She rose and crossed the room to wrap her arms around him. A hug wasn't much, but she'd craved them often enough and done without while growing up to want to offer the comfort the simple gesture provided.

Alex's arms banded around her so tightly she could barely draw a breath. She leaned back to look into his eyes. "What can I do to help?"

He pulled her close again and kissed her temple. "I wish I knew. I feel as if I have a live bomb in my hand. Someone has set the timer, but I can't read it. I have no idea how much time I have left before it blows everything to hell and back."

He'd feel even worse when he learned her secret. The only thing she could do was try to prove she loved him with actions, not words, and then if Murphy's Law did strike and she turned up pregnant maybe he'd trust her to do the right thing for their baby and for them.

That staggering thought took her aback when she realized she was actually considering having Alex Harper's baby and trying to build a family with him.

With her relationship track record that wasn't just risky. It was a potential catastrophe on a grand scale. But some chances were worth taking.

Amanda cupped Alex's tense jaw. It was late. Well past midnight. But she couldn't wait. "Make love with me, Alex."

And it would be love. For the first time in her life she would be truly making love. Not just having sex. Not just suffering from infatuation. She realized now that what she'd felt for Heath, Douglas and Curtis had been nothing more than blind infatuation.

What she felt for Alex was the kind of emotion musicians, novelists and poets wrote about, the kind that filled her with anticipation, excitement and fear.

Especially fear. But that fear gave life an exhilarating edge. This could go so badly. Or it could be wonderful. She intended to shoot for wonderful.

Alex turned his face into her touch and covered the back of her hand with his. He planted a kiss in the heart of her palm. His lips trailed to her wrist and any lingering tiredness she might have had from her day of hustling vanished.

His mouth burned a trail to the inside of her elbow, up to her shoulder, then to the side of her neck. Amanda tilted her head to the side to grant him better access. She adored the way he nuzzled her neck, creating a swirl of desire in her belly. His other hand cupped her waist, holding her close while he sipped and nipped his way from her neck along her jaw to her mouth.

She leaned into him, savoring the strength of his hips and thighs. His tongue sought hers, stroked and swirled, carrying her into a maelstrom of need. One big hand caressed her back. The other splayed over her bottom and pressed her against his growing erection. She shifted against him and his breath hissed.

She needed to touch him. All of him. To absorb as much of him into her being as she possibly could. His scent. His taste. His heat. Amanda reached for the buttons of his shirt and quickly freed them. His chest was firm and hot beneath her hands. His tiny nipple beaded under her tongue. She rapidly dealt with his belt and zipper and impatiently shoved his clothing to the floor.

Alex kicked off his shoes. Amanda marched him backward until the back of his legs hit the sofa. She shoved and he sat. She knelt before him and peeled off his black socks. Pressing his knees apart, she made a place for herself between them. His thick shaft stood tall and tempting in front of her. Her mouth watered, and her inner thighs warmed and wanted. She licked her lips, but as much as she needed him inside her, she had a better idea.

He wasn't ready to hear the words, but she'd show him how much she loved him, beginning with a foot massage. She captured one big foot and dug her thumbs into his sole. Alex groaned and leaned against the cushions. She kissed the arch of his foot while her fingers plied his flesh, and then she painted a circle around his ankle bone with her tongue.

She repeated the process with his other foot and then, working her way up from his foot, she massaged his calf and up his thigh. Her lips trailed close behind. Inside his knee. Up his inner thigh. His muscles grew tenser with each inch her hands and mouth climbed. The dark hairs on his legs tickled her lips and skin. She licked the tender sac beneath his penis.

"Amanda," Alex growled, but he didn't stop her explorations or protest when she drew intricate patterns with her tongue.

She licked the length of his rigid flesh and his fingers speared into her hair. He cradled her head gently, but his hands trembled. She found the swollen head of his arousal and took him into her mouth. She tasted, sucked and stroked, pleased that she could make him quiver the way he did her.

She loved him with her mouth, caressed him with her hands. His breath whooshed out in a half groan. His knees clamped on his shoulders and his legs clenched. She savored the harsh rasp of his breathing, the spasm of his fingers in her hair. His hips flexed and then he clamped down on her head and pulled her away.

"I wasn't finished," she protested.

"Neither am I," he rasped as he stood, cupping her elbows and pulling her to her feet with him. He quickly removed her clothing, and then he swept her into his arms and laid her on the sofa.

One hard kiss pressed her head against the cushion. A second branded her left breast. He drew her nipple deep into his mouth, rolled it with his tongue and razed it gently with his teeth. His hand found the other, plucking, teasing it.

Her middle melted like paraffin wax. She bit her lip on a moan and arched her back. Alex traced a line down the center of her belly with his fingers. He delved into her curls and found her slickness. Using her own moisture, he fondled, caressed, buffed her sensitive center and then plunged his fingers deep inside her. Hunger rolled through her. Her knees opened involuntarily to give him better access and her heels dug into the sofa, lifting her into his touch.

He shamelessly took advantage. She squeezed him with her internal muscles, silently begging for more. His tempo quickened, rushing her to a rapid ascent and then sending her crashing over. One release followed another without giving her time to catch her breath until, weak and gasping, she covered the hand buried in her curls.

"Alex, I need you." She cupped his nape and pulled him forward. He took her mouth in a kiss so deep and carnal and on the edge of control it stopped just shy of painful.

With a groan he disconnected, grabbed his pants,

fished in his pocket and found a condom which he quickly applied. Alex looked like a man on a mission. Determination hardened his jaw. Passion blazed in his eyes.

She wanted to slow him down, to savor making love for the first time while being in love. "Wait."

He paused, each muscle bunched and quivering.

"I want to be on top."

His eyes closed. His head fell back. He sucked a deep breath through his nose and then lay back on the sofa. Amanda climbed over him, straddled him and without taking her eyes off his face, eased down to take him into her body, into her heart, into her soul.

She loved this man. He stretched her, filled her, completed her. In all of her wild and crazy, detour-ridden life, this was the only time she'd ever been absolutely certain she was exactly where she was supposed to be and with whom she was destined to be.

No matter what happened from here on out, Alex would always be a part of her life. He'd left his mark on her. And baby or no baby, she would never forget him and never, ever be free of his memory.

She needed to find a way to make him feel the same.

"Amanda?" Alex called out Sunday morning from Amanda's shower. "I need soap."

Silence greeted him and he remembered her mentioning as she climbed out of bed while he'd been still half-asleep that she wanted to dash out to Park Café for a couple of her favorite chocolate muffins. A smile tugged his lips. She had a thing for those muffins.

And he had a thing for her. More than a thing, he decided as the hot water beat down on his back.

He'd fallen in love with her.

Love. Not an emotion he'd ever expected to experience.

But he and Amanda were a damned good team. Her understanding last night had put the final nail in the coffin of his determination to remain single. She was good with Zack, got along with his parents, drove him wild in bed and was an asset to his career. Look how she'd salvaged the evening last night after Chelsea's appearance had turned his mood sour. If not for Amanda he would have blown the alliance he'd made with the senator and killed the party spirit for his employees.

And then there was the way she'd tackled him on the sofa after they returned to her place. His grin turned salacious and his blood simmered. He'd need a cold shower before she returned if he kept up that line of thought, or she wouldn't get to eat her muffins before the chocolate chips cooled.

He wasn't going to let her go.

The realization sobered him. Keeping her meant marriage. He'd never planned to marry, never planned to trust another woman not to screw him over. But he'd tie himself to Amanda in a heartbeat. He loved and trusted her.

"Amanda?" he called out again. He wanted to tell her how he felt.

On second thought, not yet. He had to come up with something big, a grand gesture a woman who planned events for a living would appreciate. And he had to buy a ring. Maybe Zack could help him choose one.

Alex eyed the tiny, almost transparent sliver of soap in his hand. It wasn't going to get the job done and if Amanda wasn't here he'd have to find a new bar himself.

He pulled back the shower curtain and stepped onto the lavender bathmat. Steam slowly filled the room from the hot water running behind him as he knelt to open the vanity cabinet and scan the contents. No soap. He shifted lotions, tampons, shampoo, a leg-waxing kit and a jumble of other woman products. This was why he didn't cohabitate. Women had too much junk cluttering up the space. Good thing his bathroom in Greenwich was large enough to accommodate all of Amanda's paraphernalia.

He didn't see what he needed, but a bag in the back of the cabinet snagged his attention. He made out the shape of a rectangle through the plastic. Soap? He snagged the handle, opened the top and looked inside.

A pregnancy test.

The hairs on the back of his neck prickled. He dismissed the reaction and started to shove the bag back where he'd found it. Julia had probably left the item behind. But the corner of the receipt tucked inside the bag caught his eye. Checking the date to confirm his suspicions wouldn't hurt. He grabbed the corner, yanked out the white strip and scanned the print.

An Arctic chill swept through him when he saw the date.

The test kit had been purchased four days ago. *Four days.* It wasn't Julia's.

Why would Amanda need a pregnancy test?

Denial screamed through him and a sense of déjà vu seized him by the throat. Amanda wouldn't plot to take him to the cleaners the way Chelsea had.

Or would she?

Hadn't every woman he'd become involved with over the years eventually pulled some kind of manipulative crap to keep the relationship going long after the embers had cooled?

Amanda was short on cash and she'd been tense lately. Had she cultivated the friendship with his parents to use them against him? If so, she'd learn he wasn't a powerless teen who ran from his responsibilities anymore.

He heard the front door open, stood and whipped a towel around his hips. After turning off the water, he grabbed the kit and stormed out to meet her.

Amanda saw him and stopped. A slow, wicked smile slid across her lips and her gaze glided over his face and bare chest, skidding to a halt on the box in his hand.

Her eyes widened and her lips parted. Her shocked gaze locked with his. Color flooded her cheeks—guilty color—and then leeched away to leave her ghostly pale.

"When were you going to tell me?" he forced himself to say.

"I—I—I don't know if I am yet. I haven't taken the test. There's nothing to tell."

He'd wanted her to deny it and when she didn't, his muscles tensed even more. "How late are you?"

She blinked and swallowed twice the way a witness did when buying time. "Only a few days."

"Is it mine?"

She flinched. "If I am pregnant, then yes, it's yours. I haven't been with anyone else in a long time."

Fury boiled inside him along with betrayal. "Did you set me up?"

Her eyes widened even farther and then anger stormed her face. She strode into the room, the Park Café bag clutched in one hand. She dropped it on the coffee table. "Set you up? Do you think I want to be pregnant?"

"You wouldn't be the first woman to see me as a ticket to Easy Street."

"I'm not Chelsea. And it took two of us to create this situation. You didn't wear a condom that first time."

He searched his mind for details and recalled he'd been so eager and impatient to have her that night he'd taken her standing up. Damnation. That was exactly the kind of idiot mistake he always warned Zack not to make.

"If there is a child I want joint custody."

She closed her eyes tightly, inhaled, exhaled, then lifted her lids. Worry darkened her grey eyes to almost charcoal. "Let's not panic prematurely. We don't know if there is a baby yet."

"That's easy enough to find out." He thrust the box toward her. "Take the test."

Looking horrified, she staggered back a step and the box fell to the sofa. "Alex—"

"Do it now."

The door buzzer sounded. Amanda startled and then looked relieved by the interruption. She hurried to the intercom. "Yes?"

"A Zack Harper is here to see you," the doorman's voice said.

Zack? Uneasiness crept up Alex's spine. Why would Zack track him down unless something was wrong?

"Send him up," Amanda instructed and then turned back to Alex. "Why would Zack come to my place and so early on a Sunday morning?" She stashed the pregnancy test behind an oversize pillow on the sofa.

"My thoughts exactly."

"Alex, you might want to get dressed."

Right. He hustled to Amanda's room and jerked on his

tux pants and shirt. He didn't have anything else to wear. A knock at the door had him hurrying back to the living room barefooted.

Zack looked like hell. His hair was disheveled, his face drawn with fatigue.

Amanda rested a hand on his shoulder. "Are you okay?"

Zack looked up and spotted Alex. "Tell me it's not true."

The pain in Zack's voice ripped into Alex like a knife. He knew. Somehow Zack had discovered the truth.

"Tell me you're not my father." He confirmed Alex's worst fear.

A heavy weight settled on his chest. "I can't do that, Zack."

"Why? Why did you lie?" Zack shouted.

His obvious pain twisted the knife in Alex's gut. "How did you find out?"

"Does it matter? You lied to me."

Amanda wrapped her arm around Zack's tense shoulders, pulled him into the apartment and closed the door. "Zack, Alex had good reasons for making the decisions he did. And you need to hear them."

Amanda's support surprised Alex, especially given what he'd just accused her of doing.

She led Zack to the sofa and sat beside him. "Tell us how you found out."

"Mom and Dad were arguing last night about some woman wanting money. My *mother*—" His voice broke. Amanda took one of his fists in hers and slowly unclenched his fingers to hold his hand in both of hers. "They said as long as she knew who my real father was she would keep coming back for more money. She's bribing them."

Alex realized Amanda and the detective were right. He should have told Zack the truth sooner. It was always better to avert a crisis than to clean up after one.

It was time to come clean. "I was your age when I got Chelsea pregnant. I was young and selfish and I wasn't ready to be a father."

Zack inhaled sharply. "You wanted to get rid of me?"

Lying would be the kindest thing to do. But he'd lied for too long already. "I thought my life would be over if I had a child. No college. No friends. Yes, I tried to convince Chelsea to terminate. She went to my—*our*—parents instead. They wanted to adopt you and made plans to do so. It was the best decision anyone could have made, Zack. But I was too young and too stupid to know that at the time. And I was very fortunate to have been allowed to watch you grow up and be a part of your life. I don't regret one second of that."

"Why didn't you tell me?" Anger and hurt still filled Zack's voice and his eyes.

"I didn't want to hurt or confuse you. But I've done that anyway. I'm sorry."

"Zack." Amanda waited until Zack looked at her. "You're dating now. How would you feel if one of your girlfriends turned up pregnant?"

Zack jerked. "Rotten…scared. Angry."

"And maybe a little bit trapped and panicked? You'd worry about not being able to do all the things you'd wanted to do, wouldn't you? You're excited about going to college at Harry and Alex's alma mater, aren't you? But you'd have a baby coming about the same time all of your friends would be packing their bags and heading for orientation. They'd be leaving you behind."

The frown on Zack's face deepened. "Yeah."

Amanda squeezed his hand. "Unless you decided not to become a father. That's what Alex faced. He was in a tough spot. Making difficult choices is part of life. Making mistakes is human. We all do it. Fixing them, owning up to them and making the best out of a bad situation are signs of maturity. Listen to Alex. Let him explain his side of the story. He's a pretty great guy. But I think you already know that."

Amanda rose. "I need to take my shower. I'll leave you to talk."

Alex watched her walk out of the room. Why had she stood by him after he'd treated her like crap?

Because that's the kind of person Amanda Crawford was. And he'd blown it.

He turned to Zack. He saw the pain and confusion in the eyes so like his own. His throat burned and his heart ached for the pain he'd caused Zack. He crossed to take Amanda's place on the couch.

"I'm sorry, Zack. I've wanted to tell you for years. I probably should have. But I was afraid I'd screw up the bond between us. I'm proud of you, Zack. You've turned into one hell of a great kid. And I'd like to think that I've been a part of that even if I couldn't be your father."

Tears filled Zack's eyes. He blinked them away. "I wish you'd told me."

"Would it have made a difference? We have amazing parents. We couldn't do better."

"But you're my father."

"Biologically, yes. In my heart, absolutely. But otherwise, no. Harry Harper is your father—*our* father—in every way that counts."

And it damn near killed him to admit that. All these years he'd believed he could have been a good parent if the power hadn't been taken from him, but he finally had to admit he'd never be a better father than his had been. And it had nothing to do with power and everything to do with being there.

"Do the folks know where you are?"

Zack shifted uncomfortably and looked away. "No. I spent the night at your house. I tried to call your cell phone. You didn't answer. I used my key and let myself in. But you didn't come home."

"As you've guessed, I stayed with Amanda. But then you always were a smart kid." Alex snagged his tux jacket from the back of the chair and retrieved his cell phone from his pocket. He checked for missed calls and found ten of them, some from his parents, some from Zack. He'd never heard it ring. "I had it on vibrate and I left my jacket in here last night."

"Did you love her?"

Alex stiffened. He'd barely admitted his feelings for Amanda to himself. Was he ready to share them with Zack? No. And did her hiding her possible pregnancy from him change how he felt? Yes. No. He had no clue.

But Zack had used past tense. "Did I love who?"

"My mother. My *birth* mother."

Alex shoved a hand through his hair and expelled a relieved breath. Zack wasn't talking about Amanda.

*Tell the truth.* "No. We were just two kids screwing around and we got caught."

"That's why you always harp about safe sex."

"I don't harp."

"Yes, you do. Repeatedly. Jeez, you even bought me condoms before I kissed a girl the first time."

Alex grimaced. So maybe he'd been a little overzealous. "You're the best thing that's ever happened to me, Zack. Don't ever doubt that. And when I think about what could have happened..."

"But it didn't. What is it Amanda always says? Everything happens for a reason and we each have to find our path even if it isn't the beaten one?"

"Amanda says that?"

Amanda said a lot of things. Things that should have clued him in to the fact that she was nothing like Chelsea. She hadn't set him up. Her patching it up between him and Zack was a perfect example of Amanda's priorities.

He'd falsely accused her. Twice. First for sending the extortion note, and second for trying to trap him. Amanda was all about people. Their feelings. Their hearts. Not their bank balances. She would never do anything to deliberately hurt someone. His lack of trust could very well cost him the best woman he'd ever known.

"I like her. You should keep her." Zack reached for the muffin bag Amanda had dropped on the coffee table. The kid was a bottomless pit where food was concerned.

Alex rested a hand on Zack's shoulder. "I intend to. And for that, I might need your help."

"You mean work as a team?" Zack shrugged. "Sure. I'm in. But only if you swear to tell me the whole truth from now on."

"I will."

"What do you need?"

"Forgiveness. I said some things to Amanda that she might not be willing to forgive or forget."

"I'll put in a good word for you, but Amanda isn't the type to hold grudges."

Alex laughed. How could a kid half his age be wiser than him about women? "I hope you're right."

Because if Amanda wouldn't forgive him he wasn't sure what he'd do. One thing was certain. He wasn't giving her up without a fight.

# Eleven

*Amanda Crawford, you're a hypocrite.*

Amanda stood in her bedroom listening to the low hum of Alex's and Zack's conversation and scolded herself. How could she preach about owning up to mistakes when she wasn't willing to face or admit hers?

First thing Monday morning she'd call Alex's associate and sic him on Curtis. It might be embarrassing initially, but in the long run it was the right thing to do. If she didn't stop Curtis, what was to keep him from doing to someone else what he'd already done to her?

And she needed to take the pregnancy test…but it was in the living room. She wasn't going to tromp in there and interrupt their conversation to fetch it. The last thing Zack needed was to have the bomb dropped on him that he might be a real brother soon.

She'd do the test as soon as she returned from visiting her parents.

But before she could take those giant steps, she needed to call her parents and come clean. Pleasing them was an impossible task. She needed to quit wasting her time on the effort. From now on she had to live her life and find her path to happiness. She'd said that often enough to others. It was time she took her own advice. And if her parents couldn't handle that she was human and made mistakes, then tough.

Alex had no idea how lucky he was to have parents who supported him no matter how big his blunder. She hoped her parents would learn to accept her decisions—the good ones *and* the bad ones—one of these days. If they chose not to, then missing out on their grandchild—if there was one— would be their loss. She wouldn't expose any child of hers to the bitter negativity she'd endured while growing up.

Before she could chicken out she picked up the phone and punched in her parents' number. Her mother answered.

"Hi, Mom. I need to talk to you and Daddy. Today."

"Amanda, we're booked for couples tennis with—"

"Mother, make time for me or read about what I'm going to tell you in the paper."

Silence stretched through the airwaves. "Be here within the hour."

"I'm on my way."

Amanda disconnected and headed for the door. She didn't put on makeup or change her clothes. Her mother would have a lot to say about that. But who cared?

This visit was all about acceptance. It was time her parents realized she was her own person and she had no desire to be a little clone of either of them.

Alex and Zack looked up as she entered the living room. "I'm going out. Lock up when you leave."

Before they could respond, she tossed Alex her spare key, stepped into the hall and closed the door. He didn't need the key to secure the apartment. Giving him one was symbolic of her willingness to let him into her life. Would he get the message?

As soon as she dealt with her parental issues, she'd have to return and deal with the much larger issue of Alex…and the pregnancy test.

But she could jump only one hurdle at a time, and she wasn't sure which item on the agenda scared her the most. Opening her heart to Alex or taking the test. Funny, it wasn't facing her parents' disapproval. A week ago it would have been.

A quick cab ride dumped her at her parents' apartment on Fifth Avenue. The housekeeper let her in—another new one, she noticed. Because Dominique Crawford was demanding and impossible to please, staff turnover was frequent. Amanda had learned long ago to never get attached to Crawford employees. They never lasted long.

She found her parents in the morning room, gathering their belongings to leave even though they'd known she was coming.

"You need to sit down and listen instead of acting like I'm the least important part of your life and you'd rather be elsewhere."

Amanda watched her mother's eyebrows rise and then turned to her father. He laid his tennis racket on the glass-topped table and resumed his seat. "Your rudeness does not impress me, Amanda."

She bit down on the urge to apologize. It was way past

time for her to stand up to them, and she was through apologizing to them for not being the daughter they'd wanted. It was time they accepted her, warts and all, instead of trying to mold her into something else.

"In the next few months the Crawford name might make it into the papers." She ignored their disapproving scowls and continued. "I ended my affair with Curtis Wilks not because he dumped me like I told you, but because he had embezzled from Affairs by Amanda. I was too embarrassed up until now to admit that or to pursue legal action against him. Tomorrow that changes. I'm going to call an associate of Alex Harper's."

"Amanda, another escapade? Honestly, how do you keep finding trouble?" Her mother's questions raised Amanda's hackles.

"Is a public scandal necessary? You'll cost your mother and me credibility."

"Daddy, I have to do what's right for me, and for once I'd like your support instead of your fault-finding."

Dominique stiffened. "We don't—"

"You do. You refuse to accept that I'm not interested in fashion, and Daddy hates the fact that I'd rather pluck out my eyelashes one by one than read ticker tape all day. Why can't you just accept that I'm good at what I do? Affairs by Amanda is growing steadily every year. I love my job and I'm a success, just not in your chosen fields."

While her parents silently digested her statements, she gathered her courage to lay the big news on them.

"There are a couple of other things you need to know. One, I've fallen in love with Alex Harper."

"That's wonderful," her mother replied with a blinding smile. No surprise there. Amanda had known they'd approve of Alex given his income, lineage, occupation and address.

"Don't get excited. Something has happened to make him distrust me…and there's no guarantee we'll have a future together." She took a deep breath. "I might be pregnant with his baby. And he thinks I got that way deliberately."

Shocked silence greeted her.

"If he won't marry you, you'll terminate, of course," her mother pronounced.

"No, Mother, I won't." She paused to silently reaffirm the decision she'd made in the taxi on the way over here. "I've decided that if I'm pregnant I'm keeping this baby. I want this small part of Alex. I know it won't be easy to be a single parent. But I won't tie Alex to me against his will by trying to force him to marry me. It isn't the right thing to do."

"Do you realize how badly a bastard grandchild will reflect on me?" her father groused.

"I'm sorry if you feel that way, Daddy, but this is not a business decision. This is a personal one. And we no longer live in the Dark Ages. Nearly forty percent of births these days are to unmarried mothers. It doesn't carry the stigma it used to."

Her mother gave a snooty sniff. "That's what people say to your face. Behind your back they say something else entirely. How soon will you know if you are?"

She wasn't going to call them the moment she had the test results. She'd need time to digest them, whatever they were. "Tomorrow morning."

"We want to know immediately," her mother said.

"You'll find out after I tell Alex. He and I are the ones

that matter most in this. Your support would be nice, but you've taught me I can live without it."

And that, she realized, was the lesson she was meant to learn from this experience. She didn't need her parents' approval to live her life.

It was funny how life never delivered the lessons until you needed them most.

A seductive smile replaced the surprise on Chelsea's face seconds after she opened her door to Alex later that Sunday.

"Alex, how wonderful to see you. Come in." She opened the door wider for him to enter. He didn't miss the calculating glint in her eyes. No doubt she was trying to figure out how much she could get out of him this time.

Even on a Sunday afternoon her makeup and clothing were flawless, and she didn't have a hair out of place— a far cry from Amanda, who had dashed out of her apartment this morning makeup-free and wearing jeans and an old Vassar sweatshirt. That didn't mean she hadn't looked mouthwateringly attractive, especially since he knew she never wore a bra under her sweatshirt.

Chelsea, on the other hand, was like Alex, always intense and prepared to close the next deal or wow the next client. Amanda was just Amanda. Relaxed, comfortable, easy to be with. She relied on her natural charm and her warm smile rather than props to win people over. She was someone he should have known he could take at face value without having to worry about ulterior motives behind her smile.

How could he have been blind to those qualities?

He followed Chelsea into her living room. Her cloying perfume filled his nose, making him wish for Amanda's pure scent, not heavy perfume. The difference between the women didn't stop there, he realized as he looked around Chelsea's showplace space and noted many of the pricey antiques she'd purchased, probably with his family's money. Chelsea was the epitome of a material girl. She had always believed in the adage "She who dies with the most valuables wins."

Amanda, on the other hand, had filled her apartment with colors and textures and treasures she'd bought not because of their resale value but because they'd caught her eye. She didn't dress herself or her home to impress others but to please her own taste.

She was genuine and honest, which made her keeping the secret about her late period out of character. The contradiction nagged at him. Why had she remained silent? And why hadn't he bothered to ask before she'd run out instead of just accusing her of having an ulterior motive?

By the time he'd taken Zack back to Greenwich and hashed the situation out with his parents, he hadn't been able to locate Amanda and she wasn't answering her cell phone.

"Did you reconsider making an investment in Auturo? Here's an example of his work." Chelsea gestured to a large abstract oil painting on the wall. It wasn't bad. But it wasn't great, either. He couldn't imagine Amanda liking the muted colors or lack of emotion in the piece. Was it a nude? Was it Chelsea? Could be. Chances were the artist was her latest live-in lover.

"I'm not interested in 'investing' in anything else with you ever again. Zack knows about us, Chelsea. You've lost the leverage to keep extorting money from me or my parents under whichever guise you choose to call it."

She inhaled quickly. "The blackmailer went to the press? Do they know I'm his mother?" She sounded horrified.

"No. But I will go public if necessary. Zack understands the situation and my family is willing to back whatever actions I deem necessary."

"But, Alex—"

"It's over, Chelsea. Don't contact me again unless you want to meet our son. But let me warn you, if you ever do anything to hurt him or make him uncomfortable I will come after you and tie you in so many legal knots you'll never get free. You've held the reins far too long and we've given you too much power. Rest assured, your actions have been well-documented, and you've left enough slack to hang yourself."

Worry tinged her eyes. "You wouldn't."

"You'll find that there's nothing I won't do for the ones I love. Zack. My parents. Amanda. Don't cross me."

He pivoted on his heel and stalked out of the apartment. One problem down. But the most important one loomed ahead.

He had to win Amanda back.

"Hello, Senator," Amanda said as she reached across the window table at the River Café in Brooklyn.

The senator stood and shook her hand. "So glad you could make it on short notice, Amanda."

"I'm happy to accommodate you. Your phone message mentioned an urgent party?"

Coming home to that message intrigued her. When added to an invitation for dinner at a place known for its delicious seafood and impressive view of New York Harbor and the Manhattan skyline, she couldn't say no.

The outing would provide a nice distraction from wondering where Alex was and how his meeting with Zack had gone, and worrying about that blasted pregnancy test that was still waiting for her and if Alex could forgive her for keeping her secret.

Yanking her thoughts back to the present, she took the seat the server held out for her. With her back to the door, she faced the gorgeous view.

Why would Michael Kendrick invite her to the restaurant voted most romantic in New York City? She surveyed the room again, this time with a professional eye. The space could easily hold anywhere from thirty to a hundred, depending on the type of party. She'd yet to use it as a venue, but she'd like to. But why was theirs the only occupied table? And why were there pedestals holding red rose bouquets in every corner? Surely the senator hadn't reserved the entire room for this meal?

A frisson of unease skipped down her nape. She knew he'd recently separated from his wife. Surely he didn't consider this a date? Not that he wasn't attractive, but he'd known her parents for years, and he was...well, old enough to be her father.

"Alex mentioned you were very good at short-notice events, and last night's party proves that statement." Kendrick sat back in his chair. "I have a very special occasion in mind. I'm told you are the only one equipped to handle the details."

A trickle of excitement wound through her. "Thank you for that vote of confidence. What kind of event?"

"I'd rather not say."

Strange. "It will be hard to plan without a few more details."

"We'll get to those momentarily."

She'd dealt with eccentric people before, but until now she hadn't considered the senator to be one of them. She'd thought him straightforward and conservative. But she could play along. She pulled her PDA from her purse. "As long as it's not illegal, I can work with you. What's your time frame?"

"That's where this gets a little bit tricky."

How could it get any trickier than planning an event for which she had no details?

"Excuse me a moment, Amanda, and I'll get that information for you." He rose and left her alone in the private dining room.

How odd. Had he left the data in his car?

Moments later she heard the senator's footsteps return. He reached his seat and she looked up from her calendar. But it wasn't Senator Kendrick standing across the table from her.

A grave, somber Alex looked down at her. Her pulse kicked erratically. He wore her favorite Brooks Brothers suit, charcoal grey with a subtle white pinstripe, a white shirt and a pink tie. Pink? Conservative Alex in pink? Pink might be her favorite color, but she'd never expected to see it on him. "Alex."

"Hello, Amanda." He lowered himself into the chair Kendrick had vacated.

"Where's the senator?"

"I wasn't sure you'd agree to meet me, so I asked Michael to help me out."

She frowned. "Why wouldn't I see you?"

"Because I unjustly accused you of trying to extort money from me and then of trying to trap me. Two strikes."

An unsteady breath shuddered into her lungs and back out again. "Yes, you did, and I won't deny it hurt. But after hearing what Chelsea has done I can understand how you might jump to the conclusion that I'd do the same. I did borrow money from you and use your connections. I have two strikes, too."

"You have no strikes with me. If anything, I owe you for showing me where I've gone wrong. I've been working insane hours trying to regain the power I lost when Chelsea became pregnant with Zack. I believed that being the top dog meant having all the control. But power is useless if the people you care about are not safe and happy."

His eyes searched hers. Keeping his hands in his lap, he sat straight and tense. This wasn't the charmer she'd come to know, the one who could talk her out of her clothes in record time.

"How did it go with Zack?"

"Not bad. We still have some issues to work out, but we should be fine, thanks to the way you explained the situation. As always, you managed to find exactly the right approach and say the right thing. You have a talent for reaching people on their level and for making them see what's important. You put him in my shoes. I would never have thought to do that."

His praise warmed her. "What's going on, Alex?"

"I need you to plan something for me."

She sighed. "You didn't need to go to all this trouble to offer me a job."

"It's a special event. A once-in-a-lifetime affair. Two of them, actually. And I'm giving you carte blanche."

Confused by the tension she read in him, she bit her lip. "I'm going to need a little more to go on than that."

"It's an engagement party followed by a wedding."

Her stomach did a queer little roll. She swallowed. "For whom?"

"Us."

Her heart skidded to a halt and then beat its way up her throat. "Us?"

He lifted one hand from his lap and covered hers on the table. "I've learned the hard way that women can rarely be trusted."

Ouch. She tried to pull away but his grip tightened around her wrist and held fast.

"Chelsea wasn't the only one to work me over for money or my connections."

Double ouch. But she had no idea where he was going with this so she didn't speak.

"I never planned to fall in love or get married."

*What?*

"And then I met you."

She couldn't make her lungs work.

"I've fallen in love with you, Amanda. Any way you look at it we're a damned good team. I want you in my life. Not temporarily. Permanently."

Those were the words she longed to hear, but… "This isn't because I'm late, is it? Because I might not be pregnant."

"This has nothing to do with that. But why haven't you taken the test? Don't you want to know?"

Good question. "I've been stalling because I wasn't sure how I'd handle the answer. I needed to weigh my options and decisions. And I wasn't sure how my parents would handle the news. But you know I finally figured out it doesn't matter what they think. This is *my* life. I get to live it *my* way. And if I make mistakes, it's okay because I'm living it instead of sitting safely on a fence and watching life pass me by.

"I was going to take the test as soon as I returned from my parents' this morning, but the senator's message said, 'Extremely urgent.' I had to dash right back out again."

"And you've made your decision?"

She took a deep breath and slowly exhaled. "Yes. If I'm pregnant, then I want to keep this baby."

He inhaled sharply.

"But, Alex, I would never use a child to tie you down or extort money from you. I have an inheritance from my grandparents coming soon. I won't need financial assistance. Yours or anyone else's."

"If you're carrying my baby then you'll get it anyway. And you'll have me by your side every step of the way. I'd like to raise children with you, Amanda."

The intensity of his voice made the hairs on her arms stand up. "If we got together now I'd always wonder whether it's because of an unplanned pregnancy."

"If we get together and we love each other, does it really matter how it happened?"

She flinched and warmth steamed her face. Had she been completely transparent? "I never said I loved you."

A lazy smile tilted his lips. "You've shown me with your actions, but I was too blind and distrustful to see that before now. I don't need words, but I wouldn't mind hearing them when you're ready."

Her heart pounded faster. "Alex—"

"I want you to plan the wedding of your dreams, Amanda. No limitations. No budget. Whatever you want, you can have it. As long as I'm the man waiting at the end of the aisle for you."

What he said sounded so good she was afraid to believe him. "That sounds like a bribe."

"Do I need to bribe you?" He reached into his coat pocket and then reached across the table. He opened his hand to reveal a blue Tiffany ring box.

Stunned speechless, she stared at the box. Hope fluttered to life in her chest.

"Marry me, Amanda, whether or not we've made a baby together." He lifted the lid to reveal an exquisite pear-shaped pink diamond flanked by two pale lavender tanzanite baguettes.

Pink. Her favorite color. Lavender, runner-up. And Alex hadn't had to ask. He'd taken the time to notice.

"Let me spend the rest of my life showing you how incredibly unique and special you are and why you're perfect."

"I'm far from perfect."

"You're perfect for me."

Her eyes stung and happiness swelled within her until she thought she'd burst with it. "I do love you, Alex."

He rose, came around the table. He took her hand, pulled her from her seat and into his arms. His lips brushed her forehead, her temple and finally her lips in a tender, lingering kiss. "Then say yes."

"Yes." How could she say anything else? Because as Alex had said, they were perfect for each other.

"Let's go home and take that test. After we make love."

She cupped his jaw in her hand, relishing his scent, his nearness, but mostly the love in his eyes. "And if making love takes all night?"

The naughty twinkle made her heart skip. "Then the

test will wait. Because we're going to be together regardless of the outcome."

Alex led her toward the door. Amanda couldn't keep the smile off her face. For the second time, Alex had shown her that she was right where she was supposed to be and with whom she was destined to spend the rest of her life.

\* \* \* \* \*

# THE BILLIONAIRE IN PENTHOUSE B

ANNA DePALO

**Anna DePalo** discovered she was a writer at heart when she realised most people don't walk around with a full cast of characters in their heads. She has lived in Italy and England, learned to speak French, graduated from Harvard, earned graduate degrees in political science and law, forgotten how to speak French and married her own dashing hero. A former intellectual property attorney, Anna lives with her husband and son in New York City. Her books have consistently hit the bestseller lists. She has won an *RT Book Reviews* Reviewers' Choice Award for Best First Series Romance and has been a finalist for the Golden Quill, Golden Leaf and Book Buyer's Best awards. Her books have been published in more than a dozen countries. Readers are invited to surf to www.desireauthors.com, and can also visit Anna at www.annadepalo.com.

Dear Reader,

I was excited to be invited to write the final book in the PARK AVENUE SCANDALS continuity series. It was fun to be writing a story set in my native stomping grounds, New York City, as well as one featuring a British heroine (since I studied in the United Kingdom after college).

I hope you enjoy Jacinda and Gage's story. Jacinda is as daring as I've sometimes wished I was. And Gage—well, Gage can be remote but his outer shell is a cover for hidden depths. Watch Jacinda uncover the seductive man behind the mask!

Enjoy!

*Anna*

For my aunt and uncle,
Corsignana and Michele Dagostino.

# Prologue

*5 months earlier*

He had the lean, uncompromising face of a corporate warrior, the need to conquer stamped on his dark features.

But was he a killer?

Jacinda Endicott absorbed it all. The thick, dark brown hair, the intense brown eyes, and the granite jaw.

He wore a tux that outlined broad shoulders, and negligently held a champagne glass in one hand.

A dapper Cary Grant or George Clooney.

Still, he was unsmiling, nearly brooding even. He stared straight at the camera, a small but inescapable distance separating him from his companions. With his impressive height, he easily topped the couple on his right and the two men on his left.

Jacinda stared at the photo on her computer screen.

Gage Lattimer was enough to jump-start any woman's pulse, she thought, feeling an unwelcome kick in hers and frowning.

The billionaire venture capitalist and CEO of Blue Magus Investments kept a low public profile, but his air of quiet, self-assured power was nearly palpable.

He was the sort of man she could imagine her younger sister, Marie, being attracted to…before their affair had turned deadly.

Her heart squeezed.

It was hard for her to believe Marie was gone. Two weeks now. She kept waiting for the nightmare to end, but each morning, even before she opened her eyes, a feeling of dread coiled in her stomach.

She wondered whether things would ever be right again.

According to police, Marie had jumped from the roof of her swanky Park Avenue apartment building.

A suicide, the cops had said.

But Jacinda refused to believe her pretty and vivacious sister had taken her own life.

No suicide note had been found—and wasn't there almost always a note? Plus, the autopsy had found no drugs in her sister's system.

Jacinda shook her head. It didn't make sense.

Her sister had moved from London to New York right after graduation from the University of St Andrews, propelled by a sense of adventure. Marie had left her immediate family an ocean away, lured by the thrill and glamour of life in the orbit of *Sex and the City*.

In New York, her sister had landed a job as a commercial real estate broker, but had eventually left to start her own firm. With hard work and a sparkling personality, she'd soon netted several lucrative accounts.

And now Marie was dead. Cut down in the prime of life at twenty-five.

Because no matter what the police said, Jacinda knew in her heart her sister hadn't jumped. She'd been pushed.

But the question was, by whom? And why?

Jacinda's first clue had come by chance, when she'd flown to New York with her parents and brother right after they'd received a call from Detective Arnold McGray of the New York Police Department with news of Marie's shocking death.

At her sister's office, she'd met a broker that Marie had hired to work with her, and the woman had mentioned that Marie had been having an affair with a super-rich, powerful loner. Her sister had refused to name the man but had described him as tall and dark, with fathomless dark eyes and an adorable dimple.

Jacinda had latched onto the information. She'd also felt hurt—hurt that Marie hadn't confided in her about the relationship. But then she'd concluded Marie had probably assumed she'd disapprove of the man for some reason.

Of course she'd have disapproved if she'd had any inkling Marie's boyfriend had the potential for murderous violence.

Marie had been a free spirit and sometimes impetuous. She'd dated a guy with a nose ring in high school, and also a rocker with a mohawk.

Even so, Jacinda had never known her sister to choose a boyfriend as unwisely as she might have this last time.

Naturally, she'd gone to the police with the information her sister might have been having an affair. But the police had told her they needed more information—a lot more—to make the leap from a possible lover to a would-be murderer.

So, she'd combed through Marie's possessions… and come up empty-handed. As the police had already noted, there were no strange e-mails and no phone calls to an interesting number. Nothing.

The affair had either been a phantom or extremely clandestine, with a lover cunning enough to remain anonymous.

Desperate, she'd dug deeper, willing to look at anything. And that's when, in her sister's offices, she'd come across Marie's file on Blue Magus Investments.

Her sister had been trying to find new offices for the venture capital investment firm.

Scanning the file, her eyes had alighted on a name, Gage Lattimer, and her sister's neat, handwritten notations in the margin: *billionaire, well-connected* and *reclusive.*

*Rich. Powerful. Loner.* It had been enough.

Back at her hotel, she'd gone to Google and pulled up what little information existed on Gage Lattimer.

Now, Jacinda stared at her computer screen again. Physically, Gage Lattimer fit her sister's description, right down to how he towered over his companions. And though he wasn't smiling in the photo in front of her, she thought she could discern the indentation of a dimple.

He was thirty-five, divorced and eligible.

Through an online, people-finder service, she'd soon discovered Gage lived in a penthouse at 721 Park Avenue. Her sister's last address.

Bingo, she'd thought.

The coincidence had been too much.

For her, at least. The police were a different matter.

She knew she had to come up with more concrete evidence to interest the cops. They'd concluded Marie's death was a suicide, and they'd been dismissive of her claims of a secret affair.

They'd consider her batty now for accusing a powerful, quiet-living billionaire of murder.

Jacinda turned away from the computer screen and looked out her office window. But instead of seeing the rooftops and office buildings of Canary Wharf, London's newer financial district, she saw her reflection in the glass.

A classically pretty face stared back at her. Green eyes—cat's eyes, her mother called them—were fringed by thick, dark lashes, and balanced by an aquiline nose and a mouth with a full lower lip. Her long, curly brown hair was partly caught back by a crystal-studded barrette.

Marie had had similar features, but she'd been two inches shorter than Jacinda's own five-foot-eight.

If the police weren't interested in finding Marie's killer, then Jacinda would unearth the truth behind her sister's death herself. She owed it to Marie.

Her sister hadn't had a chance to embark on her life. She'd never get to travel the world. She'd never be a bridesmaid at Jacinda's wedding or meet any of Jacinda's children. She'd never get married and have children herself.

And, Jacinda thought, her sister's death two weeks ago had given a new immediacy to her own days. Suddenly, she wanted it all now—the husband, the kids, the full life.

What was she waiting for? Who knew how long she'd have on this earth?

She'd thought long and hard about what it would mean to take a leave of absence from her advertising executive position with the prestigious firm of Winter & Baker. But ultimately, with her plan taking shape in her mind, she'd known she had no choice.

She *had* to find Marie's killer. Otherwise, there'd be no resolution. Otherwise, she couldn't move forward with her own life.

Her family, of course, had been shattered by the news of Marie's death. Her parents and brother, Andrew, had been bursting with grief.

They'd been an upper-middle-class family and close-knit. Her parents' small business had generated enough of an income to send three children to well-known boarding schools.

But now Marie was gone.

Jacinda had gone with her parents and brother to retrieve Marie's body from the morgue and fly it back home, so her sister could be buried in the family plot outside London.

Unlike her, however, the rest of the family had reluctantly accepted the police's conclusion that Marie's death had been a suicide, if for no other reason than there was no evidence to the contrary.

But Jacinda hadn't been able to quell the feeling of unease inside her. She'd known Marie. Growing up, they'd been as close as any two sisters could be and, more than any other member of the family, she'd been privy to Marie's dreams and secrets.

There was no way her sister had committed suicide.

Jacinda swung away from the view outside—the office towers shimmering in London's July heat—and looked back at her computer screen.

Gage Lattimer. Was he the key to solving the crime?

Without allowing herself to hesitate, she picked up the phone and dialed the number for Marie's exclusive pre-War apartment building. Through directory assistance, she'd already tracked down the number for the reception desk in the main lobby.

When someone picked up, a man said, "721 Park Avenue."

The voice carried a distinct New York accent, and Jacinda reminded herself she'd have to disguise her own British accent if her plan was to have any chance of success.

She cleared her throat. "Hello. I'm calling on behalf of Gage Lattimer, one of your residents."

"Yes?" The man's voice held a hint of suspicion.

She assumed she was speaking with a doorman who manned the lobby of Marie's white-glove building.

Marie had moved to 721 Park Avenue only last year, and Jacinda had been there once, during her most recent trip to New York, after Marie's death.

At the time, she'd visited her sister's apartment alone and in disguise, because her plan had already started to form and she hadn't wanted to jeopardize it. She'd told her parents and brother that she didn't want to visit Marie's apartment with them because it was too painful to go there so soon after Marie's death.

"Mr. Lattimer will be returning to New York early and would like to contact his housekeeper so the penthouse is ready," she said, making her tone clipped and no-nonsense. "He's arriving with some guests."

"And you would be?"

She crossed her fingers. "His personal assistant."

"And you don't have Theresa's number yourself?"

"No," she responded coolly. "I'm new."

The man grumbled, "Just a minute."

Jacinda held her breath. She'd guessed the building staff at swanky 721 Park Avenue would know how to reach one of their residents' household help, if for no other reason than such contact information would be necessary in case of emergency.

And then, just like that, the man at the other end of the line was back, reciting Theresa's phone number.

"Thank you," she said before ending the call.

Without pausing for breath, not wanting to lose courage, she dialed the number she'd written down and crossed her fingers again.

She was done pretending to be Gage Lattimer's

personal assistant. But with any luck, she'd soon be playing his housekeeper—newly minted American domestic goddess Jane Elliott.

*2 months earlier*

Dropping his overcoat and briefcase onto a chair in the foyer, Gage walked into the vast, loft-like expanse that comprised the main living area of his modern duplex penthouse.

He'd only taken a couple of steps when he came to an abrupt halt—stopped in his tracks by the enticing vision before him.

A pert rear end, encased in low-rise jeans, moved alluringly back and forth and long, shapely legs tapered down to black wedge-heeled sandals.

His gut tightened.

He thought fleetingly that while the sandals were obviously a nod to New York City's warm July weather, at least her wedge-style heels could be considered a concession to practicality.

There sure as hell wasn't anything else practical about her, as far as he'd been able to ascertain.

She was bent over, seemingly feeling—dusting?—the underside of an end table near the fireplace.

A smile pulled at his lips before he suppressed it.

He cleared his throat.

"Find anything interesting down there?" he asked.

She straightened and whipped around, barely missing a solid glass lamp.

He watched as she placed a hand over her thumping heart and swallowed, her eyes wide.

Great, he thought. At least she was getting a dose of her own medicine. He'd been getting that pulse-racing sensation for months.

"I didn't know anyone else was in the apartment!" she exclaimed.

"I just got home."

They stared at each other, and Gage could almost hear the hum of sexual energy in the room.

Gorgeous, he thought for the umpteenth time.

She had the even, symmetrical features of a model, along with big green eyes and a mane of long, curly chestnut brown hair that had him wondering how it would look spread across his sheets.

She was above average in height, but her tall and willowy frame was audaciously balanced by round curves in all the right places.

His gut tightened again, and he wondered what she was doing cleaning apartments for a living. Even aspiring starlets who made their way to New York preferred to wait tables rather than push a vacuum.

It must be that she didn't have any connections and was too naive to exploit the marketability of her obvious assets.

She was a ripe little peach that had fallen into his lap. Except he wasn't picking from that tree anymore. A bitter divorce did that to a man.

Four months ago when his housekeeper, Theresa, had given him two weeks' notice, she'd recommended Jane Elliott for the job. Too busy to give it a second thought, and not wanting the hassle of contacting a housekeeping service and going through a series of mundane interviews, he'd agreed with the suggestion.

Theresa had been a good maid, but when she'd announced she was leaving to care for her sick mother, he'd had no doubt she could be replaced, especially with someone she recommended.

"You're usually not home this early," Jane said, cutting through the thick silence that had enveloped them.

He gave a brief nod. "I took the red-eye back from L.A. last night and went straight to the office." His lips quirked. "I'm short on sleep."

He could feel the strain around his eyes that came with sleep deprivation. In an unusual move, he'd left his Midtown office in the middle of the afternoon.

And yet despite having a demanding career, more often than was good for him he'd managed to come home to find Jane still puttering around the penthouse on one of the three days a week she was there.

He nodded behind her. "The underside of the table needs dusting?" he asked in a deadpan voice.

"Ah..."

The truth was she'd hardly been an excellent housekeeper. He'd invariably discover she'd missed something—forgetting to dust one of the rooms, for example, or not cleaning the hallway bath. It was one of the reasons why, as time went on, he'd offered her some overtime.

And yet, despite seemingly being unable to tell the difference between window cleaning spray and bathroom mold remover, his housekeeper knew her way around gourmet food and high-end entertaining.

During a cocktail party he'd hosted two months ago for some business associates, he'd noticed that she knew which cheese knife to lay out with what type of cheese and that she was familiar with imported wine labels. She'd asked probing questions of and offered knowledgeable suggestions to the caterer for the evening.

He'd liked listening to her husky singsong voice, letting it flow through him like fine, aged bourbon, even as he thought there was something about the woman he couldn't quite place.

Her accent wasn't a New Yorker's. Like a news broadcaster, she seemed to be from nowhere and everywhere.

She was a puzzle. And despite himself, he wanted to fit the pieces together. He wanted to get into her pants.

His lips firmed into a thin line. He'd been burned once, he reminded himself, and as a battle-scarred veteran of the divorce wars, he wasn't about to do something as asinine as getting himself ripped apart again over a pretty face.

Not that the face was merely pretty, he was forced to qualify. It rated as beautiful. Spectacular, even. Enough to make a guy not give a damn whether she remembered to dust his college baseball trophies.

"How did you say you and Theresa knew each other again?" he asked abruptly.

Her green eyes widened. "Theresa and my mother went to high school together."

"Right. I recall now that's what you said."

He stared at her. He couldn't help himself. She was so damn enticing, standing there in her typical work uniform of T-shirt and blue jeans. Today the T-shirt had an interesting green pattern that brought out the color of her eyes. It hugged high, full breasts that drew his attention as if he were a homing pigeon seeking to return to the nest.

He watched as she wet her lips and swallowed.

"I…I'm done in here." She turned to scoop up a disposable dust mitt lying on the couch. "And I'm nearly done cleaning the rest of the apartment. I'll be out of here soon."

After she scurried past him, he turned his head to watch her disappear through the arched entryway of the living room to the back of the apartment.

Damn. He was a masochist. Otherwise, why would he be torturing himself this way?

But who else would be willing to retain a so-so maid with a Gisele Bündchen body? Certainly not the society matrons with claws that prowled ritzy Park Avenue.

And what if Jane needed money?

Still, damningly, he had a disturbing attraction to his *maid.* He should give her a decent reference and dismiss her with a few weeks' severance. Before she really got under his skin.

Just then, Gage heard his cell phone ring and, with a grimace, he reached into the pocket of his pants.

He was reminded of the fact he was working on three hours' sleep, had finally gotten home and had had a chance to do little else but toss his overcoat on a chair and lust after his housekeeper.

A quick check of the screen identified the caller, and then he flipped open the phone. "Reed, good to hear from you."

"You won't be so happy to hear from me once you know why I'm calling," Reed responded.

Reed Wellington and his wife, Elizabeth, lived in the building's other penthouse apartment. The millionaire had been an investor in a couple of the venture capital deals Gage had put together. The mutually beneficial relationship had started when Reed's term on the building's co-op board had coincided with Gage's.

"What's up?" Gage asked, his voice sounding weary to his own ears.

"I'm guessing you didn't check your mail today."

"I just got home." Idly, he scanned the room. Jane usually retrieved his mail and placed it in a bin in his study.

"We're being investigated by the SEC."

He stopped, suddenly alert. *"What?"*

"You heard me."

"For what?" Gage set his jaw, ignoring the sting of sleeplessness at the edges of his eyes.

"The Ellias Technologies stock purchase."

Gage recalled the stock he'd recommended to Reed a few months back. He'd gotten a good vibe about Ellias—a high tech communications company—when he'd read about it in a trade publication. He'd run the name by his stock broker, who'd produced some stats for him to review and who'd agreed it was a good bet.

In short order, his faith had proved well placed. Only weeks after he and Reed had bought a sizable amount of stock, Ellias had landed a lucrative contract to provide the Department of Defense with radio systems.

Except now the Securities and Exchange Commission was sniffing around.

"We've been asked to voluntarily produce documents related to the stock purchase," Reed continued. "I'm sure your broker is being contacted."

"The SEC thinks we may have committed securities fraud?" Gage asked incredulously.

"I believe it's insider trading they're looking at, my friend."

Gage sobered. "You and I have known each other for a few years, Reed. You don't believe I recommended the stock to you based on non-public information I was tipped off to?"

"I trust what you've told me."

Gage felt some of the tension ebb from his shoulders. "Damn it. How much has each of us made off that stock? A hundred thousand or so, maybe? That's a drop in the bucket to people in our position, and it sure as hell isn't worth the headache of an SEC investigation!"

"I know, I know," Reed said, "but tell it to the feds."

"Damn it."

Reed made a sound of dry-humored acquiescence.

"Anyway, why the hell would they even think I acted on an insider tip?" Gage demanded.

"Good question," Reed responded, and then laughed shortly. "You'll never believe the coincidence."

"Spill."

"Guess who I just discovered sits on the Senate committee that green-lighted the Ellias contract?"

Gage's mind worked. He was acquainted with several public officials. Money talked, and with his kind of wealth, there were plenty of politicians who were happy to cozy up.

"Kendrick," Reed stated, not waiting for a response.

Gage cursed.

"Yup," Reed agreed.

Senator Michael Kendrick and his wife, Charmaine, had lived in their building until this past summer. Kendrick had even served a term on the building's co-op board—one that had overlapped with his and Reed's.

Gage recalled that, like a lot of other building residents, he had contributed to Kendrick's reelection campaign.

And now the SEC thought Kendrick had divulged some information about a government contract to him and Reed before it became public.

"It's worse than you think," Reed said. "Forget about the fact that Kendrick lived in the same building. I approached him about providing content for an Internet start-up that's an environmentally focused networking site."

"Damn," Gage said.

Reed's conversations with Kendrick could not have come at a worse time. They would make their connection to Kendrick look even more suspicious.

"I'm suspicious about the timing of this SEC investigation," Reed said.

"How so?"

"Remember the blackmail letter I received?"

Suddenly Gage made the same connection that Reed had. "You think the two are related?"

"Yup."

Reed had received a letter demanding he deposit ten million dollars in an untraceable Cayman Islands account, or else the world would learn the dirty secret of how the Wellingtons made their money.

Of course, the savvy investor had refused to pay. Someone of Reed Wellington III's Old Money connections and aristocratic bearing didn't get pushed around.

Gage would have relished explaining that face-to-face—or better yet, mano a mano—to the bastard behind the blackmail.

Reed had confided in him about the blackmail letter, but Gage had never fathomed the letter would come to this.

It was absurd. Beyond absurd. He had nothing to hide, and he knew Reed felt the same way. It was the reason the two of them had initially chalked up the blackmail letter as the work of some crackpot.

When you were in the billionaire's club, you got used to people trying to shake you down for cash. His ex-wife was a case in point, Gage thought, his lips twisting.

And then there were the drummed-up lawsuits, and even maybe a crazed blackmailer or two, as this case bore out.

It was one of the reasons he kept a fleet of lawyers on retainer.

Crap.

He felt the effects of fatigue and sleeplessness combining into a headache.

"Gage? Are you still with me?"

Reed's voice pulled him away from his racing thoughts.

"Yeah, I'm still here," he replied. "I need to call my broker and the lawyers. Once the SEC investigates, though, they'll discover there's no substance behind their suspicions."

When he signed off on his call with Reed, Gage swung around at a noise from the foyer, beyond the open archway of the living room.

He frowned, and a second later Jane peeked in, craning her neck beyond the limits of the archway.

"Sorry," she said, sounding breathless and looking guilty. "I was dusting a vase and accidentally sent it tottering."

Gage wondered fleetingly whether she'd been eavesdropping, and then dismissed the thought. What reason could she have to care about his personal financial affairs? If she were a criminally inclined housekeeper, she'd more likely be interested in stealing something from the penthouse.

But suddenly Jane's reappearance sent his thoughts traveling in a new direction.

Before he could debate the wisdom of the idea, he heard himself saying, "We need to discuss your cleaning schedule."

An alarmed look streaked across her face, and then she appeared fully in the archway. "Yes? Is there something wrong?"

Nothing but a case of runaway lust. Nothing that a good roll between the sheets wouldn't cure. "I'd like to offer you a live-in position."

Her eyes widened before she recovered. "Er—"

"This apartment comes equipped with maid's quarters, though they've rarely been used. Theresa stayed overnight only occasionally to clean up after a party."

"Oh."

"But I entertain more than usual in December." His lips twisted. "The holidays and all."

The fact was it was almost all business networking. Still, he felt compelled to entertain, even for business, in line with what end-of-the-year festivities called for.

She swallowed. "So the overnight position would be temporary?"

He surveyed her. Depends on how long it takes me to get over this crazy bout of lust.

"Why don't we see how things go?" he said smoothly. "I noticed during the cocktail party a few weeks ago that you did well pinch-hitting in the kitchen, and I have to admit even gourmet take-out gets boring after a while."

Her lips parted. "You want me to cook for you?"

He arched a brow. "Is that a problem? You've got me curious about your culinary skills."

She shook her head. "No. It's not a problem."

He was playing to her strengths. If she couldn't dust, at least she could cook. "It would only be occasionally. I often have dinner out with clients and business associates."

Her brow puckered. "I have a studio apartment—"

"You wouldn't need to give it up," he interjected. "You'd still have days off, though with the holiday season and entertaining, I'd prefer for it not to be on the weekends. How about Tuesdays and Wednesdays?"

Judging from her expression, she was wavering, as if trying to tally the pros and cons of his offer.

"Of course, you'd qualify for overtime pay," he said, sweetening the deal and testing his theory that she might be in need of cash. "Say, time and a half?"

"Your pay is already generous."

"I'm willing to pay for the best," he responded smoothly.

The best domestic help. The best cook. The best model-cum-housekeeper to waft around his penthouse driving him crazy.

"Well…" she hedged.

"Think about it."

She nodded. "Okay."

"Okay, you'll think about it, or okay, you accept?"

Their eyes met and held.

"Okay, I accept," she said.

"Great."

# One

*Present*

She couldn't believe she was continuing this charade, Jacinda thought, as she deposited her overnight bag on the bed and set down a bag full of Christmas decorations next to it.

It was the beginning of December, and she'd been maintaining her pretense for five months.

Five long, wearying months that had gotten her no closer to discovering the truth about Marie's suspicious death.

The only bright spot was that her brother, Andrew, had informed her a couple of months ago that the police had come around to her way of thinking and were now treating Marie's death as suspicious.

But she didn't trust them to ferret out the truth. So, she'd continued to work hard to remember who she was pretending to be and not let her guard down.

It had been difficult to maintain her phony American accent, but fortunately she was a good mimic. A fake ID—procured through a hole-in-the-wall news dealer with a black market business on the side—had done much of the rest.

She glanced around the room. The maid's quarters were located on the lower level of the duplex penthouse, beyond the kitchen. They weren't opulent by any stretch of the imagination, but they were well-appointed with a full-size bed, a dresser and a night table, and an adjoining bath.

She'd gotten used to living here. On days like today, coming back after a day off, she'd cart along some clothes with her in an overnight bag, cycling through the wardrobe she kept at the small studio apartment she'd sublet on York Avenue and Eighty-second Street.

In fact, she thought, it was arguable which was bigger—her entire studio apartment, or the maid's quarters in Gage's 6,000-square-foot penthouse.

Her eyes alighted on the nearby dresser. The only thing the room lacked was a good dusting by a maid—except, she remembered, *she* was supposed to be the maid.

When she wasn't a sleuth.

Since she'd started working for Gage in July, she'd been stymied in her efforts to connect him to her sister's death. She'd discovered nothing going through his programmed phone numbers, rifling through desk drawers and scanning his mail.

Nothing except, she recalled, thinking back to October, she'd almost gotten caught snooping once when Gage had come home unexpectedly early and, in one of her more desperate moves, she'd been feeling along the underside of the end table next to the fireplace.

He'd taken a phone call immediately afterward that had made him frown mightily but, despite her best efforts, she hadn't been able to hear anything significant from the conversation.

Aside from that scanty bit of possibly tantalizing information, there'd been nothing. Absolutely nothing.

Instead, even with the help of a robot vacuum, she'd turned into the world's worst maid. It was hard to play amateur detective and still find time to scrub the sink.

She unzipped her bag and started putting her clothes in the dresser.

It was a miracle she'd convinced Gage's former housekeeper to quit. When she'd contacted Theresa by phone, she'd played dumb. She'd said she was looking for a unique situation because she was used to working with a moneyed and discerning clientele, which was the reason she wasn't going through a traditional employment agency to find a position.

Fortunately, her friend Penelope had been able to provide a sham reference, vouching for her as a fictitional former employer. Her closest friend from school days had married a rich and socially connected viscount and was happy to help by allowing her name to be dropped.

And as luck would have it, Theresa *had* been toying with the idea of moving on. In her early sixties, she was nearing retirement age and had a sick sister living north of the city for whom she wanted to provide care. She had been wavering, debating a move…until an opportunity had landed in her lap with Jacinda's phone call.

Of course, Jacinda admitted to herself, she'd embellished the truth a little bit. After some deft questioning, she'd led Theresa to believe her mother had attended the same Long Island high school as the housekeeper. For Gage, she had stretched the truth even further to make Theresa and the fictitional Barbara Elliott not only former high school classmates but also close friends.

It had all worked out, Jacinda recalled. She'd placed herself close enough to Gage to do some snooping, but she'd also been able to maintain some distance, coming into the penthouse three times a week, mostly when he'd been at work.

And then in October, Gage had stunned her by offering a live-in maid position. Caught off guard, and still feeling flustered by almost being caught snooping and then eavesdropping, she'd accepted Gage's offer.

Later, she'd justified her decision by focusing on how much more time she'd have to keep tabs on Gage and get the cleaning done.

But in the weeks since, she'd lain in her bed at night, awake and restless, knowing Gage slept feet away, his long, powerful body perhaps sliding between the russet-colored sheets she herself had placed on his sumptuous king-size bed earlier that day.

She'd tried telling herself her feelings were natural, caused by tension and alarm at being alone in the same apartment as a possible killer, vulnerable in her sleep.

But the truth was her feelings were simple and undeniable attraction.

Gage was a good-looking guy. Powerful, moneyed and well-built, he'd have been arm candy for any woman, if he wasn't so remote.

He was a typical lone wolf.

And rather than sensing criminality in him, she saw a wariness in his gaze that spoke of past hurt. It spoke to her and made her want to reach out to him as a kindred spirit. Because she'd suffered a personal loss herself. Marie.

She shook her head to clear it.

Her intuition was telling her Gage couldn't be a killer. But was lust leading her astray?

Done with emptying her overnight bag, she picked up her shopping bag full of Christmas decorations and headed to the living room. There, a boxed up Christmas tree and other assorted decorations awaited her attention. She'd had the building staff haul some of it out of Gage's storage unit in the basement yesterday. The rest she'd bought in the preceding days with some of the household money.

Frankly, she'd been surprised Gage owned as much of the mistletoe-and-holly stuff as he did. He struck her as a bit of the "Bah! Humbug!" type, actually. But she supposed when your net worth was ten figures, even a smidgen of holiday spirit amounted to a lot.

She sighed, her mind circling back to her earlier thoughts.

She'd been trying to uncover clues but the wrong ones kept coming her way.

For months, she'd been dusting Gage's baseball trophies—okay, when she remembered to dust his trophies—when what she needed to find was evidence of a more deadly hobby. Like hunting or collecting knives.

Instead, she'd compiled a dossier on Gage that would have made any would-be girlfriend weep with envy.

He housed three luxury cars—a Mercedes, a Lamborghini and a Porsche—in an underground garage, though he relied on a limo and driver most of the time.

He owned a getaway house in Bermuda, which was a couple of hours away from New York City on a direct flight with his private jet, which he kept parked at La Guardia and which he could fly himself with his pilot's license.

The Bermuda getaway was in addition to a house in London's fashionable Knightsbridge neighborhood, and a lodge in Vail, Colorado, where he liked to ski.

His Manhattan penthouse was a study in modern design—all glass and metal and hard edges, with cathedral ceilings, granite countertops and stainless steel appliances. Hand-recognition technology at the front door and touch-screen lighting controls throughout completed the picture.

His artwork was Abstract Expressionism, and she recognized works by Willem de Kooning and Jackson Pollock among those gracing his walls.

His business clothes, mostly custom-made, were from Davies and Son and Benson & Clegg, both long-established London clothiers.

He owned five Rolex watches, all housed in a glass-topped wooden case.

His toothpaste was Kiehl's, and he preferred to shave with an old-fashioned shaving brush.

The list went on and on.

She had all the details—except they weren't the details she'd come here looking for.

Who had killed her sister?

Truth be told, she hadn't even gotten a hint that Gage was interested in hitting on women. On the other hand, at a cocktail party he'd hosted weeks ago, she'd seen a couple of women send speculative looks his way.

And once or twice she'd caught him looking at *her* with hot eyes.

She shivered, remembering, and then focused on the task at hand.

She began to unwrap a glass ornament.

Gage had asked her to buy some because he liked to vary the decor for his annual December holiday party for friends and associates, donating some of the previous year's decorations to charity.

She wished she was going to be with her family back in London as the holidays approached.

Particularly this year. Their first without Marie.

But she'd set herself a task, and if Gage wasn't the killer, then who was? And who would help her find out?

It was the music that enveloped him first. The dulcet tones of Nat King Cole singing "The Christmas Song."

Next came the aroma of baking bread, wafting around him softly and getting his taste buds working in response.

Gage let the door click shut behind him as he walked into the penthouse, his brow furrowing.

He came to a stop at the archway to the loft-like living area, arrested by the sight of a huge Christmas tree standing sentry by the fireplace.

His tree, except this one was well on its way to being decorated with pink and gold ornaments.

He never did pink.

And that's when he realized *she* was humming.

He glanced over to the kitchen area and caught sight of Jane beyond the waist-high granite countertop, her back to him as she bent over the range of his chef's oven, unaware he'd come home.

Unbidden, the cozy scene had him making comparisons to holidays past.

Breaks from his New England boarding school… his parents, civil but distant and all too perfect…the house in Greenwich, Connecticut, decorated up to the chimney but emitting no real warmth.

Unlike the scene unfolding before him.

Damn it.

He set his briefcase down on a glass-and-chrome console table, and shed his overcoat.

"I'm home," he called out.

He felt ridiculous even as the words came out. This wasn't a scene from some TV sitcom of domestic bliss.

On the other hand, something like *Sex and the City* he could deal with. A vision flashed through his mind of Jane in sky-high heels and skimpy lingerie, bracing one leg on his bed and crooking her finger at him, beckoning.

He felt himself getting aroused, and cursed under his breath.

Just then, Jane swung away from the stove, her eyes going wide, a tea towel grasped in her hands.

Abruptly, he was called back from his fantasy.

It irked him that she always looked at him wide-eyed.

He jerked his head toward the tree. "Been busy?"

"Uh…yes. Yes, I have." She came around the kitchen counter, drying her hands and then setting down the towel.

"Do you…" She hesitated. "Do you like it?"

"It'll do."

Her continued wariness, and his damned unwanted attraction, made him brusque.

Her eyelids lowered, concealing the expression in her eyes. "Good."

He sized her up.

Today, she wore sensible black pants, a jade cotton top that stretched over her breasts, and what looked like ankle boots. Her hair, as usual, was caught back with a barrette.

He'd rather see her in silk, cashmere or satin. Her hair loose…

He reined in his wayward thoughts.

She bit her lip as they stood facing each other, several feet apart, squaring off as they often seemed to do.

She gave a nod over her shoulder. "It's potatoes au gratin, filet mignon and fresh bread. I was waiting for you to get home to sear the filets in a cast-iron pan."

She could sear his fantasies, he wanted to tell her.

Instead, he raised his brows. "Sear them in a cast-iron pan?"

He wasn't even aware he owned a cast-iron pan.

Her lips tilted upward at the corners. "It's a cooking trick I learned. Sear and broil."

"You said *filets,* plural."

She blinked. "Yes. They're on the small side and the specialty market on Lex was selling them in pairs—"

"Then you'll have to dine with me."

Her eyes went wide again, as if he'd suggested she strip off her clothes.

Actually, it was an enticing thought.

"Oh, I—"

"That's what they did in medieval times, you know."

"What?"

"Have a taster for the lord of the manor." He allowed a brief grin. "To make sure the food wasn't poisoned."

He pretended to look around. "And since there's no one else, I guess you'll have to fill in as the official food taster, as well as the cook and housekeeper."

She looked flustered. "Are you suggesting I'd poison you?"

"Or allow me to choke on a cloud of dust," he returned, one side of his mouth turning up.

He'd been teasing about the poison and the dust, but as he watched her redden, he sobered.

He needed to remember who he was and who she was. His maid, for Christ's sake.

"It'll be an opportunity for us to discuss the cocktail party I'm planning for the end of the week," he said.

And he hated dining alone. On the occasional night he was home for dinner, his thoughts had always drifted to Jane in the maid's quarters.

He'd wondered what she was doing and had had an unholy temptation to make her keep him company.

But his point about the cocktail party wasn't off the mark, either.

At least as far as household matters were concerned, their relationship had hit its stride.

In fact, he'd gotten used to leaving her notes around the apartment about what he wanted done. *Need shaving cream. We're out of coffee.*

*Feel free to hop naked into my bed.*

He stopped short and rewound. Wrong memory.

Still, despite his overactive imagination, their communications had taken on a familiar rhythm as she'd left him notes in return.

*Leftovers in the fridge. I picked up your suit from the cleaners.*

Almost like love notes. Except not.

They stared at each other.

He started forward, and she simultaneously stepped back.

He reached up to loosen the knot of his tie, and he watched her gaze fix on his actions.

As he moved past her, he murmured, "Smells delicious."

Looks delicious, too, he added silently. And I'm tired of dining alone.

She was out of her mind, Jacinda thought as she cut into her steak.

The tinkle of cutlery against china was the only sound against a background of low Christmas music.

The voice of Bing Crosby singing about a white Christmas drifted around them, since the penthouse was wired for surround sound.

She stole a look at Gage.

He looked freshly showered. While she'd finished making dinner, he'd obviously taken the opportunity to wash up and change into jeans and a crisp, light blue shirt.

If Gage had been Marie's lover, she could well understand what the attraction might have been for her sister.

He seemed like a guy she herself could date, Jacinda conceded. If circumstances had been different.

And while he'd been washing up, she'd worked herself into a mild panic at the thought of dining with him.

She'd contemplated setting the long table in the formal dining room with herself at one end and him at the other, but that had seemed too formal, despite his joke about an official food taster.

She hoped he hadn't read too much into her reaction

to his joke, though her heart had nearly jumped out of her chest when he'd mentioned *poison*.

Sure, if he'd harmed her sister, she'd love to pound him senseless—or at least see him brought to justice.

But she was having more and more doubts these days as to whether he was implicated in Marie's death. And Gage was right. They did have to discuss the details of the cocktail party.

As a result, she'd decided to set plates on the more informal table out in the loft-like living area visible from the kitchen—where they'd have a view of her unfinished handiwork on the Christmas tree and of the fire burning softly in the fireplace.

They sat at right angles to each other—him at one end of the table, and her to his immediate right.

She watched as he took a sip of his wine.

A 1990 California Merlot, if she remembered the wine label correctly.

When she'd first come across his impressive wine collection, she'd run her fingers over the bottles in the rack and thought that she'd have loved preparing meals to pair with some of the vintages she'd spotted.

Little had she known. Definitely a case of being careful what you wished for, since they now sat dining mostly in silence.

Except for the crackle of sexual energy in the air.

"I had my personal assistant send out the invites to the cocktail party a few weeks ago," Gage said, seemingly unaware of her nervousness. "We've got thirty yeses and five maybes."

She nodded. "I contacted a caterer. Someone new."

He raised his eyebrows.

"You'll like them," she went on in a rush, making her voice reassuring. "They were written up in *New York* magazine. Their lamb chops are superb."

"Sampling the goods?"

She felt herself flush. "I had a tasting when I toured their kitchen."

The truth was, she was sometimes at a loss as to what to do with herself during her time off. Besides worrying herself silly about this crazy scheme she'd embarked on, that is. And mourning her sister.

Gage's lips twitched. "I trust you as a food taster."

She wished she could say something.

He put the last bite of steak in his mouth and, after chewing thoughtfully, he said, "Why don't you dress for the occasion?"

She gaped at him. "Pardon me?"

He'd caught her so off guard, her British accent had leaked through. She hoped he hadn't noticed.

He studied her. "For the party."

"Oh." Well, that was better than what she'd initially thought, which was that he was criticizing what she was wearing tonight. How else was a housekeeper supposed to dress?

Still. "Is that a criticism?"

He gave her a veiled look. "No, a suggestion. It'll be a festive occasion. I thought you'd want to blend in."

"I'll be baking brie."

Instead of answering her directly, he nodded over to the tree. "You've been busy."

"But not nearly done," she admitted.

"I'll help."

*Help*. The last thing she needed was an enigmatic, too attractive gazillionaire hanging a wreath for her—even if he owned the mantel in question.

Through the apartment's hidden speakers came the voice of Josh Groban singing about being home for Christmas.

Ordinarily, she thought with a pang, she'd be at her parents' house for the holidays, decorating with Andrew and Marie. Instead, here she was with Gage.

She pushed back her seat, ready to start clearing the table now that they were finished with dinner. "It's my job."

They'd barely finished eating, but nervous energy made her restless.

She reached for his plate, but he moved it away, stalling her.

Their hands brushed, and they both froze.

Her eyes locked on his.

His face was uncompromising, but his eyes radiated dark heat.

She was reminded again he was a powerful man—physically fit and financially out of her league.

He could use his considerable wealth and influence to crush her if he ever found out what she was up to.

A tremor went through her.

"I'll help," he stated again. "I want to."

She sucked in a breath. "Okay."

A short time later, after they'd dealt with the dishes and she'd experienced the tabloid-worthy sight of a billionaire loading his own dishwasher, Jacinda found herself standing before the Christmas tree contemplating where to place her next ornament.

She watched as Gage bent forward to hang a pink Christmas ball, and let out an involuntary sigh.

He stopped and looked at her. "Something wrong?"

"Nothing."

When he looked unconvinced, she said reluctantly, "I was contemplating that spot."

He gestured in invitation. "Be my guest."

"You give in faster than either of my siblings."

The words were out of her mouth before she could give them a second thought.

"You grew up with siblings?"

"A brother and a sister."

"And you fought over decorating the tree?"

"Sometimes," she admitted. "But you don't show any signs of someone who had to fight for territory."

"That's correct. As far as siblings go."

If everything she'd read about him was true, Jacinda thought, Gage didn't concede an inch in business.

"No siblings?" she asked, though she knew the answer.

"None."

She nodded at the tree. "And you're a decorating amateur, too."

"Correct again." He looked at her archly. "Is that your way of saying I'm doing a bad job?"

"You're handling the ornaments gingerly," she said, sidestepping the issue. "As if you're not quite sure how to do this."

His lips quirked up at the edges. "And here I thought I was doing all right, given how many pink ornaments there are."

She felt herself flush.

Okay, she'd gone a little overboard in adding to his expensive and tasteful collection of Christmas decor.

But as a consequence, she'd seen again that he could be charmingly funny when he let his guard down.

"I couldn't help myself," she said apologetically. "I picked up a few pink ornaments."

"A few?"

"A minuscule portion of your net worth, I'm sure." The words popped out of her mouth before she could stop herself.

His lips twitched. "Do you have a thing for pink?"

Her chin came up, and she informed him with mock importance, "Pink is the new navy-blue."

He arched a brow. "You're kidding? I must not be reading enough *Cosmo*."

"Women are comfortable enough to wear pink these days," she said. "They don't feel compelled to dress like men. Pink is power. It's breast cancer awareness, among other things."

For a moment, she felt as if she were back at work, giving a presentation on market trends and successful advertising campaigns.

She wore pink in her other life as an ad executive. But he wasn't supposed to know about that existence.

"I thought a pink and gold theme would be refreshingly different."

Of course, it would, she thought. The rest of his

apartment was like the king of the jungle's lair. Black and glass and uncompromising male lines.

He looked at her bemusedly. "Right."

She stepped off her soap box. He was the boss, after all. "If you don't like it, I can always change…"

He looked at the tree, and then back at her. "No, I don't think so," he said blandly. "Let's try something different."

"*Refreshingly* different," she corrected him.

"Right. How could I forget?"

"So why don't you tell me why you're such a tree-decorating novice," she said despite herself.

"The staff always put up the tree in my parents' household," he admitted. "Everything was already done by the time I came down from boarding school."

His childhood didn't sound as if it had been made up of marshmallow memories.

"What boarding school did you attend?" she asked, though she knew the answer from her research.

"Choate."

"Oh, I know—"

She cut herself off. *I have an ad client who went there.* But she wasn't supposed to be too familiar with New England prep schools. Then again, at least she hadn't called them *public schools,* in the British way.

"You know…?" he prompted.

"It's in Massachusetts, isn't it?"

He nodded. "I sit on the board of directors."

Of course. "They must think highly of you."

She'd discovered he sat on many corporate boards as a venture capitalist with money sunk into numerous and far-flung enterprises. He was always flying off to one place or another.

"School was sometimes more family than family," he said.

Nope, not a single marshmallow memory, it sounded like. "I'm sorry."

"Don't be," he said. "It's just a fact. My parents weren't bad parents. They were just older, and they insisted on a formality that was true to their generation."

She glanced back at the tree. Perhaps she should have maneuvered to dine with him weeks ago instead of hiding out in the maid's quarters. She felt as if she was finally noticing the seams in the facade of Gage Lattimer.

She cleared her throat as she hung up her ornament in the spot he'd conceded to her. "Are your parents still living?"

"Yes. They retired to a chalet in Switzerland five years ago." After a moment, he hung up his ornament in a new spot.

She longed to ask where in Switzerland, because she'd gone skiing with friends in the Alps a couple of times, but she held her tongue.

Perhaps it was the Christmas music, or maybe it was being far from home at the holidays, but she had to battle the urge to reach out to him.

She took a deep breath, deciding to take the bull by the horns. She *had* to ask him about Marie's death.

She'd run out of options, and her snooping hadn't gotten her anywhere. She was desperate.

"Have you enjoyed working here?" he asked abruptly, surprising her.

She clamped her mouth shut, and stared at him.

He looked almost as surprised as she did by the question. And almost as uncomfortable, too.

She picked up another ornament from the box she'd set down on a nearby table. "Wouldn't anyone enjoy living in an enormous penthouse in the heart of Manhattan?" she said flippantly, before knitting her brows and deliberately lowering her voice. "Of course, there have been some strange happenings."

He stilled. "Such as?"

She forced herself to look at him directly. "I heard there was an apparent suicide a few months ago." She paused. "A woman jumped from the roof?"

He frowned. "Where did you hear that?"

"Oh, you know," she said, waving the hand with the ornament. "One of your neighbors, I guess, was talking in the elevator."

His expression smoothed. "Yes, it was tragic."

"Did you know her?" Did you sleep with her?

Please God, let it not be him. Suddenly, it was crucial to her that Gage not be the one.

"She was my real estate broker."

She forced herself to play it cool. "Oh?" She looked around. "I thought you'd lived here for a number of years."

"I have. I didn't hire her to find me an apartment, but for new offices for Blue Magus."

"And that was your only connection to Marie Endicott? Was that her name?"

"You sure have a lot of questions," he said, his tone half-teasing.

She shrugged. "Simply curious."

He hung up the ornament he was holding, and then turned back to her. "Yes, she was my broker. Nothing more. But after she died, I temporarily pushed back finding new offices for my firm for a number of reasons."

"Oh." Relief washed through her.

"Why are you so curious, Jane?" Gage added in a low voice. "Do you want to know if I'm involved with someone?"

She hated to admit she did. "Are you?"

"No."

*You have me hypnotized…*

"Are you?" he asked.

*…so hungry for you I'm desperate for relief.*

"No."

He moved closer, and she forgot to breathe as he picked up a strand of her hair and toyed with it.

The air hummed as her lips parted and her eyes lowered to his mouth.

He had chiseled lips. And yet they looked soft, as if they could give and receive infinite pleasure.

"Jane."

She sucked in a breath…and then a second later, it hit her.

*Jane.* Not Jacinda. *Jane.*

What was she doing? She was living a lie.

She stepped back. "I—I have a phone call to make."

It was a lame excuse, and she could see from the expression in his eyes that he saw right through her.

She turned and bent to drop her ornament into its box.

And then she fled, driven by conflicting emotions that threatened to engulf her.

She had arrived in New York wanting to hate Gage Lattimer. But since then she'd had doubts about his guilt. And the whole matter had been clouded by her physical attraction to him.

If Gage wasn't responsible for her sister's death, maybe he could help her—if she could keep her attraction in check.

Except there was no way she could risk telling him how she'd tricked him, was there?

# Two

"*Andrew!*" Jacinda said. "H-how are you?"

Jacinda juggled her packages as she trudged along East Seventy-third Street.

When her cell phone had rung and she'd recognized the number as her brother's, she'd felt compelled to pick up.

No use letting her family worry about her any more than they already did. They had enough on their plates. Jacinda knew her mother was still seeing a grief counselor.

"I could ask the same thing about you," Andrew responded. "How are you doing?"

"I'm fine."

She'd maintained the pretense for her family that

she was in New York taking a sort of break, winding up Marie's affairs and giving herself some breathing room from work to come to terms with Marie's death in her own way.

Jacinda hurried across the street as a cab honked at her. When she reached the opposite curb, she looked up at the sky. It was an overcast and chilly day. It reminded her of London weather, actually.

"Have you heard anything more from the police?" she said into the phone, in part to deflect attention from the dangerous topic of what exactly she was doing in New York.

She relied on her brother to keep her up to date on the police investigation. She didn't want to call the police herself from a local number and raise questions about her presence on this side of the Atlantic. And she most assuredly did not want the police calling her on her cell when Gage might be around.

"It was the reason I gave you a ring, actually," Andrew responded.

"Oh?" She perked up as she rounded the corner onto Park Avenue. The trees along the avenue's center divider were decked out with holiday lights.

"I spoke to the detective on the case this morning," Andrew said. "Detective McGray."

Jacinda remembered that Detective Arnold McGray had made the first contact with her family in the immediate aftermath of Marie's death, when police had ruled it a suicide. But because she was already hatching her plan to go undercover, she'd taken care not to meet the man in person.

"And?" Jacinda asked. "Don't keep me in suspense."

"It seems there have been a number of attempts to blackmail residents at 721 Park Avenue."

"What?"

"You heard me. Some residents have gotten demands for a million dollars or more. And the police think the blackmailer may also be responsible for Marie's death."

"How long have the police had this theory?" she asked, her voice sharpening. "Surely they didn't just discover that a number of people were being blackmailed."

"They put the blackmail schemes together with Marie's death a while ago," Andrew replied, "but they only saw fit to mention it to me now."

To Jacinda, it was yet another sign the police were being slow and desultory in their investigation of Marie's death.

Still, she forced herself to keep walking despite feeling weak-kneed. "Do they have any idea who might be behind it all?"

"No, except since all the crimes involve residents of 721 Park Avenue, they think it's someone who's familiar with the building. Also, there was no one signed in on the doorman's visitors' log from the night of Marie's death."

Jacinda squeezed her eyes shut. This whole thing was getting bigger than she could manage. Their murderer might also be a blackmailer.

And then she had a sinking feeling in her stomach. *Gage.*

This could be the crucial bit of information that

ruled him out as a suspect—which meant she'd been barking up the wrong tree these past months.

A billionaire didn't have any need to blackmail people for a paltry million.

What was she going to do?

If only she could recruit Gage, she thought, her mind racing, not really thinking rationally.

If Gage was innocent, then he could be a valuable ally in her quest to find the perpetrator.

Gage had the money and the resources. The power and the influence.

*Power.*

Actually, it had been Gage's potent masculine allure that had made her feel most unsafe these past several months, when she'd found herself more and more doubting Gage could have been involved in Marie's death.

Jacinda remembered their encounter of a few nights ago in front of the Christmas tree, before Gage had thankfully left for a few days on a business trip.

Gage's gaze had rested on her, and she'd fled from the room, feeling a heat that had had nothing to do with the crackling fire.

But their sexual attraction only added complications to an already complex brew.

She'd tricked him. She'd approached him under false pretenses, masquerading as a maid with a contrived American accent and a phony background.

Something told her that a prominent and savvy guy like Gage wouldn't take well to discovering he'd been duped.

She winced.

"Jacinda? Are you there?"

"Yes." She glanced up at the green street sign at the corner. She was nearing 721 Park Avenue. "But I must ring off. I'm at my destination."

"Okay, but keep in touch," her brother responded. "And, Jacinda?"

"Yes?"

"Take care."

If only her brother knew. "I will."

After ending her call, Jacinda automatically stopped by Park Café, an upscale coffee shop at the corner of Gage's building. She did a quick scan of the shop, and noticing nothing significant, sighed and went to the counter to place her order.

When she'd first arrived in New York, she'd taken to dropping into Park Café as a way of observing Marie's neighbors. But none of them had aroused her suspicions.

She'd also struck up a conversation with the principal barista, who had recollected that Marie would stop by for a latte but hadn't recalled seeing her with anyone who looked like a date.

Even so, these days Jacinda continued to drop into the café sometimes before she went to work, hoping against hope that something interesting would turn up.

Today in particular, she acknowledged, she'd walked in hoping to win the proverbial lottery to get her out of her current mess. If only she could get a clue that led to Marie's killer, she could go to the police and then immediately leave the city before Gage was any the wiser about her deception.

But today wasn't going to be her lucky day, as a quick search of the nearly empty shop had revealed.

At the counter, Jacinda greeted the barista and placed an order for hot chocolate. She needed a comfort drink after the news that Andrew had imparted.

She realized resignedly that she was committed to a course of deception with a man who was likely innocent while she continued to search for Marie's killer. Her position as Gage's maid gave her a reason to hang around 721 Park Avenue without arousing suspicion, and that was even more crucial now that the police believed Marie's death was perpetrated by a building insider.

After collecting her hot chocolate, Jacinda exited the café and headed toward the entrance of 721 Park Avenue.

She acknowledged the doorman, Henry Brown, and then stepped inside the building.

Immediately, she was met by yapping dogs, causing her nearly to spill her drink.

After taking a moment to compose herself, she said, "Hello, Mrs. Vannick-Smythe."

She'd never warmed to the building's grande dame, and certainly not to the woman's shih tzus, who seemed to bark at everyone.

Mrs. Vannick-Smythe gave her the ghost of a smile, before commanding, "Louis, Neiman, down."

After a moment, the twin white shih tzus ceased their barking and sat back on their haunches.

Jacinda smiled gratefully at the older woman, but in return, the building's grande dame simply stared at her piercingly.

As usual, Mrs. Vannick-Smythe was dressed in a tailored suit, her silver hair cut in a sleek bob that accentuated her pale blue eyes.

If Jacinda had to hazard a guess, she'd say today's suit—a cranberry wool number with gold buttons—was either Chanel or St. John.

Jacinda shifted from one leg to the other. Mrs. Vannick-Smythe and her dogs always made her feel as if they could scent an imposter in their midst.

"Well, I'd better get to work," Jacinda muttered, and then marched to the elevator and stabbed the Up button.

Fortunately, the elevator arrived just moments later, and she stepped inside.

A man stepped into the elevator with her before the doors closed.

Jacinda groaned inwardly as she got a look at him.

Sebastian Stone, otherwise known as Prince Sebastian of Caspia. Her brother's old preparatory school classmate.

He remained tall, dark and good-looking, with strong patrician features.

She'd known Sebastian Stone was living in this building—Andrew had mentioned it after Marie had died. But Jacinda had made it her job to find out which apartment and what he looked like these days, so she could avoid him and any questions about what she was doing at 721 Park Avenue.

And fortunately, until today, she'd managed to avoid running into him. She knew he'd been out of the country for significant periods because she'd gotten chummy with his apartment sitter, Carrie Gray, who was now married to another resident, media scion and former playboy Trent Tanford in 12C.

But it looked as if her luck where Prince Sebastian was concerned had come to an end.

She just hoped now that Andrew hadn't shared any photos of her with Sebastian whenever they'd recently been in touch.

When Prince Sebastian looked at her quizzically, she tensed.

"Pardon me if I sound rude," he said, his voice betraying the hint of an accent, "but do I know you?"

"Ah…"

The man stuck out his hand. "Sebastian Stone."

Jacinda gulped and stalled.

Sebastian looked puzzled, but continued to hold out his hand.

"I'm not a resident here," she said in her best American accent, avoiding his eyes. "I'm the cleaning lady for Penthouse B."

She hoped she sounded suitably deferential and, more importantly, inconsequential.

"Oh?" Slowly, Prince Sebastian withdrew his hand. "I could swear—"

"You've probably noticed me around the building before," she muttered.

Out of the corner of her eyes, she watched him nod.

"That must be it," he said, though he sounded far from convinced.

When the elevator doors opened on the twelfth floor, and Prince Sebastian blessedly moved forward, she exhaled.

"Have a nice day," he said.

"Yes, you, too," she managed, stabbing the elevator's Door Close button as he stepped out.

Come on, come on.

When the doors closed, she sighed with relief.

Running into Prince Sebastian seemed par for the course. Today was *not* her day. First the call with Andrew, then Vivian Vannick-Smythe and now running into Prince Sebastian.

Her situation was getting more and more precarious—despite her glib assurances to Andrew.

What else could go wrong?

Then she remembered Gage's cocktail party was that night.

"Happy holidays!"

Gage smiled as he leaned down for a kiss on the cheek from Elizabeth Wellington.

"Right on time," he said, knowing the cocktail party behind him was getting under way and the musicians had just struck up another holiday tune.

"We brought a vintage Cabernet with us," Reed said, holding the bottle out to him as he stepped into the apartment. "Courtesy of the Wellington wine cellar, of course."

"Thanks." Gage gave Reed a meaningful look full of humor. "I'll put it in the pantry. I'm sure Jane will be able to use it for cooking one dish or another."

"Doesn't your own wine serve that purpose?" Reed parried. "I've been trying to elevate your tastes."

Elizabeth shook her head with mock resignation.

"Stop it, you two. It's the season for goodwill toward all men. Let's make merry."

"Ho, ho, ho?" Reed put in.

Ignoring her husband's dry humor, Elizabeth turned to Gage. "Thanks for inviting us."

Gage smiled. "I'm glad you could make it, since having a new baby is a lot of work."

"Don't be silly," Elizabeth replied. "You're just across the hall from us, after all!"

"The truth is," Reed joked, "I had to tear her away from Lucas, even though he was in good hands with the babysitter."

Elizabeth looked at her husband fondly.

Gage knew the Wellingtons were in the process of adopting Elizabeth's orphaned eleven-month-old nephew, Lucas. They carried a new aura of contentedness about them, particularly Elizabeth, not only because of Lucas but because she had recently announced her pregnancy.

Gage stepped aside. "Come on in. Some of our neighbors are already here."

"Don't tell me you invited Vivian Vannick-Smythe?" Elizabeth murmured as she passed him.

A smile played at Gage's lips. "Had to," he murmured back. "But don't worry—her dogs are at home."

"Thank goodness."

Gage looked up and noticed Jane approaching them.

His eyes swept over her hungrily, but he was quick to veil his expression.

She was wearing a sleeveless black cocktail dress that skimmed her lush curves. Her hair was swept up in a loose style, and black pumps revealed legs that could make a man whimper.

He felt his body tighten.

He was pleased she'd taken his suggestion to dress up a little for the evening. At least, he flattered himself that she'd dressed with him in mind.

Ever since their near-kiss days ago, before his latest business trip to Chicago, he hadn't been able to get her out of his mind.

In fact, he'd been suffering the tortures of the damned.

*How does a guy go about seducing his housekeeper?* It was a ridiculous question, really. It made him feel like some latter-day Regency lord tempted to take advantage of the backstairs maid.

On the other hand, he rationalized, they were both adults, and why should he give a damn that she was his maid?

After their moment in front of the Christmas tree, he knew their attraction was mutual. He knew he hadn't mistaken the light of awareness in her eyes.

He should just seduce her and be done with it. Get her out of his system, and move on.

He'd get another housekeeper. And she— Well, she could go on to conquer the billboards and catwalks of New York, if she wanted to. He'd help her.

Ever since his divorce, women had come and gone, but with everyone, Gage had been clear from the beginning that all he could offer was a no-strings affair. He wasn't one to lose his head or his heart—not anymore.

Of course, he hadn't dated anyone in over six months. Since before Jane arrived, now that he thought about it.

And after seeing the way Jane was dressed tonight, Gage thought that his seduction idea had even more appeal.

When Jane reached them, she looked from Reed to Elizabeth, a smile curving her lips. "Would either of you like a drink?" She nodded behind her at the two bartenders who had been hired for the evening. "I'd be happy to fetch you both something."

Elizabeth smiled with genuine warmth. "Hello again, Jane. Did you have a chance to visit the new specialty market on Second Avenue that I suggested to you?"

"I'm glad you did suggest it, actually," Jane responded. "Thanks to my trip, I made my first soufflé in ages."

Elizabeth slipped her arm through Jane's. "You have to tell me all about it." She looked up at Gage over her shoulder. "You don't mind if I steal away your housekeeper, do you, Gage?"

"Not at all."

Gage watched the two women move off.

He was called back from his thoughts, however, when he realized Reed had said something.

"What?" he asked.

Reed chuckled. "You didn't even hear what I said."

"Now that you mention it…"

Reed tossed him a droll look. "I said, she looks great, doesn't she? Those legs?"

Gage's brows pulled together. "Aren't you happily married?"

Reed laughed again. "It didn't even occur to you I might be referring to my wife, did it?"

*Damn.* "Forget it, Wellington."

The last thing he needed, Gage thought, was to be giving the impression that he wanted to hit on his housekeeper.

Even if it was true.

Reed seemed willing to change the subject, because he sobered a little. "Well, at least we don't have that insider trading investigation by the SEC to worry about anymore."

Gage nodded. "You got that right."

The Securities and Exchange Commission investigation back in October had unearthed an e-mail that had implicated one of Senator Kendrick's aides and two of the senator's associates in insider trading.

There had been no evidence tying Gage and Reed, to anything, so the SEC had dropped them from its investigation.

Good for him and Reed, Gage thought, bad for Senator Kendrick.

Senator Kendrick had declined his invitation to tonight's party, and Gage supposed it was because the man currently had the scent of scandal on his hands.

Gage watched as Reed's lips twitched again, and he looked at the other man inquiringly.

"And, one more thing," Reed said. "Don't worry about Elizabeth poaching your housekeeper."

"Why would I worry about a thing like that?"

Reed shrugged with nonchalance, but Gage wasn't fooled.

"From the way you were looking at Jane," Reed

said, "someone might think more was going on between you than stain removal and dust busting."

"Getting it on with my housekeeper?" Gage said in a tone of deliberately exaggerated disbelief, this time ready for the gibe. "I don't think so."

His fantasies were another matter, however.

"The way she's dressed, she looks more like a hostess than an employee," Reed observed.

"I suggested she dress up for the evening," Gage replied evenly. "She deserves most of the credit for tonight's success. Why shouldn't she enjoy it?"

Reed just raised his eyebrows before he sauntered off. "I think I'll go check on what sorry excuses for wine you're serving tonight."

"Do that."

As Reed walked away, Gage looked down at the wine bottle in his hand, and his lips twisted wryly.

A 1996 Cabernet. Trust Reed to make a statement.

He decided to walk it over to the kitchen, and soon thereafter, other past and present residents of 721 Park Avenue arrived at his door.

Trent Tanford and his wife, Carrie, came in the door steps ahead of Amanda Crawford and her fiancé, Alexander Harper.

In short order, his newly arrived guests were mingling with Vivian Vannick-Smythe and others in front of the Christmas tree, while the hired wait staff walked among them with hors d'oeuvres.

And as the evening progressed, Gage observed that Jane had apparently made friends when he hadn't been looking.

Of course, his neighbors had come to his parties in the past. But this year, since Jane seemed to be on friendly terms with nearly everyone, it seemed more like a gathering of friends.

Gage's gaze settled on Jane as she encouraged Steve Floyd, one of his business clients, to sample the smoked ham and other dishes that had been set out on a nearby table.

Steve appeared completely charmed and, in no time, seemed to be flirting with Jane.

Gage's eyes narrowed as he experienced a kick in the gut. If he hadn't known Jane would end the evening at his place, he'd have been tempted to go over and break up Steve's little tête-à-tête.

He was still tempted. But he didn't need to give Reed any more ammunition that he had it bad for his housekeeper.

But, Jane had certainly infiltrated his life, Gage reflected. Even his clients were falling under her spell.

The question was, how long would she stay out of his bed?

# Three

As the evening wore on for Gage's holiday cocktail party, Jacinda found herself standing next to Gage among a group of past and present 721 Park Avenue residents.

She thought the party was going exceedingly well. And Gage seemed to be enjoying himself, too. Well, except for when she'd caught him frowning while she'd been speaking to Steve Floyd.

Glancing around her now, she noted that Elizabeth and Reed Wellington were standing in an informal little circle with her and Gage, as well as Carrie and Trent Tanford, and Amanda Crawford and Alexander Harper.

Jacinda had made it her business to get friendly with as many people as possible at 721 Park Avenue— except for Sebastian Stone—in the hopes she'd pick up some clue about her sister. Unfortunately, she'd gotten nowhere.

Everyone had concurred that Marie's death had been tragic. Not surprisingly, those of her neighbors who had known Marie better had remembered her as an upbeat, energetic young woman. But when Jacinda had suggested that perhaps there was a boyfriend or significant other who was mourning Marie's death, no one could remember seeing her with a regular date.

Jacinda hadn't even gotten any good information from the doormen—not even the most regular of them, Henry Brown, who'd been rather tight-lipped about the whole issue of Marie's death, as if gossiping went against his porter's code of discretion.

"Are you expecting anybody else we know to show tonight?" Trent Tanford asked, breaking into her thoughts.

Gage shook his head at Trent. "Max and Julia Rolland had to decline my invitation because Julia is due to give birth any day. They're holed up at home."

"Julia can't wait for the baby to be born," Amanda chimed in. "I spoke with her this morning and she swears all she can do is waddle like a penguin at this point."

Jacinda knew Julia and Amanda had been roommates in Apt. 9B until Julia had married in July—shortly after Jacinda's own arrival in New York—and moved out of the apartment.

And then last month, Jacinda had noticed Amanda sporting an engagement ring. When she'd inquired, Amanda had confessed to being engaged.

"I invited Senator Kendrick," Gage added, "but he'll also be a no show."

Jacinda was familiar with the name. She recalled Marie had been volunteering with Senator Michael Kendrick's reelection campaign. She'd seen flyers in her sister's apartment and office.

"I didn't know you were friendly with the senator," she commented to Gage.

Gage glanced at her, and then leaned in to add for her ears only, "I don't socialize with him, but I added him to the guest list for tonight to keep up an important connection."

Jacinda nodded, feeling a tingle down her spine at Gage's nearness.

"What about Prince Sebastian and Tessa Banks?" Carrie asked.

"They also sent their regrets," Gage replied. "They're flying out to Caspia tonight for a few days to continue arranging their upcoming wedding. Because of Caspian business, the prince and his bride have been forced to delay the ceremony till spring."

Jacinda knew from the newspapers that society tongues had wagged when it had been announced in September that the Caspian heir to the throne would be marrying his American personal assistant.

"Speaking of weddings," Trent said, giving his wife a smile, "I hope you've all received mine and Carrie's wedding invite for New Year's Eve. We're tying the knot again—this time with a church wedding."

"Twice in one year?" Alex Harper joked. "You've got nerves of steel, man."

"We're doing it right this time," Carrie put in as Trent gave her a quick squeeze. "It'll be a big evening wedding, instead of a more impromptu affair."

"Congratulations," Jacinda murmured.

The *New York Post* had belatedly published photos in early August of Trent Tanford nuzzling and holding hands with her sister at hip Manhattan nightspot Beatrice Inn. There'd been dark speculation by the media and even the police.

But Jacinda had known they'd been barking up the wrong tree. Marie had confided to her that she'd gone out a couple of times with the renowned playboy when she'd first moved into 721 Park Avenue, but nothing had come of the dates. And when Jacinda had combed through her sister's possessions after her death, she'd been unable to locate any evidence that Marie had continued her relationship with Trent.

Instead, Jacinda believed what Marie's coworker had told her—that Marie had been seeing a super-rich, powerful loner whom she refused to name.

Moreover, Trent Tanford wasn't a loner. He'd been a world-class playboy for whom women came and went until his marriage in August to Carrie, who'd been apartment sitting for Prince Sebastian.

Marie had in all likelihood been nothing more than one in a long series of women with whom Trent had amused himself.

And on top of it all, Jacinda had seen evidence of Trent's playboy ways herself when she'd begun working at 721 Park Avenue. She'd run into Trent more than once with a different woman on his arm.

Of course, later on in August, she'd been surprised by Carrie and Trent's sudden and unexpected marriage. Jacinda knew Carrie had taken a dim view of Trent's antics. Even so, she hadn't felt close enough to the other woman to ask her about swiftly tying the knot.

"Do you think you'll be able to attend on New Year's Eve, Gage?" Carrie asked.

"Planning to," Gage responded with a smile.

"And who knows?" Reed put in with a sly look. "Maybe Gage will surprise us and bring a date."

Gage quirked an eyebrow at Reed, and Jacinda caught Amanda smiling at her.

Jacinda looked down into the glass she was holding.

Did Gage's neighbors suspect something was going on between her and her tight-lipped billionaire employer? If so, wouldn't they be surprised to discover her true identity!

"It's so nice to have some good news in this building, after Marie Endicott's tragic death last summer, poor girl," Elizabeth commented.

Jacinda suddenly tensed.

"The police think it was foul play," Reed said. "But they're still looking for the missing videotape of the roof from the night in question."

"Of course, they think it's foul play!" Amanda put in. "They know someone has tried to blackmail us, and, of course, Julia. Something fishy is going on."

Jacinda supposed the building residents around her were comfortable discussing the blackmail schemes amongst themselves because they'd all been targets.

"The police investigation has been frustratingly slow," Carrie noted.

Silently, Jacinda echoed those sentiments. She'd had her own issues with the police.

"Detective McGray is overworked and underpaid," Elizabeth said, "and he's the one looking into both the blackmail and Marie's death."

Gage nodded. "They'll get to the bottom of it soon."

Over Gage's shoulder, Jacinda noticed Vivian Vannick-Smythe slip away from the party and head toward the front door.

She'd hardly had a chance to say anything to the older woman all evening, but she supposed it was just as well. What would they have to talk about anyway? She'd always gotten the uncomfortable sense Vivian could see through her facade.

"Unfortunately, I need to leave," Amanda said, checking her watch. "I'm working with a new client tomorrow who's throwing a big bash at the 21 Club next week." She looked at Jacinda and winked. "Great party. If you're ever looking for a new line of work, let me know."

"I'll do that," Jacinda heard herself respond. She felt like such a phony.

Soon thereafter, the other guests began to take their leave, and Jacinda went back to the kitchen area to supervise the caterers and bartenders as they cleaned up.

At some point, she looked up to see Gage chatting at the front door with a couple of the lingering guests—Carrie and Trent Tanford. And a little while later, she noticed Gage assisting in the winding-down effort by helping the musicians put the furniture back to rights after they had broken down their equipment.

Not for the first time, she reflected that Gage was surprisingly down-to-earth for a billionaire to-the-manor-born.

And again the thought made her smile.

Half an hour later, however, she found herself feeling less relaxed.

The last of the hired staff for the evening had just departed, and she was alone with Gage.

Christmas music played from the speakers in the apartment, and she could see Gage in the kitchen, fiddling with a bottle of wine and a corkscrew at the kitchen counter.

He looked up, and she swallowed against a suddenly dry throat.

"Well, I'm going to head to bed," she said.

*Bed.* Wrong word. Especially since she'd been having shocking and recurring thoughts of Gage and a bed for too long.

Gage's lips twisted into a smile. "Stay and have a celebratory drink with me for a party well-done."

"You don't need to thank me," she said, wetting her lips. "It's my job."

"Okay," he responded agreeably, "so let's say instead we're having one last one for the road."

"We're both sleeping here," she pointed out. Together but in separate beds.

"So we are," he replied with another easy smile. "But it's a big penthouse, and it can be a long walk back to the bedroom."

She was defenseless against this new charming and flirtatious Gage.

"Okay," she heard herself say.

Gage picked up the uncorked wine bottle in one hand and two glasses by the stems in the other. "Come sit on the couch."

The couch? She was in trouble.

"I saved the best for last," Gage said as he came around the kitchen counter.

"What?" she squeaked.

He looked at her innocently. "My best wine label."

"Oh, right."

How silly of her to think he'd meant anything else…

Outside, the lights of Manhattan twinkled back at them, visible through the draped French windows of Gage's living room.

Inside was another matter, Jacinda thought. As the sound of Johnny Mathis filtered through the apartment, she was much too tense to play in a winter wonderland. She was too aware of Gage's long, lean body settling down next to her on the couch, after he'd handed her a wineglass.

"Good party," Gage said. "Congratulations."

She took a sip of her wine to ease her nerves. "It's easy to throw a good party when you have an almost limitless budget."

His eyes crinkled in amusement, his dimple showing. "I wouldn't say limitless," he demurred. "And the party was some work. Don't sell yourself short. I just hope you enjoyed yourself a little, too."

"I did."

He tilted his head. "Yes, I saw you speaking with Steve Floyd."

A smile rose to her lips. She hadn't had a date since…well, since before Marie's death. It had been nice to forget her troubles for a moment and allow an attractive man to flirt with her. Plus, ever since starting her masquerade as a maid, she'd had a soft spot for anyone who treated the hired help well.

"Steve's wonderful," she said. "He's got the most outrageous only-in-New-York stories."

"Don't like him too much," Gage replied. "Steve's a notorious love 'em-and-leave 'em type."

"And you're not?"

The words were out of her mouth before she could stop them.

He looked at her meaningfully. "Sweetheart, I haven't had a date since before picnic blankets dotted Central Park last summer. In case you haven't noticed, I've been traveling a lot in the past few months. Work's been…well, work."

The word *sweetheart* shimmied down her spine in a bold caress, and then hot pricks of awareness zipped through her.

Was he flirting with her?

As if in answer to her question, Gage cocked his head. "You know you intrigue me, Jane."

"Do I?"

Gage nodded thoughtfully. "You're obviously skilled and knowledgeable, and you have a keen mind. Why be a housekeeper?"

Before she could answer, however, he looked her over. "How old are you?"

"Twenty-nine."

And he was thirty-five, as she'd discovered while compiling her dossier on him.

"You've got your whole life ahead of you," he said.

Yes, she thought. Unlike Marie, who'd had her life snuffed out.

She felt her heart squeeze, and sudden emotion clogged her throat at the thought of her sister.

It was the holidays, and she was hundreds of miles away from her remaining family, on a mission that had so far gotten her nowhere.

She cleared her throat.

"Maybe I'm a bit of a free spirit," she said with forced flippancy. "I get to live in an ever-changing series of luxurious homes that are well beyond what I could afford on my own."

Her response sounded convincing to her. She hoped he thought it was, too.

Before he could respond, though, she turned the conversation in a safer direction.

"What about you?" she asked. "You're working hard. You admitted you haven't had a date since before summer."

He took a sip of his wine. "Ah, but that's the result of having had a taste of betrayal that's not easily forgotten."

She wondered whether he was referring to his ex-wife. If he'd had a taste of female treachery, what would he think of her masquerade?

He added, "So, you could say my situation is more

a deliberately chosen path rather than an aimless wandering."

"Ah."

He bent forward and set his wineglass down on a nearby surface.

Then he turned and took hers from her suddenly nerveless fingers and set it down beside its companion.

When he turned back to her, she sucked in a breath at the look in his eyes.

Her heart beat faster as he leaned forward and cupped her face in his hands.

"W-what are you doing?" she asked.

"Making another deliberate choice," he murmured against her mouth. "It looks like my path's led to your door. Consider this the kiss hello."

Her eyes closed as his mouth settled over hers. His lips stroked in a slow, sensual greeting.

The kiss sent tingles of awareness shooting through her.

His fingers combed through her hair, cupping her head and bringing her closer.

Her mouth opened to him, letting him take the kiss deeper and stoke the attraction between them. He tasted of wine, and she picked up a scent that was warm and all male.

Jacinda thought hazily that she hadn't felt this good in a long time. She leaned into Gage and sighed, feeling her nipples harden.

Eventually, Gage slowed the kiss down, lightening his touch, and when they broke apart, Jacinda became aware of the heavy, rhythmic beat of her heart.

"Let's just grab at some happiness," Gage murmured against her mouth, his eyes heavy-lidded.

Why not?

They were the first words to spring into her head.

She was having a hard time remembering why she should resist her attraction to him. She was almost certain now that Gage wasn't the perpetrator of her sister's murder or of the blackmail at 721 Park Avenue.

The truth was they were two souls alone and lonely at the holidays.

And she'd fought so hard against her attraction to Gage for the past several months. Why deny herself some comfort now?

She gave the barest nod of her head, and it was all the encouragement he needed.

And then they were kissing again, with renewed urgency this time.

Her arms moved around his neck, and he pulled her forward across his lap.

His tongue entered her mouth, encouraging her to mate with him in an erotic dance that was a precursor of another.

She couldn't get close enough to him. She felt his erection against her and shifted even closer.

Being in his arms was a surprising oasis of light and calm in a world that had been topsy-turvy for the past six months.

She felt herself floating up, carried on the wings of pleasurable sensation, as she shed all the troubles that had been shackling her, weighing her down, for the past half year.

He slowed enough to toy with her mouth.

"Gage," she breathed.

His eyes were hooded, dark with desire.

"Yes," he said huskily. "Sweetheart, let me pleasure you. I've been wanting to for so long."

His words thrilled her. "Yes, Gage."

He stood and swung her up into his arms.

"What are you doing?" she asked, her voice breathy.

"Taking you to bed," he responded in a tone rough with desire. "My bed."

Yes.

In the background, Dean Martin crooned "Baby, It's Cold Outside."

Yes, it was a cold world out there, but here, inside, she was sheltered in Gage's arms.

He carried her up the stairs to the penthouse's upper level, and all the while she reveled in the strong, steady beat of his heart against her.

When he reached the upper floor, he strode along the corridor and kicked open the door to the master bedroom, and then deposited her next to the bed.

Jacinda had been inside Gage's bedroom dozens of times, and now the impressions came back to her without effort. Recessed lighting, polished wood floors, and modern furniture. A large bed resting on a mahogany platform. Five-hundred-count luxury French linens.

Gage stepped behind her, and Jacinda felt little shivers of awareness dance along her skin.

Gently, he moved her curtain of hair aside so that it rested over one shoulder, the back of his hand caressing the side of her neck as he did so.

And then his hands closed over her bare shoulders, and he trailed moist kisses from the base of her neck to the hollow behind her ear.

She moaned, and her head fell back, giving him better access.

When he nipped her earlobe, and then blew softly in her ear, hot sensations shot through her.

She leaned back against him.

"Easy," he breathed.

She felt him find the zipper that started at the back of her neck, and then listened to it rasp downward as cool air hit her back.

She trembled.

"Cold?" he murmured.

She wanted to tell him it was what *he* was doing that was giving her goose bumps.

Before she could react, however, the gas fireplace along the wall behind her roared to life, and she realized he must have hit a switch somewhere.

He pushed the dress off her shoulders and it pooled at her feet, around her black pumps.

She felt vulnerable…and excited.

His hands trailed over the indentation of her waist, smoothed over the curves of her thighs and then caressed her stocking-clad legs.

Eventually, they wandered back up to cup her breasts, and she felt his erection press against her again.

He trailed the tips of both index fingers along the top edges of her black demi-bra cups, and then underneath, along the underwire.

She didn't have the most voluptuous of figures, but he made her feel wild and wanton.

"Ah, sweetheart," he said. "You tempt me."

*And he made her ache.*

When he finally cupped both breasts, she sighed and then savored the feeling of him stroking and kneading them.

As if sensing her complete capitulation was near, he nipped her earlobe, and then ran the tip of his tongue along the delicate shell of her ear, rocking against her from behind.

His hands stroked over her body, igniting a fire as they went.

She groaned and reached up behind her to cup the back of his head and draw him closer.

He nuzzled her neck. "So good."

"Mmm…"

Her legs felt rubbery, as if they'd give way at any moment.

His hands smoothed down over her hips, taking her underwear with them. And then one hand splayed across her abdomen while the other cupped her intimately.

She moaned and shifted, affording him better access as her eyelids lowered.

His fingers played in her moist heat, making her dizzy with passion.

"Gage, I don't know how much more I can take."

"We're just getting started."

"That's what I'm afraid of." Lava flowed through her veins.

He gave a low chuckle. "Step out of those naughty give-it-to-me heels."

"Is that a demand?" she asked breathlessly.

"Take it however you want it, sweetheart, but know the chase is over."

She did as he asked, and then pulled off her thigh-high stockings, as well.

He reached to the middle of her back and unclasped her bra. As she lowered her arms, the garment slithered to the floor, and he turned her around.

She watched as his heated look traveled down her body and then back up to meet her eyes.

"You're beautiful...and sexy as hell."

He made her feel beautiful. Instead of replying, however, she bunched her fist in his white shirt front and pulled him toward her.

She kissed him with all the passion he'd stoked in her.

At first, she tasted surprise in his kiss, but it was quickly replaced by an intense ardor.

When they finally broke apart, they were both breathing deeply.

She kicked off her shoes, and everything—shoes, dress and underwear—went sliding across the polished wood floor.

He picked her up then and laid her on the bed, and she savored the feeling of being cradled in his arms again.

When he straightened, standing at the foot of the bed, he made rapid work of his own clothes, his eyes glittering down at her, full of passion and fire.

His movements were clipped, rough, as he unbuttoned his shirt and yanked it off. His undershirt came up over his head, and he tossed it aside.

She soaked in the sight of him shirtless, admiring the defined muscles in his arms and chest.

He undid his watch and tossed it on the bed. Then his hands went to his belt, and once he'd removed it, he kicked off his shoes and socks and lowered his black trousers.

Her breath hissed in as she took in the sight of him in black banded briefs.

But suddenly he looked beyond her, toward the other side of the bed, and frowned. "Damn it, I don't remember where I put protection."

"Second drawer, night table on the right," she replied.

She knew where she'd last seen some condoms. She was familiar with everything about his apartment.

Gage studied her, and then his face broke into a grin, his dimple showing through. "I knew there were benefits to sleeping with my housekeeper."

She arched a brow. "Done it before?"

He grinned again. "Sweetheart, you're my first."

He looked boyish and carefree, so different from his usual, guarded self that her heart flipped over.

She watched as he reached over and pulled open the nightstand drawer, searched inside for a moment with his hand and then pulled out a foil packet.

When he turned back to her, he tore open the packet and she sat up on the bed and reached for him.

Without waiting for an invitation, she pulled down his briefs and let his erection spring free.

She watched as the muscles of his stomach tensed, and then she reached out and began to stroke him.

The breath hissed out of him, but when she looked up to meet his gaze, his hooded eyes were full of lambent fire.

"Sweetheart, ah…"

Moments ticked by, and his breathing grew more harsh, fevering her own arousal.

Finally, he grasped her wrist and stilled her.

He quickly donned the protection and tossed the foil wrapper aside.

As she leaned back, he stretched out on the bed beside her.

Her hands played over the muscles of his shoulders and back while he caressed and kissed her.

When she was desperate for him to take her, however, he surprised her by moving her to her side and shifting behind her, spooning her.

Hooking her upper leg over his, he tested and found her moist heat. As she gasped, he nipped her neck and then slowly slid into her welcoming warmth.

"Gage…" Her voice trailed off as liquid fire suffused her. This position was new to her.

His hand stole around to touch her from the front, making her experience every exquisite sensation in a burst of color.

He slid in and out of her, and they both moaned with every brief joining.

Jacinda had never gotten aroused so quickly, had never experienced such a rapid and heady spring to complete abandon.

"Give yourself to me," Gage murmured.

His rough words were her undoing, and she flowered for him, moving against him, in a sudden burst of energy.

Her long, drawn-out moan made his muscles tense.

He gripped her hip and his fingers flexed as he drove into her with a harsh groan.

Moments later, they both sagged against the mattress.

It was then that the notes of "Have Yourself a Merry Little Christmas" reached her, and tears sprang to her eyes.

# Four

He woke up feeling sated.

No, even better, Gage corrected himself as he opened his eyes. He felt content.

And it was all due to Jane.

He glanced over at the other side of the bed—which was empty.

Jane had already gotten up, which was quite a feat since he was an early riser himself.

Raising his head, he noted the clock on the bedside table revealed it was half past six. And since he could smell coffee brewing, Jane must already be getting breakfast ready.

Gage settled back against his pillow and stretched.

One thing was certain in the clear light of day. He

should have given in to the attraction between him and Jane a lot sooner.

He'd never cared what other people would think of him sleeping with his housekeeper. He was rich enough not to give a damn, and long past the point of needing social approval.

And Jane was genuine—the real deal. Unlike so many women he knew. Unlike his ex-wife, for example.

Now, he didn't know why he'd fought against the attraction to Jane for so long.

Turning his thoughts in an even more pleasant direction, he contemplated whisking Jane off to his hideaway in Bermuda for the forthcoming weekend. They could both get a respite from Manhattan—which overflowed with tourists during the holiday season—and escape to a balmy climate.

He wondered what Jane would say to the plan, and then grinned. At least he wouldn't have to worry about her work schedule. He'd be more than happy to give her a few days off to get away from it all with him.

With that thought, he rose and threw on some sweatpants.

When he padded downstairs, he discovered Jane in the kitchen, her back to him and talking in a low voice into her cell phone.

It was apparent she hadn't heard him come down.

His gaze swept over her, and he felt the kick of arousal.

She must have found some clothes in her room because she was dressed in a knee-length satin robe. The robe, however, did little to hide her assets. Instead, it showcased an hourglass figure and outlined a rounded bottom.

Her hair tumbled over her shoulders, and slim, shapely legs seemed to go on forever.

Desire slammed into him.

He wanted to take her again right here, right now.

Then a couple of her words reached him, and abruptly he frowned.

He was standing a few feet away, and he realized he didn't recognize the voice she was using.

Her accent was…British.

He stepped closer.

"Do the police know anything else about Marie's death?"

Gage stilled.

"It's so frustrating. I know our sister didn't take her own life."

Gage's eyes narrowed. What the hell did Jane mean by *sister?*

She was obviously talking about Marie Endicott—the broker whom he'd hired and whose death the police had ruled suspicious.

But if Jane was Marie's sister, why hadn't she said anything?

His mind zipped through the possibilities, and he didn't like any of them.

And as his suspicion grew, so did a simmering anger.

It was looking like he'd been taken for a ride. By a woman. Again.

He must have made a sound, because suddenly Jane whirled around, her eyes wide.

Shock flitted across her features, but was quickly replaced by alarm.

Gage would have thought the reaction was comical, if he hadn't been at the receiving end of it.

"Andrew, I must go." She spoke into the receiver, but her eyes were fixed on him.

As soon as Jane ended her call, he didn't wait for an invitation.

"Who the hell are you?" he demanded.

Her lips parted. "I—"

He could practically see the wheels turning in her head, as if she was trying to guess how much he'd heard and come up with something to say.

The realization only made him more furious.

"Wait, I know," he said sarcastically, answering his own question. "You're Marie Endicott's sister."

He watched as Jane went pale. Except, he realized, he wasn't even sure anymore that her name was Jane.

She seemed to come to some kind of resolution, and her chin lifted. "My name is Jacinda Endicott."

"Nice British accent," he commented. "Now, mind telling me what the hell you're doing playing maid?"

She squared her shoulders. "I can explain, if only you'll let me."

Under other circumstances, he might have admired her bravado. But this situation hit too close to home. He'd let her get under his skin, damn it.

He folded his arms. "This ought to be good."

She took a deep breath. "I came here because I knew from the beginning my sister couldn't have killed herself. But I was desperate because the police had ruled it a suicide."

She spoke quickly, as if she believed that at any moment he'd give her the boot from the apartment. In that, he acknowledged, she wasn't too far off.

"What does this have to do with me?" he demanded.

"I decided to take matters into my own hands—"

"By posing as a maid in the building so you could do some snooping?" he finished for her.

She hesitated, then nodded. "Yes."

She looked vulnerable and sexy as hell. Even now, he couldn't help his instinctual reaction to her effortless sexuality.

"Why me?" he demanded. "Out of all the residents in this building?"

"I discovered you and Marie had known each other," she admitted in a low voice.

He nodded curtly. "Right. She was my real estate agent. I was impressed by her energy and hired her despite the fact that she was young and relatively inexperienced."

He watched as Jacinda bit her lip.

"I thought you and Marie were…involved."

Realization dawned, and with it, his anger kicked up a notch. "Are you telling me you suspected I had something to do with your sister's death?"

When she nodded, he stared at her disbelievingly.

He'd trusted her, damn it.

"You slept with me and all the while you thought I had something to do with your sister's death?" he asked incredulously.

"I'd ruled you out by that point," she said, her voice suddenly heated.

"Oh, yeah? How? By finding the killer?"

"Aside from being a client, I couldn't find any evidence linking you to Marie!"

"Great, just great. I've been legit with you from the beginning and, all the while, you've been playing detective."

She hugged herself. "The longer I looked without turning up anything, the less likely it was you were the...one responsible."

His lip curled. Apparently she couldn't bring herself to say the word *murderer*.

"I've searched Marie's apartment," she went on, "and so did the police, to no avail. I've also been to my sister's old office, where her coworker took over the lease and is still running a real estate business. Nothing."

He'd heard murmurings through the building grapevine that Marie's old apartment on the sixth floor hadn't been sold yet. Now he knew why. Jacinda was still hoping for clues.

"So that's what you were doing when you forgot to dust the bookcases or scrub the sink around here," he accused, piecing it together. "And here I was wondering why you were a maid instead of an aspiring starlet, like everyone else in New York. I didn't know you were already putting your acting skills to good use!"

She started, a guilty look on her face, but then continued determinedly, "Yesterday I got a call from my brother in London, who's in touch with the police. He told me about the attempted blackmails in the building, and how the police's new theory is that an insider was behind both the blackmail and Marie's murder."

He arched a brow.

She dropped her arms. "I knew you couldn't be a blackmailer. You don't need the money. It didn't make any sense!"

"And do you also know I was a victim of one of the blackmail plots?" he asked icily.

She shook her head, looking at him helplessly.

"Oh, yes, indeed," he said, his voice dripping sarcasm. "Reed Wellington was blackmailed, and when he refused to pay, it appears someone went to the Securities and Exchange Commission with the false story that he and I had benefited from an insider stock tip."

They stared at each other.

His jaw hardened. "I should fire you on the spot."

He could fire her, but, he acknowledged, he couldn't as easily eradicate her from his life. Her scent was on his skin. Her stamp was on his apartment. She'd infiltrated the inner sanctum of his life.

"How did you get Theresa to recommend you?" he demanded, having a perverse urge to know all the details, now that her secret was out.

She opened her mouth, and then hesitated.

"Don't even think about not telling me the whole deal," he ordered.

She stopped, blinked, her brow furrowing. "I got a friend to provide a false reference, and I let Theresa think my mother had attended her high school alma mater on Long Island."

"Clever." He didn't mean it as a compliment, and

she seemed to know better than to acknowledge it as such.

"I was going to tell you..."

"Sure," he snarled. "And should I assume last night was about softening me up for your pitch?"

He had the satisfaction of seeing her turn pale again.

"Last night, when Marie's death came up, you said nothing," he said, his voice clipped.

"I wasn't going to tell you who I really was in front of half the residents of the building!"

"And all that stuff about being a free spirit," he went on, his lip curling. "It was all a pack of lies."

Alarm and then guilt crossed her face.

"It's actually a bit of a family trait," she said, barely above a whisper.

"The free-spiritedness or the lying?"

She blanched, and his jaw tightened.

"Why the hell would you make the leap from Marie being my real estate broker to thinking I had something to do with her death?"

He couldn't get himself to say *murderer*, either.

She looked close to tears. "Marie was having an affair. She was so closemouthed, I only discovered it after her death, from one of her coworkers. Marie had described the man as a very rich and powerful loner. Someone who was tall and dark, and had a noticeable dimple."

"And from that you concluded the man was *me?*" he said incredulously.

"I thought it was the perfect cover. The phone calls ostensibly about finding new real estate for you when in reality—"

"We were conducting a clandestine affair?" he said in disbelief. "Did it ever occur to you that where there's smoke, there may not be fire?"

"I know it sounds batty now—"

"It's off the wall!"

"—but I was overcome with grief at losing my sister. I knew she didn't kill herself."

"And that's your explanation for lying and deceiving me?" he demanded. "For coming here under false pretenses?"

"I need your help," she pleaded.

He admired her audacity, while her nerve infuriated him.

He spread his hands. "Sorry, can't help," he bit out. "Until recently, I was a suspect, remember?"

"I don't know where else to turn," she said, her voice tinged with desperation. "The police now think Marie's death is suspicious—"

"So I've heard."

"—but they don't have any leads."

"Yeah," he taunted, "and if you'd come clean about who you were, maybe we'd have linked Marie's death to the blackmail schemes earlier."

"Would you have listened to me?" she flung back at him, and then shook her head, as if answering her own question. "No, I don't think so. Even the police were maintaining Marie's death was a suicide."

Would he have listened to her? The truth was, he let himself acknowledge, he'd have been leery of another blond bombshell with an agenda.

He contemplated her. She was supplicating, on the point of begging him, really.

She was also the woman who'd made sweet, passionate love with him mere hours ago. The woman he'd let his guard down with.

And despite his best intentions, he wasn't unmoved by her plea. He still wanted her.

He cursed under his breath.

Then he realized that while he might still want her, she *needed* him. And with that, an idea started to form.

He wiped his face clean of emotion—the way he often did with an adversary across the bargaining table.

"You need my help," he said calmly.

She nodded, her expression wary.

"I could lean on the police, use my contacts—"

She nodded again. "Yes, exactly."

"For a price."

Her eyes widened.

"I don't have anything to give," she said, startled. "If it's money—"

"No."

She shook her head. "I make good money as an ad executive, but nothing on the order to tempt a billionaire." She paused. "What do you want, then?"

"You," he said flatly. "I want you."

She sucked in a breath. "What?"

"You heard me," he said, his voice hard. "I want you in my bed."

She looked astounded. "You want to buy me...like an investment property or an art object?"

"I prefer the term *mistress*," he said dryly.

Her mouth opened and shut.

"Are you married? Engaged? Steady boyfriend?" he asked brusquely.

She shook her head.

Some of his tension ebbed. "Well then, there should be no problem."

"You can't be serious!"

"You want my cooperation, that's my price. Of course, I'll hire a cleaning service to take over maintenance of the apartment."

Their eyes locked, and several taut moments passed.

Finally, she said in a low voice, "I'm willing to do whatever it takes."

His gaze swept over her. "Oh, sweetheart, you have what it takes."

And then he decided to give her a taste of what to expect.

He reached out and pulled her into his embrace.

He took in her wide, startled eyes and parted lips before his mouth crushed hers.

The kiss was hard and unyielding. A stamp of possession neither of them could mistake.

Her soft curves pressed against him, making him want, making him burn.

His tongue swept into her mouth, and fireworks erupted, just as they had the night before.

But after a moment, he let her break free.

She stepped back, and covered her mouth with her hand.

They stared at each other and moments later, she lowered her hand.

"Make no mistake," she said. "You'll get my body, but that's all you'll get."

She brushed past him, and he turned and watched as she fled toward the back of the penthouse.

Toward the maid's quarters, where she no longer belonged.

Crossing a billionaire had been even more ghastly than she'd expected, Jacinda thought, still in the process of straightening up the kitchen counter.

It was past ten in the evening, and she was restless. Gage had left a note this morning saying not to bother with dinner for him because he'd be meeting a business associate.

She found it lonely, rattling around by herself in an apartment that was bigger than many homes.

Outside, the city lights twinkled, and inside, the Christmas decorations cast a warm glow.

Most visitors to New York would be enjoying themselves right now. It was the season when thousands of tourists flocked to the city for holiday shopping and shows, filling restaurants and hotels, and spilling into the streets and onto double-decker tour buses.

But Jacinda knew her feelings had nothing to do with the season, and everything to do with a certain billionaire.

She squeezed her eyes shut for a moment as she remembered her confrontation with Gage two days ago.

She'd made a mess of things. She'd gone about it all wrong from the beginning.

She should have confessed to Gage who she was before he'd found out himself in the worst possible way.

She winced as she thought back to how angry Gage had been.

Then again, she tried telling herself, even if she had come clean, Gage would have been just as furious at being duped. The only thing she could have hoped for was that when she begged for his help, he would have been swayed a little by the fact she'd come forward by choice.

She placed a couple of pots back in the cupboard.

As it was, she'd bargained with the devil.

*I prefer the term mistress.*

His words came back to her, reverberating in her mind, as they had for the last forty-eight hours.

She'd sold herself in exchange for his help.

"Billionaire's mistress." She tried out the title on her tongue.

Never, never, never in her wildest dreams would she have thought she'd acquire that title. But then again, six months ago, she hadn't known any billionaires.

If only her friends and colleagues could see her now.

Of course, her family would be aghast. One daughter dead, and now the other a kept woman.

Her family would think she was out of her league with Gage Lattimer—which was, of course, true.

*Gage.*

She couldn't believe his cold-bloodedness.

He'd propositioned her with cool calculation.

She could well understand now how he'd made hundreds of millions betting on and trading in start-up companies. He had a quick, analytical mind, true, but he was also one cool customer.

While she'd been doing her best not to fall for him these past months, he'd apparently been unmoved. As soon as her real identity had come out, he'd switched to propositioning her, without missing a beat.

She was mortified...and angry.

Oh, she knew she wasn't an innocent party herself, but even though her head was telling her to be rational, her heart couldn't help feeling hurt.

Had their night of passion meant nothing more to him than a roll between the sheets with the hired help? Apparently so, since he'd handed her a take-it-or-leave-it offer.

And she'd had to take it. She didn't have much confidence in the police cracking this case—at least not without help and outside pressure—and she was willing to do whatever it took to see that Marie got justice.

She *needed* Gage's money, power and influence.

But more than that, the most damning thing was she didn't mind as much as she should going back to Gage's bed.

Their night together had been a revelation. She'd never felt such a swift, overpowering attraction to a man before. A man who had proved to be an expert, imaginative lover.

She heated up as images from their night of passion in Gage's bed flashed through her mind. After their initial coming together, they'd woken up and had sex once more. Gage had caused responses from her body that she didn't know it was capable of.

She was glad now, however, that she'd vowed to close her heart to him. He might get her body, but he wouldn't get anything else.

Fortunately, he hadn't pressed the matter since their confrontation. She'd gone back to the maid's room and stayed there.

It was as if he sensed they both needed a cooling off period—like two boxers going back to their corners.

Or more aptly, like two lovers recovering from a spat.

As if conjured by her thoughts, she heard the front door click and turned to see Gage step inside the apartment.

He stilled when he spotted her, and then proceeded to shed his coat.

"We're going to Bermuda," he announced without preamble.

Her lips parted. She'd expected more of the cool distance of the past forty-eight hours. Not this.

He deposited his coat and briefcase on a nearby chair.

"First thing in the morning," he elaborated as he moved toward her. "I have a house there."

Of course, she knew that. She knew all about his various and far-flung real estate holdings.

"Ever been?"

She shook her head.

His lips twisted in the semblance of a smile. "Well, don't worry. You'll feel right at home. They drive on the right side of the road, like in London."

Of course, she knew. Bermuda was a British territory in the Atlantic.

He stopped on the other side of the kitchen counter. "Where's your luggage?"

She found her voice. "It's at the studio apartment I sublet on York Avenue."

He nodded curtly, as if absorbing an additional detail about her and her elaborately planned masquerade of the last few months.

"You can use one of my suitcases," he said.

"I don't have much here appropriate for Bermuda's warm weather."

His lips twisted again. "Don't worry. You can buy stuff when we get there and charge it to me."

She felt herself flush at the reminder of the arrangement she'd agreed to. "Why are we going?"

He looked at her penetratingly. "Because I've been working too hard, and I need some R & R."

She wondered what else he needed besides rest and relaxation, and she could tell from the look on his face he knew where her thoughts were heading.

She schooled her features, refusing to give him the satisfaction of knowing he'd rattled her. "And how are we getting there?"

"My jet. From La Guardia. You could say I'm driving."

Of course. She knew he had a pilot's license.

"I see."

"Don't worry," he added, his voice mocking. "There's also a copilot and a skeleton crew."

She finally felt a rise of anger. "That's not what I'm concerned about. I thought you were going to help me solve my sister's murder."

"And I thought *you* agreed to becoming my mistress."

"Yes, but not to jetting off to Bermuda," she replied.

"Worried about the Bermuda Triangle? Don't fret, sweetheart. I've flown through it a couple dozen times. You're in good hands."

"Oh, of course," she retorted. "I mistakenly assumed this was a plot to get rid of me."

He flashed her a mirthless smile.

"What I meant is," she went on coolly, "how are we going to solve anything if we're in Bermuda?"

"I've already spoken to the police. Detective McGray."

She stared at him in surprise. "What? When?"

"From work." He looked at her mockingly. "You didn't expect I'd have you sitting nearby, listening in on every word, did you?"

Damn him. "What did you tell him?"

"Nothing about your little masquerade." He added dryly, "I doubt McGray and the NYPD would appreciate knowing you've been encroaching on their territory by playing detective."

She supposed she should be thankful to him for not betraying her. But the words stuck in her throat.

"I informed Detective McGray that I've taken a very personal interest in the Marie Endicott case," he elaborated, seeming to have some mercy on her, "and I want it solved. I don't care how many detectives they need to throw at it. I also let it slip I'm good buddies with the mayor, the police commissioner and everyone in between."

Her shoulders lowered as some of her tension ebbed.

Gage shrugged. "I contribute generously to political and charitable causes in the city."

"Thank you for your help," she said huskily.

He nodded curtly, and then moved by her toward the stairs.

"Sweet dreams, Jacinda," he said. "I'm looking forward to our trip."

As Jacinda watched him go, she thought he might as well have said, *I'm looking forward to having you uphold your end of the bargain.*

Any other woman would have been thrilled at the prospect of jetting off to an island paradise with a good-looking, virile billionaire.

Not her, she told herself. Not under these circumstances.

Life had a quirky sense of humor, she acknowledged, even as, at the same time, she felt an odd flutter at the thought of a romantic idyll with Gage.

# Five

He was a bastard.

And the one thing about piloting your own private jet for a couple of hours, Gage thought, was that it gave you plenty of time to dwell on just what a bastard you were.

He stared out the cockpit at the endless sky before him, checking monitors and controls regularly as he did so. His copilot—one of the private contractors who often worked for him—had stepped back into the cabin for a brief break.

But Gage knew his fiftyish copilot would be back soon. In a short while, they'd begin their descent to Bermuda.

In the meantime, he could sit back and try to enjoy flying. Usually he loved the sense of freedom that came with it. He thrived on it, in fact. It was a brief respite from feeling tethered to his numerous responsibilities.

But, on this trip, there was one responsibility he *hadn't* left behind.

She was, in fact, sitting in the cabin behind him, no doubt contemplating the bargain she'd struck.

Jacinda.

He was still getting used to her name on his tongue—after she'd sidelined him with her bombshell revelations.

Jacinda. Her real name.

It suited her better than Jane. *Jacinda* came from the Greek for *hyacinth,* he knew, for once grateful for having been forced to study the classics at prep school.

It seemed appropriate she was named after the fragrant flower. He intended to savor her scent—and everything else—during this trip. He wanted to make her bloom for him.

These past couple of days, he'd also discovered he liked her natural British accent a lot more than her contrived American one, and grudgingly admitted she must have a good ear for accents to be such a good mimic.

In fact, he found her British voice sexy and distracting.

He ought to be mad as hell at her deception. He was, but the initial searing anger had passed. Unlike his ex-wife, at least Jacinda had been motivated in her deception by overwhelming grief.

He supposed, if he'd had a sister, he'd have been just as intent on discovering the truth behind her tragic death.

Even the police now believed Marie's death to be suspicious. And with good reason, Gage thought, his expression darkening as he recalled the blackmail plots that had come to light.

He thought back to his call to Detective McGray, a midlife veteran of the NYPD.

Gage was familiar with the career detective's type. As soon as he'd made it clear how connected he was, he knew he'd gotten McGray's attention. In no uncertain terms, he'd delivered the message that he expected the guy to stop hitting the snooze button on this case.

And by the middle of the call, Gage could have sworn he heard the detective's feet hitting the floor from their position on some battered metal desk.

He told himself all of it had been done in return for Jacinda becoming his mistress.

He'd been so furious with her when she'd poured forth the truth. Furious at her for her deception. Furious at himself for wanting her all the same.

So he'd decided punishment was in order, though it was a toss up as to whom he was punishing by demanding she become his mistress.

She hadn't been too happy about his proposition. And for his part, he'd have to continue fighting getting overpowered by a bad case of the hots.

He'd never felt such a swift, overpowering lust for any other woman. It kicked in at the mere sight of her, and their round in bed a couple of nights ago had served to sharpen his desire rather than quench it.

As his copilot stepped back into the cockpit and Gage prepared the jet for the descent to Bermuda's L.F.

Wade International Airport, he wondered how far he was willing to take his arrangement with Jacinda.

He wasn't any closer to an answer hours later, after they'd landed and arrived at his villa along Bermuda's southwest coast.

He did, however, instruct the staff to place Jacinda's suitcase in the master suite. He watched as after a brief hesitation, Jacinda walked toward their shared bedroom to unpack.

Afterward, the two of them had lunch, and then he had to take some business-related calls.

At some point, he observed through a window that Jacinda was exploring the house and grounds.

When the sun was ready to set, however, he found her curled up with a book in the sitting area of the master suite.

She was dressed in a knee-length sleeveless cotton sundress with a flower print and halter-top. He'd called ahead and made sure his staff had made some rudimentary purchases for her so she'd have something appropriate to wear when she first arrived.

He'd changed and showered also since their flight, and had donned some sand-colored chinos, an open-collar blue shirt and a pair of nautical-style brown moccasins.

"Come sit out here and watch the sunset with me," he said, sliding back the doors leading from the master suite to an outdoor terrace. "We'll sip some wine before dinner."

He watched her hesitate before nodding and coming toward him.

"Planning to ply me with alcohol before you have

your way with me?" she asked tartly as she stepped onto the terrace along with him.

He saw beyond the false bravado. She was nervous.

He set down an ice bucket with a bottle of white wine and two glasses that he'd had a member of the staff deliver to the master suite earlier.

"Now is that any way to show your gratitude?" he asked mildly, his tone faintly mocking.

He was mocking not only her, but their situation.

He added, "I see you found some of the clothes I instructed the staff to purchase."

"Yes, it was…thoughtful of you."

"I admit to being surprised you chose the halter-top."

She was clearly braless underneath, and the airy cotton fabric skimmed her trim figure.

He felt a kick-start and then a tightening in his gut.

"I decided to dress the part."

Neither of them needed to give voice to what part she was referring to. Mistress.

His lips quirked up. "You're doing a good job."

She met his gaze. "Or at least, what I think is the part. I have no idea how to act like a mistress."

A half smile crossed his lips as he poured the wine into two glasses.

"Likewise," he said, handing her a glass. "You're my first."

She looked surprised as she took the glass from him. Their hands brushed, causing her to bobble the glass for a second.

"Ex-wife, yes. Mistress, no," he elaborated.

"How is that possible?"

"Simple," he said. "I date discriminately, but I haven't had any interest in having a particular woman at my…disposal."

Until now. For a price.

He watched as she flushed at the reference to her new status as a kept woman—her bills paid, her needs taken care of.

"How did you know my dress size?"

"I checked the clothes in your room before we left New York."

She gaped at him.

"Did you think you were the only one capable of rifling through someone's personal possessions?" he asked.

She flushed again.

The truth was he'd done some extensive digging of his own.

"I also know you're an ad executive with Winter & Baker back in London," he said.

"Currently on leave."

"Right," he responded, inclining his head. "Impressive position, though."

"I'm good at what I do."

He raised his glass to her in silent salute. "I've always admired people who can spot trends. Make them, even. I guess you could say that's what advertising and venture capitalism have in common."

She took a sip of her wine. "How did you find out about my job?"

"Simple online search," he replied before quirking a brow. "I wanted to make sure you weren't lying this time."

A guilty look crossed her face.

It was too easy to bait her—though she showed plenty of signs of fight in her, he thought with respect.

"What else did you learn?"

As she turned to sit in a wicker chair, he did the same.

He watched her close her eyes and turn her head to the warm ocean breeze.

"Your tastes tend toward romantic tunes. Celine Dion, Natalie Cole and Alicia Keys."

She opened her eyes and looked at him. "You learned *that* from an Internet search?"

"No," he admitted. "From the favorites list on your iPod. I took a look while you were out earlier."

"Payback?"

"Just curious."

And he meant it, he discovered. He wasn't gratuitously snooping. He was genuinely curious about her. Hungry for details about who she was. The real woman behind the masquerade.

"What else have you learned?"

"You live in London. You have an older brother named Andrew who is a trader at Schroders, the British investment firm. And two parents, Eleanor and George, who own their own party-supply business."

"Very good," she murmured.

He sipped his wine. "Courtesy of local news articles in the aftermath of Marie's death."

"That's what I would have expected."

"You have a preference for MAC cosmetics, French cheeses and Stella McCartney tops."

"Only her budget line," she replied. "Especially in my recent incarnation as a housekeeper."

"We'll get you the designer duds, I promise."

As he expected, she went straight for the bait.

"You've done more than enough shopping for me already. Thank you."

"You're welcome, but the offer still stands."

Her lips compressed.

"You attended Woldingham School and then read English Language & Communication at King's College London," he continued unperturbed.

He'd gotten her *curriculum vitae* from the Winter & Baker web site.

"So sorry the names are not as tony as Choate or Princeton," she returned. "Even so, I hope my qualifications suffice for the job of mistress."

His lips quirked. "They'll do."

"What a relief."

This time he let himself grin. "You should know I don't find sarcasm a turnoff."

"You forgot I like to ski," she replied, ignoring the loaded comment. "I've been to the Swiss Alps several times."

"Great. Then you should feel right at home in Vail. I have a lodge there."

"I know," she said with dry humor.

He cocked an eyebrow, and a shared moment of reluctant amusement passed between them.

"You're a fine cook…and a rotten housekeeper."

"I was otherwise occupied," she said.

This time it was his turn to say, "I know."

Their gazes held for a moment, before he turned and looked out past the terrace's rail.

He nodded in front of them, and then glanced back at her. "The sun is about to go down."

"Yes."

He watched as her eyes lowered and she breathed in deep of the ocean air, a smile curving her lips.

"Like it here?" he asked.

She turned to look at him. "It's beautiful. Peaceful."

He was glad she liked Bermuda. He was a fan of the place himself—blue, blue ocean and the endless vista of sky. And now she added to the beauty of it. For him.

"I saw you wandering the grounds earlier," he observed.

"It's an impressive house."

"The perfect location," he countered.

He'd seen the place and bought it, lured by the privacy and tranquility and location on one of Bermuda's best beaches.

The estate boasted its own pool, tennis court, guest and staff cottage, and landscaped gardens.

Jacinda turned to look at the sun's last rays, and Gage studied her face, the setting sun giving it a warm glow.

She truly was beautiful. Her classic features were smooth and relaxed, her curly brown hair loose and down around her shoulders. Her green eyes were rendered even paler by the reflected light of the sun and were fringed by thick, dark lashes.

She was suited to be *in* an ad as well as *creating* one.

But though she'd accused him of wanting to purchase her like an art object to add to his menagerie of beautiful things, the truth was he wanted to possess both her body and soul.

He looked out over the water.

They sat in silence, watching the sun disappear over the horizon, with the ocean's lapping waves as its parting gesture.

When the light had almost completely receded, leaving stillness behind, Gage looked down at his glass and then over at Jacinda's.

They'd both finished their wine, a damn fine Chardonnay.

But more importantly, the wine should have relaxed her. And judging by the companionable silence, it had worked.

Still, he wanted her.

He stood.

"Come on," he said, reaching for the wine bottle with the hand that wasn't holding his empty glass. "It's almost time for dinner."

She looked up at him blankly for a moment and then stood, apparently roused from her thoughts.

He stepped to one side, and she slid by him to enter the suite.

Once inside, he placed the wine bottle and glass down on the table she'd used for her own glass.

She was peering at the time on the bedside clock when he walked up behind her.

He cupped her upper arms and placed a kiss on her bare shoulder.

"We have to make sure you get some sun on this trip," he murmured.

She stilled. "In what?" she said, her voice coming out breathy. "The skimpy bikini I found among the purchases waiting for me?"

"There's a skimpy bikini?" he asked. "What color?"

"Emerald green, if you must know."

"Mmm," he replied, his voice laced with humor. "Remind me to give the staff a special bonus."

He nuzzled her neck, the shell of her ear and the tendrils of hair at her scalp.

"I thought you said it's time for dinner," she said huskily.

"Almost time," he corrected. "I wouldn't mind a little prelude first."

"Don't you mean interlude, as in 'romantic interlude'?" she replied as his hands went to the knot holding up her halter-top.

"Both."

The top fell away from her, and his hands came up to cup her bare breasts.

He kneaded, fueling his arousal.

When he circled over the peaks of her breasts, she moaned and slumped against him. She reached back and grasped his muscled thigh for support.

"Ah, Jacinda," he said in a low voice. "We may not trust or even like each other, but we always have this, don't we, sweetheart?"

She wet her lips. "I don't know what you mean."

He flicked his tongue over the shell of her ear and bit down lightly on her earlobe. "Liar. I think you do."

In the next instant, he turned her in his arms and pushed her back against the wall behind her, his mouth coming down on hers.

Her breasts pressed into his shirt, her dress held up below her chest by the zipper on her lower back.

She moaned again as his tongue swept inside her mouth, her arms sliding around his neck.

He pulled up the skirt of her dress so that it bunched at her hips, and one hand slid up her soft thigh.

She smelled of flowers and sun and surf. And she was making him crazy.

Pushing her panties aside, he parted her moist folds and delved into her waiting heat, stroking her.

Lifting his head, he watched her lips part and her eyes cloud as she gazed back at him.

"Let me fill you," he said deeply.

"That was the deal," she responded, her voice throaty.

He stilled for a second.

What had he expected? They *did* have a deal. She'd agreed to become his mistress.

But damn, her business-like response irked him.

He wanted to engage her mind, her emotions and her deepest fantasies.

He wanted her complete and utter capitulation, deal or no deal.

Aloud, he said, "That's right, sweetheart." He circled over her nerve center, making her gasp. "And I want you to enjoy it as much as I intend to."

"Gage." She moved restlessly against him.

"Ah, Jacinda, let it go," he coaxed.

There was nothing more erotic for him at the moment than having her come apart in his arms.

He pressed, swirled and then pushed inside her, flicking his thumb over her core, leaving them both breathless with want and pulsating need.

Her hands moved down to dig into his arms.

"Gage…"

"Yes?"

And then he watched with pleasure as she arched her back and came apart for him with a low moan.

Moments later, he kissed her softly. "I think I got my answer," he said in a low voice.

He stepped back and his fingers went to work on the buttons of his shirt, his need for her overwhelming him.

As they both undressed, they kissed again, repeatedly and with increasing desperation.

When they'd both shed their clothes, he sat back on the bed, drawing her to stand in front of him.

Then he leaned over to the night table and pulled out the foil packet he knew was there.

But before he could open it, she took it from him.

His eyes closed with pleasure as she sheathed him.

He leaned back then, taking her with him, so that she sat astride him.

He caught the look of surprise in her eyes.

"Aren't we ever going to have sex the traditional way?" she asked.

"What? Plain vanilla sex?" he asked. "Not if I can help it."

He positioned her and himself, and then watched

her shudder as she slid down over him. He savored the sensation as much as she did.

"Move for me, Jacinda," he murmured, before he lost his mind in a tidal wave of lust and desire unlike anything he'd felt with anybody else.

She moved, sinking down on him again and again, and his mouth closed over one breast, urging her on.

Their pants and gasps filled the otherwise silent room.

He turned his attention to the other breast, determined to take her with him when he came.

Their movements became more urgent.

And then suddenly he felt her squeeze around him. "Oh, Gage."

Her climax claimed her, and she shuddered.

His hands sank deep into her hips, and he raised up, pumping into her.

A second later, with a hoarse groan, he followed her over the edge.

# Six

The next morning, Jacinda was forced to come to terms with her new status.

Billionaire's mistress.

She'd slept with Gage and was officially a kept woman in every sense.

She ought to be appalled, and she tried hard to summon the appropriate amount of outrage.

But the truth was she'd enjoyed going to bed with Gage.

The first time hadn't been a fluke. He was a wonderful lover, and last night again they'd been like a match set to parched wood.

She looked over at him, lounging next to her on a deck chair beside the pool, scanning a fax that had come through that morning.

Minutes before, he'd spread sunscreen on her back, and it was all she could do not to purr from the effect of his hands smoothing over her skin as he murmured his approval of her emerald-green bikini, his voice smoky with promise.

She was still recovering from the result of his touch, trying to keep her mind off of his smoothly muscled body laid out before her and the memory of running her fingertips over his back with sunscreen.

He, on the other hand, had apparently switched to work mode without missing a beat.

How was it possible, she wondered, for one man to revert from impassioned lover to cool corporate titan so easily?

Gage had said he'd had a taste of betrayal. Could that at least partly explain his guardedness, his ability to close up so quickly?

Curiosity overtook her. "It's occurred to me…"

He glanced up inquiringly.

"It's occurred to me," she started again, "that while I was pretending to be someone I'm not, you're actually the master of disguise."

He put down his fax. His eyes were still shielded by sunglasses, as were hers, but she could tell she had his complete attention now.

"And how do you figure that?" he asked.

"You hold your cards close to your chest."

"Some people call that a business asset."

"You're enigmatic," she tried again.

"That's all you can come up with after months of

snooping?" he teased, his tone gently mocking. "I'm disappointed."

"Guarded, I should have said."

"Most blackmailed billionaires are."

She shook her head. "I think it goes back further than that. You said you've tasted betrayal."

He sobered. "That's right. You could say I've had trouble with deceptive women before your recent acting routine."

"Your ex-wife?"

His lips twisted mirthlessly. "She came up on the Internet search, did she?"

"Google is an amazing thing."

"I should have figured."

"I hear the founders are billionaires today."

"And betraying the fraternity by giving up personal info on the other club members," he said with affected mournfulness.

"Too bad for you."

"I'm even more sorry I didn't get the chance to bankroll them when they got started," he responded, making her smile.

He sat back, his expression turning glib. "So what information about the redoubtable Mrs. Gage Lattimer would you like to know?"

"You divorced after less than two years of marriage." She made it a statement, but with an implicit invitation to elaborate.

"Yes, and that was eight years ago." The corner of his mouth turned up. "Back when I was a mere millionaire but still considered a good catch."

"No doubt."

"The trouble was I was also too love-struck to think about asking for a prenup when I met Roxanne," he continued. "She was an aspiring singer looking for her big break. I realized too late she thought her big break was me."

Ouch, Jacinda thought.

"When she asked for a divorce a year later and tried to take me to the cleaners, my divorce lawyer did some checking." Gage paused. "It turned out she'd hidden some interesting details about her background."

A weird premonition coiled in Jacinda's stomach.

"Credit card fraud coupled with a pattern of chasing men with money," Gage went on. "In other words, she was what some might label a 'gold digger'. Unfortunately for her, that little characteristic lowered the divorce settlement a bit."

"But you've done well for yourself since then," she offered.

"I haven't acquired any more wives," he replied, tongue-in-cheek.

"She must be sorry she didn't stay since you're a billionaire today."

"Maybe," he conceded, "but at the time, she had bigger fish to fry. I was her entrée into society, but once she was there, she didn't need me anymore. Divorcing me meant she was free to pursue rich types who had the same priorities—hitting the party circuit and keeping tabs on their social standing."

"I see."

The trouble was she *did* see, and all too well. Albeit belatedly.

With her masquerade, she'd hit a sore spot with Gage.

No wonder he'd been so furious when he'd discovered her subterfuge. In his eyes, she was another woman who'd approached him under false pretenses. But instead of being after his money, she'd been after information.

It must have taken something for someone like Gage, raised by formal and distant parents, to open up to another person. After his ex-wife betrayed him, he must have withdrawn again.

Gage only propositioning her to become his mistress suddenly made sense, Jacinda thought. He'd already learned to be guarded and cynical.

"So when you discovered I'd tricked you," she ventured, drawing her conclusion aloud, "you decided to punish me."

He quirked a brow. "Did last night feel like punishment?"

She felt herself heat up.

"Since we're on the subject, let's talk about the person who's influenced *your* life. Your sister."

The topic of Marie made her smile sadly. "My sister was impulsive...but always full of energy. She came along when I was four, and she was a dynamo from day one."

He tilted his head, regarding her. "You look alike. I should have seen the resemblance right off the bat. The curly brown hair, the big green eyes."

She shifted, feeling a ripple of awareness under his

scrutiny, and then nodded. "Yes, except Marie was a couple of inches shorter than I am."

"And you've always been the responsible older sister."

"Sedate, boring," she said with a laugh.

"Not in bed."

She could just make out his eyes behind his sunglasses at that moment, and they held hers.

She sighed. "I couldn't believe Marie was having a secret affair—one she didn't even tell *me* about."

"She must have had her reasons."

"And I'm afraid those reasons are why she wound up dead."

He nodded.

"Do you understand why I need to find out who this man is?" she asked. "Will you help me?"

"I said I would."

She drew in a breath, and then because there didn't seem to be anything else to say, she nodded at his fax. "Anything interesting with work?"

He glanced down, too. "Just a company I'm involved with. They need some marketing help, badly, at this point."

She pasted on a winning smile, lightening the mood. "Try me. I'm good with slogans."

He laughed. "Got anything that rhymes with Mandew? It's the founder's last name, and they're a computer start-up."

"'Can-do Mandew, We Do Great Things for You?'"

He laughed again. "Not bad for an on-the-spot idea. I see the beginnings of a great partnership."

Jacinda's breath caught.

Just what type of partnership they would have remained to be seen, she thought, but their relationship was getting more complicated by the day.

By the time they got back to New York, Gage was feeling more relaxed than he'd been in ages.

A getaway with Jacinda to his Bermudan hideaway had been just the ticket to rejuvenate him. He'd won a game of tennis but she'd made him work for it, and they'd also found time to go sailing and waterskiing. As for the last, he'd been tempted to say the hell with it, lay her on the floor of the power boat and make passionate love to her while the sun's rays beat down on them.

At night, they'd dined by moonlight and gone into town for music and dancing. And of course, they'd ended up in bed for more passionate bouts of lovemaking.

Along the way, he'd learned some interesting things about Jacinda. Like him, she enjoyed challenging herself with crossword puzzles. She was funny, especially when cornered, and smart as a whip. She could talk about anything from world affairs to the latest health topics knowledgeably.

They'd arrived back in New York late last night, in time for the start of the weekend.

Now, Gage poured himself a cup of coffee in the kitchen and took a sip, waiting for Jacinda to finish getting showered and dressed and come down the stairs.

As he studied the Christmas decorations she had put up, a smile played at his lips.

Maybe tonight he would whisk her to Radio City Music Hall for the annual holiday show. He could get one of his assistants to scrounge up tickets for good seats, or instead they could catch a Broadway show.

Jacinda might like either. He wondered whether she'd ever been to the city during the holidays, and somehow he doubted it.

This afternoon, they could do some holiday shopping. Barneys, Bergdorf and Tiffany all came to mind.

Gage smiled. He could picture how much Jacinda would protest if he bought her a bauble from a famed jeweler, and somehow he relished her reaction. He was enjoying getting a rise out of her these days—almost too much.

Still, since her secret was out, there was no longer any reason for her to hide her light under a bushel by dressing like a maid for his sake.

He could get used to keeping a mistress, Gage thought. Except right now the only woman he could picture in the role was Jacinda.

But he wasn't attracted only to her body. She had a fine mind—cagey but fine. She'd been smart enough to maintain a masquerade that had had him fooled for more than five months.

She challenged him, intrigued him and made him want her all the more.

The sound of footsteps roused him from his reverie.

When Jacinda came into view, he noticed she was wearing one of those pairs of jeans that had driven him crazy the past few months. They hugged all her curves and were paired with a fitted wraparound top in a burnt orange color. Black leather boots completed her ensemble.

Her hair was down and loose. He'd noticed she was wearing it that way now and was glad.

"Hi," he said. "Coffee?"

"Yes, please."

He reached for a new mug. "I was thinking about what we could do today. I thought you might like to do some holiday shopping." He poured some coffee into the mug. "Okay, if we start at Tiffany?"

He watched as she frowned.

*Here we go,* he thought with a hidden smile.

"Actually, I thought we'd go to Marie's apartment."

His humor faded. When he'd thought about possible itineraries for today, one thing that had never occurred to him was scouring Marie Endicott's old apartment.

"And why would we do that?" he asked without inflection.

She shrugged. "The apartment is still filled with Marie's things. I know it sounds batty but—" she shrugged again "—I thought we could take another look, in case there's something that's been overlooked the past few months."

"You know the police have been in there."

She nodded. "And so have I, but—"

He put the mug on the counter rather than hand it to her. "Jacinda, let the police do their job."

Her chin set at a stubborn angle. "You said you'd help me."

"And I have. I've leaned on the police."

"But the case remains unsolved."

"Right," he replied. "And there could be a murderer on the loose. You don't need to be taking risks."

The thought of Jacinda exposing herself to danger made him tense.

"How is it dangerous to visit my sister's old apartment?"

"If the crime was an inside job, and the police now think it was, someone in the building is dangerous. If he knows you're snooping, he could get nervous."

Her lips compressed, and he read mutiny in her expression. "I've been discreet."

"Nobody's seen you entering or leaving Marie's apartment?"

"No one," she confirmed, and then hesitated. "Well, except for once, when Amanda Crawford was in the elevator when I hopped in on the sixth floor."

He quirked an eyebrow. "My point exactly."

She looked exasperated. "You don't believe Amanda—"

"No, but someone at another time may have seen or heard you without your being aware of it."

She turned on her heel. "I'm going with or without you."

He trotted around the counter and took her arm. "Then it's with me. But at least let's have breakfast first."

He was never outmaneuvered, but she'd boxed him in. He wasn't going to let her go to Marie's apartment alone, not given what he knew about the crimes in the building.

She relaxed under his grasp. "I'll get breakfast."

"No, I will," he responded, smiling at her look of surprise. "I can make a mean cheese omelet."

"This I have to see."

"I've kept my culinary prowess a secret until now," he joked, "because I enjoyed having you cook for me."

"I should have guessed."

An hour later, after a delicious breakfast, they both slipped into Marie's apartment.

Gage walked around the space, taking in his surroundings.

The apartment was decorated in bright, cheery colors and comfortable furniture. A tidy kitchen was near the front door and was followed by a good-size living room. On either side of the living room were two bedrooms, one with a queen-size bed that had apparently been where Marie had slept, and the other with a smaller double bed presumably for overnight guests.

The two-bedroom apartment resembled a cozy bachelorette pad. But though the furniture and personal possessions were all there, someone had made some inroads in packing things up. Open and half filled cardboard boxes lay on a number of surfaces.

Pausing beside one box in Marie's bedroom, Gage noticed a framed photo lying on top of the packed contents. He pulled it out and studied it.

Marie and Jacinda smiled into the camera. Young and carefree, they had their arms around each other.

Jacinda came up beside him.

"That was taken while on holiday in the Canary Islands."

"You were obviously close," Gage remarked.

Jacinda nodded, and when he glanced at her, Gage noticed tears in her eyes.

*Damn it.*

Another reason why he hadn't wanted to come down here. He knew it would upset her.

"Let's get the job done," he said gruffly.

Jacinda nodded around them. "Just look through things, and pick up anything that seems interesting. You're a fresh pair of eyes. You might spot something the rest of us have missed."

He looked at the empty surface of a nearby desk. "My first inclination would be to start with electronic stuff, like e-mails and computer files. But I assume the police have their hands on it now?"

"Yes," Jacinda confirmed. "I know from Andrew that they came and took Marie's computer and cell phone once the investigation turned to possible murder. I've been left with packing up personal possessions."

She shrugged. "It's not much, but I don't want to leave any stone unturned."

"Okay then, why don't I look through stuff while I help you pack?" he said, making his tone comforting and upbeat. "I'll start in the living room, and you can work in here. Deal?"

Jacinda nodded.

Gage doubted they'd find anything interesting, but a deal was a deal.

With that thought, he went back into the living room, grabbed an empty box and started toward the built-in bookshelves along one wall.

Bookshelves, he thought, were the perfect place for tucking away slips of paper and other interesting stuff.

Half an hour later, though, he wasn't feeling nearly as sanguine.

He'd gleaned that Marie's reading tastes ran to popular fiction, real estate and some classics. But he hadn't discovered much else.

After tucking a couple of paperbacks into a cardboard box, he grabbed the next item on the shelf—a leather-bound copy of *Wuthering Heights*.

His lips quirked. According to family lore, his mother had, at one point, wanted to name him Heathcliff—or Heath, for short.

With idle curiosity, he opened the book and thumbed through the pages.

And then froze.

Instead of page after page of printed type, the book was filled with handwritten and dated entries in a feminine hand.

It seemed to be a diary. Marie's diary.

He swore under his breath.

Jacinda poked her head out of the bedroom. "Did you say something?"

He looked up, and the blank look on his face must have told her something because she walked over to him.

"What are you looking at?" she asked, looking down at the book in his hands.

He watched as her eyes widened.

"I think it's your sister's diary," he said.

Jacinda shook her head disbelievingly. "I didn't even know she kept one."

"Not only did she keep one," he said, flipping the volume closed, "but she took the trouble of hiding it in what looks from the outside like a leather-bound copy of *Wuthering Heights*."

Jacinda sucked in a breath, and then her eyes welled.

"Oh, Marie," she murmured. "Why all the subterfuge?"

"We have to turn this over to the police."

"Not before we read it!"

"Jacinda…" he began warningly.

"Not here," she replied more urgently. "Upstairs in your apartment. We'll need to call the police and hand it over. But before that, we have time."

# Seven

The minute they got back to Gage's apartment, Jacinda flopped down on the sofa and opened the volume in her hands.

"The first entry is from early last year," she said, aware of Gage sitting down next to her. "I'd recognize Marie's handwriting anywhere!"

Hungrily, she scanned the first page, which was filled with details about a night partying at the Limelight. Still, nothing too revealing.

Even so, Jacinda felt a nervous tension grip her, as if she might burst out of her skin.

They might have found the key to Marie's death!

She couldn't believe it, and fought a tremor in her hands.

She flipped to the next page and the next and the next.

She couldn't seem to skim the pages fast enough, so she jumped to the end of the volume.

The last entry was from two days before Marie's death. It contained some ho-hum details about one of her potential real estate deals.

Frustrated, Jacinda turned the book so it opened at an early entry and flipped pages several at a time.

*...visited the Met...*

*...bought fabulous dress at Saks...*

*...thinking of moving to larger apartment...*

*...called home today...spoke with Jacinda...*

Seeing a reference to herself in her sister's hand gave her a pang. Oh, Marie.

She turned pages rapidly...until Gage reached out and stilled her hands.

"Jacinda," he said, "this isn't doing anyone any good. You're overwrought."

She pulled her hands out of his grasp, and then shot him a mutinous look. "I have to!"

After a moment, he sighed, apparently prepared to let her quest run its course.

She stared back down at the diary and continued to flip pages.

*September 6$^{th}$—I'll have to call him Ted because I don't dare write his real name even here.*

Jacinda froze. Ted must have been Marie's secret lover.

At her sudden stillness, Gage leaned in and read over her shoulder.

As her finger traced down the page, she felt Gage go immobile, too.

*Our tryst was at one of NYC's premier hotels.*

*He has the manners of another era, unlike most of the men I meet. And great in bed!*

*I knew it was wrong. He's married. But I couldn't help myself.*

Jacinda felt her stomach plummet as if in free fall.

Her sister had been having an affair with a married man. A rich and powerful *married* man.

No wonder her sister had been so secretive.

And it may have cost her her life.

Oh, Marie.

"Marie was having an affair with a married man," she said in a choked voice, as if saying it aloud would make it easier to believe.

"I know," Gage said quietly. "I was reading along with you."

She looked up at Gage in anguish. "Why didn't she tell me?"

"I'm sure she didn't want to disappoint you."

Sympathy, kindness even, was etched on Gage's face. If she hadn't been so shocked and distraught, she would have marveled at this latest glimpse of the man behind the master-of-the-universe facade.

She nodded at him but emotion welled up anyway, refusing to be kept at bay.

As sobs wracked her, Gage removed the diary from her hands and pulled her into his arms.

"Go ahead and cry," he murmured. "You've been strong and brave."

She burrowed her head into his shoulder, and he rubbed her back.

She'd thought she'd shed all the tears she was capable of over her sister's death, but this latest shocker had sent her reeling, stripping her of her defenses and leaving her vulnerable.

How ironic, she realized amidst her jumbled thoughts, that she was being comforted by the man she'd once suspected of being responsible for Marie's death.

But there was no other place she'd rather be right now than in the shelter of Gage's arms. There was a haven there that was both unexpected and welcome.

Jacinda put her head down against a strong wind blowing along Park Avenue as she headed toward number 721.

Soon after her crying fit yesterday, Gage had called Detective McGray of the NYPD, and then she and Gage had gone over to the police precinct together.

Gage had introduced himself and then her as Marie's sister. From the look on Detective McGray's face, it was obvious he was surprised to see them together.

Without further elaboration, she had explained that she'd been packing up things in her sister's apartment and Gage had been helping her.

The detective's surprise had soon been replaced by interest in their new find. Marie's diary.

Detective McGray had absorbed the news that they now had solid evidence of Marie's secret affair with an impassive expression.

But with a glance at Gage, he had promised to do all he could to crack the case.

Jacinda dug her fingernails into her palms.

*She'd been right, and the police had been wrong.*

Now, as she turned under the green awning of 721 Park Avenue and stepped into the building lobby, Jacinda noted absently that there wasn't a doorman in sight.

Crossing the lobby to the elevator bank, however, she heard voices coming from the mail room.

And from the tone of those voices, it sounded like two people were arguing.

She slowed and then, because she couldn't help being curious, she stopped once she reached the doorman's wide mahogany desk.

Her footsteps had been muffled by the Oriental rug covering the center of the ivory marble floor, and judging by the steady staccato sound of the voices, it seemed neither party in the mail room was aware of her presence.

The sound of the disagreement was startling. No one argued, not even in a furious whisper, in 721's lobby, which reeked of wealth, luxury and hush-hush class.

And she couldn't be sure, but it sounded like the voices belonged to Henry Brown and Vivian Vannick-Smythe.

Jacinda wondered what Vivian was complaining about, and she only marveled that Henry was responding. Perhaps Henry had been in his job long enough that he didn't fear the wrath of the building's icy matron.

She strained to catch a word, but after several moments without being able to make out anything, she relaxed.

She was eavesdropping, and she really ought to move on.

In the next moment, however, instead of proceeding toward the elevator bank, she found herself tiptoeing closer to the mail room entrance.

She'd taken four or five steps, however, when Vivian's voice reached her.

"...Marie Endicott..."

Jacinda froze.

Why would Vivian mention Marie's name during an argument with Henry?

She shook her head.

Were her ears playing tricks on her? Was she so desperate to solve the mystery of her sister's death after this many months that everything seemed somehow connected to Marie?

She heard a rustling sound, as if someone was moving about, and hurriedly decided to resume her stride.

She looked over her shoulder in time to see Henry Brown emerge from the mail room and frown when he saw her.

She gave the young dark-haired man a sunny smile.

"Hello," she called. "Cold today."

"We'll get some snowflakes tomorrow," he responded, his expression clearing but still not cracking a smile.

A second later, one of Vivian's shih tzus appeared at Henry's side and started barking.

"So I've heard," she responded over the dog's barks, and then hurried forward to punch the button for the elevator.

From the corner of her eye, she noticed Henry making a production of shuffling some paper at the doorman's desk while the dog at his side growled at her.

She breathed a sigh of relief when the elevator arrived and she was able to step inside and bid *adieu* to the yapping ball of fur.

It was only when the doors closed, however, that she realized Vivian had yet to emerge from the mail room.

The minute she got upstairs, she called Gage at his office.

"Hi. Everything okay?" he said.

She took a deep breath. "Actually…"

"What's up?" Gage asked, his tone sharpening.

"I just came through the building lobby, and I heard Vivian Vannick-Smythe arguing with Henry Brown in hushed tones in the mail room."

"So?" Gage asked, his tone relaxing. "Vivian is grouchy enough to light into one of the building staff."

"I can't be sure, but I think I heard her mention Marie's name."

"And?"

"And I think Henry and Vivian may know something we don't about Marie's death."

After a moment, Gage's sigh was audible. "Jacinda, stop playing amateur sleuth. Just because Vivian mentioned Marie's name doesn't mean she had something to do with your sister's death. The whole building's been speculating about Marie's death off and on since it happened. Everyone knows the police are investigating."

"You don't believe me?" She felt a stab, as if Gage's opinion mattered more than most.

"You said yourself you couldn't be sure it was Marie's name that was mentioned."

"Have you noticed Vivian's dogs never bark at Henry?"

"No."

"I think those two have a connection they're hiding."

"Of course the dogs don't bark at Henry. He's the doorman. They see him all the time, and they recognize someone familiar."

"I think there's more to the story."

"Jacinda, stop it." He added with sudden suspicion, "Did anyone catch you eavesdropping?"

She hesitated. "Henry emerged from the mail room and spotted me heading toward the elevators."

She heard Gage swear under his breath.

"Jacinda, for the last time, let the police do their job."

"And I do mine?" she retorted. "Namely, taking care of you?"

"That's not what I meant."

"Then what did you mean?"

"We recently found Marie's diary, and you're eager for more leads. But let the police investigation run its course, and don't let your imagination take flight in the meantime."

He sounded so reasonable, so convincing, so sure.

Perhaps Gage was right, Jacinda thought.

After all, her instincts had already been proven wrong once—when she'd thought *he'd* been responsible for Marie's death.

Since then, she'd done a complete about-face. In fact, these days, more than anything, she feared falling in love with him.

"Sit tight until I get home," Gage said.

She sighed, and then responded reluctantly, "Okay."

"Oh, and Jacinda?"

"Yes?"

"I may be home a little later than usual."

"Right, okay," she answered.

After ending the call, Jacinda looked around the penthouse.

She'd find something to do with herself. What was a mistress supposed to do with her time?

Shop? Do lunch? Avail herself of the chauffeured car that Gage had put at her disposal?

She didn't know anyone well enough to invite to lunch. Elizabeth Wellington next door seemed quite nice, and she knew Gage was friends with Elizabeth's husband, but Elizabeth had her hands full with a baby these days. Besides, no one knew she'd morphed from being Gage's housekeeper to his lover, and it would look odd for Gage's maid to be issuing invitations to lunch.

And as far as shopping, what would she do? Go looking for a tiara and gown? Those were for a princess, not a mistress.

Of course, the one thing she was itching to do was solve the mystery of her sister's death.

Maybe she could take a stroll. And so what if her meanderings happened to take her to the door of the police station?

What could it hurt to mention to Detective McGray what she'd overheard?

Wouldn't the police appreciate all the leads they could get, even if some of them ultimately proved false?

She'd told Gage she'd sit tight, but that didn't mean a stroll around the neighborhood wasn't in the cards.

After the call with Jacinda, Gage stared at his office phone for a few moments.

Making up his mind, he picked up the receiver and dialed the number he'd taken down two weeks ago.

"McGray here," a gravelly voice announced.

"It's Gage Lattimer."

"How can I help you?" the detective said, sounding more alert.

"Jacinda Endicott just overheard an argument in the building lobby between one of the building residents, Vivian Vannick-Smythe, and one of our doormen, Henry Brown."

"Yeah?"

"The argument apparently involved Marie Endicott," Gage elaborated.

"Interesting."

"I think so, too," Gage replied blandly.

"Might be time for another chat with Mrs. Vannick-Smythe and Henry Brown."

"Maybe so," Gage agreed. "And, Detective?"

"Yes?"

"If you do find anything interesting, I'd appreciate your letting me know ASAP. I'm in touch with Jacinda Endicott."

Not only that, I'm sleeping with her.

"Will do," McGray responded before they ended their call.

After replacing the receiver, Gage stared at the phone thoughtfully.

The lead might not go anywhere. On the other hand, it just might.

# Eight

It was a bittersweet Christmas Eve.

Her first without Marie. Her first with Gage.

Jacinda sprinkled pine nuts on the fillet of sole on the kitchen counter in front of her.

When it had become clear Gage would be spending Christmas by himself in New York, Jacinda had made up her mind to stay, as well.

It wasn't that Gage had demanded she remain in New York. But Jacinda told herself that with recent breaks in Marie's case, she couldn't afford to leave town.

Of course, the more complicated story, which she refused to fully acknowledge to herself, was that Gage himself was a draw to remaining in New York.

She enjoyed his company, and she was powerfully attracted to him.

Under other circumstances, she would have been ecstatic at meeting a man like Gage. But she was his temporary bargained-for mistress until Marie's case was solved.

She steeled herself for that day, because while Gage had shown every sign of enjoying their affair, Jacinda knew he'd been burned in the past. And she didn't kid herself that Gage had forgotten she was another woman who'd come into his life with a hidden ulterior motive.

She sighed as she dusted pine nut crumbs from her hands.

Mouth-watering aromas filled the penthouse from her baking and cooking, and the sounds of a Christmas medley floated in the background.

The cooking was a way to channel her restless energy, because no matter how much progress had been made, there remained a big question mark next to Marie's death.

Jacinda knew her family hadn't been too happy when she'd announced she was staying across the Atlantic for the holidays. They'd sounded worried, too, as if they were concerned she continued to be consumed by grief. Jacinda hadn't wanted to raise false hopes by telling them of recent breaks in the case, namely, the discovery of Marie's diary, and perhaps the conversation between Vivian and Henry.

Because her family had appeared not to know of the diary, she assumed Detective McGray had trusted her to pass along the information.

At the thought of Detective McGray, she recalled when she'd stopped by his office the other day.

He had been dismissive of the argument between Vivian and Henry, just as Gage had.

Miffed but willing to hold her tongue in the interest of keeping the police's cooperation, she'd accepted the detective's opinion with outward equanimity.

But privately, she still found herself clinging to the belief that something important had transpired in the conversation between Vivian Vannick-Smythe and Henry Brown.

So, here she was trying to direct her energies toward something positive, preparing meals that would make a *chef de cuisine* proud.

Tomorrow, she'd present a traditional English Christmas dinner. Roast turkey with stuffing, roast potatoes and bread sauce. Also, parsnips and swede, Brussels sprouts and chestnuts. And of course, the traditional Christmas fruit pudding, which she'd prepared weeks ago, even before it had become clear she and Gage would be spending Christmas together in New York.

But tonight, she reflected, she and Gage would dine on lighter fare. A delicately prepared fillet of sole with pine nuts and chives. A side of asparagus tips and seasoned couscous.

She was just sliding the prepared sole into Gage's top-of-the-line sub-zero refrigerator when voices reached her from the front door.

She turned around in surprise, but before she could react, Gage stepped inside, followed by Detective McGray of the New York Police Department.

Gage looked grim, and Jacinda tensed.

*This* could not be good news on Christmas Eve.

Minutes ago Gage had gone down to the lobby to retrieve the mail.

Now, he halted and nodded over his shoulder. "Jacinda, you know Detective McGray. He was walking into the lobby when I got downstairs."

She walked out of the kitchen. "Detective McGray."

"Ms. Endicott," the detective said gruffly with a nod of his head.

If Detective McGray thought it was odd he'd found her cooking in Gage's kitchen, he didn't remark on it.

"May I take your coat?" she asked.

It was ridiculous. She knew the detective was here to discuss something momentous, but she felt as if she were having an out-of-body experience.

"I'll take care of the coat, Jacinda," Gage said as the detective shed his. "Why don't you and Detective McGray get seated?"

At her questioning look, Gage added, "There's been a break in the case."

She and Detective McGray walked over to sit on facing couches in the living room, and after dealing with the detective's coat, Gage came to sit down next to her.

Not for the first time, Jacinda noted Detective McGray looked like any other overworked and underpaid veteran of the NYPD.

"Ms. Endicott, earlier today we arrested Senator Michael Kendrick for the murder of your sister," the detective said without preamble.

Jacinda felt as if someone had knocked the breath out of her. "What?"

"We've recovered the security camera videotape of the building roof from the night of your sister's death. It appears your sister and Senator Kendrick had some sort of altercation, and he pushed her to her death."

Jacinda sucked in a deep breath, and then felt tears sting the back of her eyes.

Finally. *Finally.* The truth was out.

Gage stroked her arm. "Are you okay?"

She nodded, momentarily unable to speak.

At last, she said, "How? You had a theory it was a building insider who was behind the crime."

"You didn't know?" Gage responded for the detective. "Kendrick lived in 8C with his wife until July. They moved out and put their co-op on the market."

Right when Marie died, Jacinda thought. And right before she assumed her persona as Jane Elliott.

"We've got evidence the senator was romantically involved with your sister," Detective McGray said. "The senator's wife was aware her husband was cheating—though not with whom. That's probably why they separated. When we arrested the senator earlier today, Charmaine Kendrick came forward with love letters she'd discovered between her husband and his anonymous lover."

Jacinda frowned. "I'm surprised Senator Kendrick's wife was so willing to cooperate. She doesn't sound like the typical political wife."

"You've never met Charmaine, have you?" Gage

asked rhetorically, looking at her. "I got the feeling she was unhappy with Kendrick for a long time. And being the wronged wife, selling him out gives her more leverage in divorce proceedings."

Gage added dryly, "And believe me, divorce is something I know a lot about."

"How did you find the building tape after all this time?" Jacinda asked Detective McGray.

"Vivian Vannick-Smythe produced it."

At Jacinda's look of surprise, Detective McGray cleared his throat. "Mrs. Vannick-Smythe in 12A and her lover, Henry Brown, have been blackmailing the residents of this building."

Jacinda gaped at the detective. "What? How did you discover that?"

It was a bombshell.

"When we questioned both Vivian and Henry about the happenings in the building," Detective McGray said, "they both initially denied any involvement."

Jacinda nodded. "Of course."

She couldn't imagine the icy matron on the twelfth floor conceding anything. Vivian Vannick-Smythe had probably bristled at even being accosted by the police.

Detective McGray looked cynical. "But Vivian got nervous once we told her we were also questioning Henry Brown at the station house. So she decided to cut a deal. Once she'd summoned her lawyer, of course."

"Let me guess," Gage said.

Detective McGray gave a curt nod. "She was willing

to cooperate once she'd gotten a guarantee we'd go easy on her."

"So she decided to sell out her lover," Jacinda concluded.

"You could say that," Detective McGray replied. "As far as we can make out by putting together Vivian's and Henry's stories, the truth is both of them were in on the blackmail schemes from the beginning. The videotape of the roof from the night of the murder was one thing they were using to blackmail Senator Kendrick. That's why they were holding on to it."

Jacinda's nails dug into the palms of her hands. Vivian Vannick-Smythe was a mean-spirited shrew.

To think how much she and her family had suffered these past several months while all along Vivian had held the key to solving her sister's murder!

"Vivian gave us the evidence to arrest Kendrick in exchange for our agreeing not to prosecute her for blackmail and withholding evidence," McGray said in a gravelly voice.

"And Henry caved and talked?" Gage asked.

Detective McGray shifted his gaze from Jacinda to Gage. "Only once we told him Vivian had fingered him as the perpetrator of the blackmails. He confessed he'd been Vivian's lover and that she'd convinced him to engage in the blackmail with her."

Jacinda felt a twinge of sympathy for Henry. He was on the hook for several felonies while Vivian would be let off easy for her cooperation. It must have been Henry who'd answered the phone back in July when she'd placed that fateful call from London seeking information about Gage's former housekeeper.

"You said the tape was *one* thing they were using to blackmail Kendrick," Gage pressed. "There's more?"

Jacinda looked at both men perplexedly. "Why? Why did he have to kill my sister? It doesn't make any sense."

"Unfortunately, it does," Detective McGray responded, a hint of sympathy entering his voice. "One possible motive for the killing is that Kendrick believed your sister was the one blackmailing him."

Jacinda sucked in a breath. The news sent her reeling.

"You see," Detective McGray elaborated, "Henry admitted he and Vivian initially blackmailed Kendrick by threatening to expose his extramarital affair and ruin his political career."

"And since Kendrick had been so careful, so discreet, about his affair with Marie," Gage guessed, "he must have figured Marie could be the only source of the blackmail letter."

"Exactly," Detective McGray said.

Jacinda shook her head in disbelief. "How did Vivian and Henry even discover the affair?" She looked at the detective. "You and I didn't find anything, and we both looked through Marie's things."

"Henry admitted he and Vivian snuck into the Kendricks' apartment when they lived in the building. My guess is they got hold of a love letter or two, like Mrs. Kendrick did."

"But why didn't we find any letters in Marie's apartment?"

McGray shrugged. "It's possible Kendrick destroyed them. After he was blackmailed and got nervous, he must have been inside Marie's apartment at some point and gotten his hands on them."

Jacinda shook her head again. "How could he and Marie be so discreet and yet leave love letters?"

McGray coughed. "The love notes were signed with pet names and must have been hand-delivered somehow, or at least hidden in places only the other party would know about."

"So Vivian and Henry knew Kendrick was having an extramarital affair with *someone*," Gage mused, "but they didn't realize with *whom* until they got hold of the videotape."

"That's probably right," McGray agreed. "Too bad for Kendrick he didn't realize the roof was being videotaped."

Jacinda perked up. "Has Kendrick confessed to killing my sister?"

McGray snorted with disdain. "Kendrick is a politician—and a powerful one. He hasn't admitted anything, but he's got a lawyer. This thing's going to blow big once it hits the papers. It's going to make Kendrick's problem with his staff and the ongoing SEC prosecution seem like small potatoes."

"I remember now that Marie mentioned she was volunteering with Senator Kendrick's reelection campaign," Jacinda mused out loud. "And of course, the two of them living in the same building provided the perfect cover."

It all made sense, she thought, why she and the police had been unable to find a paper or electronic trail from Marie to the senator. The two had lived in the same building, so there hadn't been any need for long-distance communication. All the senator had had to do was knock on Marie's door.

Jacinda recalled coming across Kendrick's reelection campaign material in her sister's apartment. It hadn't seemed remarkable at the time that Marie would be volunteering for the senator's reelection bid. And as a result, any calls from Marie to the senator's campaign office wouldn't have looked suspicious.

It must have been audacious and reckless for the senator to have both his wife and his mistress under the same roof. But also extremely convenient.

The evidence had been right under her nose, Jacinda thought.

Why hadn't she suspected anything? Had she been too naive to believe her sister could have an affair with a married man? A powerful elected official?

Oh, Marie.

"According to Henry Brown's confession," Detective McGray said, "Senator Kendrick was the only 721 Park Avenue resident to pay the blackmail money. Everyone else refused and went to the police."

"Kendrick is an idiot," Gage muttered.

Jacinda looked over at him. "More than an idiot. A murderer."

Now that the initial shock of discovering who had killed her sister had worn off, she felt the gates open on her pent-up frustration.

She'd waged a lonely battle for six months. Her initial hunch had been correct—her sister had been murdered. She'd been right, and the police had been wrong.

And rather than volunteering his assistance, Gage had offered her the role of mistress in exchange for his help.

"I'd like to see the videotape," she said thickly, addressing Detective McGray.

The detective hesitated. "Are you sure you're ready? And that you want to? We try to spare families the graphic details."

Jacinda raised her chin. "Tell me."

Detective McGray looked down and studied the rug. "Your sister and Kendrick appeared to be arguing," he said gruffly. "I'm assuming he lured her up to the roof with the promise of a lovers' tryst, but he intended to confront her about the blackmail. In any case, on the tape, Marie looks as if she's shaking her head in denial just before…"

The detective trailed off.

"Just before Kendrick pushed Marie off the roof," Jacinda finished, tears stinging the backs of her eyes.

No wonder Detective McGray thought Kendrick had assumed Marie was blackmailing him. The videotaped argument certainly supported that theory.

She looked from Gage to Detective McGray. "Everyone discouraged me, but I knew, *knew,* right from the beginning that my sister hadn't killed herself."

"Ms. Endicott," Detective McGray said, "I can understand why you're upset right now—"

"I've been upset for six months," she shot back, and

then stood. "Thank you for stopping by, Detective. I appreciate your coming here to tell me the news yourself."

Her tone was cold, impersonal.

After a momentary look of surprise, and after shooting a glance at Gage, the detective stood, too. Gage followed suit.

"I'm sorry for your loss, Ms. Endicott."

Jacinda nodded numbly.

"I'll show the detective out," Gage said.

"Thank you," she said to no one in particular, and then turned to walk toward the back of the penthouse.

She was done with the police—and with Gage.

"Are you all right?" Gage asked in the doorway to the master bedroom.

"Fine," she said, not looking up from gathering some toiletries into a case.

"You don't look okay."

In fact, she felt as if she'd gone nine rounds with a phantom opponent, Jacinda thought.

The fight was over, however. Marie's killer had finally been found.

But while she'd slowly been coming to terms with the loss of her sister over the past several months, now she was facing losing Gage, too.

Her heart ached.

Then she shook herself.

The twinge didn't make sense. She was mad at him.

He'd made her pay for his help. Then he'd dragged his feet, more interested in continuing their affair than in helping her solve a crime.

But now that Marie's case was solved, and their bargain was over, she wouldn't let him put her aside like another cast-off plaything. She'd protect herself by beating him to goodbye.

"It's late in London," she said, "but I'll need to call Andrew...my parents..."

"There's time for that," Gage replied.

"That's always been your philosophy, hasn't it?" she replied sharply.

Gage frowned. "Meaning?"

"Meaning you were never too keen on solving Marie's murder." She mimicked, "'Let's go to Bermuda, Jacinda. Let the police do their jobs, Jacinda.'"

Gage's brows snapped together.

"In fact, you were happy for the investigation to drag on as long as I continued as your mistress!"

Jacinda watched in satisfaction as Gage's scowl disappeared and his face went blank.

"You just wanted satisfaction—to continue punishing me for deceiving you!"

"Is that what you believe?"

"That's what I *know*," she said, zipping up her case and picking up her handbag from the bed. "Marie's case has been solved, so according to the terms of our bargain, our affair is over."

She headed toward the door.

"Where are you going?" Gage demanded.

"Home, to get my luggage and pack," she said without glancing at him. "If I hurry, I may even be able to get back to London before Christmas is over."

Tears threatened, but she held them back. "What a gift that would be!"

What an utterly depressing Christmas, all around, she thought.

Still, she kept walking, marching down the penthouse stairs, even as her lips quivered.

It was only when she got to the pavement outside, and raised her hand for a taxi instead of letting one of Henry Brown's fellow doormen do it for her, that she let the tears flow.

# Nine

Damn it.

As soon as Gage heard the front door close behind Jacinda, he felt the strange silence of being alone on Christmas Eve in a city of upward of eight million people.

He was tempted to go after Jacinda, but he reined himself in.

She'd floored him with the accusation that he'd made halfhearted efforts to solve Marie's murder because he was content with her as his mistress.

His initial reaction had been to deny it, but then he'd caught himself.

He'd forced himself to confront motivations he'd previously been unwilling to stop and examine.

Jacinda's accusation was true. At least partly.

Gage raked his hand through his hair in frustration and looked around the master bedroom.

Jacinda had left her stamp on the room.

Some of her things lay about, and her scent still hung in the air.

Gage glanced at the bed and remembered the impassioned nights the two of them had spent there.

He'd found a release—no, a freedom—in her arms that he hadn't in any other woman's.

She was ambitious but warm—exactly what he was looking for.

She'd used stealth to infiltrate his life and slip past his defenses. But once inside his home, she'd become a part of his life he couldn't do without.

And now she was gone.

*Our affair is over,* she'd said.

It was true, he'd struck a bargain with her—one that he wasn't too proud of, in retrospect. And now that Kendrick had been arrested, there was no reason for Jacinda to stick around.

There was no way to get her to stay…unless, maybe, he put everything on the line.

It was time to let go of the past, Gage realized. To let go of the fact that their relationship had started on the wrong foot, with a crime followed by deceit and a devil's bargain. And even more, it was time for him to let go of baggage from his divorce that had helped sour his relationship with Jacinda.

Gage checked his watch. It was a few minutes after four.

If he hurried, he'd have time to pick up a new Christmas gift for Jacinda, and then get to her apartment before she left for the airport. He was betting it would take her some time to pack and contact an airline.

If necessary, though, he'd follow her to London.

He'd already picked out an expensive but tasteful gold watch for Jacinda, but he decided to save that gift for tomorrow. If he had tomorrow. Today he needed to pull out the works.

He was also betting his usual chauffeur would remember Jacinda's address. He'd had Jacinda use his car and driver in the past to run errands and pick up stuff from her studio apartment.

Striding out of the bedroom, he found his cell phone and called his driver, asking him to be ready immediately.

He grabbed his coat from the entry closet and, shrugging into it, opened the door of his apartment…and came face to face with the Wellingtons across the hall.

They turned to look at him in surprise. Elizabeth was holding Lucas, and Reed had his key in the door. They were obviously on their way in or out.

"Happy holidays, Gage!" Elizabeth said.

The holidays didn't seem so cheery to him at the moment, Gage thought, but he was hoping to fix the situation.

"Have you heard the news?" Reed asked. "We just got a call from the police."

So, Detective McGray and his fellow cops at the NYPD had wasted no time, Gage thought. News was spreading fast. It would break in the media soon—if it hadn't already.

"I've heard," Gage said shortly.

"Another reason to be thankful at the holidays," Elizabeth said as the baby waved his arms and chortled.

Reed looked at him more closely. "Anything wrong? Did the police call you?"

"In fact, I got a visit from Detective McGray himself."

Reed raised his eyebrows. "Surprising."

"Not really," Gage replied, "when your housekeeper happens to be Marie Endicott's sister."

Reed's face registered surprise, and Elizabeth's eyes widened.

Reed recovered first. "Crime solving in your spare time, were you?" he said with dry humor.

"I knew there was more to your relationship with Jacinda than met the eye!" Elizabeth exclaimed.

Gage leaned over and stabbed the button for the elevator. "At the moment, I've got to catch up with Jacinda before she boards a flight to London."

He straightened and belatedly took in the heart-warming domestic tableau that the Wellingtons presented. A happily married couple, one baby and another on the way.

*This* was what he could have. *This* was what he wanted. Suddenly, he saw his future.

If he hurried.

Reed eyed him. "Of course. Don't let us hold you up."

"Good luck!" Elizabeth called as the elevator doors opened and Gage stepped inside.

"Thanks," Gage shot back before the doors closed.

His driver arrived a few minutes after Gage got downstairs. And fortunately, his chauffeur remembered driving Jacinda to York Avenue and Eighty-second Street a couple of times to collect her belongings.

After they made a quick side trip to pick up Jacinda's gift, the driver headed toward York Avenue.

The going was slow, however, because rush hour had begun and there was significant holiday pedestrian traffic.

Gage thrummed his fingers on the leather-upholstered armrest of his seat.

When they arrived at Jacinda's apartment, he hopped out and cursed under his breath when he saw the building had a security camera but no doorman.

He looked at the doorbells and was relieved that the name Elliott was taped under the buzzer for Apt. 5B. It looked as if Jacinda had gone to some lengths to make her identity as Jane Elliott appear real, and for once, Gage was thankful for it.

He knew she wouldn't be inclined to let him upstairs, but he punched the buzzer anyway and waited.

When there was no answer, he tried again…and again.

Was she ignoring him? Or—dread slammed into him—was he too late and she'd already headed to the airport?

He was spared further debate, however, when a resident of the building happened by.

He smiled at the older man, and lying through his teeth, apologized for not being able to find his key.

The older man took one look at his expensive suit, and with a curt nod, held the door open, allowing Gage to follow him in.

As Gage rode the elevator up, he thanked the powers that be for unquestioning New Yorkers.

When he got to the fifth floor, he stopped in front of 5B and knocked.

When there was no answer, he glanced at the crack between the door and the floor.

No light. No sound.

Damn it.

She could swear there wasn't a free cab on the whole island of Manhattan at the moment.

Jacinda trudged along Eighty-second Street, pulling her wheeled suitcase behind her.

She was still in shock over everything that had transpired earlier in the day.

Senator Kendrick had been arrested for her sister's death.

Once she'd reached her studio apartment, she'd pulled up the senator's picture online. The minute she'd seen Kendrick's photo, everything had clicked for her. Kendrick was tall, dark-haired and dark-eyed. And he had a noticeable dimple.

Afterward, she'd called her parents in London to let them know Senator Kendrick had been arrested for Marie's murder.

The call had been an emotional wringer. She'd shed copious tears along with her mother, an ocean away.

At the end of the call, she'd told her parents she would try to get a stand-by seat on a flight to London, however much the odds were stacked against her.

One thing she hadn't counted on, though, was how difficult it would be to find a taxi to the airport.

On Christmas Eve, Manhattan was thronged with

tourists and shoppers. On top of it all, she was cold, miserable and getting more dispirited by the second.

Of course, she could try the airport shuttle train, or one of the buses that departed from Forty-second Street to the airport. But she'd have to take the subway to either of those, and the nearest subway stop was a long way from York and Eighty-second Street.

Still, she was starting to realize she might not have a choice.

Turning the corner of Eighty-second onto York, she looked up…and stopped short.

The breath went out of her.

Gage.

He was bent, leaning into the passenger side window of a black limo with tinted windows, apparently speaking with the driver.

She stood frozen in place as he straightened and looked up and down the street.

His eyes came to rest on her and he stilled.

Jacinda didn't think she could bear facing him again. Why was he here?

After a moment, Gage walked toward her, his face unreadable.

When he came to a stop, he looked down at her suitcase and then back up at her. "Need a ride?"

His offer was heaven-sent. Or not.

She lifted her chin. "I need to get to JFK."

"That's what I figured," he replied.

She eyed him warily.

"You won't catch a cab here."

"Are you going to force me to accept a ride from you just like you coerced me into becoming your mistress?" she retorted.

His jaw tightened and then relaxed. "I guess I deserved that."

His mea culpa took her by surprise.

He gestured to the car behind him. "However, the offer still stands."

She wavered, and then reluctantly moved toward him. "Since you're my only option, I accept."

When she drew near, he reached down and grasped the handle of her suitcase, stopping her progress.

"I'll get your luggage," he said.

She looked up at him, their faces inches apart, and swallowed. "Fine. Thank you."

There was nothing like having a billionaire help you with your luggage, Jacinda thought. Her girlfriends and coworkers back in London would think she was bonkers for leaving Gage behind.

Then she shook herself. She was not bonkers. He was a jerk, she thought, her resolution hardening.

After Gage had deposited her suitcase in the trunk of the car, he opened the car door for her and she got in, making herself comfortable in the plush leather-upholstered interior.

Gage came around and got in himself after a quick word to the driver.

After noting the privacy partition separating her from the driver and obscuring the view ahead, Jacinda decided her best course was to stare out the passenger window.

She watched the shoppers hurry along with bags of gifts, and her heart ached.

The whole world seemed to be happy—except for her.

"Jacinda."

"Hmm?"

"Look at me."

She turned her head around. "Is that an order?"

"It's a request."

"How generous of you."

"I know I hurt you."

Her lips parted. "Marie's death hurt me."

"I've been an ass."

"Well, points to you for being able to concede that much!"

"You should know, though, that I went to the police with your suspicions about Vivian and Henry."

His declaration surprised her. "You did?"

He nodded, and for the first time, she thought she detected a hint of vulnerability in Gage's face.

"Detective McGray was so dismissive of my suspicions when I told him," she said.

"Probably because it was old news to him by that point," Gage said. "I called him right after the call with you about Vivian and Henry."

"Oh." So Gage hadn't been completely dismissive of her suspicions.

"Henry admitted to the police that he and Vivian were having a disagreement over his cut of the senator's blackmail money," Gage went on. "Henry's deal with Vivian was for twenty-five percent of the money from the blackmail schemes, but when no one but the senator paid up, Henry thought he was entitled to more. That was the argument you heard in the mail room."

Gage added dryly, "I should have known you wouldn't listen to me and sit tight."

"Of course, and I was right to go to the police."

"You accused me of not being interested in solving Marie's death because I wanted to prolong our affair," Gage countered.

"Yes."

She felt herself flush because she knew now she'd been somewhat unfair in her accusation. "Why didn't you tell me you phoned Detective McGray? Why did you suggest I was letting my imagination get the better of me where Vivian and Henry were concerned?"

Gage sighed. "After thinking about it a little more, I realized the conversation you overheard was an angle worth pursuing. But I didn't want you putting yourself in danger. There was a murderer on the loose, and the police thought someone in the building was responsible."

"I see."

She felt a shiver of emotion shoot through her. Gage cared about her.

"And you were only partly right in your accusation," he said.

Catching the look in his eyes, Jacinda held her breath.

"I did want to prolong our affair, but not to continue punishing you," Gage said, looking deep into her eyes. "It was because I wanted you. I was falling for you."

Her lips parted.

"I'm in love with you, Jacinda."

Her heart thudded inside her at his words.

"I've been an ass, but I'll spend the rest of my life making it up to you, if you'll let me."

She felt the pinprick of tears.

"But it's your choice," Gage went on, that hint of vulnerability she'd seen earlier reappearing in his eyes. "I'll take you to the airport, let you go home to your family, and we never have to see each other again, if that's what you want."

"You can't be in l-love with m-me," she said in a choked voice.

The tears gathered as she took in the tender look on Gage's face.

"Why not?" he asked, his dimple appearing. "We're used to being two guarded people, but we let our guards down with each other."

"You can't…"

"What'll it take to convince you?" Gage joked, and then patted his clothes as if searching for something. "Maybe your Christmas gift?"

As Gage reached inside his pocket, Jacinda's eyes widened.

"I had something picked out for you," he said, "but I realized when you left the apartment that this was more appropriate."

"I don't have your gift! I—"

"Tossed it into the trash bin?" he finished for her, his tone droll.

"I left the tie at the apartment."

Gage smiled. "Just what I need. Another tie."

She blinked back her tears. "What do you recommend getting a billionaire?"

"I've got several suggestions about what you could give *this* billionaire that would make him very happy," he replied seductively.

She heated up at his suggestive tone.

Gage pulled out a jewelry case and flipped it open, and Jacinda felt her heart stop.

A round diamond in a beautiful latticework setting twinkled back at her.

"It's a family heirloom," Gage explained. "My ex-wife never wore it, because she was interested in something shiny and new. On the way here, I stopped by a jeweler who's a friend of mine and keeps a few things in his safe for me."

Emotion clogged her throat. "It's beautiful."

Gage took her hand. "Jacinda, will you marry me?"

"I haven't said I love you!"

"I'll take you on whatever terms I can get."

"Don't you ever stop?" she said, her laugh coming out as half a sob.

"Not when it's something I want badly. I love you, Jacinda."

Tears rolled down her cheeks. "Then aren't you lucky I'm in love with you, too!"

"Ah, sweetheart," Gage said, catching one of her tears with his thumb. "Don't cry."

"I can't seem to help it."

And in the next instant, Gage folded her into his arms and was kissing her senseless.

When they finally broke apart, Gage wiped at her tears, and she braced her hands on his chest.

"How will this work?" she asked, sudden worry tingeing her voice. "You live in New York, and I live in London."

"I've got a house in London," he replied. "We'll make it work if we want to."

She nodded, and then offered, "My firm has a New York office. I could always ask for a transfer."

"You'd do that for me?" Gage asked deeply.

"I'd like to keep my job, but I'm still willing to be your kept woman," she teased.

Gage groaned. "I'm going to have to work hard to live that one down."

Jacinda sobered a little. "I'll sign a prenup. I know your ex-wife—"

"I don't want a prenup with you," Gage interrupted. "Sweetheart, I'm willing to stay love-struck by you for the rest of my life."

Jacinda gave a watery laugh.

"Do you still want to head to the airport?" Gage asked, gazing into her eyes. "Because I'll understand if you want to spend Christmas with your family, especially since—"

Jacinda shook her head. "I called them and broke the news to them already."

She added more softly, "I want to spend the twenty-fifth with you, Gage. My family is already together and getting comfort from each other, but I can't think of a more comforting place for me to be right now than with you."

The look in his eyes warmed her heart.

"But I'd love it if you'd come to London with me soon to meet them."

He grasped her hand and raised it to his lips. "Of course. How does right after Christmas sound to you?"

"It sounds perfect."

After instructing the driver to turn the car around and head back to his apartment, Gage drew her to him. "Come here, and let me show you how to deliver an early Christmas gift I'd really appreciate."

Jacinda laughed, and then shot a glance at the front of the car. "Gage, we're not alone!"

"That's what the privacy partition and the tinted windows are for," he replied, dimpling.

And then they were too lost in each other to say anything more.

# Epilogue

"What are you doing?" Gage asked, curious.

Jacinda stopped looking around them. "Taking notes."

He arched a brow. "On what?"

They were at Carrie and Trent Tanford's second wedding—a big, black-tie affair on New Year's Eve. After a church service, everyone had moved to a sit-down dinner at the Metropolitan Club, a two-story, white-marble space with a double staircase at one end and an enormous fireplace on the other.

Jacinda looked around where the two of them were sitting. "Wedding details. I want to get ours right."

Gage looked around, as well. Everything had been decorated with both a wedding and New Year's Eve theme in mind: silver, gold and white.

"Thinking of going with pink and gold for your own wedding?" he asked, unable to resist teasing her.

"Laugh if you want to," she responded, an expression of mock affront on her face.

Gage noted with satisfaction that, momentary teasing aside, Jacinda's expression lately had been all sunshine and light.

Once Kendrick had been arrested for Marie's death, Jacinda had acknowledged being ready to move on with her life in a way she hadn't been able to do for the past six months. And when her real identity had been revealed to the other residents of 721 Park Avenue, they had readily taken her into their inner circle, treating her as another victim of the crimes that had been perpetrated at their building.

For his part, Gage was glad Jacinda's future would include him.

"You know, I'm taking notes, too," he said, his eyes caressing her.

She looked surprised, happy. "On what?"

Leaning close, he whispered in her ear, "On how I'm going to get you out of that dress."

He grinned as he straightened, and she playfully slapped his arm.

His gaze raked over her.

She really did look terrific. Her claret V-neck satin dress was one he'd bought for her at Saks a couple of days ago, handing over his Amex Black Card with pleasure at money well-spent. The sleeveless dress showed off her shoulders and neckline to perfection.

Of course, he'd insisted on completing her look for the evening with a diamond-and-ruby necklace and earring set, which he'd surprised her with right before they'd departed for the wedding.

"What are you two lovebirds tweeting about?" Reed asked from the other side of the dinner table.

"The same thing you and your wife tweet about, Romeo," Gage retorted, getting a laugh from everyone around them.

Carrie and Trent had seated many of their fellow 721 Park Avenue residents at the same table.

"I doubt it," Reed shot back while Elizabeth, next to him, smiled. "Not unless you're talking about ways to relieve morning sickness, or teething pain in an eleven-month-old."

Gage had never seen Reed look more content. Parenthood seemed to agree with the Wellingtons. They'd been loving toward each other all evening, on one of their rare nights out without baby Lucus.

Still, Gage couldn't resist ribbing his neighbor. "A likely story. Tell it to the tooth fairy."

There was another round of laughter.

"Actually, Reed," Julia said, speaking up, "why don't you give a holler if you're up at two o'clock in the morning? Emma kept me and Max up last night until three."

Gage knew from photos he'd seen earlier in the evening that the Rollands had produced one cute baby.

"Ah, what we have to look forward to," Alex put in with a mock groan, squeezing Amanda's shoulder, his arm around the back of his fiancée's chair. "Makes me weak-kneed with gratitude that all Amanda and I are doing is planning a little bitty wedding."

"Can it, Alex," Reed responded good-naturedly. "We've been watching you dance attendance on Amanda all evening. When the time comes, you'll be pacing the floor with a howling bundle like the rest of us, and liking it."

"Busted," Amanda joked, but Alex just smiled easily.

"Speaking of weddings," Sebastian said, "Tessa and I hope you all will be attending ours in a couple of months in Caspia."

Jacinda clapped her hands. "I know Gage and I wouldn't miss it for the world. It's not every day we get invited to the wedding of an heir to the throne. I'll bet press from around the world will be there—"

"Stop," Tessa joked weakly, holding up a hand. "You're making me queasy just talking about it."

"Well, we can all do with some media attention of the upbeat variety, for a change," Gage put in.

The press had been all over Senator Kendrick's recent arrest.

"I'll second that," Trent Tanford agreed.

Gage turned his head and noticed the bride and groom approaching their table.

"Shouldn't you two be mingling with the guests?" Reed called.

"You are the guests," Trent shot back.

Carrie smiled as she stroked Trent's arm. "And anyway, we came to tell all of you there'll be a midnight dance in a few minutes to ring in the New Year."

"It's bound to be a good year for all of us," Gage

responded. "Vivian has put her apartment up for sale and is already living somewhere else."

"No kidding!" Sebastian and Trent said in unison.

Gage nodded in confirmation, knowing both Sebastian's and Trent's apartments were on the same floor as Vivian's, and guessing that the two men hadn't been looking forward to continuing as her closest neighbors. "The only reason Vivian isn't behind bars is that she cooperated with the police by offering up evidence against Senator Kendrick and implicating her lover, Henry Brown."

"What I want to know," Julia said, "is how and why. How did she do it?"

"Good question." Gage looked around the table. "Many of you probably don't know this, but Vivian's family used to own 721 Park Avenue. Though the family had to sell the property when their fortunes declined, they held onto ownership of one apartment—Vivian's. According to the police, Vivian's late husband used to be head of security for the building."

Reed's lips twisted. "So Vivian the ice queen had a track record of sleeping with the hired help."

Gage inclined his head, observing he had everyone's rapt attention. "I'll agree it's interesting. It also meant she was acquainted with security for the building."

Reed guffawed at the double meaning in Gage's words.

"So," Max said, finishing, "Vivian knew how to get access to everyone's apartments in order to use people's indiscretions against them."

"Exactly," Gage responded. "In fact, I think that's

why the SEC started investigating me and Reed for insider trading a couple of months ago. Vivian must have snuck into Reed's apartment or mine and misinterpreted, perhaps deliberately, some notes relating to a stock sale by the both of us. When Reed refused to pay blackmail money to keep his supposed financial misdeed hush-hush, Vivian retaliated by bringing the stock sale to the attention of the SEC."

Trent nodded. "It all makes sense. She and Henry must have sneaked into my apartment and found photos of me out with Marie. They must have copied the memory card on my digital camera and put it back before I discovered it was gone." He looked thoughtful. "When I refused to be blackmailed, they must have released the photos to the media."

"She or Henry must have gotten into all of our apartments," Max said in agreement. "That's how the blackmail schemes all started."

"But why?" Julia asked. "Why would she try to blackmail us?"

Gage grimaced. "The million-dollar question, if you don't mind another bad pun. According to the police, Vivian was pinched for cash after her husband's death. To support her lavish lifestyle, she took to blackmailing wealthy residents with Henry's help."

"To think I was afraid of her yapping dogs," Elizabeth Wellington said.

"Well, you won't have to worry about them any longer," Trent replied. "None of us will."

Jacinda was glad for that. Even so, she couldn't help letting her thoughts stray to what might have been.

"If Vivian hadn't been up to no good," she said sadly, "my sister might still be alive. Vivian's blackmail is what pushed Kendrick over the edge. He thought Marie was blackmailing him with a threat to make their relationship public. It looks as if he, like the rest of us, never suspected Vivian or Henry."

Elizabeth touched her arm sympathetically. "Jacinda, I'm so sorry. You've suffered even more than the rest of us in this whole episode."

There were murmurs of agreement around the table.

"Thank you," Jacinda replied, squeezing Elizabeth's hand. "Fortunately, I've gotten resolution now that Senator Kendrick is behind bars."

She looked around the table at all the faces offering sympathy and support. Her neighbors. Her new friends. "And I hope this will mean a new chapter in the life of 721 Park Avenue."

"Now that the rats among us have been eliminated, you mean?" Max asked rhetorically.

Jacinda smiled. "Not only that, but there's a parade of wedding bells and stork deliveries to look forward to."

She looked at Gage. He'd opened up and, these days, acted far from the guarded man she'd met six months ago.

She glanced back around the table. "For starters, Gage and I will be holding a regular open house at our apartment for Friday night TGIF drinks."

Gage raised his eyebrows, and then gave her a wink.

"Of course, the maid will be cleaning up before your arrival," she added teasingly.

Everyone laughed.

"I thought I recognized you when I bumped into you in the elevator," Sebastian put in.

"Sorry," she responded, "but I had to lie."

At Amanda's quizzical look, she explained, "Sebastian went to prep school in England with my brother. We hadn't seen each other in years, but when I ran into him in the elevator recently, he thought he recognized me. Of course, I had to convince him that I was Gage's maid so I could unearth the real story behind my sister's death."

"And you and Gage fell in love in the process," Tessa added with a grin. "How romantic. Like two spies falling for each other."

"Gage, you sly dog," Sebastian put in. "And here we all suspected you were just shagging the maid. It was even more complicated than that."

As Gage smiled enigmatically, Jacinda bit the inside of her mouth to keep from laughing.

No use telling everyone about how she had conned Gage, too, until recently, Jacinda thought. She was happy to let them think Gage had been in on her charade from the beginning.

After all, she'd gotten her hero.

However, she couldn't resist teasing by adopting an expression of pretend shock. "You all suspected Gage was shagging his housekeeper?"

Elizabeth laughed. "Yes, his disposition improved!"

"Yeah, we thought he must be getting some," Reed added with a sly grin.

Jacinda felt herself flush, but beside her, Gage laughed knowingly.

At that moment, the band began to play again, intruding on the conversation.

"I think that's our cue," Carrie said to Trent.

Amid a round of applause, Carrie and Trent walked over to cut the cake.

A short time later, after the cake cutting, Jacinda walked out onto the dance floor with Gage and the other couples of 721 Park Avenue to join the bride and groom and other guests for the midnight dance.

As the band began to play, all the couples swayed in a slow dance.

Gage's body pressed against hers, and Jacinda sighed, closing her eyes and resting her head on Gage's shoulder.

"Happy?" Gage murmured in her ear.

"Is it showing?" she whispered back, a smile curving her lips.

Gage laughed softly. "Only in the best way." He nuzzled her temple. "And speaking of showing, the baby boom in the building is giving me ideas."

She raised her head to look at him, even as her heart did a little flutter at his words.

She wanted to have a baby with Gage, she realized. He'd be such a good father. Attentive, loving. Everything he'd revealed himself to be already with her.

She tilted her head, and asked teasingly, "But aren't we getting married first?"

They'd agreed to have a May wedding in London, and then make 721 Park Avenue their home base. In fact, she'd already asked for a job transfer to the New York office of Winter & Baker.

Gage gave her a devilish look. "Yes, but we'll need to practice. Lots."

"Yes, please," she responded, and he laughed.

It was looking as if she'd be asking for another indefinite leave from Winter & Baker sooner rather than later.

Last week, after Christmas, she and Gage had flown to London and then on to Switzerland for a brief trip to break the news of their engagement to their parents.

Of course, both families had been delighted to hear of the engagement.

Jacinda reflected that her family in particular had welcomed the happy news at the end of a very difficult year. When she'd admitted she'd really been in New York sleuthing for the past six months, her parents had been taken aback and then belatedly concerned—even though she and Gage had spared them the details of how she'd masqueraded as his housekeeper without his knowledge. But even that wrinkle had soon been smoothed over, lost in the happiness over the engagement.

Now, as the last notes of the song faded away, the lead singer of the band took the mike.

Along with Gage and the other guests, Jacinda turned to look at the stage.

"It's the final seconds, folks," the singer announced. "Ten, nine…"

"Here it comes," Gage said in a low voice.

Everyone around them had started counting.

"…six, five…"

She looked up at Gage. "I'll love you just as much next year."

"Good to know," he replied, his dimple coming out. "…one…"

Gage's lips closed over hers as the crowd around them erupted with "Happy New Year!"

And there was no doubt in Jacinda's mind that this year *would* be a happy one for her and Gage. The first of many, she hoped.

They had a lot to look forward to—a wedding, children and a lifetime together.

They'd found each other.

\* \* \* \* \*

# Special Offers
## Great Value Collection

721 Park Avenue—Manhattan's ultimate address for high-society secrets & affairs!

**PARK AVENUE Scandals**
MAUREEN CHILD · LAURA WRIGHT · JENNIFER LEWIS
On sale 17th February 2012

**PARK AVENUE Secrets**
BARBARA DUNLOP · EMILIE ROSE · ANNA DEPALO
On sale 16th March 2012

# Save 20% on all Special Releases

Find out more at
**www.millsandboon.co.uk/specialreleases**

Visit us Online

0312/10/MB367

# MILLS & BOON

## Book of the Month

## We love this book because...

Rafe St Alban is the most dark-hearted, sinfully attractive rake in London. So get ready for fireworks when he sweeps prim Miss Henrietta Markham off her feet in Marguerite Kaye's compellingly sensual story of redemption!

**On sale 4th May**

*Visit us Online*

Find out more at
**www.millsandboon.co.uk/BOTM**

# Special Offers

Every month we put together collections and longer reads written by your favourite authors.

Here are some of next month's highlights— and don't miss our fabulous discount online!

**All I Ever Wanted** — kristan higgins
On sale 20th April

**MICHELLE REID and ABBY GREEN — POWER**
On sale 20th April

**THE SANTINA CROWN — THE PRICE OF ROYAL DUTY — PENNY JORDAN**
On sale 20th April

## Save 20% on all Special Releases

Find out more at
**www.millsandboon.co.uk/specialreleases**

Visit us Online

0412/ST/MB369

# The World of Mills & Boon®

There's a Mills & Boon® series that's perfect for you. We publish ten series and with new titles every month, you never have to wait long for your favourite to come along.

**Blaze®** — Scorching hot, sexy reads

**By Request** — Relive the romance with the best of the best

**Cherish™** — Romance to melt the heart every time

**Desire™** — Passionate and dramatic love stories

*Visit us Online* — Browse our books before you buy online at **www.millsandboon.co.uk**

## What will you treat yourself to next?

**HISTORICAL** — Ignite your imagination, step into the past...

**INTRIGUE...** — Breathtaking romantic suspense

**Medical Romance** — Captivating medical drama—with heart

**MODERN™** — International affairs, seduction and passion

**nocturne** — Deliciously wicked paranormal romance

**RIVA™** — Live life to the full – give in to temptation

You can also buy Mills & Boon eBooks at **www.millsandboon.co.uk**

*Visit us Online*

## Mills & Boon® Online

Discover more romance at
**www.millsandboon.co.uk**

- **FREE** online reads
- **Books** up to one month before shops
- **Browse our books** before you buy

*...and much more!*

---

**For exclusive competitions and instant updates:**

Like us on **facebook.com/romancehq**

Follow us on **twitter.com/millsandboonuk**

Join us on **community.millsandboon.co.uk**

*Visit us Online*  Sign up for our FREE eNewsletter at **www.millsandboon.co.uk**